R. L. SNYDER

Printed in the United States of America.

ISBN: 978-0999517970

First edition: April 2, 2020

Published by: MECROSS Publications

P.O. Box 1061

Gorham, Maine 04038

Also by R. L. Snyder

The Branwen Saga
Branwen

The Shadow War
The Blocker
First Dragon
Oathsworn

Watch for more at www.branwensmajor.com.

To Laura

For helping to keep me on track.

And to Rob

For your help making sure everyone was where they were supposed to be.

Cover Design: Fiona Jayde Media

PROLOGUE

Cleveland 1979

The sudden sound of a police cruiser triggering its siren disturbed the stillness of the deserted alley. The reflected display of flashing blue lights quickly receded into the night as the black-and-white patrol car sped off in pursuit of its quarry.

A gentle wind stirred the loose trash of old newspapers and cigarette butts that littered the asphalt floor of the narrow roadway. Not one of the multitude of homeless the city chose to ignore sought shelter within the confines of the dim avenue. A feeling of uneasiness within the canyon of brick walls ensuring they settled elsewhere.

The alleys only occupant, a lone rat, turned and considered seeking shelter in the open space between a pair of overstuffed dumpsters. The hair on the little beasts back bristled. Changing its mind it scampered down the alleyway towards the relative safety of the street.

A shadow emerged on the wall between the dumpsters, quickly swelling into an emptiness of stygian blackness. Movement, like dark water rippled within the ebony abyss. A lone figure stepped from the void and looked up and down the dark corridor. Satisfied the alley was empty he placed a leather briefcase on the ground. Settling the trench coat draped over his shoulders with a shrug he removed his brown fedora and ran his fingers through his long dark hair.

A sudden wisp of air signaled that the wall had returned to its original state. Replacing the hat he reached down and recovered the briefcase. He began to whistle while he strolled toward the street.

The driver of an idling sedan jumped from behind the wheel and hastened to open the rear door as the man approached. Reaching for the case he asked, "Would you like me to take that, sir?"

"I will hold onto it, thank you. Is all in readiness?"

"Everyone is waiting, sir."

"Good." He turned and looked back down the alley. As he did, a dirty streetlamp momentarily caught his profile. Handsome, almost beautiful, except for the eyes. Blue orbs that glistened like wet ice. Cold, unfeeling, malevolent. Not altogether human.

The new arrival stepped into the car. Closing the door the driver hurried around the vehicle returning to his place behind the wheel. As he reached for the ignition the sleeve of his jacket pulled back exposing a tattoo. Three straight lines radiating evenly from the center like the foot of a bird, surrounded by a circle. Some considered it a peace symbol. It was not.

"Will it take long to reach the facility?" The passenger asked.

"About an hour, sir, depending on traffic. Roads are pretty quiet this time of night."

"Thank you. What should I call you?"

"Name is Jimmy, sir."

"Nice to meet you, Jimmy. No need to be so formal. We are going to become good friends you and I. You may call me Cain."

"Thank you, Mr. Cain."

"Just Cain. Were you told what to expect?"

"Uh, yes, sir."

"And you are doing this willingly."

"I am, sir. I mean, Cain. I want to serve Him."

"And He appreciates your desire to serve. His reward will be great I promise you."

Turning in his seat Jimmy asked nervously. "Will it hurt?"

Cain smiled reassuringly. "Maybe a little at first, but it is over quickly. Are you ready?"

"What do I need to do?"

Cain removed a metal container from the valise the shape and size of a large thermos.

"Just sit there. Don't move."

He unscrewed the top of the container and placed it on the seat next to him. For a moment nothing happened, then a dark mist appeared around the lip like a layer of thick smoke. It slowly rose and as it did a shadow formed, not upon any solid object but floating in the open space between the seat and the roof of the vehicle.

Jimmy stared over his shoulder at the shadow. It hesitated, then jetted forward striking him in the eyes. Jimmy jerked forward striking the steering wheel then recoiling onto the seat as if he had been pulled by a string. He sat, unmoving, the whites of his blank eyes staring at the roof of the car.

Cain wondered if his neck had been broken. "It is done? He lives?"

"He does. We are one." A voice answered. It was Jimmy's, but then again ... not.

"You have control."

"I do. He is frightened but cooperating."

"He is uninjured?"

"He is ... functional."

"Then take us to Mentor."

"It shall be done."

Cain screwed the cap back onto the container and placed it next to the other five that rested in the valise. He leaned back in his seat and closed his eyes.

"Wake me when we get there."

CHAPTER ONE

A young man walked along the edge of the wood, the shadows of the trees presenting relief from the unrelenting heat of the sun. He stopped for a moment and regarded the city less than half a mile away. It was like looking at a painting from another era. The distant buildings with their magnificent columns reminiscent of a time when Sparta prepared to delay the onslaught of the Persians at Thermopile. This was Olympus, the home of Zeus.

"It is an impressive sight is it not?"

Startled, his hand falling to the hilt of his sword, he turned towards the voice.

"I am sorry. I did not wish to startle you. I am not a threat I promise."

Leaning against a nearby oak a young woman, not much older than his twenty years, smiled at him. "You are the First Dragon, are you not?"

Relaxing a little he dropped his hand from the sword and flexed his fingers. "Sorry. I didn't know anyone was there. Guess I'm a little jumpy. You surprised me."

The stranger chuckled. "That was not my intent. I am used to observing while not being observed. You have surprised me as well. Few seem to notice me anymore."

Arthur smiled. "Well. you're good at it. I'm not often caught off guard."

"You mean since your awakening."

"Uh, yeah."

"It is a burden for one so young to have so much responsibility thrust upon him."

Arthur examined the stranger. She was stunning. Tall, athletically built with long red hair and sparkling blue eyes. She wore a simple dress, something like an ancient Greek stola with a wide elaborately designed belt encircling her slim waist. Resting in her hand was an exquisitely carved bow, the image of Medusa etched into the riser while the locks of serpents wrapped themselves up and down the limbs. From her shoulder, a simple leather quiver rested. The wooden shafts of several arrows protruding more than a foot from the opening.

"Out hunting?" Arthur asked pointing to the bow.

"In-a-way, but I find you more interesting than my typical quarry."

"Would it be rude for me to ask who you are?"

"Not at all. I am Artemis. I think you know my brother, Apollo. I have overheard him speak often of you. He believes you a true hero. A warrior with both wisdom and compassion. A rare combination."

"He is too kind."

"Oh Apollo can be kind I suppose, but I do not believe that is the case. He and his fellow warriors are honored to follow the true First Dragon. It takes much to impress my brother."

"I'm flattered."

"Do not be. From what I hear his praise is well earned. Even that fool Hercules brags about being one of your oath-sworn."

"He is a good friend."

She nodded. "To many of us."

"Have you heard how he is doing? I haven't seen him since he was wounded."

"I understand the wound would have killed a normal man. Of course, Hercules is anything but normal. I believe he will recover. And remember, First Dragon, what happened to him was not your fault. Hercules is a warrior. He fights because he believes in this cause, as do all that serve you. There will be casualties as there are in all wars. But I have heard you make wise decisions which result in victories. Success always saves more lives in the long run then it costs."

She smiled at him causing him to feel ... relaxed. Something he had not felt in a while. The stress of the last few months seemed to flow from him at her words.

He was used to sharing his thoughts with Michael, working out his anxieties. But Michael was gone, reunited with his family, no longer the entity residing within his head. And the others ...

Kathleen was away, busy training to control her new power as a Blocker. His oath-sworn, those he had become close to, that he thought of as friends, were taking their duties too seriously, leaving him without the relaxed companionship he had grown accustomed to.

"It will work out, Arthur. Your friends, your love, they are adjusting to their new roles. Give them time."

He looked at her wondering how she knew what he was thinking.

She chuckled. "I do not read minds, First Dragon. It is obvious things have changed for you. That your world has changed. You miss what you had. Anyone can see that. I remember when my brother first joined our military. He was lonely, miserable. He missed his family and his friends. In time, however, he discovered new friends, a new family that cared as much about him as he did those he left at home. And he found happiness in his new life. Give it a little time. You will adjust to your new reality. And I believe you too will find happiness."

"I know. In my head I understand. It's just that things have happened so fast."

"You cannot return to what was. You must strive to move forward. You have a lot of help. Accept it."

"You're right. I guess I've just been feeling a little sorry for myself."

A dog howled from deep within the woods. She turned. "It sounds like Cerberus has caught the scent of something. I best get back to my business. He at least acknowledges me. It has been an honor to meet you, First Dragon." She raised the beautiful bow as she turned. "Until we meet again."

Arthur watched until she was absorbed by the trees seeming to fade into the forest. When he could no longer see her he turned towards the city, a smile developing as he began to work his way back. He started to hum a tune. One he did not recognize. Weird he thought, but he felt better than he had in days. It was like a heavy burden had been lifted from his shoulders.

"Arthur!" Loki waived as he jogged toward him. "Where the hell have you been?"

"Sorry. I needed some time to think."

"Well, you can take all the time you need, but not alone. Not any more. You may be able to sense Shadows, little brother, but not their followers. I kind of doubt we have gotten rid of them all, even here on Olympus. We don't need a repeat of what happened on Asgard. That bastard almost killed you. You don't have Michael to help you heal anymore."

"I know. Sorry. I'll make sure I let you know before wandering off again. Any word on Hercules?"

"Just got off the horn with Sif. She said she heard from Helen that he is still unconscious, but the docs are hopeful. One of those big spears from our new friends went right through him. Damned if I know how he lived long enough for the medics to reach him."

"He is a strong man."

Loki laughed. "And stubborn, stayed alive just to annoy the SOB that gutted him."

"And to allow his legend to grow. I doubt we will ever hear the end of this one."

"Right up there with the hydra story."

"Do hydras exist?" Arthur asked.

"Not anymore."

They looked at each other for a moment, then burst out laughing. They started to walk toward the city.

"How's Kathleen doing with her training?" Loki asked.

"Doing well I guess. She won't let me watch. Says I make her nervous. Merlin wants to get her back to Earth as soon as possible but doesn't want her to go until she can defend herself."

"From Shadows you mean. That girl doesn't need a lot of help with solid beings."

"Maybe not." Arthur thought about the wound she received during the invasion. The one that he thought killed her until the man on the hill brought her back, back with the power of a Blocker awakening within her.

"I think we should all go back, little brother. And soon. We have been here for several days already. Too much time has passed on Earth. The gods themselves only know what Satan and his minions have been up to. Speaking of Satan, decided if you are going to meet with him?"

"No."

"No you haven't decided or no you aren't going to meet?"

"If I'm going to meet with him."

"Well if you decide you have to, you will not do it without us. I don't care what the son-of-a-bitch said. That would be suicide. You know as well as I that it's a trap."

"Not so sure, Loki. Satan may be evil incarnate, as my sister would say, but I believe he has some sort of weird sense of honor. If he says he will be alone and only wants to talk, I believe him."

"And if not?"

Arthur smiled. "Then I will have my oath-sworn nearby. I'm trusting, not stupid."

"We don't even know where this meeting is to take place."

"I'm sure he will find a way to let us know."

"Arthur," a tall man with a dark well-trimmed beard called running towards them. "Odin wishes to speak with you, my lord."

"Damn-it, Rex, how many times do I have to tell you I am not your lord?"

"Technically, little brother, you are," Loki said. "You are a prince of Asgard and the First Dragon of the Alliance. You are royalty whether you like it or not. And as your oath-sworn, you are his liege lord."

Arthur stopped and grinned. "So does that make me yours as well?"

Loki slapped his shoulder. "Never, little brother."

"But you are my oath-sworn."

"Different rules."

"What rules?"

"Mine, of course."

Arthur chuckled, "Of course."

"He awaits you in Zeus's conference room ... Arthur," Rex said.

"That's a little better. Can't have the original King Arthur calling me that."

Rex smiled. "I am no longer a king and I have willingly sworn an oath to serve you. Besides, it is you that carries Excalibur, not I."

Choosing to ignore the comment Arthur started to walk to the hall. "Any word from Thor?"

"He has not returned and there has been no word."

"That is weird," Loki said. "My brother is usually very prompt in his reports. Takes every task seriously. Even a simple recon."

"Millie with him?"

"Yes, Arthur, and Lancelot. Michael wanted to go but felt his appearance might cause a bit of a disturbance on the streets of Cleveland."

"Ya think," Loki said. "You mean an eight-foot dude with blue hair might make some of the locals take an interest?"

"What about Lucifer?" Arthur asked.

"I said Lancelot accompanied them. Somehow Lucifer's image as Lancelot returned as he announced his intent to go with Millie. He seems to have the ability to change his appearance at will."

"And the others don't?"

"They have not done so as of yet," Rex said.

"Strange. I need to talk to Michael about that. Is he at the hall?"

"Everyone is there. They await your return."

"Kathleen?"

Rex smiled. "She and her father are there. I overheard her tell Freya she needs to discuss wedding plans with you after the meeting."

"Oh."

Loki laughed. "Getting cold feet, little brother?"

"No. And stop calling me that. It makes me feel like I'm seven years old."

"I will do what I can, adopted sibling of lesser age."

"Asshole!"

As they entered the conference room Ares called out, "The First Dragon."

All rose to their feet.

This is something I am never going to get used to, Arthur thought. *Michael, I wish you were still here to help me with all this protocol crap.*

"I am, Arthur."

He froze. *"What!"*

"When we are near I can hear you and you, me. It is something my people have been able to do for a long time."

"You mean you can read my thoughts. The others can too?"

"Only when you wish us to. As when we were one, I can only hear what you think when you address the thoughts to me."

"How? I'm not one of you."

"Perhaps it is because you are the First Dragon."

"How close must we be?" Arthur asked.

"For us, it is a few yards. I would assume it will be the same with you."

"Good. I've missed you."

Arthur could feel the chuckle. *"And I you. Remember the others can hear you only if you address them. Think of whom you wish to speak to and they will hear."*

"Everything okay, Arthur," Loki asked. "You look like you just saw a ghost."

"Just talking to a friend."

Loki looked towards Michael who stood with his siblings, Ezekiel, Gabriel, Remiel and Ariel.

"Again. How?"

"I'll explain later."

"Damn right you will."

"First Dragon," Odin said. "All is well I hope."

"I am fine, sir. Thank you." He looked around. "Why are we all here? I thought we were not going to meet again until this evening."

"That was the plan," Freya said. "But plans are fluid. They flow in the currents of time."

"Things have changed that need your immediate attention, Art," Charlotte said as she moved forward and stood beside Freya. It surprised him that his mother stepped into her role as Freya's second as if born to it.

"What has changed? Shadows"

"No, son, people," Paul said maneuvering his wheelchair next to his wife.

"People?"

"Disciples we think," Odin said. "We have just heard from Thor. He has been looking into reports of several atrocities that have occurred in and around the Cleveland area."

"What kind of atrocities?" Arthur asked.

Zeus leaned on the table. "Attacks on children. A shooting during a church service, dozens killed and wounded, an explosion in the home of a family sponsoring a meeting of young boys and their fathers, no survivors, and several children and their parents killed and injured in a shooting during the matinee of a movie in Strongsville."

"All happening at almost the same time," Ra added. "Can't be a coincidence, so Thor and the others looked into it."

"What did they find?" Loki asked.

"At the theater, a squad car happened to be passing just as the shooting started. They were able to stop most of the shooters as they exited the building. There was a violent exchange of gunfire. One officer was badly wounded, and all but one of the shooters was killed. One escaped. On the arm of each of the deceased was a tattoo. The mark of Nero."

"But I thought we decided after the Boy Scout incident that these were not directed by the Shadows but by some want-a-be cult."

"We may have been mistaken," Odin said.

"I don't understand. Satan said he would do nothing until after we meet. And only if I decided not to take him up on his offer. And children are not normally his targets."

"Maybe this is a warning," Apollo offered. "To ensure you accept his offer."

"Doesn't make sense. I need to get back."

Kathleen gripped his arm. "We all need to get back. You will not face him alone, Arthur. We go with you. I go with you."

Falstaff moved next to them. He placed his hand on Kathleen's shoulder. "My god-daughter speaks for all of us, First Dragon. We are your oath-sworn, the oath-sworn of the First Dragon. Where you go, we go. Besides, my little princess intends to marry you. I will not allow her to be disappointed because you got yourself killed playing the hero."

"But he said I must meet him alone."

"Bullshit," Loki said.

"He will not meet me if you are there. At least if he knows you are there. I have an idea."

CHAPTER TWO

"*Michael, can you hear me?"*

"Yes, Arthur."

"Would you and your family remain after the others leave?"

"It shall be done."

"What is going on, Arthur? I've seen that look on your face before," Merlin asked.

"An idea that may help. Still working on the details. I will explain when I get it all sorted out. I promise."

"Are you going to meet him, Art?" Charlotte asked.

"I think I have to, Mom. If Satan is behind what is going on I need to find out and try to stop him."

"Do you have any idea how?" Paul asked.

"Not a clue, Dad. But I have to try something."

"This isn't all on you, Art," Gwen said stepping beside her mother.

"I know. This isn't about my ego, Gwen. But I believe I've been given the power of a Blocker and found the other Blockers and those of you that can resist Shadows for a reason. I think we are meant to do something together. Something important. I don't know what yet. But I know I am different from Blockers of the past, we are different. That difference may be our chance to finally put an end to this war."

"That may be true. I hope it is so, but how?" Odin asked. "For centuries we have battled this evil, doing what we could to contain it. Never stop it. Why now? What has changed?"

"I don't know. There are a lot of questions that I don't have answers for." Arthur hesitated, the words of the man on the hill haunting him. "But before we can go forward we have questions to be answered, puzzles that need to be solved. Why the introduction of new players, Millie, Kathleen, the Friends and of course Michael and his brethren. How can the Shadows create multiple portals while we are restricted to the two on each of our worlds? Shadows can reach Earth seemingly anywhere and yet not able to reach the other dimensions except through one of our portals. Why? These things are important. I don't know how but I believe if we can answer these questions we will discover a way to end this. Possibly for good. But we need time to solve the puzzles. My meeting with Satan may buy us that time."

"And it may get you killed," Loki said.

"Maybe. And maybe that is why we have Lancelot, Millie and now Kathleen. In case."

"Don't say that," Kathleen said.

He looked into her deep green eyes and smiled. "In case we need to combine our strength," he lied.

"Oh. I thought ..."

"I know what you thought. Nothing is going to happen to me. I have a wedding to attend."

"Damn right," Loki said. "So now what?"

"I will meet you at the large portal. I need to talk to Michael for a moment."

"We will wait outside," Loki said. "oath-sworn, remember. Get used to it. You don't go anywhere alone. Not anymore."

Arthur chuckled. "Fine. Out front."

When the others had departed the room he closed the door and turned to Michael. *"Can everyone hear me?"*

"Yes, First Dragon."

"I want to speak to you without the others hearing what I say. The fact that we can communicate this way I would like to keep secret as long as we can."

"Merlin suspects," Arthur heard Michael say. *"And I think Loki."*

"I know. I will talk to them about it. They will understand what I am trying to do. Do you think Satan or his folk could hear us? I know he heard you when we were together, Michael."

"I do not believe so. We were as one at the time and whether you intended to or not you did address him. Unless one of us intends to speak with him I do not believe he could hear."

"Good. Let's hope not. I understand that Lucifer took on the form of Lancelot when they returned to Cleveland. Is that something that you all can do?"

"No, First Dragon," he heard Gabriel say. *"We were all surprised when he transformed."*

"Did he do it purposely? Can he control it?"

"I do not believe so," Ariel said. *"It is strange. I heard him say thank you to someone as it happened."*

Arthur smiled. *"Then there is a chance. I would like you all to come with me when I return to Earth. But you will be able to stay only if what I suspect happens."*

"Do you think He is helping?" Michael asked.

"*He?*" Ezekiel asked.

"*He who awakened the power of the Blocker within our young warriors. He who speaks to Arthur alone.*"

"You mean ..." Remiel asked.

"I'm not sure who he is, Remiel. But he has done some pretty fantastic things and there is no doubt he is helping us," Arthur said.

"If we can transform, what would you have us do, First Dragon?" Ariel asked.

"*When we are alone like this, please call me Arthur, and in answer to your question, I'd like you to be my radio.*"

Apollo poked his head through the double doors. "The others await outside, First Dragon."

"Thank you, I'm on my way."

"If you would give me a moment before you go, First Dragon."

"Sure, Apollo. What can I do for you?"

"You can accept my oath."

"Your oath?"

Loki pushed the door open and the remainder of the oath-sworn entered. "Listen to him, Arthur."

"I wish to join the fellowship, First Dragon. I wish to give you my oath."

"But your position here. Your responsibilities to Zeus. To Olympus."

"I have spoken to my father. He has released me from my duties and has given his blessing. As with Hercules, I wish to serve the First Dragon as a representative of Olympus."

Michael placed his hand upon Arthur's shoulder. As do we."

Arthur looked at the warriors from Haven. He hung his head. "I do not deserve this."

"But you do, Arthur. You are First Dragon of the Alliance of Worlds. You represent all of us and it is only fitting that each of the member worlds serves the Dragon," Michael said.

"But you are not a member."

Gabriel smiled. "We are now."

"Which is why we are here as well," a voice called from behind the group standing in the doorway.

"Sorry, Arthur. They were waiting outside. This is Bast," Kathleen said joining the others and introducing the woman who had spoken. She was taller than Kathleen, skin like polished mahogany, athletically built, and very beautiful. Behind her stood a man, as dark as her, as tall as Loki and as muscular as Hercules.

"And this is my brother, Anubis. Ra is our uncle and he has permitted us to join you," Bast said. "To represent Duat."

"Do you understand what you are asking?"

Anubis smiled. "We understand the oath, First Dragon. I will enjoy watching my sister swear to serve a man. My uncle thought it amusing as well. No one in the family thought she would ever say those words."

Bast slapped her brother on the shoulder.

Falstaff laughed looking at Kathleen. "I know what you mean."

"Uncle!"

Arthur was silent for a moment. "You all understand what this means."

They nodded. No one spoke.

"Then I am honored." He drew Excalibur. Michael stepped forward and the others fell in behind him.

"I Michael ...." And so it began. One after the other they came forward and repeated the words. At the end of the line, his mother appeared pushing his father's wheelchair. She smiled and Gwen stepped from behind her.

"It is what she wants, Art," his father said carefully rising to his feet. "She is an adult and knows her own mind. And we give our blessing."

Gwen approached her brother and kneeled. Loki handed her his sword.

When she had given her oath Arthur returned Excalibur to its scabbard. "I am honored. I am humbled. I am resigned that this group of warriors, this fellowship, my friends, my family, shall prevail against the evil we face. And I give you my oath that from this day forth I am yours. Our fates are intertwined. We are as one. You are not just my oath-sworn, we together are The Oathsworn."

"We are so proud," Charlotte said.

"Yes, Art. Now take this group of heroes and stop the bastard." Paul said settling back into the chair.

"I believe it is possible now, Dad."

Charlotte turned and pushing the chair with his father, followed the others as they left the building. Taking a deep breath to still the surge of emotion he felt Arthur looked about the hall. He stopped when something on the wall caught his attention. A beautifully carved bow suspended above a brass plaque. The form of Medusa prominent.

"It belonged to my sister," Apollo said from behind him. "She was a great warrior."

"Was?"

"She disappeared about ten years ago."

"Disappeared?"

"In Ohio. On a mission. We were looking for what we believed was a group of disciples that had murdered a family. It was brutal and ritualistic. We tracked them to a large gorge near Akron. Artemis was a great hunter and was tracking the killers for us. We were doing our best to follow their trail near a stream that flowed down the rocky floor of the gorge. Artemis and one other scouted ahead. Someone she was training. One she cared for. We found him alone suffering from a stab wound to the abdomen. He told us that they found not a group but a single individual who turned on them and stabbed him before he could react. My sister stepped between them trying to protect her friend. She drew her blade and they fought. I don't know why she didn't shoot him. She was wounded and fell to the ground unable to continue. I was surprised because I knew of no man that could defeat Artemis with a sword or bow. The man picked her up, and before carrying her into the black doorway that appeared, gave her wounded companion a message."

"What did he say," Arthur asked.

"He told him to tell Zeus that it was Cain that has defeated his daughter. That she now belongs to him.

"The only thing I found of her was that bow."

Arthur was quiet for a moment. "And the wounded man?"

"His name was Ari. He died before we could bring him out of the gorge."

Arthur was about to tell Apollo of his encounter in the woods but decided better. Now was not the time. And he had to figure out what it meant first. Or that it was even real.

"Arthur?"

He turned. Gwen stood with Kathleen. They had been listening.

"We should go," she said quietly.

Arthur looked again at the bow. "I suppose we should.

"You know, Art. I almost feel sorry for Satan," Gwen said as they stepped outside.

"You do?"

"Sure. I doubt he has any idea what's coming."

"And what is that?"

"Us. The oath-sworn of the First Dragon. I'm sorry, The Oathsworn. Think about it. He is about to face Thor and Loki, Falstaff, and Sif, gods of Asgard. The daughter of Merlin the Magician and Gwenivere, Sir Lancelot, and King Arthur himself. Hercules and Apollo, Bast and Anubis, the kin of Ra, the archangels of Haven, Millie the Blocker, maid of China, and of course the First Dragon and his beautiful sister. He ain't got a chance."

CHAPTER THREE

The passenger rolled down the window and listened as the waters of Lake Erie lapped softly along the sandy shore. He smiled when he noticed the long, slim cigarette boat tied to the aluminum dock, its red hull bumping gently against the rubber tires. Two men stood next to the boat armed with shotguns.

The driver opened the door and Cain stepped out. Wrapping his arms around him and bending over he stretched his back. "I hate these damn things." He reached inside and recovered his briefcase. He turned to the driver. "Follow me."

They walked to the dock. "The boat is prepared?"

"Yes, sir. Fueled and ready to go."

Cain turned to the driver of the car. "Get in the boat. Start it up and wait for me. I won't be long."

"Yes, sir," The driver jumped into the boat, taking a moment to regain his balance as it rocked from his added weight, then took a seat, reached for the ignition, and started the powerful engines.

Cain turned and walked towards the warehouse. As he approached the door opened and a man stepped out. Holding the door he nodded as Cain stepped across the threshold. Neither man spoke.

One of the guards on the dock looked at his partner. "Scary dude."

"Wait 'til you meet his boss," the man in the boat said with almost a cackle.

Cain walked swiftly towards the raised platform that stood at the far end of the room. More than two hundred people, draped in long white robes, hoods obscuring their faces, remained silent as he strolled through them, parting the crowd as if he were an icebreaker slicing a steady path through still icy waters. Cain climbed the thirteen steps onto the stage which resembled, by no accident, a gallows, complete with post and noose. He placed his bag on the metal table attached to the wooden pillar and turned to the crowd.

"I am Cain. I bring greetings from our master. He wishes to assure you that He knows of your loyalty and sacrifice." He was silent for a moment. "He rewards the faithful and the rewards shall be great I promise you!"

A cheer rose and Cain raised his hands to still the crowd.

"He wishes you to know that the time is nearly come. No more shall you be ridiculed and punished for following the one true god. No more will the rules of the society of this faithless world apply to you. All of you shall be rewarded with the power of Him. You will rule as kings. You will take what you want, destroy what you want, kill without fear of retribution. This world will be yours to do with as you wish!"

The crowd began to scream and dance, the shadows of their actions reflected upon the walls looking for any not of the faith, like a scene from hell. Demons escaping the depths. Dante's warning brought to life.

Cain raised his hands again and all movement stopped as if a switch had been thrown. He smiled. A sinister movement of the muscles of the face. Nothing more.

"Not long ago this hallowed place was attacked by those that oppose us. Many of the faithful perished that day and our doorway to this world was closed. But we are back. They cannot stop us. There are other doors and his forces will soon join you in this holy war. The unbelievers will suffer and perish. Even now Satan himself is preparing to destroy the most powerful of our enemies. The Blocker. The one they call First Dragon."

Another cheer from the crowd. Focused on Cain no one noticed as a single figure worked their way towards the door at the end of the hall.

"I come here today to reward five of you that have proven themselves truly worthy. Their actions have succeeded in drawing the attention of our foes away from what will prove to be a pivotal moment in our righteous and holy war."

Reaching into the bag he carefully withdrew five metal cylinders. Gently unscrewing the tops he called out, "William Beck, Samuel Warren, Cynthia Woodall, John Franklin, and Steven Halter, please join me."

There was a rustle in the crowd as five figures moved through the multitude of worshipers until they reached the stairs. The lone figure in the back of the room hesitated with their hand on the handle of the door.

As the five stepped upon the stage Cain lined them up facing the audience. He smiled at each as he gripped them one-by-one ensuring that ally could be seen.

"Are you prepared to become one with Satan? To help lead the forces of the faithful to victory?"

"We are."

Cain turned to the crowd. "These five have given the world a demonstration of the power of our lord. Attacking the children of our enemies has created terror within the hearts of our foes. Through terror, we will weaken the resolve of those that oppose us. Fear and chaos shall reign. For this, they are to be rewarded with a precious gift. They shall become as one with Him."

"Satan!" The crowd screamed.

Cain smiled when he heard the name. As he turned he whispered, "You fools."

"Do you willingly accept this gift?" He asked the group.

"We do."

He pointed at the five silver vessels on the table. "Rise."

From the open mouths of the cylinders, dark vapors began to appear. Remaining separate the misty clouds rose higher thickening until five distinct shadows hung menacingly behind their chosen vessels.

Cain nodded and as one they shot forward into the back of the necks of their chosen hosts. It was over in mere moments. The newly possessed turned their heads as if one being and looked at Cain. He nodded. They moved to the steps and began to chant.

"Satan is our master, Satan is our lord ..."

The lone figure slipped out the rear of the building unnoticed while the sole guard focused on the events taking place on the stage. She rushed to the woods dropping the white robe from her slender shoulders as she ran, terror trying to sap her strength.

"Oh, Merlin. What is happening?"

Cain walked to the boat, the five possessed following silently. When he reached the dock he turned. "You know what you must do. It is time."

He stepped onto the boat. "Take me to Cleveland."

CHAPTER FOUR

The Havenites stepped off the platform and Arthur smiled. "Well, that worked."

"I know who they are. I can see them," Kathleen whispered. "I mean who they really are. I don't understand."

"You mean you see through them."

She chuckled. "I suppose that's what I mean. I know who they are and yet they are someone else. We will need to get them new clothes though. They look like they are wearing tents."

"Welcome to my world. Strange things happen to a Blocker. And you're right about the clothes. Especially Ariel."

"I guess I never understood what you... I don't know... went through."

"It doesn't always work this way." He nodded towards Millie staring at the newcomers. "I'm not sure all Blockers have the same abilities."

Noting the strange look on Millie's face Kathleen nodded. "I guess not."

"You are..." Millie looked at Michael.

He looked down at himself and then at his siblings who were examining each other.

"It is I, Millie, Michael." He turned to Arthur. "Like Lucifer."

"Lancelot," Arthur said. "Lucifer is not a name that will encourage confidence here."

Lancelot nodded. "Nor does Lancelot. You should refer to me simply as Lance."

Millie took his arm. "I'm not sure which I prefer. Tall dark and human or taller, lighter and way more exotic."

"I am who I am regardless of how I appear."

Tightening her grip on his arm she simply said, "I know."

"These forms we now find ourselves in," a tall, exquisite looking blond woman asked holding her loose robe to her breast, "How?"

"I was hoping that the same thing that happened to Lucifer would happen to you," Arthur said. "Fortunately it did."

"Do you believe it was Him?" Gabriel asked.

Michael shrugged his shoulders. "It is possible, brother. But I am not sure it is truly who you believe him to be. But this is good. We can walk about this world without causing undue alarm."

"You mean by people seeing seven-foot aliens with green hair walking the streets," Arthur said with a chuckle then stopped.

"Something wrong?" Kathleen asked.

Arthur looked at those from Haven. "No. Just... never mind. It isn't important."

"Well," Gwen said. "They may look like they belong around here but there is still a problem. Ariel and Michael are common enough names but I'm not sure about the others. Not a lot of folks around here use handles like Remiel or Ezekiel. Well unless you're from Idaho or someplace like that."

"True enough," Arthur agreed.

"I do not use my real name here," Millie said. "Helps me fit in better."

"You feel my name might cause people to view me differently?"

"It might, Remiel," Arthur said. "How about Bob? Simple and easy to spell."

"Bob? It is simple. You believe it is a name that will not draw attention?"

Gwen giggled looking at the big man. "You are built like Hercules and your dark curly hair and blue eyes are enough to melt the heart of any girl you might meet. I'm not sure people will even pay attention to the name. But Bob is good."

"Gabe is okay for Gabriel and maybe Zeb for Ezekiel," Millie said. "And I agree with Gwen. You guys are knockouts."

"Knockouts?" Gabriel asked.

"It means you're a pleasure to look at," Michael explained.

"And I couldn't get a date at home," Ezekiel said. "I may just stay here."

"What about us?" Bast asked.

"Something to think about on our way to Cleveland," Arthur said, "Maybe Bea for now."

Bast smiled. "Bea, I like it."

Arthur stepped back as a large van pulled up. "I think our ride is here."

Loki took Arthur's elbow and pulled him from the group as they were loading into the van. He looked around the edge of the wood. "Something isn't right."

"I noticed. Looks like a battle took place within the last few days."

"But we've been gone that long on Olympus. Weeks should have passed here. Maybe months."

"I know." He nodded to the van. "We should go. And Loki, let's not talk about this right now."

"Understand. But we need to be careful."

As Loki stepped into the back of the van Arthur looked once again at the woods.

"Are you okay?" Kathleen asked. She had moved to the center of the bench seat to make room for him.

"Oh, ah, yeah. I'm fine. Just thinking."

"Well think on the way back. The driver said he heard from my father and he needs to see us right away."

"He's here?"

"Came via the small portal along with Odin and Freya."

"It must be something important."

"I agree, Michael."

Arthur closed the door. He smiled at Kathleen. "Sorry. Lost in thought."

He turned towards the back of the van. Loki looked at him and then Michael. He smiled and gave a small nod of understanding.

"Everyone ready?" Arthur asked. He turned to the driver. "Let's go."

"What is your concern, First Dragon?" Michael asked.

"Did you notice the area around the portal?"

"You mean the damage?"

"Yeah. I would have thought it would have been cleaned up by now."

"Unless the battle happened but a few days ago."

"That can't be. Weeks should have passed while we were gone. Maybe even longer."

"It is curious."

The van passed a scorched area of the wood line, the remnants of a helicopter protruding from the charred debris.

"This makes no sense."

"What makes no sense, Arthur?" Kathleen asked. "Are you sure you are okay?"

He took her hand and gave it a gentle squeeze. "I'm fine. But something isn't right."

She looked at the wreckage. "Many good people died during the fight, Arthur. It was not your fault. And those your father asked to join us wished to end their lives this way. To them, it was a blessing. An honorable death."

"I know. That's not what concerns me ...."

The windshield shattered.

"Brace!" Arthur screamed as the van began to slide down the embankment throwing the driver's bloody head against the side window. The van came to a stop and rolled onto its side.

"Ambush! Everybody out. Stay low." Arthur struggled to push the passenger door open. Reaching for Kathleen's hand he drew her up onto the side of the van and they tumbled to the ground.

"You okay?" He asked catching his breath.

"Just bruised. Nothing broken. What happened?"

"An ambush."

"Need some help here," Loki called.

Arthur crawled onto the van and helped Loki pull Ezekiel through the side door. They handed him to Gabriel who lowered his unconscious brother gently to the ground.

"Banged his head. I think he'll be all right," Loki said jumping down.

Clutching her robe Ariel asked, "What is happening?" She looked at Ezekiel. "Is he all right?"

"Someone shot the driver. Ezekiel is just knocked out I think." Arthur jumped down beside Loki. "Thor, Kathleen, get everyone behind the van. Loki, come with me. I want to see if we can locate the shooter."

"Or shooters," Loki said.

"Always the optimist, let's go."

Loki chuckled. "Damn wish we had thought to bring guns."

Michael reached into his robe and withdrew a small cylinder not much bigger than a toothpaste tube. A red stripe around one end and a small black button on the other were the only markings. "Will this help?"

"I don't know. What is it?" Loki asked.

"A weapon. Point the red end at the target and press the black button." He smiled at Loki. "Remember my friend, point the red end at the target."

"Everyone is a comedian."

Thor crawled up beside them. He handed another of the toothpaste tubes to Arthur. "Remiel said to give this to you."

"Anyone else hurt?"

"Just some busing."

Arthur took the tube, surprised at the weight. "Thanks. Loki and I are going to crawl up to the edge of the embankment and see if we can spot the shooter. I need you and the others to keep watch and cry out if you see movement anywhere else. Did anyone call for help?"

"I did," Thor said. "It's on the way."

"How is Ezekiel?"

Thor smiled. "Awake and angry."

"That's a good sign," Michael said. "I should get back with the others. I'm not going to be much use in this baggy clothing."

"Thanks, Michael."

"Arthur?"

He turned to find Kathleen working her way around the edge of the upturned van. "What is going on?"

"Loki and I are to try to locate the sniper."

"I'll go with you."

"No. Kathleen, I need you to stay here."

"But ..."

"I don't have time to argue. You swore an oath to follow the First Dragon and as much as you don't like it I need you to do what I ask." He shook his head. "Sorry. I did not mean for that to come out the way it did."

She looked at him for a moment. She turned to Thor. "Tell me what I need to do."

As they crawled along the bank Loki shook his head. "I wouldn't do that too often, little brother."

Arthur grimaced. "I know. I think I'm going to pay for it later."

"You damn sure are. Now let's see if the lesser of the dangers you are going to face today is still up there. Lucky for you he is only trying to kill you."

As they neared the road a crack sounded from across the highway and the blacktop in front of them exploded into chips of hardened blacktop.

"Shit! That was close," Loki said cringing. "See 'em?"

"Yeah, two of them. They were creeping towards the road when they saw us. Thank God he fired as he was taking cover or one of us would be sporting a new eye."

"So now what?"

"Go down the road about ten yards and wait. I'll draw their fire and you see if you can get at least one of them with that thing."

"No, you are the First Dragon. Not me. I'll draw their fire. It's my job to risk my backside for you, not the other way around. Get used to it."

Arthur looked at him for a moment then nodded. "Fine. But watch your ass. It's a lot bigger than mine."

"Asshole."

Arthur worked his way down the sloping bank for about ten yards then stopped. Climbing to the edge of the road and keeping his head down, he waited. Loki poked his head up and dropped back just as a bullet zipped past and struck the tree behind him. Arthur sat up when he heard the crack and saw the muzzle-flash. Holding the tube with two hands he pointed the small weapon and pressed the black button. A quick snap sounded almost like that of a bullwhip and the man with the gun was gone, the rifle clattering off the edge of the roadway.

Loki stood and as the other man turned to run, fired with the same result.

"Son-of-a-bitch!" he said grinning. "Nothing to clean up."

Arthur ran to join him. "Do you think there are any more?"

"Doubt it. This was done in a hurry. But we should be careful just the same."

"Agree. I wonder how they knew we were here."

"Did you notice the uniforms?" Loki said. "Like the ones, Millie told us about. Maybe they have been hiding out since the fight waiting for a target of opportunity"

"But that was weeks ago for them."

"Was it? I saw you looking at the chopper. Something is wrong with the timeline. It's like Earth and Olympus are synced."

Arthur looked up at the sound of approaching helicopters.

"Great."

CHAPTER FIVE

Arthur looked around the conference room. Only his oath-sworn was present.

"I don't understand," Kathleen said placing her hand on his.

Giving it a gentle squeeze Arthur smiled. *I guess I'm forgiven.* "I don't know. You said that your father wanted to see us as soon as we got back."

"That is what the driver said before he was killed."

"Look, Kathleen, I'm sorry about what ..."

She released his hand. "We will talk about that later. First Dragon."

I guess I'm not forgiven.

"First Dragon." Merlin stepped into the room followed by Freya, Odin, and Patricia. Nodding a greeting to Apollo and Lancelot he stopped when he noticed the five people standing next to Millie.

Raising a single eyebrow he asked, "And these are?"

"Tis I, Merlin. Michael. And these others are my kin." This is Ezekiel, Gabriel, Remiel, and the beautiful young lady is my sister Ariel."

"But how?" Merlin asked.

"We don't know," Arthur said.

Gwen walked over to Ariel who was holding her oversized robe closed while fingering her long blond hair. "We need to get you some clothes that fit." She smiled. "Soon."

"I think you are right. Thank you, Gwen. I like this color."

Merlin stood silent for a moment. "This just gets stranger all the time." He turned to Arthur. "Our friend on the hill?"

"I would suppose so but he didn't make an appearance. Who knows anymore?"

Merlin bowed to Ariel. "I will have you taken to wardrobe as soon as this meeting is over if that meets with your approval."

"It does. Thank you."

Merlin walked to the head of the table. He held out his hand and took that of a dark-haired young woman. "Patricia has brought us some disturbing news."

"The witches are back," she said. "At the warehouse in Mentor."

"How? Lancelot and I closed that doorway," Arthur said.

"I don't know, but there are a lot of them and they are planning something."

Freya smiled at Patricia. "I will explain. You have done enough." She turned to those seated around the table. "Patricia has risked her life infiltrating the disciples of Satan once again. She was lucky not to have been discovered."

Merlin squeezed Patricia's shoulder. "No more."

She looked up at him and smiled. "I promise."

"Patricia's contacts," Freya continued, "notified her that the atrocities that have been occurring in the last few weeks are linked to the people that organized the crossing in Mentor. When she heard of this she resumed her role as one of the witches, convincing them that she was the sole survivor of our attack. It made her somewhat of a celebrity allowing her to get close to the leaders. Yesterday she attended a ceremony in the warehouse. The guest of honor was Cain."

"That can't be. I saw him die," Lancelot said.

"So we all believed. However, there was no doubt it was him."

"How?" Lancelot asked. "He had a bullet hole in his forehead."

"I put it there," Loki added. "The bastard was dead."

"I have no idea but he is back and stirring up trouble. According to Patricia, it was he that was behind the recent attacks on the children. Disciples carried out the actual strikes but it was orchestrated by Cain. He rewarded them for their good work." She turned to Patricia. "He offered Patricia one, which she graciously declined stating that she did not feel worthy."

"Thank all that is holy for that," Merlin said looking at Patricia and taking her hand.

"Rewarded them?" Arthur asked. "With what? Medals."

Patricia leaned on the edge of the table. "Cain had what looked like coffee thermoses. Bringing the people forward that were to be rewarded he asked each if they would accept a gift from their god. They nodded, almost as if in a trance. He opened the canisters and Shadow drifted out and possessed them."

"How many?" Loki asked.

"Five."

"He carried them in daylight in a thermos?" Thor asked. "I did not know that could be done."

"No one did," Freya said.

"But why now? Arthur asked. "Satan said he wants to meet. We have a truce. At least until after we meet. These attacks sure look like an escalation to me."

"I agree," Odin said taking a seat next to his wife. "It is strange. There is no incentive for you to risk a meeting with him. There is no advantage for either of us."

"Maybe he doesn't know about them."

Everyone turned towards Ariel. "Is it possible that Cain could do this without the knowledge of Satan?"

The room became still. Odin looked at Lancelot. "Who was Cain with the day you believed he was slain?"

"Bael."

"And he serves Satan?"

Merlin looked at Odin. "So we thought."

"He was shocked when Arthur told him he had confronted Satan," Loki said.

"What happened to Cain's body?" Freya asked.

"When Bael opened the portal he took it with him," Lancelot said.

"Are we fighting more than one enemy?" Gwen asked.

"I think a more interesting question would be, is Satan?" Arthur said. "I think it just became more important than ever for me to meet with him."

"It could be a trap. This could all be an elaborate ploy to lure you to the meeting, Arthur," Loki said.

"I don't think so. I need to meet with him. If nothing more than to find out why he asked for it. Don't worry, Loki, I have a plan or two myself. I am not going in unprepared." He looked at Kathleen. "We have plans."

"This is stupid. You think you can trust a Shadow?"

"Satan is not a Shadow, Kathleen."

"Then what is he?"

"I'm not sure. But I think it is important we find out."

"Have the Friends been able to tell you anything?" Freya asked.

"They have tried," Arthur said. "We are still working on expressing concepts. The idea of family, home, relationships, have different meanings. Every time I think we understand each other I discover we are speaking about apples rather than oranges. Sometimes it is hard to keep them on the subject."

"What does that mean?" Merlin asked.

"Well," Kathleen said. "They like to talk. Ask questions about us. They are very curious. A lot were very personal questions." Her cheeks gained a little color. "Then they would explain the differences between us. For example, we, ah, found out they don't procreate as we do so some of our ideas on family are different for example."

"Okay, I'll bite," Loki said. "How do they procreate?"

"They do so without intercourse."

"They don't have sex!" Falstaff said. "That is not right!"

"Literally," Arthur added. "They have no males or females. They think the way we do it is barbaric, inefficient, and ... messy."

"Barbaric! So what do they do? Smile at each other?" Loki asked.

"No," Kathleen said. "They hold hands."

"They what?"

"They sit in a circle and hold hands, Loki," Arthur said. "The way I understand it, each individual shares a part of themselves through the contact and a new individual is created from the combination of... whatever it is they share. As I said, we are having some concept problems."

"So what, they hold hands and a baby just plops from their fingertips?" Gwen asked.

"Not exactly. Something just grows within the circle. Not a child. Another... Friend appears." Arthur shrugging his shoulders. "An adult."

"They have no children?" Gwen asked.

"No. The idea is confusing to them," Kathleen added.

"This is all very interesting, and unsettling," Merlin said. He looked at Kathleen and Arthur. "And I can see how it could be embarrassing, but did they tell you anything we can use to defeat our mutual enemy?"

"I think the Friends come from a different world than Satan's people. The Shadows as well. From what I understand, Satan's people have a portal system that connects them as we do with our worlds. The Ot's, or whatever they are called, seem to — harvest the Shadows and the Friends and bring them back to their world. I'm not sure, but I think they can only reach Earth from Ot. But the Shadows are not Shadows when they are harvested. Those from Ot take something from their world and process it in machines which create what we call Shadows."

"But the others, the Knights of Satan and the big red beings?" Odin asked.

"The knights are created using some kind of technology I think. The others are of Satan's race, they don't possess others to exist. They control the Shadows and those they possess."

"But what about the thing that possessed you. Samnu. Wasn't he from Ot?" Kathleen asked.

"I don't think what was in me was him. I mean not the real him. I think it was kinda like a projection or something. A piece of Shadow that absorbed some of him. I'm not sure. We have a lot to learn about them."

"It was a lot simpler when we thought the enemy was just the Shadows," Apollo said.

"And I don't think their portals work like ours do. At least not completely. I think they are created by some kind of machine," Arthur said.

"Not our magic circles of stone?" Loki asked sarcastically.

"That would explain their ability to create them in multiple locations," Lancelot said.

"Those from Ot seem to have technology that far exceeds our own," Arthur said. "But only in some ways. To be honest, the way things work there doesn't follow the same rules of science we have here. It is very confusing. I'm not sure they come from a parallel world like the ones in the Alliance."

"What do you mean?" Merlin asked.

"Well, science works the same way on all of our worlds." He looked around the room. "To include biology. We are all basically the same."

"Except for those from Haven," Gwen said.

"True," Arthur said. "But we are similar."

"Do you guys have sex?" Falstaff asked.

"We are not as the Friends," Ariel said coldly.

Arthur turned towards Michael. "How were you able to project your mind into Excalibur?"

"We have developed technology that allows us to separate our essence from our material bodies."

"Astral projection?" Freya asked.

"Something like that," Michael said.

"And how did the rest of you arrive here? Did you use a portal of some sort?"

Michael was silent for a moment. "Not exactly. We have equipment that allows us to travel long distances."

"It wasn't given to you as ours was?" Arthur asked.

"No. Ariel and Remiel developed the technology that allows us to travel within a hole in space."

"How many moons does Haven have?" Gwen asked quietly.

"I begin to see where this is going," Ariel said. "We have three."

"And the planets in your solar system?"

"There are six. Only Haven holds life," Gabriel said.

The room was quiet for a moment.

"So you are not of what we would call our Earth," Millie said.

"Or any of our worlds," Merlin said.

"And I think the same is true of Ot," Arthur said.

"Shit," Patricia said. "We are being invaded by aliens from other planets now."

"Looks that way," Arthur agreed.

"Well then what do they want? I always thought it was souls," Rex said.

"They call us food, but I'm not sure that is what they mean," Arthur said. "Once again concept. I'm beginning to wonder if what makes us, us, could be some kind of drug to them. Or something they need to power their technology."

Merlin nodded his head. "We need to stop thinking of them as we do ourselves. What drives us does not drive them."

"You mean they may not be evil?" Gwen asked.

"Oh, they are evil, Gwen," Arthur said. "What they do is wrong no matter what drives them. They enslave, destroy, torture. The Friends and the Shadows are slaves that are used and abused. They are as evil as you can get."

"So how does any of this help us?" Thor asked.

"I'm not sure yet. But knowing your enemy is key to defeating him," Arthur said. He chuckled. "I read that somewhere."

"Good to know you can read," Loki said.

"So what do we do now?" Odin asked.

"I guess I meet with Satan."

CHAPTER SIX

Arthur studied the unobtrusive structure that lay across from the Federal Building. Taking a deep breath he pushed his way through the revolving glass door. He stopped and glanced up and down the remarkably quiet boulevard. *"See anyone?"*

He heard Michael respond, *"Everything is quiet. A car drove by a few minutes ago but did not stop. That was the last we saw and there has been no pedestrian traffic."*

"The locals were told there is a gas leak. Dangerous to be in the area until fixed," Arthur said. *"Patricia's idea."*

"Do you believe this will work? How will Satan know you are coming?" Ezekiel asked.

"I'm pretty sure he knows. I get the feeling that we are under constant surveillance."

"Be careful, First Dragon,"

"I will, Michael. You just be ready."

"We shall remain vigilant. If you call all of us will respond."

"I'm counting on that."

Arthur strolled across the street, his hand in the pocket of his long trench coat, his fist wrapped around the handle of an automatic, the other brushing the scabbard of Excalibur.

I don't know if I'm supposed to be James Bond or Matt Dillion, he thought with a chuckle.

Stopping in front of the office building he looked around, pleased he was unable to see any of the others.

"I will come alone. But I won't be alone," he whispered.

"*You will not,*" he heard Michael respond.

"*We await your call, First Dragon,*" Gabriel said.

"*We are ready,*" Ariel added.

"Thank you all."

Pushing the doors open he stepped into the cool and very quiet lobby. It was empty. No hustle of busy men and women moving about, no friendly banter as they continued with their daily activities. The stillness gave him a sense of loneliness.

A few stray pieces of paper drifted gently across the polished floor encouraged by the circulation of the air-conditioning. Arthur approached the doorway leading to the basement. He pushed it open remembering the last time he had entered the stairwell. The doors and the walls had been repaired and repainted.

Reaching out with his senses he felt nothing. No Shadow. Didn't mean there couldn't be a disciple waiting below. He pulled the pistol from his pocket, slipped off the safety, and held it against his leg.

He stopped at the bottom of the steps remembering the blood that had covered the floor. It was gone. Scrubbed clean. The terror of facing Satan suddenly vanished. He was nervous but not frightened. Stepping around the corner he entered the main room. It suddenly grew cold. A dark shadow materialized on the far wall which quickly turned into a pitch-black archway. Satan stepped through. He was alone.

"You can put that away. I am here to talk, not fight" He looked around. "I see you have kept your word and come alone. I also see that the thing in your head is no longer with you."

"I have done as you asked," Arthur said coldly.

"As have I. You are safe young man. I do not go back upon my word. I have brought none with me. As long as there is no aggression directed toward me, there will none toward at you."

Arthur slipped on the safety and put the pistol back into his pocket. He drew Excalibur. Satan smiled.

"Although not necessary, an understandable precaution."

"I keep the sword. Although you claim you have keep your word there have been attacks by your minions upon my people. Something you said would not happen. Hard to trust you."

"I have directed no such attacks. You must be mistaken."

"I'm not. They were orchestrated by one of yours. Calls himself Cain. And he has brought Shadows with him."

Satan was silent.

I was right, he didn't know.

"I was not aware of such activity. If what you say is true it was not by my orders. I have not broken my word."

"Then maybe you should get a better grip on your folks."

Satan stepped forward and an ebony blade materialized in his hand. His eyes flared and Arthur could feel the fury as a tangible force.

"Do not push me, child. I do not tolerate insult."

"And I do not tolerate treachery!"

Satan stood as if carved from marble. The muscles of his arms like spring steel ready to snap. Arthur prepared for the strike. Fear finally drawing a cold sweat.

The ebony sword faded and Satan took two steps back. "You have grown since last we met, Young Dragon."

"What is it you want?" Arthur demanded.

Satan took a deep breath never taking those emotionless eyes off of him making Arthur regret not bringing the others.

"Watch your tone, boy. I come with a proposal. Call it a business arrangement."

"A business proposal? What could you possibly offer me?"

"The lives and the freedom of the people of this world."

"Their lives?"

"For eternity."

"And in return?"

"Safe passage."

"Passage? A passage where?"

"The other dimensions."

"You're kidding me."

"I do appreciate humor, First Dragon. But I am very serious about this offer. The people of this world will never be attacked by me or my kind again. I would give you my word."

"Like now?"

The anger started to return. "As I said, I am never forsworn. That situation will be taken care of."

"Then maybe we should discuss this proposal when you have your house in order."

The sound of a gunshot followed quickly by many others, made both look towards the stairwell.

"Arthur, several men have arrived. They are armed and are trying to reach the stairwell. We are doing our best to prevent that. I would suggest you conclude your business and leave." Michael said.

"What is that?" Satan asked.

"It seems that some of your folks don't want me to leave."

"They are not mine! How do you know ....?"

Before he could finish his question a dark portal opened and several large beings with blue skin and black eyes burst into the cellar armed with ebony swords and axes. Three quickly moved towards Satan while two more threw themselves at Arthur.

"I'm in trouble down here!" Arthur called out while raising Excalibur to a defensive position. He quickly stepped aside as a long black blade slid down the forged steel of Excalibur and struck the floor.

Arthur spun as the other being lunged at him with a massive ax missing his shoulder by the thickness of his shirt. As he completed the turn he brought Excalibur across the back of his assailant opening the thing from shoulder to hip. It fell between him and the first attacker causing it to pause. Dark blood pooled on the concrete floor threatening secure footing.

Carefully negotiating the blood of its companion, the second beast brought its sword up seeking a weakness in Arthur's defense. The two danced from side-to-side seeking an opening when Arthur heard flesh stuck from behind him. Was it Satan that had received the blow? His back began to itch but he could not afford to take his eyes from his opponent. Raising his hand Arthur prepared to send a blast of power to quickly end the fight afraid he was about to be attacked from behind.

"Do not kill him, First Dragon. I need him alive. I need to ask questions."

Satan stepped past him and approached the blue figure. Flicking his hand droplets of black liquid spattered onto its face. As they touched its flesh there was a loud sizzle and the thing screamed grabbing at its face. Satan walked over and delivered a vicious uppercut causing the huge being to fall to the floor and remain still. He turned to Arthur.

"This was not my doing. I believe we both were their targets."

Arthur raised his arm and before Satan could react threw Excalibur in his direction. Satan's sword reappeared as the steel blade flew over his shoulder. Reacting quickly, Satan turned just as another of the blue-skinned figures dropped a long dagger and fell to the ground, Arthur's sword protruding from its chest with little more than the hilt left exposed.

Satan turned and looked at Arthur. The sword disappearing in his hand just as Loki, Rex, Michael, and Lancelot rushed around the corner of the stairwell. Arthur held up his hand.

"Wait."

Satan pointed at Excalibur. "Take it."

Arthur walked over and recovered his sword.

Satan reached down, grabbed the arm of the prone figure, and without taking his eyes off Arthur, walked back towards the black doorway.

"Consider my offer, First Dragon. I would suggest you not wait too long."

He stepped into the doorway and vanished.

Arthur looked down at the bodies littering the basement floor. They began to hiss, then melted into the concrete leaving only a cloud of fine black dust.

"Did I see you save Satan's life?" Loki asked incredulously.

Arthur chuckled. "I guess you did."

"Why the hell would you do something like that? The bastard was done for. That thing had him cold!"

"It was the right thing to do at the time. I think."

"You think?"

"I know this may sound crazy, Loki, but I believe we need him right now."

"Need him how," came the cold stone voice of Lancelot. The look on his face reminded Arthur of the history Lancelot and Michael had with Satan. Of the death of one's sister and the other's wife.

"I'm sorry. For the moment I think he may be the lesser of two evils. There is conflict on Ot. I think someone is attempting a takeover. Maybe if we let them kill each other for a while they will leave us alone. And I think that no matter which side wins they will be weaker for it."

"You are sure of this, Arthur," Michael asked.

"Pretty sure. He didn't know about the attacks orchestrated by Cain. He was pretty pissed. It seems keeping his word is important to him."

"A strange monster," Rex said.

Arthur smiled. "He is that."

"What offer was he talking about?" Loki asked.

"I'll tell you when I have everybody together. What happened upstairs? You started shooting and the big bad blue guys stepped out of the wall at the same time."

"Several vehicles ran the barricade and stopped in front of the building. Many people stepped out. They were armed," Michael said.

"So I shot one and all hell broke loose," Loki added.

Michael looked at Loki.

"Was I supposed to let them in? Zeb, Bob, and Gabe were the only ones inside. What if they couldn't stop them before they reached Arthur? There were a lot of them."

"I was not criticizing, Loki. Just stating the facts."

"Yeah, you were stating facts the way my mother used to tell Odin I had been creative again."

Michael shrugged.

"Art!" Gwen threw herself into his arms. "You okay?"

"I'm fine."

Kathleen stood at the base of the steps. Gwen stepped aside. Kathleen continued to stare at him unmoving. He reached out his arms and she came running. They embraced and she drew her lips to his. After a few moments, she stepped back taking a deep breath. "I heard you call for help. I was unable to break free. I was afraid you ..." She smacked him on the shoulder.

"Ouch."

"You will not do something like this again without me. Is that understood?"

"My poor Arthur," Loki said. "And you thought Satan was a problem."

He smiled. "I understand, Kathleen. We will discuss this when we are alone."

"Yes we will but it will not change things."

"What happened, First Dragon?" Odin asked stepping into the room. Behind him were his wife and Merlin.

"A lot, sir. An opportunity has arisen I think. One we may be able to take advantage of. Let's get back to the Federal Building." He looked around. "I don't want to be here any longer then I have to and we have a lot to talk about."

"Are you going to seal the room?"

"No, Merlin. I may need it again."

CHAPTER SEVEN

"He wants you to what!" Falstaff asked.

"He wants me to agree to allow him free access to the other worlds. If I agree to his terms he promises to leave the people of Earth alone."

"Why?" Merlin asked. "Why offer a deal at all. If he occupied Earth or even controlled a large portion of the population, the other worlds would be within his reach."

"We could close our portals," Apollo said taking a seat.

"And abandon those of this world. That has not worked well for us in the past," Anubis said. "And I believe there are still some of our own that follow him. I doubt we have unmasked them all. Besides, he would most likely be able to send several of his warriors across before we knew of the arrangement. By then it would be too late."

"We would have to sever all contact with each other as well to ensure our security," Sif said. She turned to Michael. "And what of your people?"

"We do not use a portal. I do not believe it would interfere with us reaching any of you." He turned to Ariel. "You are our scientist. Would there be a problem?"

"Not technically. But that is not the point. We cannot allow this. We cannot abandon any of you."

"And we won't," Arthur said. "I would never consider allowing that monster and his kind free access to feed upon anyone." He leaned against the wall and crossed his arms. "Especially not friends and family. The question that I have is why is he even offering this deal?"

"Maybe he has no choice," Gwen said.

"What do you mean?"

"I don't know, Kathleen. Maybe they are running low on food. Art said Satan did not know about Cain and the attacks that took place during the truce. Maybe someone is trying to overthrow the dark lord using the shortage as an excuse. Been done before."

"So why try to kill Arthur? I mean they had to know Satan would try to stop it. He had given his word. He almost died as well. Pretty sure he didn't orchestrate that."

"Maybe," Rex said. "But what if First Dragon wasn't the primary target. What if he was the bait and the real target was Satan."

"Please call me Arthur, Rex, and you may be right. The beings that attacked us came from his world and they went after him more than me."

"There was the attack in the lobby," Ezekiel said.

"True." Remiel stroked his chin. "They had to be there for Arthur. I doubt they would try to attack their god with guns."

"Then both of us were targeted."

"I would assume that is the case," Odin agreed.

"Cain?" Lucifer asked.

"Maybe," Michael said. "He is a good suspect."

"But what the hell is Cain doing?" Loki asked. "He is human."

"He has not been human for a very long time," Lancelot said.

"Okay. So the not-human asshole is smuggling Shadows here without letting his boss know he is doing it. You think he is the one trying to usurp Satan?"

"No, Loki," Lancelot said. "I believe Cain is merely a puppet."

"Then who?" Kathleen asked.

"It has to be Bael," Lancelot said. "He has always pulled Cain's strings."

"You think Bael is trying to take Satan down?" Arthur asked.

"He is almost as powerful as Satan himself. Remember what he said when we met them in the woods where I thought I had killed Cain. He implied that he was stronger than Satan when it came to you."

"A little overconfident, but a coup?"

"I suppose it is possible, Arthur," Merlin said. "We have no idea what their social or governmental structure looks like."

"If they have a social structure," Kathleen added.

"If Bael is planning to overthrow Satan why use Earth as his battleground? Why not do it on his own world?" Arthur asked.

"A good question. One that deserves consideration," Odin said. "But the immediate problem we face is the half a dozen Shadow possessed lunatics running around being supported by a bunch of fanatics hell-bent on creating terror right here in Ohio. Killing children."

The room became quiet.

"What about our home worlds?" Freya asked.

"Our home worlds?" Odin looked at her.

"Have they got assets on our home worlds with a similar agenda?"

"A good question," Merlin said. "We need to let our people know what is going on here and have them increase security. I will go to Avalon and let the king know."

"And the others?" Apollo asked."

"I will return home and ensure all is well," Odin said. He turned to Apollo and Bast. "I will let Zeus and Ra know what is happening. I will take the main portal. I want to ensure it is properly secured and send additional forces if necessary."

"Thank you," Arthur said. "We will do what we can here to find Cain and his people and hopefully contain this thing."

"You mean kill the bastards," Falstaff said.

Arthur stood for a moment then nodded. "Cain at least."

"Or try," Lancelot said.

Freya placed her hand on Arthur's shoulder. "I will accompany Odin. I shall inform your parents you are well and see what your mother thinks about Cain's plans. She has proven herself a remarkable intelligence analyst and has a better grasp on the way this world works than I. She may be able to provide insight as to what Cain's next move might be. Maybe we can get ahead of him."

"Do the guards at the portal have power rods?" Arthur asked.

"If they do not I will ensure some are provided," Freya said.

Odin stepped beside his wife. "And what of Satan's proposal, First Dragon?"

"Pretty dumb to believe I would consider it but then I don't know how his mind works. Let him stew for a while. Once we figure out what Bael and Cain are doing then I will contact him with my answer."

"Then we should be going." Odin offered his arm to Freya and escorted her to the door.

"I should go as well," Merlin said stepping to Kathleen and kissing her on the cheek. "You be careful."

"I shall, Father."

With Merlin's departure, Arthur took a seat at the head of the table. "I guess we should get to work. Anyone got a suggestion of where to start?"

For the next hour, they tossed around ideas as to what to do to find and stop Cain and his people. The problem of Satan and the Shadows almost forgotten. An urgent knocking at the conference room door ended their discussion. Gwen got up. She listened as a member of the clerical staff spoke softly but urgently. Arthur came to his feet when she turned and he saw the look on her face.

"What's wrong?"

"Odin and his party were ambushed as they turned off the main road towards the portal."

Loki jumped up knocking his chair back. "My parents?"

"They live. The guards at the portal heard gunfire and sent a party to investigate. The ambushers were killed but not before several of Odin's party and portal guards had fallen. Your parents were wounded. They are in Asgard. The guard commander does not know their status but he reports their injuries appeared grave."

Sif took Thor's arm and Fallstaff placed his hand on Loki's shoulder. Arthur turned to them. "Go. Take the small portal and go to your parents. We will seek out Cain. He will pay I promise you. Keep me informed as to their condition. They are my family as well."

Loki could not speak and just nodded. Thor looked at Arthur. "I will stay."

"No. You must go. I have plenty of people to look out for me."

Thor stood still for a moment. Sif squeezed his arm. He nodded and they left the room. Arthur turned to Falstaff who did not follow them.

"I stay. Odin and Freya would not wish me to leave. There is little I can do for them there."

Kathleen took his arm. "It is okay, uncle. We understand. No one will fault you for going to them and Arthur has plenty of people around him to keep him safe."

He smiled down at her. “No, princess. Odin would not wish me to abandon my responsibility.” He turned to Arthur. “They would both want me to fulfill my oath. And to watch over you, little one.” He slammed his fist on the table his voice cracking. “They would want me to stay and make these bastards bleed.”

The room was quiet for a moment. Arthur placed his hand on Falstaff’s arm. “Arm yourselves. We leave for the portal in fifteen minutes. Patricia, would you please make arrangements for transportation. A helicopter would be nice but whatever is available.”

“I will go with you.”

“No,” Kathleen said approaching her. “You are a brave woman and I am happy you and my father have found one another. But you are not a warrior. You can help us most by staying here and acting as our liaison.”

Arthur placed his hand on her shoulder. “Kathleen’s right. You’ve been a great asset to us but the skills required for what we must do are not yours. Use the small portal. Seek out my mother and help her. The last I heard she was on Avalon.”

“But I have never used a portal. I have never visited any of the other worlds.”

“In all this time?” Kathleen asked. “What is wrong with my father?” She smiled. Well, if you are going to be family someday then it is about time you did. I will take you to the portal myself. For now, why don’t you see if you can get us that transportation.”

“Okay, everyone, let’s saddle up,” Arthur said.

“Saddle up?” Apollo asked.

“I will explain on the way to the armory,” Lancelot told him. “It has something to do with a warrior called John Wayne.”

“Who?”

“I will explain.”

The people from Haven remained as the others departed.

“You need to draw weapons.”

Michael smiled. “We used your weapons when dealing with those on the street. Did not want to draw attention to ourselves. But now we wish to use our own.”

“Got a spare?”

The door opened and Patricia looked in. Lancelot stood behind her. "There is a helicopter on its way. It will land on the roof."

"What kind?"

"A Huey."

"The others are in the arms room. They will be ready shortly," Lancelot said.

"Thank you.

"Patricia, find Kathleen and have her take you to the small portal. Find my mother, and Merlin," he added with a smile.

"Thank you."

Ezekiel handed Arthur one of the white tubes and grinned. "I always carry a spare."

"Thanks. These things are cool. How do you reload them?"

"You don't. They work off the energy of the sun. Leave it exposed for ten or fifteen minutes and it will be fully charged."

"How many times will it shoot between charges?"

"It is designed to be fired fifty times before recharging, however, it can be charged at any time so it basically can be fired indefinitely," Ariel said.

"And if it is cloudy?"

Ezekiel smiled. "That is why I carry a spare."

"Fantastic.

"A Huey will not carry us all. You five will come with me. Lancelot, you and Millie go with Gwen. I'll have her drive one of the vans and take Falstaff, Rex, Anubis, and Bast. Kathleen and Apollo will come with us."

Lancelot nodded. "I will tell the others. Shall I notify Kathleen and Apollo?"

"If you don't mind. Kathleen is taking Patricia to the portal. You will find her there." He clapped his hands. "Okay then. Let's go."

Arthur started to follow the others out of the room then stopped. He closed the door and sat on the edge of the table. "I don't know if you can hear me but any help you can provide will be appreciated. Things are getting a little complicated here."

"They are."

A man in a business suit and trench coat stood near the closed door. It was the same man that had visited him in the hospital.

"I seem to be facing more than one enemy."

"You are facing only one enemy."

"I don't think so. There are the Shadows, Satan and his warriors, and now Cain and probably Bael and his followers. Not to mention their disciples."

"There are many factions to your enemy, but there is still but one."

"I'm sorry, but these riddles aren't helping."

The man in the suit smiled. "Your enemy has many faces, Arthur. But the evil they represent remains the same. Terror is their weapon. Chaos is their goal. You and your friends must prevent them from reaching that goal. The people of this world cannot realize what you know to be the threat. To do so would be its downfall. You and your friends must prevent that at all costs. A rational explanation for all that transpires is essential to your success. Cain and his warriors must be a priority. Seek allies from your new friends and old enemies. As a man of this world once said, the enemy of my enemy is my friend" He tilted his head. "At least for now."

Arthur was about to ask another question, but the man was gone.

"Great. More riddles."

There was a knock at the door. Michael stuck his head in.

"The helicopter has arrived and Gwen and the others have departed in a van." He looked at Arthur. "Are you well?"

Arthur shook his head. "Outside of being totally insane, I'm Fine. We should go."

CHAPTER EIGHT

The helicopter orbited the wood line that surrounded the large portal. Several men and women stood near the stone circle. There did not seem to be a sense of urgency to their movements.

"Looks like they have everything under control," Apollo said looking out the window of the closed door.

Michael pointed to the line of covered bodies. "It seems that not all is well."

Arthur pressed the push-to-talk button on his headset connecting him to the pilot. "Could you circle the area? Slowly? I would like to take a look."

"You want to see if anyone else is down there," the pilot asked.

"Yeah. Can you do that without us getting shot down?"

The pilot chuckled. "I will do my best. Loki would remove my manly parts if something happened to you. My wife would not appreciate that."

"I'm sure she wouldn't. Thanks."

Pulling the headset off, he raised his voice over the roar of the turbine engines. "We are going to circle the area. Keep your eyes open. There is a chance some of the shooters are still around. I don't want any surprises when we land."

Crowding to the windows the others began to scan the trees as the pilot guided the helicopter in an ever-widening circle. He turned and tapped his head indicating that Arthur should put his back on.

"How low do you want me to go?"

"Low enough we can see if there is movement in the trees But don't take any unnecessary chances. Remember your wife."

The pilot gave him a thumbs up. "Got it. I'll keep it at five hundred feet. We can cover more territory that way and still see if we have uninvited guests lurking around."

Arthur leaned forward and looked out the window at the pilot's feet.

"I think that is Gwen," Ariel said pointing at the van turning off the main highway.

"Look there," Ezekiel said. "Movement near the intersection."

Little flashes of light appeared in the trees and the van suddenly veered off the road striking a tree.

"Get us down there!" Arthur screamed as Apollo and Ezekiel slid the side doors open.

As the helicopter began its rapid descent Michael drew his weapon and pointed. "Over there!"

"Set us down wherever you can." Arthur turned to the others. "I need a prisoner. Can these things stun someone?"

Ariel pointed to a small wheel on the weapon she held. "Turn it to the left to incapacitate. As the dial moves to the right the intensity of the beam increases."

Arthur noticed hers was pegged to the right. He nodded as the pilot brought the helicopter to a quick landing at the intersection of the main road.

"Let's go!"

They leaped from the aircraft as the skids kissed the ground. As soon as they were clear, the helicopter lifted off concealing them in a fog of dust. Using the cover they quickly ran to the trees. Kathleen to Arthur's right, Michael and Apollo flanking them. Ezekiel and Gabriel followed Michael and Remiel and Ariel spread out a good ten yards to either side. No commands were given. Everyone knew what needed to be done and where they had to be.

They ran towards the report of gunfire hoping to come up behind the ambushers. Apollo grabbed Arthur's shoulder. He pointed toward six armed men firing rapidly in the direction of the crashed van.

"Lancelot. Can you hear me?"

"Yes, First Dragon."

"Is everyone okay?"

"Falstaff has a wound to his arm. Gwen has a bump on her head and is bruised from striking the steering wheel. The rest of us are uninjured."

"We are behind the shooters. We will engage in a count of twenty. Cease firing then so you don't hit us. Then keep your heads down."

"I understand."

He pointed to the shooters. "*I will stun the one in the middle. The one leaning against the tree with the wounded leg. I want him alive.*"

"And the others?" Aril asked.

"I don't care. They just tried to kill my sister and my friends."

He started to count. As he reached twenty he fired. The forest became very quiet. The wounded man lay unconscious. There was no sign of the others.

Kathleen tapped his arm while sliding her pistol back into the pocket of her short jacket. "I heard you speaking to the others."

"You did?"

"Now that I can hear, I would suggest you be careful what you think when near me."

Oh shit.

"I heard that."

He and Kathleen walked toward the limp figure of the would-be assassin. Kathleen kneeled next to him and tearing a piece of his shirt wrapped it tightly around his leg.

"Won't be able to answer any questions if he bleeds to death."

Arthur sensed a presence just as Kathleen and Millie yelled a warning. He turned. as a shot rang out from beside him just in time to witness a man drop his rifle and slump to the ground. A dark mist materialized from the third eye the attempted assassin now sported. It burst into a shower of black ice as Arthur hit it with a blast of energy.

Kathleen stood, the smoking pistol in her hand.

Arthur looked at the gun. "I didn't sense him until he stood. Nice shot."

"Thank you. Nor did I. I saw him before I felt him. How can that be?"

"I don't know.

Lancelot stepped from the cover of the trees. "I believe the Shadow was weak."

"Weak?"

"I believe that the Shadows Cain brought with him are not as strong as the ones we have been dealing with."

"But even a scout is stronger than this one was."

Gwen stepped up beside him. "The Friends said that the Shadows were not natural creatures. Satan's people do something to them. Maybe these were removed from the process too soon. Before they were complete. And thanks for the rescue, big brother."

Arthur grabbed Gwen and pulled her tightly to his chest. "Are you all right?"

"I was before you grabbed me. Ease up, Art. My ribs are bruised."

Releasing her and stepping back he smiled. "I'm sorry but I am damn glad you weren't hurt."

"Well, I was. Just not as bad as these guys wanted me to be." She looked around. "Where are the rest of them?"

"All around you," Ariel said waving her hand. "They have been reduced to their basic components."

"Really? How? Oh, God, they aren't in my mouth are they?"

I do not believe so," Ariel said with a smile. "All should have settled by now."

Arthur showed her the Haven weapon. "With this. Cool, huh?"

"Can I have one?"

"Maybe later."

"You left one alive?" Falstaff asked looking at the unconscious figure on the ground. He was holding his left arm, blood oozing between his fingers.

"Are you all right, Uncle?"

"This? Tis nothing, princess. Just a scratch."

"Which needs attention before you bleed to death."

"There is a first aid kit in the van," Rex said. "I'll get it."

"Why is this thing still breathing?" Falstaff demanded.

"I am hoping he will provide some answers as to Cain's plans."

"I will question him, First Dragon. But when I am done, he dies. He tried to kill Odin and Freya."

Arthur almost felt sorry for the prisoner. "Let me try first." He turned to Michael. "Would you and the others sweep the area and make sure there aren't any more of these bastards milling around?"

"Of course."

"And be careful."

Michael smiled. *"Always*

Millie looked at him a little surprised. "Did you just say something to Michael?"

Kathleen chuckled. "Welcome to the club, Millie. Lancelot is going to be a little surprised when he finds out what you can do."

The prisoner groaned.

"Our guest seems to be waking." Apollo stuck the muzzle of his rifle under his chin. "Friend, my lord is going to ask you a few questions. If you answer them honestly I will do my best to keep the big fellow," he nodded towards Falstaff, "from separating you from your arms."

Rex arrived with the first aid kit. Kathleen took it and stepped up to Falstaff.

"Uncle, please come with me and allow me to see to your wound."

Falstaff looked at the prisoner.

"I believe Arthur will have a better chance of getting answers without him worrying about his arms."

"Do not kill him. Please. I wish some time alone with him."

"I will do my best." Arthur turned to the prisoner. "Of course, that will be up to him."

The wounded man's terrified eyes followed Falstaff and Kathleen as they walked away. Arthur kneeled in front of him. Apollo placed the business end of his rifle along his temple.

"What is your name?"

"Bobby. Bobby Johansson."

"Well, Bobby Johansson, my friends are not very happy with you. Right now the only thing keeping them for tearing you apart is me. Consider me your best friend. Do you understand?"

He looked around. "Where are the others?"

"Gone"

"Gone where?"

"Where you will go if you don't cooperate. You were working for Cain?"

"My boss was."

"And your boss is?"

"Jimmy Hart. He had one of those things in him. A demon."

"He was with you?"

He nodded towards the dead man.

"I see. And do you know what your boss was told to do?"

"We were to kill a one-eyed man and a woman when they went to the stone circle."

"And then what were you to do?"

"I don't know. Jimmy only told us what we needed to do when we were to do it."

"I see. Where were you supposed to go after you killed the one-eyed man and the woman?"

"I don't know. Back to the temple in Mentor, I guess."

"Is that where Cain is?"

"No. I mean I don't think so. He left and I don't know if he is back yet. Took off in a boat. Had some of the demons with him."

"Do you know where they went?"

"No."

"Can you guess? Did you hear anything? Think carefully, your physical well-being may rely on it. The one-eyed man and the lady are very important to the big guy."

"Cleveland. I heard Jimmy say they were going to Cleveland. Some big shot was supposed to be there and they wanted to kill him."

"Do you know who this big shot is?"

"They didn't say. But I heard Jimmy talking to some of the others. He said he thought Cain was scared of the guy."

Arthur was quiet for a moment, then he stood. "Thank you, Bobby. You have been most helpful." He started to turn away then looked back. "Were you involved with any other of Cain's recent operations?"

He was silent and looked down at the ground.

"Well."

"Just one."

"Which one?"

"Some girl scouts. But I didn't hurt any of them. I just drove the truck."

"I see. I was unaware there was a driver. I was told however that one of the shooters escaped."

Bobby stared at him terrified.

"The area is clear, Arthur," Michael said looking down at the prisoner.

"Thank you, Michael."

Rex looked at Bobby. "What do we do with him, First Dragon?"

Arthur stared at the man for a moment, turned his back, and started to walk towards the portal. "Give him to Falstaff."

CHAPTER NINE

Arthur stared at the bodies. Almost a dozen draped with blue capes. Apollo kneeled and lifted the cape that covered one of the Olympian warriors.

"His name was Philip. His father is Ajax. I was there the day he graduated from the military command school. I stood beside Ajax as they awarded him his gold laurel. He was so proud." He rose and looked at the others. "They must have been surprised or there would not be so many killed."

"It looks to me like they gave more than they got," Falstaff said looking at dozens of poncho covered bodies.

"True. But it still hurts. I will have to tell his father. It will be better if the news is delivered by a friend."

"Go," Arthur said." And pass on my condolences, please."

The Asgardian guards stepped aside as Apollo mounted the stone. "Olympus," he said. Lights flashed and he was gone.

"Not something I would wish to do," Arthur said.

Kathleen took his arm. "No one does but it is better coming from a friend."

"What do we do with the bodies?" Falstaff asked.

"The Olympians go home." He handed him his Havenite weapon. "Use this on the others. I don't want to have to explain them to the authorities."

The portal began to glow and Loki materialized.

"What are you doing here? You should be with your family."

"You are family, little brother. My father and mother live. There is nothing I can do for them there. Freya is out of surgery and the doctors say she will recover. She is awake and angry. The bullets struck her leg. They went through and no major vessels or bones were struck."

"And Odin?" Falstaff asked.

"He remains in intensive care. His injuries are more serious. One bullet struck his neck and one glanced off his skull. He lost a lot of blood. It is the head wound that is troubling the doctors. There is swelling in his brain. They are doing all they can."

"Then you should remain with him." Arthur placed his hand on Loki's shoulder.

"Thor and Sif remain. Freya insisted I return to be at your side."

Kathleen looked at him. "How?"

"How what," Loki asked.

"How can you be here? I mean now. How can Odin and Freya just be out of surgery? You have only been gone a few hours. I did not expect to see you for weeks?"

Loki looked confused. "I don't know."

"It is as Merlin suspected," Michael said. "The time separation between dimensions is shrinking. Asgard and Earth now share a common flow in time."

"Then this is the end of our guardianship of the portals," Loki said. "On your world, Arthur. We will now age at the same rate as they do. No longer will we be able to watch as the decades pass. It will fall to others to continue our work."

"Don't be hasty, Loki," Bast said. "We still age at a much slower rate than those of this world. We will be able to continue for many years to come."

"And then the responsibility will pass to our children," Anubis said.

"I hope that will not be necessary. But how did this happen? I mean for centuries there has been a major difference in the way time flowed on our different worlds," Arthur said. "Why has this changed now?"

"Maybe it is no longer necessary," Gwen said. "Maybe because we can fight these things on our own. Me, Arthur, Millie, and even Rex know what we face and have acquired the tools to fight them. We, I mean those of us born on Earth, know about the other worlds now." Taking Loki's hand she continued. "You don't have to keep your presence a secret from us anymore. Who you really are."

"Not from you, but I do not believe the rest of your world is ready for the truth."

"But someday soon."

"Maybe."

Remembering what he had been told by the man in the suit Arthur shook his head. “I agree with Loki. What we are doing needs to be shared with as few people as possible. We need to come up with plausible explanations for recent events. The last thing we need is for the press to start asking questions. Terrorism maybe. And the Havenite weapons will help.

This may work to our advantage. Coordination between the dimensions will be easier.” He turned to Michael. “I never asked. Does your time pass differently from ours?”

“No,” Ariel said. “It flows as it does here.

Millie looked up at Lancelot. “But then how could you have been at the first battle? That would mean you have lived for centuries.”

“Time affects us differently,” Ariel said.

Kathleen turned to Ariel. “If you live for centuries then what about children? I mean you could have thousands by now. If they live as long as you where did you put them all?”

“Those of Haven do age, but at a slower rate than any of you. They have few children. A child is born only when a member of their society dies."

“That is an extreme birth control program you guys have,” Gwen said.

“It is not by design. They do not make the decision not to have children. It just happens,” Michael said. “The population remains stagnant.”

“You said you are siblings,” Arthur said. “Do your parents still live? Did six people die so you could be born?”

“I do not know,” Michael said. “We never knew our parents.”

“How the hell could you not have known your parents?” Loki asked. “Were you all born at the same time? I mean what would that be, sextuplets? And then what, raised by a great aunt?”

“We six do not remember childhood,” Gabriel said. “We have always been together just as we are.”

“You keep referring to the others of your world as them,” Gwen said.

Michael looked at her. “We are not the same.”

“Do you have any children?” Millie asked looking up at Lancelot.

“No.”

“But you have been married,” Gwen said.

“Many times,” Remiel said.

Arthur turned to Michael. "Just out of curiosity, any of your people, besides you, able to transfer their consciousness as you did with me?"

"No. Only we six."

"Are you sure you are from the world as the rest of your people?" Kathleen asked.

"Something we have discussed many times without coming to a satisfying conclusion," Remiel said. "Haven is the only home we have ever known."

"Do you look the same as the others on your world?"

"We do," Ezekiel smiled. "Of course we now look like you."

"Oh, this just got weird," Loki said. "The Friends don't have sex and you guys just showed up one day, centuries ago, all grown up."

"Just got weird?" Rex asked. "Loki, this is all weird to me. It has been so since I woke. I'm still getting used to hot showers."

"Well, whoever you are we are most grateful that you are with us," Arthur said.

"True. We are most fortunate." Millie looked up and took Lancelot's hand.

"Anyone got a radio?" Arthur asked. "I think we need to call for a ride."

"Back to Cleveland?" Bast asked. "Why not use the portal?"

"It can take us to Cleveland?"

"No, First Dragon. But we can go to one of the other worlds and then use it to take us to Cleveland."

Arthur looked at Loki. "You knew this?"

"No. I mean, not really. To be honest, I don't think anyone thought of it."

Arthur shook his head then looked at Bast. "Thank you. I think that is a great idea. We will return to Asgard, check on Odin and Freya, and then go on to Cleveland."

As they turned towards the stone circle Arthur heard Kathleen whisper to Gwen, "It takes a woman to state the obvious."

"Speaking of the obvious," Gwen said smiling at Kathleen then turning to Arthur. "What happened to the helicopter you came in?"

"It can't take us all."

"No, but I was thinking it might take some of us to Mentor."

Mentor?"

"The dude back there said he thought they were all going back there after the assassination. Maybe we should check it out."

Arthur smiled. "I guess it does take a woman to state the obvious. Kathleen, please call the helicopter. Have it land here.

"Michael, you and the others take the chopper to Mentor. Millie, you and Rex go with them. The rest of you come with me. We will take the portal and get back to Cleveland. The prisoner said Cain was heading there. We need to find him and stop him."

"Is it wise to split up? We should stay with you."

"Right now we can do more by splitting up, Rex. Don't worry. I have more than enough security. I'll be fine." He turned to Michael. "Hang on to the chopper. I need you to get back to Cleveland as soon as you can. Make this quick. Check things out but if it gets too hot then leave."

"And Satan?" Falstaff asked.

"I don't think he will be a problem. I have a feeling he is pretty busy right now."

Loki turned to Arthur. "I can't believe we are chasing the same bad guy."

"As you said, things have gotten weird. Now let's go. I don't know what Cain has planned but whatever it is we need to stop it before any more innocents die."

CHAPTER TEN

The helicopter settled on the sand only yards from the dock. The guards squinted as the skids touched the ground and the rotor wash peppered them with sand wondering if their leader had returned. They realized their error when the door slid open and Lancelot stepped out. Before they were able to level their weapons both disappeared.

"Saves disposing of the bodies," Rex said charging his M16.

"It also prevents questions from the local authorities," Lancelot said lowering his weapon.

Millie looked at him about to say something.

"We will only use force when threatened. If no weapons are pointed in our direction we will stun them. Once they are incapacitated we secure them and notify the local authorities that the FBI has rounded up a few more domestic terrorists. Is that okay?"

She nodded and smiled.

Michael tapped on the pilot's window. "Can you wait?"

"It would be better if we don't. You can call us when you're ready. We make too big a target."

"I understand."

He stepped back and in a cyclone of flying sand the Huey lifted off.

"He will come back when we call."

They walked unchallenged towards the large warehouse. Lancelot opened the door, the white tube in his hand ready. Two stunned guards fell to the floor before they were able to shout a warning or raise their weapons.

Michael stepped over them. "Please take their weapons, Rex."

The warriors from Haven walked towards the raised dais, their progress only slightly delayed as flashes of light from their small weapons littered the floor with fallen worshipers.

Lancelot stunned the last two figures who stood on the stage. As they hit the floor a man jumped from behind the dais, an assault rifle in his hands.

Michael shot him before he could fire. Instead of falling he simply took a step back. Quickly resetting the weapon Michael fired again. The assault rifle struck the ground as the man disappeared.

Lancelot pushed Michael aside. "It is a Shadow! Get behind me." He raised his hand as an ebony mist rose from the vacant space the man had recently occupied. A beam of intense light jetted from Lancelot's extended fingers and struck as the dark vapor solidified into the shape of a faceless figure. The Shadow flew apart only to slowly coagulate and reform. The sinister form of the shade seemed to look at him, tilting its head in curiosity.

"A knight," Lancelot whispered. "He is not one of the five!"

Millie stepped beside him and they raised their arms. A blade of sun bright-light, thinner than a razor blade and three feet wide, flew from the extended fingers of the two Blockers and struck the Shadow. It screamed as it was sliced in two, each half bursting into shards of black ice that clattered upon the floor.

"A knight?" Millie asked as she tried to catch her breath.

"One of Satan's Black Knights. The most powerful of the Shadows. I have never seen one do that before."

"What was it doing here?" Michael asked. "I mean if Cain is involved in the attempted coup of Satan, why would one of Satan's most powerful Shadows be here?"

"To kill Cain, maybe," Millie said. "Do you think Satan sent him?"

"I do not think so. I believe it was trying to aid those on the stage. This is disturbing," Lancelot said. "And why come back here after all these years."

Ariel approached, careful not to step on any of the prone figures that lay at odd angles upon the floor. "What do we do with all these bodies?"

"They are going to wake up eventually," Ezekiel said joining her.

"We could just make them disappear," Remiel said smiling at Millie.

She looked up at Lancelot, "No."

"He was not serious, Millie. It is simply his attempt at humor."

"Leave them for the local authorities, "Michael said. "I will call and report that the FBI has taken down the terrorists responsible for the attack on the movie theater. I will let them know where to find them. Take their weapons and we will lock them in." He turned to Rex. "See if you can get the helicopter back here, please."

Rex nodded and stepping over several of the inert bodies muttered to himself. "Weapons that make people disappear, machines that fly, little boxes that send signals farther than a man can see: I was asleep for a very long time."

"This is not good."

"No, Lucifer, it is not." Michael looked at the others securing the prisoners. "If Cain and his puppet master control even a few of the Shadow Knights ... " He turned to Lucifer. "We need to get back. We need to warn Arthur."

Arthur looked at the two warriors that stood guard outside the door to the hospital room occupied by Freya.

They understand that the threat is real, even here. That's good.

One of the guards opened the door. "The First Dragon."

Freya smiled as he entered. Her leg was heavily bandaged and elevated. She held a small computer tablet in her lap.

That's cool. Never saw one so small.

Thor and Sif stood to the side of the bed.

"First Dragon. Well met," Freya said.

"It is good to see that you were not more seriously wounded, my lady."

"I have had more severe injuries teaching my sons to cook." She smiled at Kathleen and nodded at the others. "Going to get a little crowded in here if all of your oath-sworn are with you."

"The Havenites, Rex and Millie have gone to the warehouse in Mentor. Seems they are still using the building. Thought it would be a good idea to check it out."

Kathleen nudged his arm.

He looked at his sister. "I mean Gwen suggested it."

"Good. This conflict between Satan and the others may work for us or it may make things a lot worse. I'm not sure. The more information we have the better. Have you asked the Friends if they know anything about what's going on?"

"I have not," Arthur said. "But that's a good idea. We're still trying to figure out how to get them home. Where it is. For now, they remain guests of Zeus. Ariel thinks that Satan's people use a similar technology to theirs rather than a portal to travel between worlds. That's how the Friends got here. She believes it might explain how they can cross in so many different locations. Why they don't need a fixed point."

"But not why they are restricted to your dimension. We need to figure that out," Freya said. "It could be useful. Hell, it might prove critical. Maybe we can find a way to stop them from traveling altogether."

"I know that my father has his scientists working on it," Kathleen said. "You might consider having Ariel work with Merlin's folks, Arthur."

I think she is letting me know that I should have thought of that.

"I will try, but she seems intent on sticking with us. Her oath and all."

"It is not her oath alone, Art," Gwen said. "That lady likes to fight."

"A woman after my own heart," Freya said. "But she may be able to help us more working with Merlin's scientists."

"I will mention it to her." Arthur turned to Thor. "Any more on your father's condition?"

Sif took her husband's hand. "There has been no change."

Freya looked up at her son. "I want you two to go with Arthur. There is nothing you can do here to help me or your father. If there is any change in his condition I will send word."

Thor took her hand. "I have a duty to my family, Mother."

"And Arthur is your brother and the First Dragon, who you swore an oath to serve. Remember that. There is nothing you can do to help us, so go. We are safe enough here. As soon as I can move I will join you." She turned to Arthur. "I will have your mother come to you. She is a fantastic intelligence analyst and can work in my place until I can get out of here. Which better be soon."

"You have heard about the time shift?" Arthur asked.

"I have. Curious but I believe it will work in our favor. I have checked with the other worlds. It is a universal change. Any idea how or why it happened."

"None."

"Do you think your friend from the hill has something to do with it?"

"Probably, but I don't know why, or why now."

"Maybe it is no longer needed. A puzzle to be solved at a later time. For now, Satan and Cain remain our primary concern."

"And whoever is pulling Cain's strings," Loki said.

"Lancelot thinks it is Bael," Kathleen said. "Millie told me he is certain of it."

"Then we should find out what Bael plans. And stop him. One thing we don't need is to have his war with Satan fought on Earth," Freya said. She looked up at Falstaff. "How is the arm?"

"It is fine, my lady. No more than a scratch."

She looked at Kathleen who shrugged her shoulders.

"Good. Now all of you, get out of here. You have work to do."

Thor, Loki, Sif, and Kathleen took turns kissing her on the cheek. Arthur smiled when Falstaff stepped forward.

"You try and I will remove your manhood."

Laughing he leaned down and kissed her on the forehead. She smacked him. "Get out of here, you oaf."

Arthur leaned on the door as the last of them left.

"You have seen him again?"

"Yes. He told me we should consider working with Satan. And keep things from as much of the public on Earth as possible. He said that if my world was to discover what was going on, who we were fighting, it would be its downfall."

"Did you tell the others?"

"Not yet."

"Why not?"

"I figured they had enough to worry about. They know we have to stop Bael. The idea of working with Satan, even for a little while, is something I'm not sure they would all agree to. I know Michael and Lancelot would find it difficult. He was responsible for the death of Michael's wife and Lancelot's sister. Bael killed them, but it was on Satan's orders."

"They are your friends, Arthur, and more importantly, your oath-sworn. They accept that you know what you are doing. Do not underestimate them. And remember, you are First Dragon. You cannot take a vote every time a decision needs to be made. You make it, they obey. That is the way it works. Seek advice, but only you can make the final decision."

"I understand my responsibility. But thanks for reminding me."

"You are welcome. Now kiss your adopted mother on the cheek and get out of here. You have things to do."

CHAPTER ELEVEN

Arthur and Kathleen stepped from the platform of the small portal. As they did the lights immediately began to swirl and Loki and Gwen materialized.

He turned to the operator. "Cut it a little close didn't you?"

"Sorry, First Dragon, but you have urgent messages from your oath-sworn Michael and my lord Ra. I am to tell you that you must contact him immediately upon your arrival."

"Which him?" he asked with a smile.

"Sorry, First Dragon, Lord Ra."

"Is he here?"

"No, sir. He and a small contingent of warriors from Duat are in the city of Kent in response to a report of a shooting at the advanced schooling center there. They are in the guise of FBI agents."

"You mean the university. Do you have a radio?"

As he handed him the radio, Thor and Sif stepped from the platform and approached Kathleen. Thor looked at Arthur.

"Is something amiss?"

"I don't know. Ra wants Arthur to contact him right away. I believe something is happening at some sort of school."

"Do you think it is a Shadow?" Arthur stood still for a moment. "How many dead?" He listened again. "And the shooter?" He looked at the others. "Thank you, sir. We will join you as soon as we can." He handed the radio back to the warrior. "Is there transportation available?"

"Yes, sir. The helicopter is on its way back from Mentor but will not arrive for some time so I asked the Sheriff for assistance. He offered one of his."

"Good man. When will it be here?"

"It is on the roof now. We have weapons and FBI vests waiting. My Lord Ra ordered them to support your cover as members of the Hostage

Rescue Team. The helicopter will only accommodate four people, however." He turned to Loki. "He asked me to ensure your bag was included, sir."

Loki smiled and nodded his thanks.

"Okay. Thor, Loki, and Apollo will come with me. The rest of you wait for those coming from Mentor. Tell them what is going on. I will let you know if I need you."

"What is happening, Art?" Gwen asked.

"There is a gunman in a tower on the campus of Kent State University. Three people have been shot. One was killed instantly, a campus policeman. The other two are students and have been rushed to the hospital in critical condition. The shooter is still in the tower. Ra and his people have contained him. He believes that the shooter may be possessed."

Loki draped his arm around Gwen's shoulders. "You think it is one of Cain's Shadows?"

"No way to tell."

"Why do they suspect it is a Shadow?" Thor asked.

The warrior from Duat looked up at him. "Sorry, sir. Lord Ra said I was to tell the First Dragon that a student reported seeing a dark ghost. She and her boyfriend were in the lobby when a man rushed in with a gun. A campus policeman confronted him and when the man pointed his gun at them the officer shot him. The young woman said a ghost came out of the man, possessed her friend, who then picked up the rifle, shot the guard, and rushed up the stairs."

"Was she hurt? "Kathleen asked.

"No, my lady, she said he just smiled at her and then ran up the stairs."

"I think Ra is wise in considering the presence of a Shadow," Thor said.

"Ya think," Loki said.

"Where did it come from?" Sif asked.

"They don't know, my lady."

"I will go with you, Arthur," Kathleen said.

Arthur took her hand. "You can't, Kathleen. The police are expecting members of the HRT. There are no women on the team."

"That is ridicules. I am a warrior as is Sif."

"I know, and you are right. But right now, here on Earth, in America, there are no women warriors. Someday that may change, it should, but that is the way it is now."

He turned to the others. "Okay, everyone knows what needs to be done. Let's do it."

Sif looked at Kathleen. "This is a backward world."

"Tell me about it," Gwen said. "I've lived here my whole life. Women get little respect. Things better change soon or there will be a female revolution."

"One I would enjoy joining," Kathleen said.

"Why didn't he take me," Falstaff asked. "I'm a man."

Sif laid her hand on his arm. "You are too big to fit into their small aircraft."

Ra waited until they had cleared the rotor wash and the helicopter lifted off. "Well met, First Dragon. The shooter remains in that tower."

Arthur gripped his forearm. "Damn. How am I going to get to him up there?"

"That is the same question we have been asking."

"Are you sure he is possessed? Maybe the girl was in shock and imagined what she saw," Thor said.

Ra pointed to a man with a high-powered rifle equipped with a scope. "Because one of my men put a bullet in him and he did not fall."

"That'll do it," Loki said looking at the large rifle.

"Did you see anything?" Arthur asked. "Any Shadow when he was hit?"

"Too far away to be sure," Ra said.

"I thought I saw something, First Dragon," The sniper said.

"What did you see?"

"A dark mist that encircled the man for a moment. I thought I was seeing things until it flowed back into him through the hole I put in his chest. I have never seen a Shadow but I would guess that is what it was."

"Right, that is what it would look like." Arthur turned and pointed at the dozens of police officers sheltering behind their cruisers. "Think any of them saw it?"

"I doubt it," Ra said. "He is pretty high up and they have no snipers with them as of yet."

"Did they see him hit?" Loki asked.

The sniper shook his head. "I don't think so. They were mostly helping the wounded and getting the students to safety. If they had I think there would have been some kind of reaction. There wasn't. I guess they figured I missed."

Arthur thought of the words of the man in the suit. "That's good. We need to keep the idea of him being possessed quiet."

"So how the hell do we do that?" Loki asked while taking a Marlin large-bore sniper rifle from his bag.

"Maybe we could cause a diversion." Arthur looked at one of the police cars parked nearby. "To draw everyone's attention away from the tower" He turned to Loki and Ra's sniper. "Do you think you two could take out his knees, make him fall?"

Loki looked at the sniper who nodded. "If he is standing, no problem, if not, there are other body parts we can hit. But how is that going to help? Even if the guy falls from the tower and smashes his head into mush, the Shadow will survive and seek another host. There won't be any hiding that."

"I'll take him out as he falls."

"Don't you think someone will notice a solar flare coming from your fingertips?" Loki asked. "Not something the average Joe sees every day I mean."

"That is what the diversion is for. And I'll keep it tight."

"What diversion?"

A shot rang out. The windshield of the police car Arthur had examined shattered causing everyone to duck. Arthur smiled. "Something like that."

Another crack and a bullet struck the same cruiser low and near the trunk. Liquid leaked from beneath the car where the bullet had exited.

"Gas," Ra said.

"Yep, all it will need is a little help and poof," Arthur said.

"That should do it," Loki said. "Cops would have time to move as soon as they see the poof." He turned to the sniper. "The left knee is mine.

Another shot rang out followed by a loud crash as a van struck a nearby tree. Falstaff burst from the driver's door of the damaged vehicle and pulled the sliding side door open. "Out! Move it!"

The remaining oath-sworn tumbled from the van and sought shelter just as another shot rang out. Falstaff fell and Kathleen and Sif ran to him and began helping the big man towards a nearby dumpster.

Loki placed his rifle to his shoulder and fired three times in quick succession. "Help me keep this bastard's attention away from them."

The Duat sniper nodded, fired, and worked his bolt so fast it seemed like he was firing a semi-automatic rifle. The shooting from the tower stopped.

Sif called from the dumpster. "He will live but it will be a while before he can sit comfortably."

"It will be a long time before he lives this down," Thor said laughing.

Arthur looked at Kathleen. "How did you get here so fast?"

"Portal, Asgard, portal, van, no traffic, Falstaff driving."

Arthur shook his head. "And those from Mentor?"

"Did not wait."

"Well that isn't going to help us keep this quiet," Apollo said pointing to another van pulling into a nearby parking lot. Channel 7 news stenciled along its side.

"Okay, we need to do this before they get set up." Arthur turned to Apollo. "Work your way over to that police car and warn the officers that their vehicle is leaking gas. Get them to move."

"Ra, as soon as your sniper and Loki are ready I want everyone to shoot at the tower. I need to draw attention away from the car so sees us light the gas. When the car explodes I expect everyone will either look or duck. That's when the snipers will knock him from his perch. I will take care of the Shadow as it falls." He turned to those hiding behind the dumpster.

"Kathleen. Listen, we don't have much time. Can you see Apollo?"

"Yes. He is helping several police officers move to other cars."

"Can you see liquid leaking from the car closest to me?"

There was a hesitation and then, "Yes."

"Do you think you can ignite the gasoline without making it obvious how you do it?"

"My light can do that?"

"Yes. Just will it so."

"Okay. Then yes, I can light it but I can't be sure no one will notice."

"When the shooting starts I believe everyone will look towards us. When they do, you set off the gas. Understand?"

"I do, and it will be done subtly."

"Thank you. Get ready." He turned to Ra. "As soon as the shooting starts I need the snipers to make him fall. Timing is everything. Ready? Okay. On three. One ... two... "

Ra's people and Thor began shooting at the tower. The news people stopped what they were doing and turned towards them. The police car exploded. As Arthur hoped everyone either ducked or turned to look at the burning car. The two snipers fired. Arthur raised his hand and a thin bolt of concentrated light struck the falling assassin. The body struck the ground with a muffled thud followed by a rain of black ice. All the shooting stopped. The FBI agents rushed to the fallen sniper.

Ra turned to the police. "He's down. Threat has been neutralized."

Silence overtook the scene. Then the news people began to run towards the police.

Arthur pulled Loki to him. "Call the helicopter. We need to get out of here before the press reaches us.

"Can you handle them, Ra?"

"I can. I will explain you had to leave because the identity of the HRT must remain secret for you to properly do your job." He turned to the remainder of the oath-sworn. "I will provide them transportation."

"Thank you."

"Are you going back to Cleveland?"

"Yes."

Kathleen rushed towards him. He held up his hand and she stopped.

"You must not let these people know we are together. I need you to get back to Cleveland as soon as you can. Ra will provide transportation. Act as if you are a reporter. Try to interview him."

He turned to go and then stopped. Without turning around he said quietly, "Great job, Kathleen. Thank you." He hesitated and then added. "I love you."

Gwen looked at Kathleen. "We are reporters?"

"So it seems."

"You heard him?"

"Sure did."

"Good thing for him that he remembered to say that."

"There are times I'm proud of my big brother. He is slow but apparently, he can learn."

Kathleen turned to Ra. "We are from the Cleveland Plain Dealer. What happened here?"

CHAPTER TWELVE

The panel truck moved slowly down the small alleyway. Piles of trash littered both sides of the road next to overfilled trash cans. A calico cat ran across the street in pursuit of a large overweight rat. No people were about. The alley was swathed in shadow from the multistoried homes and apartments that flanked the small roadway making it seem like late afternoon rather than mid-morning.

"How far to the Federal Building?"

"Not far. End of the alley and around the corner," the driver said.

Cain looked into the back of the panel truck. The floor was covered in fifty-five-gallon drums held in place by nylon straps. Around each, a bundle of dynamite attached with bands of electricians tape. A detonation cord connecting each of the bundles lay upon the floor leading to the driver's seat.

"You know what to do?"

"Yes."

"When you reach the target all you have to do is move from the seat."

"I understand."

"Remain in this body if possible until a suitable host can be found, then make your way to the safe house and wait for me."

"My host is concerned. He did not realize that by volunteering he would lose his life."

Cain looked at the driver. "Satan rewards all that serve. This life is nothing compared to what awaits you. You will be reborn. The rewards will be great. Does he understand?"

"He does. He is pleased."

Cain looked out the window. "Let me out here."

The van stopped. Cain climbed out and the truck pulled away. He turned onto the main boulevard and began to whistle an old tune content in the knowledge that his plan was moving forward.

As the driver approached the intersection on the opposite end of the alley a large dog burst from around a dumpster. Instinctively he slammed on the brakes throwing him forward onto the steering wheel. As he left the seat a massive explosion rocked the alley. Cain was thrown to the pavement from the concussive blast as the vehicle disintegrated in a ball of flame. Bricks and burning pieces of shattered wood landed on his back concealing his presence. Slowly rising to his feet he brushed the dust and debris from his clothing while extinguishing the flames that threatened to engulf him. Wiping blood from his eyes he stepped to the alley and looked at the twisted metal that had been the truck. Reaching into his pocket he removed a handkerchief and wiped the blood from his eyes then shook his head to still the ringing in his ears.

Several buildings were burning, cars on the main roadway lay on their sides while flames licked at the twisted metal. Several bodies littered the street, some moving, some not. A stillness filled the air, suddenly replaced with screams.

"Incompetent fool."

Cain watched as a dark fog gradually moved across the rubble until reaching the still form of a woman. The mist melted into the body. Slowly she rose to her feet, the twisted remains of her left arm hanging at her side.

Reaching into his pocket Cain withdrew a small black box. Checking to ensure no one was looking he pointed it at the wall, a dark doorway materialized and he stepped through. The doorway folded into itself and he was gone.

Pushing a fluorescent light and the remains of a ceiling tile from his back, Arthur painfully climbed to his feet. The room was dark and he could hear others about him choking on the dust.

"Kathleen?"

"I'm here," She said between coughs. "I'm okay."

He reached out and feeling her hand took it. "Anyone hurt?"

"Just my pride," Loki said. "I think Thor landed on me."

"Sorry, Loki," Falstaff said from the dark. "I think that was me."

"Really? I'm lucky to be alive. How's your ass?"

"Hurts."

"Does anyone have a light?" Merlin asked. "Someone is lying at my feet. I think they are hurt."

Suddenly the room was bathed in bright light. Arthur looked down at his hands.

"I didn't know you could do that," Michael said.

"Either did I."

Merlin climbed to his feet. "Quickly, the conference table has collapsed and Millie and Lancelot are trapped under it."

Falstaff and Thor lifted the end of the large table. Gabriel and Remiel pulled the two still forms free.

Merlin leaned down and placing his fingers first along Millie's and then Lancelot's neck nodded. "They are alive."

"What happened?" Sif asked wiping the dirt from her face with the back of her hand. "Was it an earthquake?"

"Some kind of explosion I think," Arthur said. He turned to the door to the main office. "Someone check on the others?"

"I'll go," Rex said. He began to work his way over the tossed chairs and fallen ceiling tiles. The emergency lights flickered twice then came to life. The glow from Arthur's hands faded as they did. The door hung at an angle held in place by a single bent hinge. Rex pulled it free and stepped into the office.

Lancelot seeing Millie lying beside him quickly came to his knees and pulled her into his arms. "Millie!"

She coughed and opened her eyes. She smiled. "I'm okay. What happened?"

Lancelot turned to Arthur.

"We don't know. Some kind of explosion upstairs I think."

"Gas line?" Gwen asked.

"Maybe."

Rex poked his head in. "Everyone is all right out here. Just shaken up. A few cuts and bruises. I'm to tell you the phones are dead and the elevator isn't working."

"The radio phones?" Merlin asked.

"No signal."

"What about the emergency staircase?" Sif asked.

Rex turned and asked someone in the office. "The door is jammed. They can't get it open."

"How do we get out of here?" Apollo asked.

"Let me see what I can do with the door," Thor said as he worked his way over the debris.

Falstaff pushed aside a broken chair. "I'll help."

Thor stopped. "Not with that arm, my friend. It is bleeding again."

"Just a scratch."

"Never-the-less, let me do this."

Falstaff shrugged his shoulders.

The ventilating system hummed back into operation drawing the dust from the room. The lights flickered and then they too resumed normal operation.

"What about the portal?" Kathleen asked. "Can we use it to get out of here?"

"If we can reach it," Merlin said. "And if it is not buried."

The sound of tearing metal interrupted any further comment. Thor called out. "The door is open but the hallway to the staircase and the portal is blocked. The ceiling and one of the walls have collapsed."

Arthur climbed over the damaged door to the office. "Can we clear it?"

"In time. Maybe a lot of time. And I do not know what lies beyond."

"Then I guess we better get to it."

"We will need to be careful," Thor said. "I do not know how stable the remainder of the structure is."

"What about the elevator shaft?" Gwen asked. "If it is clear we might be able to climb up that way."

"Good idea," Arthur said. "Thor, do you think you could open the doors?"

"I will try."

He walked to the elevator and griping the doors tried to push them apart. The muscles of his back and shoulders strained the material of his shirt. The doors started to move but stopped when only two inches apart.

"Let me help," Falstaff said.

"Your arm," Sif said. "You will reopen the wound."

"Not to mention your ass."

"Enough about my ass, Loki."

"I'll do it," Anubis said. "Thor, you take one door and I will pull the other. Let us see if we can open this thing."

Placing their backs to each other they put their hands along the edges of the doors.

"Ready?" Anubis asked.

"I am," Thor said and began to push.

The doors groaned. Inch-by-inch they moved apart as the two men exerted more and more pressure. When a gap, a little under a foot appeared they stopped. Catching his breath Thor said, "Something is blocking the doors. I am afraid this is as far as they will go."

"A little tight," Loki said. "Not sure we can get through that."

"I know I can't," Falstaff said.

"I think I can fit," Millie said stepping towards the opening. She stuck her head in. "Really dark in there. Can't see if it's clear but I'm pretty sure I'm looking in the car and not the shaft."

"Wait," one of the clerks said and rifling through her purse withdrew a small flashlight. "Will this help?"

Taking the light Millie nodded. "Thank you." She turned it on. "It's the car." She squeezed into the elevator.

"Be careful," Lancelot said. "We don't know how stable it is."

"I will. Seems solid enough. I can see a trapdoor on top but I can't reach it."

Kathleen moved to the opening. "I can help." She squeezed into the elevator car.

"I think I can too," Bast said.

Gwen stepped forward. "I think I can too."

Loki laughed. "It looks like it is up to the ladies to save us."

"Not all the ladies, brother," Sif said. "I will not fit."

"Nor will I," Ariel added.

"That's okay. I think we will be enough." Gwen worked her way into the elevator. As she pulled her leg in there was a loud groan and the sound of grinding metal.

"It's falling!" Thor yelled.

Dust flew into the room as the car dropped then everything became still. Arthur looked into the open shaft. The car was gone.

"How deep does this go?" Arthur asked.

"I don't know," Merlin said. "We are on the bottom floor but I don't know how much farther the shaft goes down."

"We need to do something," Lancelot said.

"We are okay," a muffled voice called out.

"Gwen?"

"Yep. We are all okay, Art. No one's hurt. Just took our breath away for a moment. The car fell about ten feet I would guess. Scared us is all. We hit something and stopped. Must be machinery at the bottom. We are going to try and get the trapdoor open and see if there is a way to climb up. Hang on."

"Thank God," Merlin said.

After a few minutes, a beam of light appeared from below.

"We are through," Millie said. "I'm standing on top of the car. It looks like the cables are still intact and I think there is a ladder along the wall. Can't tell if it is blocked up above though. Can't see the top. We are going to try the ladder."

Some noise from below and muffled voices drew everyone's attention to the shaft. A light flashed blinding Arthur as he stood near the opening.

"Sorry. The ladder is on the opposite wall. Just wanted to let you know we were on our way up," Millie said.

Arthur rubbed his eyes. "Be careful."

"We will," Kathleen's voice echoed from the dark. "Millie and I are going to climb up first and make sure the ladder is safe."

"Do the walls look stable?" They heard Gwen call

"So far so good," Kathleen said. "Still can't see anything up above."

A moment later Kathleen called down. "There is a ledge up here. We will wait for you."

"On our way," Gwen said. "How about some light."

The moving beam from the flashlight showed a metal ladder fastened to the wall.

"Okay. We will wait here," Kathleen said. She coughed. "Lots of dust in the air. Smells like something must be burning up above."

"Gwen, wait," Arthur said. He turned to the others. "Anybody got water?"

"I have some in my office," Thor said. "If I can get into it I'll bring it."

"Gwen, we are going to get some water."

"Kathleen, Arthur is going to send some water up," Gwen called.

"Good. We could use some. The air is rather thick."

"I got it," Thor said handing Arthur two plastic bottles of water."

"Gwen, I have the water. Two bottles. If I reach in can you get it?"

"Do my best. I'll let you know when I'm ready."

A minute later Bast called out, "I'll take one."

"Wait," Millie called down. She flashed the light down the shaft and Arthur was able to see Bael reaching out. He leaned into the opening as far as he could.

"Can't reach. If I toss it can you catch it?"

"Let's try," Bast said.

"Here it comes." Arthur tossed the bottle underhand. Bast leaned out from the ladder.

"Got it."

"I'm next," Gwen said. "Move up, Bast, I'm right behind you."

Arthur could see Bast move up the ladder and then he saw Gwen.

"Be careful."

"Always, big brother. Now toss the bottle."

He lobbed the water towards her outstretched hand.

"Nice catch. Put it somewhere so you can use two hands."

"Back off, Art. I'm not stupid," she said chuckling.

"Ready?" Millie called down.

"On our way," Gwen said and the light moved away from the opening.

"This ledge must have been for some kind of maintenance work," Kathleen said as Bast reached the platform. Millie helped her step on. "There is room for all of us. Let me have some of that water, please. The smoke is hurting my throat."

She took the bottle and after taking a long drink offered it to Millie.

Gwen climbed onto the ledge and opening the other bottle took a drink then offered it to Bast.

Millie flashed the light above.

"Pretty dark up there," Gwen said.

"Yes, it is. I don't know if the shaft is blocked or it normally looks like this."

"With all this smoke you would think that we would see some kind of fire," Kathleen said.

"Hey, it looks like something is moving up there," Millie said.

"Where?" Gwen asked.

"Over there on the side of the wall opposite the ladder. It looks like something is disturbing the smoke."

They stared at the odd movement then Kathleen screamed, "Shadow!"

Before any of them could move the Shadow launched from the opposite wall straight for Bast. Gwen jumped between Bast and the Shadow wrapping her arms around her. The Shadow enfolded itself around the two women and Gwen lost her balance. She and Bast fell from the platform taking the Shadow with them.

"Gwen!" Kathleen screamed as she heard the bodies strike the top of the elevator.

Millie shone the flashlight down the shaft illuminating the still bodies that lay upon its top. A dark mist swirled around them.

CHAPTER THIRTEEN

"What was that?" Arthur yelled.

"A Shadow has Gwen and Bast. They fell," Kathleen said.

"They fell? How?"

"The Shadow attacked Bast and Gwen jumped to protect her. They fell off the ladder."

"How far did they fall? Are they all right?"

"A long way, Arthur. I don't know how badly they are hurt. We are working our way down to them now."

"What about the Shadow?"

"It looks like it's wrapped around them," Millie said. "It is still moving. I can't see them through it."

"Burn it!" Lancelot yelled. "Quickly!"

"But the girls," Loki said.

"They will be all right. The blast will not hurt a person unless they are possessed. Gwen cannot be possessed."

"And Bast," Anubis asked.

"The fact that they still see the Shadow means it has not yet possessed her," Arthur said. "Gwen must be preventing it."

A sudden burst of light radiated from the opening in the elevator followed quickly by another.

"It's gone," Kathleen said. "It was pretty strong. We both had to hit it."

"How are the girls," Lancelot asked.

"In a minute. We are almost there," Kathleen said.

They heard a thump as either Millie or Kathleen jumped from the ladder and landed on the top of the elevator. Another thump and Kathleen called out.

"They are alive but I'm afraid to move them. Gwen is on top of Bast and ..."

"And what?" Loki demanded.

"Her neck doesn't look right. I'm afraid if I move her it might cause more damage."

Arthur turned to Thor. "Is there a cervical collar with the first aid kit?"

"I'll check. We keep a lot of stuff here."

How is Bast?" Arthur asked trying to hide his concern for his sister.

"Breathing," Millie said. "Until we move Gwen there isn't much we can do. There is a good deal of blood under her head." She hesitated. "I just don't know, Arthur. I'm sorry."

"Here!" Thor said handing Arthur the collar. He pushed it through the gap between the doors.

"I have a cervical collar for Gwen. Can you see it?"

A beam of light flashed up the shaft. "I see it," Millie called. "Toss it toward the center. That way it won't miss the elevator."

Arthur tossed the collar.

"Got it," Kathleen said.

"Gently put it around her neck then check that her back is okay before you move her," Arthur said.

A moment later Kathleen called up. "We have rolled her off of Bast. She is lying flat on her back. She's breathing okay and I didn't see or feel any other injuries. But she is unconscious."

"And Bast?" Anubis asked.

"She is bleeding from the back of her head. I think her right arm is broken. She is unconscious but her breathing is steady. Can you send something down we can put on her head?"

"Here," Thor said handing Arthur a small bag. "There are bandages in there."

Arthur took the kit and nodded his thanks. "Coming down." He tossed the kit.

"Got it," Millie said.

"Now what?" Loki asked. "We need to get them out of there."

"I know," Arthur said. "Is there any other way into the shaft?"

His question was met with silence.

"Even if we could get down there, how would we get them out?" Lancelot asked. "And then what? They need a hospital and we are trapped."

The phone rang on one of the desks. Sif grabbed the receiver. "Hello."

She smiled. "We are okay but Gwen and Bast have been injured. They are trapped at the bottom of the elevator shaft."

She hesitated for a moment then turned to Arthur. "It is your mother. She wishes to speak with you."

"Mom? How did you get here?"

He listened, "Okay. Tell them to be careful. Kathleen and Millie are on top of the elevator as well. Make sure nothing falls."

He listened for another moment. "Thanks, Mom. We will be ready. "Freya sent my mother through the large portal to coordinate the Intel collection effort. My father and Randy are with her."

"Randy?" Loki asked.

"Yeah. Said he wants to help. They got here shortly after the explosion. She says the fire department is in the garage and is going to try to open the doors. If they can they will send help down to the girls and then to us. My mom is coordinating our rescue."

A large fireman pulled at the doors. "They're jammed tight. I think that the whole damn building must have shifted in the explosion. Might be the frame is bent." Taking off his white helmet and wiping his arm across his forehead he spoke to the man behind him. "Frankie, get the jaws and have the EMT standing by. The lady out there says there are injured at the bottom of the shaft. Better get a backboard, rope, and tackle."

"Got it, Chief."

As the man ran off the Fire Chief pulled his radio from his belt. "Bill, any word on what blew up?"

"Don't know yet, boss. Ain't a gas line though. Cops are thinking maybe it was some kind of bomb."

"A bomb?"

"That's what they said. We are helping them cordon off the area in case there are any more."

"How about casualties?"

"At least eight dead and another two dozen injured. Some of them ain't going to make it. Getting dogs from the Sheriff to check out the rubble for more victims and the guys at the airport are sending one to sniff out explosives."

"Okay. I'll be up shortly to relieve you. Soon as the EMT's and the climbers get here I'll be up. Did you call for backup?"

"Didn't need to. Departments are arriving from everywhere. As soon as this hit the news everyone started offering to help. It's a damned circus up here."

"I bet. Have the outside departments work the fires. We need to get them contained before they spread to the rest of the city. Remind our friends in blue that this falls under our purview. We run the show. Ask them to keep the damn press away."

"Believe it or not they don't want it. Maybe it's because it looks like half the city is on fire. Plus there are a bunch of FBI guys running all over the place. I'll let them know about the press."

"Okay. I'll be there shortly. Do me a favor."

"Yea, Hal?"

"Call my wife. Let her know I kind of doubt I'll be home for dinner."

"You got it."

"Hey, Chief?"

The Fire Chief turned to a man in a blue uniform with EMT embossed in white over his left breast pocket. The new arrival placed the two large bags he had been carrying on the floor.

"I'm Jordan. I understand there are injured?"

"Yeah. Good to see you, Jordan. I know who you are. Got a good rep. Where's your partner?"

"He's coming with the backboard and the rest of the gear. I brought the med gear. Anyone hurt upstairs?"

"No. Building was empty except for a few on the ground floor and the ones down below. It's been cleared. Federal holiday. There are folks trapped on top of the elevator which is at the bottom of the shaft. Two injured needing immediate care and Evac. I understand one of them has a neck injury. Bunch of FBI agents trapped on the subbasement floor. Priority is to the victims in the elevator shaft. Get them out and transported. I'll have a couple of guys take care of freeing the others once you're clear."

"Got it, Chief. Any of the trapped folks injured?"

"Not that I know of. If they are we will take care of them once they're free."

"Okay. We'll get the others."

"And, Jordan..."

"Yes, Chief?"

"Be careful. This may have been a bomb and if so the nut job that set it off may still be around. I'll see about getting a cop in here."

"Much appreciated."

A younger man in a similar blue suit joined them with climbing gear wrapped around him and carrying a backboard.

"This is Billy Creager, Chief. He may look young but he's working on his nursing degree. He's a good man."

The Chief nodded. "Good to hear. Okay. I'll leave you to it." He looked as two firemen arrived carrying a Jaws-of-Life.

"Get these doors open for the EMTs. And get them another backboard. Once they get the people off the elevator, go down and get the people on the bottom floor. I'll send some more guys with more climbing gear."

The Chief walked past the damaged cars and debris strewn around the underground garage. He stepped around the body of a woman with a mangled arm. The injury to her head leaving little doubt she was dead. As he worked his way towards the chaos of the main street a middle-aged woman stepped from behind a pillar. She was accompanied by a man of similar age. Behind them stood a young man in the uniform of a police officer. The Chief nodded as he offered his hand.

"Mr. and Mrs. Earsterdrak, we will have them out soon. I understand that you are with the FBI?"

"Yes. I'm a profiler. This is my husband, Paul. He's a lab tech."

The police officer was not introduced.

"Your daughter is one of the injured I understand."

"That's right. Gwen."

"She an agent?"

"Yes."

"Keeping it in the family. Well, two of the best EMT's in the city are going to get her out. If it was my daughter down there these are the two I would want to rescue her."

"Thank you. And the others?"

"As soon as the injured are recovered we will get them out. They seem to be okay."

He stepped aside as several firemen and two of Cleveland's finest ran past.

"Now if you will excuse me, I am needed up top." He touched the front of his helmet.

"Of course," Charlotte said. "Thank you."

As the Chief walked away Paul looked towards the damage in the garage. "This was one hell of a big explosion. Think Art and the others were the targets."

"It would make sense," Charlotte said.

"Satan?"

"I don't know, Paul. From what Freya has told me this isn't the kind of thing he does. And he and Art are under a truce."

"Bael or Cain then?"

"Good possibility. But I think Cain is responsible for everything that has been happening lately. He has been seen."

Randy looked around. "You're pretty sure this is one of them. Couldn't it have been an accident or some nut job? There are plenty around. Maybe a ruptured gas line or a propane truck."

Charlotte shook her head. "I wish that was the case, Randy. But I'm afraid this was an attack on Art and his friends. If Cain is working for Bael and their intent to overthrow Satan, they would need to get rid of Art first. They probably feel he is the easier target."

Paul laughed. "Then they don't know our son."

Charlotte smiled. "No, they don't."

Randy looked around. "I'm still having a tough time accepting all this. I mean demons and the devil himself. Art now some kind of magic-wielding warrior; Thor, Merlin, Avalon, Olympus. It's nuts."

"It is hard to accept I know," Paul said. "But you have seen it. It's real."

"I have. And I know it's real. That's what makes it so scary. It's also why I wanted to come along. I need to do something to help."

"This isn't the kind of thing you are used to dealing with, Randy," Paul said. "These are not the type of bad guys you've dealt with before. Maybe you should have stayed with Liz and kids."

"They are with Becky, and the folks in Avalon are taking good care of them. They're safe. I wouldn't have come if I thought they weren't. I mean, they are surrounded by Knights of Camelot and Vikings from Asgard. It's like some crazy fairytale. They are in a castle and staying in Merlin's house until other arrangements can be made. The house by-the-way."

"It does take some getting used to," Paul said.

Randy nodded. "I think they are as safe as anyone can be right now."

"You know you don't need to stay there anymore," Charlotte said. "Now that our times flow at the same rate you and your family could go home."

"With what I know now? No, Mrs. Earsterdrak. I need to do something to help stop this threat. For my family. Hell, for my world. And I think they are safer where they are. The kids are loving it."

"It does draw you in," Paul said.

"Iona tried to explain this oath-sworn thing to me. Do you think Art will let me join?"

"It's not some kind of club, Randy," Paul said. "These people have sworn to defend Art to the death. It is not something to be taken lightly. And you cannot change your mind once you have done so. The oath is for life."

Randy was quiet. He looked down the open aisle of the garage. Then he smiled. "Like King Arthur and the knights of the round table. Crazy, but I do understand. I still need to talk to Art."

"Make way.

They stepped aside as Jordan and Creager approached carrying Gwen on a wooden backboard. She lay strapped in, a cervical collar around her neck, and an IV line attached to a bottle carried by a fireman walking beside them. Another two firemen followed with Bast on a stretcher, her head swathed in bloody bandages. Neither of the girls moved.

Kathleen and Millie walked behind Bast and seeing the Earsterdrak's stopped.

Charlotte watched as they passed, a tear in her eye. Paul took her hand.

"Go ahead, Millie. I'll meet you at the hospital," Kathleen said.

Millie nodded and followed the firemen.

"Mr. and Mrs. Earsterdrak ..."

Charlotte took her hand. "Call us Mom and Dad, Kathleen. Or if you are more comfortable, Paul and Charlotte. Please. We are soon to be family."

Kathleen smiled. "Thank you. I am sorry about Gwen. You can be proud of her. She threw herself around Bast when she was attacked by a Shadow. She succeeded in preventing her from being possessed. But she was knocked from the shelf and fell. It was a brave thing to do."

"Did the Shadow succeed?" Charlotte asked.

"No."

"How bad are they hurt?" Paul asked gently.

"Bast has a possible fracture of her arm and maybe her skull. She has yet to wake. The medics don't know how bad the head wound is. If she will wake. Gwen ... well, she ..."

"Go ahead," Charlotte said wrapping her arm around her. "It's okay."

Kathleen started to cry. "Her neck is broken. It's pretty bad. If she lives she they think she will be paralyzed."

CHAPTER FOURTEEN

Brushing the dust from his clothing Arthur looked up and seeing his parents rushed towards them. “Mom, Dad. Have you heard anything about Gwen or Bast? The guys that pulled us out didn’t know anything.”

Charlotte placed a hand on his shoulder. “They have been taken to the hospital. We waited for you before going. Are you all right? You’re not hurt?”

“I’m fine, Mom.” Turning to his father he smiled. “You are looking a lot better. How are you feeling?”

“I’m doing well. The doctors in Avalon are impressive. Intend to get rid of this cane in a few days.”

“How bad are they hurt?” Loki asked.

“We aren’t sure. Bast hurt her head and Gwen has a neck injury,” Charlotte said.

“A neck injury?”

Doing her best to hold back tears, Charlotte wrapped her arms around Loki. “It is broken, Loki. We don’t know how badly.”

Loki turned to Arthur. “We need to get to the hospital.”

“We will,” Paul said. “We have a van parked two blocks down. We got here right after the explosion but couldn’t get any closer. It’s pure chaos out there. Two warriors from Asgard keeping an eye on the van. Freya sent them to watch us. We had to work our way here through all the police and firemen. It’s a good thing Freya provided us with the credentials she did. They allowed us to get through.”

Noticing Randy for the first time Arthur offered him his hand. “I didn’t expect to see you here. Shouldn’t you be with Liz and kids?”

“They’re safe and I wanted to see you.” He looked around. “We can talk later. Let’s get to the hospital.”

“Where is Millie?” Lancelot asked.

“She’s with Gwen and Bast. One of us was allowed to go in the ambulance with them,” Kathleen said. “She insisted.”

"Why?" he asked.

"She feels responsible. I told her there was nothing we could have done. The Shadow attacked so quickly there was no way we could have stopped it before it struck Bast. We destroyed it as soon as we could but she thinks that since she was the first on the ladder she should have detected the Shadow sooner."

"You didn't sense it?" Arthur asked.

"Nothing until we saw it."

"Strange," Merlin said. "And you said it was strong."

"Very. It took both of us to destroy it."

"Did it speak?" Arthur asked.

"Nothing."

"That is odd."

"I wonder how it got into the shaft," Michael said.

"More important," Arthur looked back at the elevator, "why was it there."

"If I was to venture a guess," Paul said. "I'd say, you. And the others. The bomb, the Shadow, I think they were targeting you."

"Satan has never done anything like this before," Lancelot said. "Never so overt."

Charlotte sighed. "I don't believe Satan was behind this. We should go."

The emergency room was packed with the injured, their families, those that were ill, and those that liked hanging out in emergency rooms. The young man tasked with keeping everything organized and under control was finding it difficult to maintain order. The chaos was about to boil over.

As soon as they stepped into the room it was obvious that they all could not stay. "Those not family might be better off waiting outside. A bit crowded here. We will see what we can find out and let you know."

"I will wait," Lancelot said.

Charlotte smiled at him. "I know you want to check on Millie but I assure you she is okay. It might be better if you wait with the others. As soon as I see her I will send her out."

Looking at what was going on in the ER Lancelot took a step back. "I see what you mean. I will wait here."

Falstaff watched as the young man rushed around the room trying to answer questions, evaluate the needs of those waiting, and prioritize their care while avoiding, when possible, the belligerent attacks by some of those that felt they should not have to wait. Falstaff turned to Thor. "Looks like the little guy could use some help. Shall we?"

The two big men walked up to the young man just as a foul-mouthed individual accosted him demanding attention. Falstaff placed a hand on the guy's shoulder and firmly repositioned him in a chair. He smiled at the ER tech. "Need some help?"

"You will sit down and remain quiet," Thor said in a voice that could melt a frost giant. Silence permeated the room. "This young man is doing his best to help you. You will allow him to do so. My friend and I will remain to assist him. Please bring any complaints you wish to express to one of us." The room became quiet.

An elderly woman, holding a badly swollen wrist, looked at them. "You tell em big guy. Make em wait their turn. Bunch of sleezebags if you ask me."

"I like you, lady," Falstaff said. "You're next."

Charlotte and Paul walked to the desk. Paul smiled. "My daughter and her friend were brought in by ambulance. They were injured in the explosion. My daughter's name is Gwendolyn Earsterdrak. That is E A R S ..."

"Arthur!"

Millie ran down the hall towards them. The nurse looked up at Paul and smiled.

"The young lady has not allowed anyone except the examining physicians to get near your daughter or her friend. There is also a very large FBI agent that is with them that insisted they are important witnesses under his protection. They have been kept isolated from everyone. He was very instant." She smiled. "I believe the young lady will be happy to take you to her. If the large agent will allow you to get close, of course."

"This way," Millie said. "Is Lancelot here?"

"He is outside waiting. If you wish to go to him we understand," Charlotte said.

"I'll take you to Gwen first."

Seeing the look of guilt on Millie's face Kathleen took her hand. "It wasn't your fault, Millie."

"Kathleen said that neither of you felt it," Arthur said. "I don't think I would have been able to see a Shadow in the dark without feeling it first."

Millie looked at Arthur, then stepping up on her toes, kissed his cheek. "Thank you. Gwen is in room three. They took Bast up to surgery. The doctor said they are waiting for a spinal surgeon for Gwen. The guy is supposed to be one of the best."

Paul took her hand. "You are a good friend to Gwen, Millie. Thank you."

"Did the doctors say anything about her condition?" Charlotte asked.

Millie was quiet for a moment. "They are worried that her spine might be severed at the base of her neck. She was having a hard time breathing so they put a tube down her throat. They gave her something so she won't wake up. They called it an induced coma. It is necessary to keep her quiet."

Loki looked at the door. Arthur placed his arm around his shoulder. "She is the strongest person I know. If anyone can beat this, it will be Gwen. Shall we go in?"

Paul took his wife's hand and nodded. "We will give you a moment."

Arthur tried to open the door. "I think it's locked."

"Oh, I'm sorry, I forgot," Millie said. "Open the door. It's us."

The door opened.

"Hercules!" Arthur said. "What are you doing here?"

"I thought you could use my help."

"But you should be in the hospital."

"I am in a hospital."

"I mean as a patient."

"I was bored. Besides, the hole is mostly closed and the doctors said I was making remarkable progress. I can make progress anywhere."

Loki went to hug him but Hercules pulled back. "Ain't ready for that. The stick the dude shoved in me was thick. Need a little more time."

"I'm sorry."

Hercules smiled. "It's okay." The smile faded and he nodded toward Gwen. "She's asleep. I'll wait outside. Give you guys some time alone."

Hercules gently hugged Charlotte. "She's going to be okay and I'm going to stay with her until she is."

"Thank you."

"You should go," Paul said to Millie. "Lancelot is waiting.

"Thank you." As she walked down the hall Kathleen noticed that she held her head a little higher.

Loki stood back from the bed. "She looks so small. You don't think it did something to her? You know, inside?"

Arthur placed his hand on Gwen's forehead. He smiled. "She is alone and her spirit is strong."

"Art?"

"Yes, Gwen."

"Never did this with you before."

"Never had to."

"I can't move and I'm having trouble opening my eyes."

"I know. You've been hurt. The doctors are keeping you asleep until they can figure out what to do."

"What's going on?" Loki asked

"I'm talking to Gwen."

He looked down at her. "Tell her ... tell her I love her."

"I will. But she already knows."

"Is Loki there?"

"Yes. He says he loves you."

"Please tell him I know."

"I already did."

"Can you let me talk to her like you did with Michael?" Loki asked.

"I don't know. Michael was in my head."

"Would you try?"

Arthur took his hand and placed it on Gwen's head. He placed Loki's on top of his"

"Loki wants to see if he can talk to you like he did when Michael was in my head. I don't know if it will work. He is here."

"Loki?"

"Did she say something?

Arthur let go of Loki's hand. "I'm sorry."

"Tell him that I know he is here."

"She wants me to tell you she knows you are here."

"Arthur, I can't lose her."

"None of us can." He turned to the door. "I need to let my parents come in. You okay?"

Wiping his eyes with the back of his hand he turned towards the wall. "Yeah. Thanks for trying and, well, you know. Letting me know she is there."

"You're welcome."

Arthur opened the door and stepped back as his parents walked to Gwen's bed, each taking a hand. Paul looked at Arthur.

"I remember what Michael did when I took your hand in the garage."

"I'm sorry, Dad. I tried with Loki."

"It was a thought. Can you reach her?"

"I have. She's a little frightened but in no pain. She knows you're here."

Paul leaned down and kissed his daughter on the forehead. "You're going to be okay, honey." He stepped back. "Thanks, Art."

Arthur walked into the hall. Hercules was leaning against the wall watching the door.

"Anyone try to get in besides the doctors?"

"No. And I've been here since they brought the two of them in."

"How did you know?"

"Folks talking about what happened even on Olympus. Seems there is no longer any difference in our times. Used the portal. Guards said they heard someone was hurt. Had them bring me here."

"Would you mind staying?"

"It will be my honor."

"You armed? If this is Cain's doing some of his followers use guns."

Hercules smiled. "Not a problem." He opened his coat exposing the hilt of a .357 magnum revolver.

Arthur smiled. "Should have known it would be something big."

"Loved that DIRTY HARRY movie."

"I'm sure you did."

Arthur walked out of the building. The others stopped talking when they saw him.

"How is she, Art," Randy asked.

"Stable. They're calling in a specialist."

"Arthur?"

He turned and looked at Michael wondering why he would not speak out loud. *"Yes."*

"Would you mind if Remiel looked at Gwendolyn?"

"Why are we talking like this? And no, I do not mind. But why?"

"I do not wish anyone to hear what I am about to say. Not yet. Remiel is a doctor. A surgeon. He has an idea but feels it is critical no one knows what it is he is proposing. It could be dangerous and he is not sure it will work. But it could save Gwendolyn."

CHAPTER FIFTEEN

Kathleen sat on the lone wooden bench outside the entrance to the ER. Arthur sat down next to her with two bottles of Coke. She looked up when he offered her one.

"Thank you."

He rolled the cold bottle across his forehead. "You're welcome."

"Any word?"

"Bast is out of surgery."

"How is she?"

"Alive. That's something. She had a clot pressing against her brain. The doctors removed it. They think she will be okay. There is some swelling."

"To her brain?"

"Yeah. Won't know for sure if it caused any damage until she wakes. They're optimistic though."

"And Gwen?"

"The specialist looked at her. Said there wasn't much he could do. The spinal cord was severed at the base of her neck. The most we can hope for is that she can breathe on her own someday. She will spend the rest of her life unable to move. A quadriplegic."

Kathleen threw her arms around him. "Oh, Arthur, I am so sorry."

"Remiel is in with her now. Michael said he is a doctor. That maybe he might be able to help."

"You think he can?"

"I don't know."

"We need to get Bast back to Duat. The doctors there might be able to help her."

"I agree."

"Where are your parents?"

"Waiting outside the room while Remiel exams her."

"Shouldn't you be with them?"

"I'll go back in a few minutes. Michael said Remiel wants to talk to me when he is done. Alone."

Kathleen started to get up and Arthur took her hand. "Please stay. There is nothing that they can say that I wouldn't share with you."

She squeezed his hand.

"First Dragon?" Anubis called as he walked toward them.

"Please, just Arthur. People around here have no idea what a First Dragon is and I would like to keep it that way."

"I'm sorry — Arthur."

"No problem. We need to try to keep a low profile."

"Like that is possible with Hercules around," Kathleen said.

"Has something happened to Bast?" Arthur asked.

"There is no change. The doctors think there is hope. That is what I want to speak with you about."

"Yes."

"I would like to take her back to Duat. To the doctors there and her family. I know that everyone here is doing what they can, but ... well ..."

"Your doctors are a little more advanced."

"Yes."

"Kathleen and I were just discussing that. Of course, if you think it is safe to take her through the portal. We will see if we can get an ambulance to transport her. It would be safer. I'll have one of our guys drive so there won't be any questions. I will tell the hospital folks she is being moved for her safety. Her life may be in danger."

"Thank you. Once she is settled I will return."

"There is no need. Stay with her. Let me know how she is doing."

"I cannot do that. My place is by your side."

"Nothing is going on right now. Go. I'll call if I need you."

"But ..."

"No buts. Go." Arthur smiled. "I am concerned about her too. We are all family."

"I'll ask my father to seek Patricia's help to arrange for the ambulance."

"You are most kind, Kathleen."

"As Arthur said. We are family." She turned to Arthur. "I will find him and be right back." She kissed him on the cheek and she and Anubis walked back toward the hospital.

They met Michael, Remiel, and Ariel on the steps to the ER. Kathleen stopped for a moment taking Michael's hand. They spoke. She nodded then followed Anubis through the double doors.

"We need to speak." Arthur heard Michael say.

"Is something wrong?"

"No, First Dragon," Ariel said. *"But what we are about to propose must remain confidential for now."*

"From the others?"

"From all but you and those of us from Haven," Remiel said.

"Why?"

"Remiel believes there may be a way to help Gwen," Michael said. *"To save her. To allow her to walk again."*

"But it is dangerous, and to be honest I am not even sure it will work," Remiel said.

"I believe it is possible. Theoretically," Ariel added.

"I have discussed it with Gwendolyn," Remiel said. *"She understands the risks and wishes me to try."*

"Try what?"

"On our world, Remiel is a skilled surgeon," Michael explained. *"He has led our medical profession to several major breakthroughs. One is a procedure that can restore function to those that have lost the ability to use their limbs due to injury."*

"You can fix a severed spinal cord?" Arthur asked.

"Not exactly," Remiel said.

"What does that mean?"

"There is a procedure that replaces the function of the spinal cord. It does not repair it. I have tried it in the lab with some success but I have never tried it on an injury as severe as Gwendolyn's. And never on one of your kind."

"Replaces the function?"

"Replaces the entire cord," Ariel said.

Arthur looked at them to make sure they were serious. *"Replace?"*

"Yes. I will introduce a series of microscopic machines that are programmed to reconstruct the damaged spine. Then replace the cord with biological fibers that carry electrical impulses from the brain to the body."

"Biological fibers?"

"Grown from stem cells collected from the host," Remiel said.

"Stem cells?"

"The basic cells of life."

"You said it was dangerous. How so?" Arthur asked.

"We have never taken one from this world through the window. Ariel believes it can be done, but as I said, it has never been tried. The well can cause a good deal of stress to a body," Michael explained. *"And Gwendolyn's is already compromised. And human."*

"I believe I can construct a containment suit for her with materials available here," Ariel said. *"Once on Haven, we will place her in a security field that will protect her from our gravity which is half again what is experienced here."*

"I will then operate through the field," Remiel added.

"Is that all?" Arthur asked afraid of the answer.

"No surgical procedure is without risk. I have to remove the damaged bones and the cord before I can start the procedure. That is a great deal of trauma for the body to contend with. Although she will feel no pain, Gwendolyn's mind will remain active. I will stay in contact with her. She will need to assist. Once the cord has been removed I will introduce the microscopic mechanical builders and the biofiliment."

"Builders?"

"The robots that will do the repairs. Gwen will need to work with them. They will construct the artificial spine around the newly introduced cord." Remiel said.

"But we must first get her there. Travel to and from is a concern," Ariel said. *"We do not know how it will affect Gwendolyn. Our technology allows us to travel through space, Arthur. Unlike your portal that is interdimensional, our window bends space, allowing us to cover vast distances to other planets. I do not understand how your portal functions. It is beyond our science."*

"Magic?" Arthur said sarcastically.

"Do not disregard the possibility of magic, Arthur. Look at what you can do as a Blocker. One being's science is another's magic. But our technology must be safeguarded. Your world is not ready for it."

"I understand," he said. *"Another planet?"*

"Another reason we feel we need to keep this quiet for now.

"And we must not let the people of our world know we are bringing her. I do not know how the news would be received," Michael added.

"You mean bringing an alien to one of your doctors?"

Michael chuckled, *"From here. Yes."*

"And Gwen understands what you want to do. How dangerous it is? That it might not work?"

"She does. I have told her of the risks."

"Is there anything else?"

"We have no idea if her body will reject the machines. I have never done this with someone of your species."

Arthur was silent for a moment. He looked up when he saw Kathleen.

"It is your decision. Tell her what you think necessary," Michael said.

"And if you do not do this?"

"Gwendolyn may die," Remiel said. *"At best she will remain paralyzed for the remainder of her life."*

"My father has phoned Patricia and she is making arrangements for an ambulance to move Bast," Kathleen said taking Arthur's hand. "Did I miss something?"

"I know not telling her will be difficult," Michael said.

"You know I can hear you. A Blocker. Remember."

Michael smiled. "I do remember, Kathleen. Forgive me."

"So what is going on?"

"They may have a way to help Gwen," Arthur said.

"How?"

"That is a little complicated. Let's just say that it is a bit unorthodox."

Kathleen looked at him for a moment realizing that was all she was going to get. "Will it work? Will she walk again?"

"She might."

"Then that is all I need to know. And your parents?"

"I will tell them what I can." He turned to Remiel. "Save her and bring her back to us."

"I will do what I can. But we need to move her. And we need to do it as soon as possible. Her life is in danger here not only from our enemy but from nature itself." He turned to Ariel. "How soon can you be ready?"

"If I can find what I need, a few hours. I will begin immediately." She turned to Arthur. "Can I get help?"

"I'll get everyone out here and you tell them what needs to be done. We will make it happen." He turned to Michael. "Where?"

"Someplace away from here. Secluded."

"The house. It's empty."

"I don't know what you need it for but it won't be empty for long," Kathleen said. "Your mother has directed that we move our operation there until we can move back into the Federal Building."

"What about the small portal?"

"Hercules is making arrangements for a squad of warriors from Olympus to secure it during the clean-up."

"I'll speak to my mother." He turned to Kathleen. "See if Patricia can get us another ambulance, please."

She turned when she heard voices. "Here come the others."

"Is everything okay, Arthur?" Lancelot asked.

"Yes. But Ariel needs your help getting supplies for a special project. It may help Gwen. Please get her whatever she needs. We need to do it quickly."

"For Gwendolyn?" Falstaff asked. "It will be done." He turned to Ariel. "Now what do you need, little lady?"

Merlin took Arthur by the arm and led him away from the others. Kathleen followed. "Are they taking her to Haven?"

Arthur looked at him then shook his head. "Why did anyone think this was going to remain secret?"

"I am not sure what he intends to do but taking her to Haven seemed logical after Remiel examined her. I do not know if the others realized that of course."

"Of course. They aren't the world's greatest wizard. Where's Loki?"

"With your parents. They are with Gwen."

"I better go talk to them."

"Do you want me to go with you?" Kathleen asked.

He leaned down and kissed her. "Thank you, but this is something I'd better do alone. Will you wait for me?"

"Always."

Arthur opened the door. His mother was sitting in a chair next to the bed holding Gwen's hand. His father and Loki were at the foot of the bed. They turned when he entered.

"Any change?"

"The doctor said it was too soon. They will try later this afternoon to wake her," Charlotte said.

Loki leaned on the rail of the bed. "They said she will never walk. I don't care. I'll carry her wherever she needs to go just so long as she is with me."

"There is something I need to talk to you about. All of you. But first I need to speak to Gwen."

He walked to her bedside and placed his hand on her forehead. *"You there, Sis?"*

"Not going anywhere. At least for the moment. Remiel talk to you?"

"He did. You okay with this?"

"Doesn't seem like I have much of a choice. Have you told Mom and Dad? Or Loki?"

"Not yet. You scared?"

"Terrified. But I'll be the first person in the family to visit an alien planet. What stinks is that I can never tell anyone about it."

"I know. Like going to Camelot. Who would believe you anyway?"

"True. Uh, Art?"

"Yes?"

"Maybe it would be a good idea not to tell them how dangerous this is."

"They will know what they need to know. Nothing more until you get back. And you will be coming back."

"I know. But just in case."

"I'll be here."

"Thanks, Art. You know that I love you."

"I do. And back at ya."

"Tell them I love them all and tell Loki yes."

Yes?"

"He asked me something. I don't think he knows I heard him. I can hear people now. Just can't talk. Be funny to see his face when you tell him."

Arthur released her hand. "She wants me to tell you that she can hear you and that she loves you." He turned to Loki with a grin. "And she told me to tell you, yes."

It was difficult for Arthur not to laugh when he witnessed the look on his friend's face. Surprise, terror, and then joy.

"Thank you."

"I'm pretty sure I know what that was all about. I'm happy for you."

"You mean he finally asked her?" Charlotte asked.

Turning a little red Loki nodded. "And she said yes."

"That's wonderful," Paul said taking his hand.

"We now have two weddings to plan," Charlotte said. "Wait until I tell Freya. She wondered what was taking you so long."

"I don't want to put a damper on this moment but I need to talk to you. I've spoken with Gwen and she asked me to explain what I can."

"What is this all about?" Paul asked.

"As you know Remiel is a doctor. He thinks he might be able to help Gwen."

"How?" Loki asked.

"It is an experimental procedure and has never been tried on one of us before. Gwen understands what awaits her if she does nothing. There is a possibility she may not survive the surgery. She is willing to take the risk."

"Risk?" Charlotte asked. "What kind of risk?"

"The surgery cannot be done here. They have to take her to Haven. Their gravity is denser than ours. And no one from here has ever traveled through one of their doorways. The surgery itself is very complicated. There are several risks involved. Gwen has decided to accept them."

"What will be the outcome if successful?" Paul asked.

Arthur smiled. "Complete recovery."

Loki shook his head. "It is too risky."

"If nothing is done she may die. And it is her decision, Loki. And she has made it. Support her in this. Honor her wishes."

He was silent for a moment then walked to the bed. He gently kissed her and whispered. "You come back to me."

"I will."

CHAPTER SIXTEEN

The large passenger van pulled off the main highway onto the acre long driveway leading to the house Odin had given Arthur. Outside of a small custodial staff, it had remained empty since the day his father had been shot. It was not vacant now. Guards appeared from the trees and while two aimed automatic rifles at the van another stepped forward. Hercules lowered his window.

"I am driving the First Dragon and his oath-sworn. There is an ambulance behind me and another van behind that."

Looking into the van the guard stepped back throwing his arm across his chest. "First Dragon. He signaled the other guards. "Let them through."

Arthur leaned across the seat before Hercules could pull away. "We are expecting no one else. Please make sure we are not disturbed."

"I understand, sir. The estate is well guarded. Your mother called ahead and Zeus and Ra sent warriors immediately."

"Zeus and Ra?"

"They await you at the house."

Zigzagging around a series of barriers designed to restrict travel along the driveway, Hercules worked his way to the house. Make-shift bunkers made of green sand-bags were numerous and obvious in the yard and the surrounding trees. Several had light machine gun crews manning them.

"It looks like we are in a war zone," Millie said.

"I'm afraid we are. The followers of Cain are human and are armed with weapons from this time. No swords and spears. And no armor," Arthur said.

Thor placed his hand on the back of the seat and leaned forward. "Speaking of armor, there are a few vests in the armory. I'm afraid the only ballistic armor available is for Arthur, Loki, and I."

"That should be sufficient," Merlin said. "I think our enemy will find it difficult to reach us with all this security."

"What if they use Shadows?" Kathleen asked. "Our warriors have no protection from them."

"They have us," Millie said.

"But how many would suffer before we could help?" Lancelot asked.

Arthur turned to those in the back. "I will speak with Zeus and Ra about getting power rods. That would at least hold them up until a Blocker was available."

"Some of us should walk the perimeter," Lancelot said. "We should be able the sense the presence of Shadows."

"I hope so. Millie and Kathleen were unable to sense the one in the elevator shaft, and it was strong," Arthur said.

Millie nodded. "I did not know it was there until I saw it. And then it was too late."

"Nor did I," Kathleen added.

"You are both still getting accustomed to your powers," Lancelot said. "And the smoke, your concern for us and each other, the concentration it took to move in the shaft and the danger you faced doing so may have contributed to your lack of awareness. It takes time to understand all the power of a Blocker. Remember, Arthur developed many abilities I never considered until he showed me what was possible. Exorcising a Shadow as an example."

"You and Millie did a pretty good job on me," Arthur said with a smile.

"Only because you made me aware that it was possible."

"And I just followed Lancelot," Millie said taking his hand.

"It may take time to fully develop your skills. Nothing to worry about," Arthur said. "I don't think it is important.

"Do you believe that?" he heard Lancelot ask in his head.

"No."

Hercules stopped the van. "We're here." Several vehicles were parked along the front of the house. Zeus and Ra stepped off the porch to greet them.

"I am happy you have arrived without incident," Ra said.

"Bast?" Arthur asked.

"She and Anubis have arrived in Duat and the doctors are with her. They are optimistic."

"Good."

Zeus placed his hand on Arthur's shoulder. "How is Gwendolyn?"

"She is in the ambulance with my parents, Loki and Remiel. Remiel is monitoring her to make sure she is stable enough for what comes next."

"Is it possible he can help her? I asked our doctors what the prognoses was for a patient with her injuries. They gave little hope. Do you believe the medicine of Haven is that more advanced than ours?"

"I don't know. But it is her only chance. Ariel has constructed a containment suit for Gwen to help with the transfer. Remiel added some medical equipment to it. I don't understand any of it but he is convinced it will keep her stable during the transfer."

The ambulance pulled up beside them. Ariel got out of the front and walked past with nothing more than a nod. Michael followed as she entered the house and shrugged smiling.

"It is not her intent to be rude, Arthur. She is lost in thought."

"No need to explain, Michael. Does she believe Gwen will be safe during the transfer?"

"She is as confident as she can be considering this has never been tried. Only we six have used the window to travel from world to world."

"The others on your world do not?"

"No.

Ariel has discussed it with Remiel and they agree this is Gwen's only chance."

"Thank them for me."

"I shall."

Gabriel opened the rear doors of the medical transport. Charlotte and Loki helped Paul step down and then pulled a floating stretcher from the back."

"Where did that come from?" Zeus asked. "I didn't know we had any here and if we did it would have been buried in the basement of the Federal Building."

"Ariel built it," Arthur said. "She is an engineer as well as a scientist."

Merlin shook his head. "And far beyond my skills in both areas."

Gwen lay encased in a silver suit, not unlike that worn by deep-sea divers. Covering her head was a solid helmet, with no visor. Arthur lay his hand on the helmet.

"Can you hear me?"

"Yes. Not as loud as before, but I can hear you. Are we there yet?"

"Funny. No, we are at the house."

"I still can't wake my body. Weird and a somewhat frightening feeling. Ariel said that when we are ready Remiel will do something that will put my mind asleep. He isn't sure how I would react to the space-window."

"He's a good man. He will do all in his power to help you."

"I know. They are all good people. But I'm scared, Art."

"I would be too. I mean, traveling to another planet."

"Yeah. But at least I get to go before you. Are you jealous?"

"Of course."

"Are Mom and Dad here?"

"They are."

"And Loki?"

"He wants to go with you."

"He can't. You need him with you and there is nothing he can do to help me."

"I know that. So does he, but that doesn't change how he feels."

"Tell him I will be okay and we will be together again soon."

"I will."

"We need to go, Arthur," Remiel said. "Michael has taken Ariel to the basement to prepare and I need to see to Gwendolyn."

Arthur took his hand from the helmet and looked at his parents. "We must go."

"I understand," Paul said.

"I'm sorry but you will have to wait upstairs."

"We know, Art," Charlotte said. "Michael explained it to us. And we have said our goodbyes to Gwen."

"She heard you."

Charlotte smiled. "Thank you."

"And we will see her again."

"I know."

Paul placed his arm around her. She had tears in her eyes.

"I'm going," Loki said.

"You can't," Arthur said.

"Not to Haven. To the basement. With you."

Ezekiel looked at Arthur then placed his hand on Loki's shoulder. "It's all right."

Arthur and Loki followed the stretcher into the house.

Remiel turned to Paul and Charlotte. "Michael said that if you wish to accompany us downstairs he understands."

Paul looked at his wife who shook her head.

"Thank you but we will remain up here. She will not really be gone if we do."

"I understand. I will do all that I can for her."

"We know," Paul said. "Thank you."

Charlotte stepped into the dining room. She looked at the people waiting. "We will set up here."

Remiel looked at the series of numbers scrolling across a lighted panel on the helmet of the suit. He turned to Ariel. "She is ready."

Ariel removed a small box from a pocket, flat and no bigger than a cigarette lighter. "Please step back."

Placing her thumb on the device she turned her hand in a pattern so fast that Arthur was unable to follow. A dark doorway materialized in the wall in front of her. She nodded at Remiel who guided the stretcher into the opening. When he was no longer visible the door folded into itself and was gone.

"Arthur,"

"I know, Loki."

"What?" Michael asked.

The doorway. It looks just like the one used by Bael," Arthur said.

"And Satan," Loki added. "More defined and a little smaller, but similar."

"You're right. I never considered it before," Michael said. "It is similar."

"Interesting," Ariel said. "You have said that Satan and the Shadows do not appear to use a portal such as yours."

"No," Arthur said. "They can open them without a platform. And they are always black holes. Like yours. I never thought that was important. I just figured ours was light and theirs dark. Kinda like Gwen always said, good versus evil, light, and darkness. We only have two functioning portals on each world and they are always on a platform. Even the one in China. The Shadows don't have any fixed point."

"I think I understand."

"Understand what, Ariel?"

"The Shadows are from another world, such as we. Not another dimension, but another planet. They have developed a space window."

"But if it is like yours, why can't they use it to go to the other dimensions?" Arthur asked.

"The device is not like ours."

"How so?" Loki asked. "Seems the same to me."

"I believe it is a crude device. Restricted in its ability. To a single point in time and space."

"But if they are that advanced, why not use spacecraft?" Loki asked.

"For the same reason we do not," she said. "Distance."

"Distance?" Arthur asked. "What kind of distance?"

"We are not talking about travel in this galaxy, Arthur.

"Where are you from?" Loki asked.

"A planet in a galaxy your scientists have yet to discover."

"Then the Shadows may be from another planet too," Arthur said. "But if they are so advanced why are they coming here? If space is so big."

"It is endless," Michael said.

"Okay, endless, so why didn't they find someplace closer to attack?"

"A good question," Michael said.

"And why don't they have advanced weapons like your little toothpaste tube?" Loki asked.

"Satan and the others seem more comfortable with swords and shields. Only their local acolytes use firearms," Arthur added.

"And magic," Loki said.

"Magic? What magic?" Arthur asked.

"Oh, I don't know, swords appear from their hands, being able to possess people, mind control, flitting around without a body. Little things like that. And of course, their primary opponent shoots lighting from his fingers."

"It's not magic."

"Then what is it? You talk to some guy that only you can see. That brings people back from the dead. That may be controlling time. That gave you and the others the power of the Blocker."

"You mean God?"

"Whose?" Loki asked. "And if he is why does he need us?"

Arthur was silent for a moment. "I don't know."

"You cannot assume that physics works the same throughout the universe. What we call science others may consider magic," Michael said. "Look at what Satan and his followers consider food. Many of your people do not believe a soul exists and yet these beings feed upon them."

"I am not sure they have the technology to create the doorways," Ariel said.

"If not them, then who? And why not come themselves?" Arthur asked.

"I don't know," Ariel said. "Magic or science, what we need to figure out right now is if Satan and his people did not develop the ability that allows them to travel here, who did? And why?"

CHAPTER SEVENTEEN

Gwen woke instantly as the warmth of a sunbeam seemed to engulf her. Rising to her feet she sought the source of the illumination.

"Hello. Is someone there?"

"I am here, Gwendolyn."

Straining to see beyond the light she tried to follow the voice.

"What is happening? Are we on Haven?"

"You are."

"I am. What does that mean?"

There was a chuckle. A pleasant sound like wind chimes finding a tune in a gentle breeze. "It is not important, child. I am where I need to be and right now I need to be with you."

"I don't understand," Gwen said. She looked around and suddenly realized where she was. "Art described what it was like when he was aware of himself within his own mind." She looked down. "Yep, no clothes. I'm not awake."

"You are awake, it is your body that sleeps."

"Who are you?"

"I am who I am."

Gwen smiled. "Art got the same answer in China."

"We are not the same."

"Well, I know that. You're a girl. Do you pick a gender to make yourself more acceptable? A man for Art, a woman for me?"

"We are not the same. I have never visited your world."

"I'm about to ask the same question my brother did and if you say yes there are going to be a lot of pissed off people when I tell them you're a woman. Are you God?"

"As I said, I am who I am as is the one that speaks to the First Dragon."

"So you know about Art?"

"Of course."

"And you know what is going on."

"I know what I know. What is important is what you know."

"That is not much of an answer." Gwen placed her hand in front of her eyes. "Any chance you could turn down the light a little so I can see who I'm talking to?"

The light dimmed and a woman appeared, a more defused illumination radiating from her form. She looked a lot like Kathleen.

"She is your friend is she not? I felt it would be easier if I appeared as someone you knew."

"So you don't look like this."

"My true form would cause you discomfort and possible harm. This will do."

"Okay. So why am I sort of awake and why are you visiting me?"

"You must deliver a message to your brother upon your return."

"So, Remiel's idea is going to work. I'm going to be able to move again."

"I am sorry, child, but I cannot say. All I can tell you is that you will return. Whether Remiel will be successful is yet to be determined. It is up to him. I may not intervene."

Trying not to show the alarm she felt Gwen asked. "What is the message?"

The figure stepped forward and placed her hand on Gwen's shoulder. All the fear, the anger, the disappointment she had felt disappeared.

"You have a strong soul, Gwendolyn. No matter the outcome of Remiel's procedure, who you are will prevail. And you are an important part of the battle to come. Your brother and his friends will need you. And you will be with Lucifer."

"Did you give him the power of the Blocker?"

"I gave him nothing. I simply awakened what was in him."

"He is a special man. I'm glad he found Millie."

"Yes, he is. They all are, these Oathsworn of the Dragon. Now when you return you must tell your brother that Satan does not act alone. It is in his home he will find the true enemy."

"I'm not sure I understand."

"That is alright. You will when the time comes."

Gwen screamed as suddenly she was consumed with a burning pain seeming to attack every nerve in her body at once.

"It has begun. I wish you well, Gwendolyn, and grant you this gift."

She fell asleep.

"Damned his incompetence. We had them."

"It is obvious that you did not, Cain. If you had then they would no longer be a problem and we would not be having this conversation. As it is, they are forewarned." Bael looked at the metallic vessel in his hand. "How many?"

"Two dozen so far."

"Any trouble finding hosts?"

"None. Dozens of volunteers. The fools think Satan will reward them for their service. They fight one another for the privilege to carry what they call a sacred demon."

"And our ... demons?"

"A few warriors. We lost our only knight. The others are not fully developed. The ones we were able to hijack are immature."

"I will provide more of the knights. Are your locals able to follow instructions?"

"Enough for our purposes."

Bael stood and stretched. "We must finish this First Dragon and his followers before we can go forward with our plans. We are not strong enough to fight two enemies at once. We finish off the weaker and then focus on Satan."

Cain shook his head. "I am no longer certain they are the easier opponent. There are now three Blockers and as many of the new abominations. Those that are immune to possession."

"Are they immune to bullets or blades?"

"No."

"Good. And how many of your disciples are available that can use those weapons?"

"Maybe a hundred. Maybe a little more. Several are former soldiers."

"And do we know where the First Dragon is?

"At the house where Heidi and her followers first confronted him. I have a man watching them."

"And those that follow him?"

"Those that are not injured are there."

Bael stared at Cain. "Send as many as are available. Ensure they have sufficient firepower. I want them all dead." He stepped to within two inches of Cain. "I do not want any excuses this time. You will lead the attack yourself. And make it bloody. I want this spread all over the news. Have some of them carve their symbols into the flesh of the fallen. Let terror reign."

Randy threw the man to the floor securing his hands behind his back with metal shackles. "I caught him hiding near the highway. The bastard was watching the place." He held up a two-way radio. "He had this on him. Was telling someone how many of us he saw." Rolling the man over with his foot he pointed to the prisoner's forearm. "Check out his arm."

Arthur looked down at the tattoo prominently displayed on the exposed skin.

"Just like the assholes that attacked my place and tried to kill Becky and her kids."

"They know where we are," Merlin said.

"But who knows?" Charlotte asked. "Satan or Cain?"

"Does it make a difference?" Hercules asked. "They want to fight, we oblige."

"Thor, let everyone know if they see anything to take no action. Just call it in," Arthur said.

Paul looked at his son. "You have a plan."

"I think so. At least one in development," he said smiling

"Sif, I want additional warriors standing by. Have them come through the portal. I don't want them seen coming from Cleveland. Have them stage in the woods on the other side of the main highway. Not too close. I don't want anyone to know they are there. They need to be available when we call but I want their presence to be a surprise."

Sif nodded then turned to a tech seated at the dining room table. "Send a message. We need a strike force. When they arrive they are to wait at the portal for further instructions."

The communications tech nodded. "Right away, my lady."

"A hammer and an anvil," Randy said.

"A what?" Kathleen asked.

"When I was in Vietnam a common tactic we used was called the hammer and the anvil. While one force perused the enemy we would send another behind them by chopper. They would be pushed by the hammer into the anvil. Nowhere to go. Pretty successful most of the time."

"I didn't know you were in Vietnam," Arthur said.

"Enlisted not long after Paul was killed. 101st Airborne Division stationed out of Camp Eagle. Got out after my first tour. Saw how our guys were being treated when they came back and decided to become a cop. Thought I might be able to stop some of the crazy's from harassing them."

Arthur took his hand. "Proud of you."

Shrugging his shoulders Randy said, "Yeah, well, different kind of war."

"Wars are all the same for the warrior," Falstaff said. "You kill theirs before they get the chance to kill you or yours. Pretty simple really."

Randy smiled. "Once you remove the politics I guess you're right. It helps if you believe in what you are fighting for."

"How about good versus evil," Charlotte said.

Randy smiled. "Good cause."

"Let Lancelot and Millie know we are expecting trouble. The first sign of Shadows they are to return here."

Arthur looked at Michael. "You and the others save your little tubes for those we identify as possessed. If there are any. Keep Loki or Rex near. In case a Shadow comes for you. Lancelot and Millie will destroy the Shadow when the body is gone. No chance of a transfer that way. They will be carrying guns so you must eliminate the host first. None of us has the power to stop bullets and not all of us have armor."

"And where will you be?" Loki asked.

"Right now I plan on Kathleen and me to standby here in case we are needed. Of course, plans change. I'll be watching for Cain or Bael. If I sense their presence, we will go after them."

Thor placed his hand on Arthur's shoulder. "Sif and I will remain with you."

"We will keep the others from you just in case," Sif added.

"And what will Hercules and I be doing while you are having all this fun?" Falstaff asked.

Arthur looked up at the big man. "Have your long guns?"

"Of course."

"Then you stay here and protect my parents. Let no one reach the house."

Hercules smiled. "A noble task. No harm will come to them. This I swear."

"Thank you."

Charlotte turned to the dining room. "Come you two. I have work to do. You may think the only fight is here but I'm getting reports that may not be true. Let's see if we can figure out what these bastards are up to."

Falstaff smiled. "I like your mother, First Dragon. Feisty."

It will be dark soon, Arthur," Kathleen said.

They were sitting on the hanging swing on the porch rocking slowly, his arm around her, an automatic rifle at his feet.

"Do you think they will come?"

"I do. I think that what happened in Cleveland was meant to kill us. They are not going to stop until they succeed."

"Will this ever end?"

Placing his hand under her chin, he lifted her head and stared into her eyes. "Maybe. Probably. I don't know. The only thing I do know is that as long as I have you with me I will never stop fighting."

"Do you believe we can win?"

"I have to. I have a wedding to attend."

Kathleen wrapped her arms around him and drew her lips to his

"Ahem. Sorry, Kathleen — Arthur," Loki said. "You are needed in the house."

"Problem?"

"Just got a report of a lot of traffic on the road."

"Anybody stop?"

"No. Several vans, two panel trucks, and a dark stretch limo. Weird convoy."

"Yep. I suppose it is about to begin."

"Seems that way."

Arthur stopped the swing and offered his hand to Kathleen. "It looks like we have work to do."

She smiled. "Seems that way."

Taking her hand he led her into the house. Rex and Randy were waiting.

"Your Mom said that everyone is ready," Randy said.

"Lancelot and Millie, along with two Asgardian warriors, will remain near the driveway entrance," Rex reported. "Thor has had several obstacles placed along the driveway to slow down any vehicle trying to make a rapid approach. Sif has automatic weapon strong-points positioned to cover the obstacles. The others have fallen back per your instructions."

"Thanks, Rex." Arthur turned to Thor. "Falstaff and Hercules?"

"Upstairs."

"Good."

"And the local police?"

"They have been told we are conducting a training exercise for the SRT. They are ready to block all traffic to or from the area as soon as you give the word," Paul said. "Good cops."

"Best do so now." Turning to his mother he asked, "Air support?"

"Icarus is standing by as is the blocking force."

"Who is leading them?"

"Isis."

"That is one tuff lady," Loki said.

"She insisted," Ra added with a chuckle. "I have never been able to deny that woman anything."

One of the warriors working communications turned to Charlotte. "We may have a problem, my lady."

"What kind of problem? And please call me Charlotte."

"Yes, Lady Charlotte."

Arthur shrugged his shoulders. "Don't fight it, Mom. You'll lose."

"The police report that a large truck passed before they were able to set up the roadblock."

"What kind of truck?" Paul asked.

"A refuse vehicle."

"You mean a garbage truck," Randy said. "That is a heavy vehicle, Art. It will be hard to stop."

"I know." He turned to the tech. "Tell the blocking force to start to move in. Not too close. I don't want them seen. And have Icarus warm up his bird."

"Yes, sir. Wait. A report. Several vehicles just pulled up near the driveway. The refuse vehicle has reached them and stopped as well." Listening he hesitated for a moment. "A man from the limo is speaking with the driver of the large truck. He has signaled to the other vehicles. Several armed people are exiting and falling in behind the truck."

"They are planning to use the truck to crash through the obstacles. Their scout must have reported them," Randy said.

"Seems that way." Arthur turned to Michael. "You ready?"

He nodded. "We shall wait near the garage until you tell us where we will be of most value."

"Thanks. As soon as I know their final dispositions I'll let you know. Everyone take your positions." He turned to Kathleen and Rex. "You two stay here. Rex, protect who you can from possession. Kathleen, deal with any Shadows. Thor, you and the others concentrate on the disciples." He stopped and looked out the front door. "Anyone sees Cain, let me know right away. He's mine."

"Arthur."

He took Kathleen's hand. "I need a Blocker with those near the house. Lancelot and Millie will watch one side and I will the other."

She hesitated, turned, and looked at Charlotte talking to the communications tech. She squeezed his hand. "I understand, First Dragon."

"And me?" Loki asked.

"Stay here and make sure nothing happens to my parents."

"But ..."

"Loki, look, I need someone that has fought these things and knows them. Someone that can stop a Shadow from possessing my parents."

"Can't I do that?" Paul asked.

Arthur looked at him.

"The one from the house. The one you drove out. It was inside me. Isn't that how Gwen and Loki became immune?"

"That's true, Arthur," Kathleen said taking his hand.

"Besides, I have this." He held up the .45 Arthur had given him

"And this," Merlin said handing him a power rod. "I shall remain with them."

Arthur was silent for a moment. Shaking his head he said, "Okay. Loki, you are with me."

The communications tech turned to Arthur. "The big truck just pulled up to the driveway, First Dragon

"Here we go," Arthur said turning to the door and the battle that awaited.

CHAPTER EIGHTEEN

The small communications device in Arthur's pocket chirped. "Yes, Lancelot?"

"The large truck has stopped. It is still on the main road. About fifty people are crowding behind it."

"What are they doing?"

"Nothing. Just standing there. Another ten or fifteen on each side of the road just stepped into the trees. I sense Shadow with the outlying groups. Nothing with those behind the truck."

"Any idea how many may be possessed?" Arthur asked.

"No. But there at least two that are warriors. Maybe even a knight. I can't tell. Too many. Strange though."

"Strange how?"

"Only the larger ones are talking. That's why I am not sure of their numbers"

"Okay. You and Millie stick with the group on the left and Kathleen and I will take those on the right."

"As you wish."

Arthur put the communications device back in his pocket. "New plan. Rex, go to Michael. Tell him there are Shadows in the trees on both sides of the driveway. Have him join me. You stay with Ezekiel and Gabriel then work your way to Lancelot. He and Millie are on the left near the highway. Protect them. Once the hosts are down the Shadows will seek new ones. Lancelot and Millie should be able to destroy them but I want you there just in case."

"I understand."

Arthur's phone chirped again. "Yes, Lancelot?"

"Those in the woods have stopped moving, they now lie on the ground."

"The main group?"

"They are still as well. Several vehicles have parked along the roadway. Their occupants have moved behind the refuse vehicle. They have stooped down. No one is moving.

"Wait. A white box truck just pulled out. It has passed the larger truck and is moving down the driveway towards you. It is picking up speed. Those behind the truck just dropped to the ground. It is all strange."

"Stop it!" Randy yelled. "Stop that truck!"

Turning Arthur asked, "What?"

"Stop it. Any way you can. It's a bomb."

"A bomb?" Arthur turned to Sif. "Stop that truck!"

Arthur turned back to Randy. "How do you know it's a bomb?"

"Seen it in Nam. Bad guys know there are obstacles ahead. Send someone with a bomb to clear it while the main force waits. As soon as it blows they will rush us."

"How can you be sure?"

"Can't. But ...."

His next words were cut off by the sound of a machine gun chattering quickly followed by an enormous explosion. The windows in the house shattered peppering everyone with shards of glass and knocking them off their feet. Although his ears were ringing Arthur heard the chirp of the phone.

"The big truck is moving."

Climbing to his feet and helping Kathleen Arthur looked around. "Anyone hurt?"

A few thumbs up and shaking heads. He turned to Randy. "You were right."

Smoke billowed above the trees and carpeted the yard. Men and women lay on the ground, some moving, many more not.

"We need to get the wounded out of there."

"I'll send someone," Ra said.

"Send the chopper in. I want all those vehicles destroyed. If there is another bomb we need to stop it. And have the blocking force move in and stand-by. Make sure none of these bastards' escapes."

"Do you want prisoners?" Zeus asked.

Arthur looked at the carnage before him and listened to the cries for help "I don't care. If they offer to surrender, fine. But tell Isis to be careful. Take no chances. If they even look like they might be a problem, kill them."

Loki smiled. "I think you are beginning to understand how our enemy fights, little brother."

"Ra, I would appreciate it if you and Zeus would organize the people we still have standing, try to stop what's coming down the driveway."

"It will be done, First Dragon."

Randy ran from the house. "Everyone is alive. Lots of cuts and bruises but all are back to work. Your mom says ..." He looked at Paul.

"I have been married to that lady for a long time, Randy. There is little she could say that would shock me."

"She said to stop those f......, ugh, bastards."

Paul laughed. "Haven't heard that one before but I agree."

A gunshot rang out from the window above them followed by Falstaff calling down, "Trucks on the way. Most of the people are staying behind the damn thing. Can't get a clear shot. Got the one on the top though. He had a machine gun. Took it with him when he fell off."

Another shot rang out.

"They put something in the windshield. Can't get the driver. Bullets won't penetrate," Hercules called down.

Another shot rang out followed in quick succession by four more.

"I'm trying for the tires but it is still coming."

Zeus grabbed Arthur's shoulder. "Go. Take care of the Shadows. We've got it this."

He picked up an M60 machine gun while Ra broke open an M79 grenade launcher. Shoving an explosive shell into the weapon he nodded to Zeus.

"Go, First Dragon," Ra said. He called to a warrior in the doorway. "You have what I asked for?"

"Yes, Majesty." The warrior from Duat held up a long green tube. Another warrior followed with two more of the LAW light anti-tank weapons.

Arthur smiled, "Guess you do." He pulled Kathleen to him and kissed her. "You be careful. Let them do the fighting. You watch for Shadows. Don't get distracted."

"I understand what I need to do, Arthur. Now go do what you have to and leave us to take care of this. And come back."

"Promise." He turned to Randy. "Stay with my dad. Watch his back in case he needs to help Kathleen. Bullets will stop the disciples."

"Got it, Art." He pulled the charging handle of his M16 rifle to the rear and released it chambering a round.

Arthur turned and started jogging towards the trees. He tried not to look back as he heard several more shots fired from the second-story windows. Moving deeper into the woods he heard the sound of a machine gun. A thump and then an explosion signaled that one of the 20mm grenades had silenced the gun.

"*Stay safe, Kathleen.*"

Loki tapped his shoulder. Arthur stopped and looked at what Loki was pointing at. Along the grassy berm that lined the driveway lay the remains of several of the warriors that had been positioned to stop the advance of the enemy. From the severity of the wounds, there was little doubt that they were dead. The burning carcass of the truck lay on its side in the center of the roadway several yards from the fallen.

The garbage truck rounded the bend and barreled toward the carcass of the burning truck. "We need to move." It crashed into the heap of metal and pushed it aside like so much trash. Trudging on the rims of flattened tires it continued its steady course towards the house. Dozens of kaki clad individuals flanked the truck firing as they ran while scores of others safely followed behind. The intensity of fire increased and several more of the Alliance warriors fell trying to stem the flow of attackers.

"I'll make these bastards pay!" Loki said through gritted teeth.

Michael threw himself into Arthur and Loki driving them to the ground just as several bullets tore the bark from the birch tree behind them. He quickly came to his knees and fired, the beam of light from his small weapon striking a figure not more than ten feet from where they lay. The body disappeared in a flash and the smoky remains of a Shadow hovered in its place. Arthur rolled and raising his right hand flung a bolt of energy towards the Shadow. It shattered.

"Thanks."

"There are more," Michael said looking into the trees. He raised his weapon and fired twice. The ebony mist of two Shadows appeared and Arthur threw light at one as the other flew at Michael. Loki wrapped his arms around the Havenite and Arthur lifted his left hand engulfing his friends in light The Shadow exploded.

Loki let go and turned aiming his assault rifle at one man while Michael fired at two more. Arthur destroyed the two shadowy forms that remained from Michael's attack. Dark ropes of living energy crawled from the holes created by Loki's bullets.

"A warrior," Arthur screamed. "Stay back."

The ropes intertwined and became the figure of a featureless man. Throwing his arms out Arthur projected a burst of light to rival that of the sun.

Catching his breath he looked around. "How many did Lancelot say he saw coming this way?"

Loki surveilled the area while keeping his rifle at the ready. "About ten or fifteen I think,"

"So maybe ten more at the most."

The gunfire from the house became frantic. Arthur was worried about his parents and Kathleen. From the other side of the driveway, he saw flashes of light accompanying the sounds of automatic weapons.

"There!" Loki shouted pointing at close to a dozen men moving through the underbrush. Hearing his shout they froze searching for who called. Loki and Michael fired and at the same time Arthur launched a massive ball of light.

"Check the bodies," Arthur said as he pulled his communicator from his pocket.

"Lancelot?"

"Yes, First Dragon."

"Your status?"

"Ezekiel has been wounded. It is not serious. Millie and Gabriel are attending him."

"And Rex?"

"He is ensuring that the disciples are no longer a threat."

There was a gunshot.

"I see. When you can, meet me at the house."

"We shall as come as soon as they have completed their ministrations."

The gunfire from the house intensified.

"We need to hurry. This isn't over."

A series of whooshing sounds erupted from the house which was quickly followed by multiple explosions.

"There goes the truck," Loki said.

"Isis," Arthur called into his communicator.

"Yes, First Dragon?"

"I think the enemy may be falling back. Be ready."

"We are prepared."

"Icarus?"

"Yes, First Dragon."

"Get ready to take out the vehicles. I don't want anyone to escape."

"Would you like me to wait until some of them are inside?"

"Your call."

"I understand."

Arthur looked back at the house. The sound of gunfire was receding down the driveway. "We should go."

The scene that greeted them as they stepped from the trees reminded him of one of the WW II movies he had watched as a kid with his father. Thick smoke lingered above the broken bodies that littered the lawn and driveway. The house was pockmarked with bullet holes. The remains of the garbage truck in flames. The smell of death almost overpowering. Kathleen ran to him, tears in her eyes and wrapped her arms around him.

"Are you okay?" he asked

"I am fine, but so many have fallen. Zeus has been wounded. He saved me, Arthur. While I was trying to stop a Shadow that had found its way into the house, a man reached the porch and shot several bullets at me. Zeus stepped between us. Your father stopped the bastard but not before Zeus was struck several times."

"Will he live?"

"I do not know."

"There was a Shadow?"

"Yes. A strong one. Your father protected him until I stopped it. It tried to possess Zeus when he fell."

"Was he hurt?"

"Your father, no. But I do not know if Zeus will survive. His wounds are severe."

"And my mom?"

"She's fine. Helping with the injured. Apollo was wounded. I do not know how he is. Ariel, Thor and Sif are with the warriors pursuing the enemy."

Stepping into the house Arthur saw Ra holding a bloody cloth to Zeus's head. The lord of Olympus was not moving. Ra looked up.

"The bullet entered his skull. He is alive but we need to get him home."

"I'll go with him," he heard Apollo say.

"You okay?"

"Armor stopped the bullets. I think I may have a few cracked ribs but I'll live. It is Zeus I am worried about."

Several explosions and a massive amount of gunfire made them look towards the street. Then all was quiet. Arthur's phone chirped.

"It is over, First Dragon," Isis said.

"And?"

"We have no prisoners. I saw no one attempt to surrender. Lancelot has ensured there were no Shadows. All is clear."

"Any casualties?"

"None."

"Thank you."

"You are most welcome. We will clean up here. Those from Haven are using their weapons to help remove unwanted evidence. I will make arrangements to have the remains of the vehicles removed."

"Please thank everyone. You have done an excellent job."

"Will do."

"Icarus?"

"Yes, First Dragon."

"I need you to set down near the house? We have wounded that need to be evacuated."

"On my way."

Taking a deep breath he looked once again at the carnage that lay before him. Doing his best not to shake he turned and entered the house. His mother was kneeling beside one of Ra's warriors bandaging a bloody arm. She looked up, tears in her eyes. He tried to smile when he saw behind her a black hole materialize. Cain stepped from the opening and reached for his mother.

"No!" Randy screamed and dove over the table striking Cain, preventing him from reaching Charlotte. The force of his tackle throwing the two of them back into the opening. Arthur watched horrified as the dark doorway closed.

"Randy!"

CHAPTER NINETEEN

"How did he do that?" Arthur demanded. "It was like he knew where it would open. That my mother was his target."

"I do not know," Michael said. "Ariel did not believe their technology was sophisticated enough to allow them to be so precise."

Charlotte took his hands. "I am so sorry, Art. Randy stopped that thing from reaching me. He saved my life."

Hugging his mother he whispered, "But why."

"Why what, dear?"

"Why did Cain come here? Why did he try to take you? It would have been much easier to just have a Shadow possess you or ..."

"Kill me?"

"Yes."

"We are assuming that he planned on opening his doorway here," Merlin said. "How would he know that your mother would be in the house, in this room? And for that matter who she is? Her relationship to you. There is no way he could have known. And to the best of my knowledge, those that serve Satan have not taken people before. Not even the possessed."

"It was Cain," Kathleen said. "Is he possessed?"

"I do not know what Cain is," Merlin acknowledged. "I am not even sure he is human." He turned, looking at the empty wall. "He did not purposely take Randy with him. That was unintentional."

"The door closed as they fell in. Did Cain close it?" Arthur asked.

"I don't know," Merlin said.

"What will they do with him? What do we tell Liz?"

Arthur stared as the wall. "I don't know, Kathleen.

The sound of a helicopter drew their attention outside.

"Get the wounded on board," Arthur said. "The most critical cases first. Tell Icarus to take them to the portal then come back. We will use what vehicles we have to move as many of the others as can be moved in the meantime."

"Isis will have transportation," Hercules said from the stairs. "I will call. She will also have field medics."

"Good. Thanks. Have you heard about Zeus?"

"I have and would like to go with him. Hera will need me."

"Apollo is with him now. Go with them."

Hercules nodded and stepped outside.

"Zeus has always treated Hercules as a son. He looks to him as a father. He never knew his," Falstaff said.

Arthur looked at the back of his retreating friend. "I know." Turning to his mother he asked, "Any word on casualties?"

"Reports are still coming in. The blocking force escaped injury but the warriors here ... many will not return home."

"When possible I would like to know the name and family status of each. Both the wounded and the ... fallen."

"There are those on each world that can take care of that," Ra said.

"I know, sir, but, I would like to know. They were here because of me. I was in command."

"No, Arthur. They were here for us all," Ra said. "They were volunteers. We have no warriors that are conscripts."

"I'll take care of it. Art," Charlotte turned to the communications officer. "I need a casualty report, please."

Paul placed his hand on Arthur's shoulder. "I heard about Randy. I'm sorry, Art."

"What do I tell Liz, Dad?"

"We will tell her what happened," Kathleen said. "She has a right to know."

"And we don't know he's dead," Loki said. "If there is any way to find him and bring him home we will do so."

One of the communications techs rose. "There is a message from Cleveland, First Dragon.

"What is it?"

"They have reached the basement and secured the small portal."

"Some good news," Loki said.

The tech continued to stand seeming uncomfortable.

"Something else?" Kathleen asked.

"Yes, my lady." He hesitated.

Arthur smiled. "There is little you can say that is going to make this day any worse. What is it?"

"They received a message, First Dragon. Satan demands to meet with you."

The room became quiet.

"Does it say when?"

"Now, First Dragon."

"Does the message say where?"

"It does, First Dragon."

"So tell me."

"He waits outside. The message says you will know how to find him."

Loki grabbed his arm. "You can't go, Arthur."

"I think I better."

"It could be a trap. You can't go alone."

"I don't think it is a trap but don't worry, I am not going alone. Never again. I take my oath-sworn with me."

Loki smiled. "That's better. I'll get them."

"Do not tell Hercules or Apollo. They need to be with Zeus."

"I understand."

Arthur walked to the door. Paul stepped beside him. "What do you think he wants?"

"Not sure. I don't think he was responsible for today's attack. We had a truce. He's dangerous, evil even, but I think his word is important to him. I don't think he broke it."

"Hell of a gamble," Paul said. "I'll go with you."

"No, Dad. I need you to stay here. You are the only one outside of the oath-sworn that can stop a Shadow from possessing someone. I'll have Kathleen stay with you."

"You will not!" Kathleen said. "Have Millie stay. I go where you go."

"I'd listen to her, son. Trust me, won't do you any good to push this."

Arthur looked at his father and then at the woman he planned to marry. He smiled. "Good point. Okay, Millie will stay with you."

"Do you wish warriors to accompany you?" Ra asked.

"Thank you, sir, but no. It will be better if they stay here. In case any of Cain's people return. I will have the oath-sworn with me."

"I have a few power rods if you wish to take Millie," Merlin said.

Arthur thought about it for a moment and then nodded. "I'll take her, but here." He handed Merlin the small weapon Michael had given him. "This might be useful. Point the red end at the target and push the button. But be careful."

"I will. I have seen them work."

"Everyone is waiting," Loki said looking in.

"Thank you." Arthur walked onto the porch. Kathleen and his parents followed. Charlotte stepped beside him and took his hand.

"Be careful. Don't trust him."

"I know better, Mom. It will be okay."

Stepping off the porch he looked at the people that waited. Legends, myths, gods, and angles. Loki, Thor, Sif, Falstaff, Michael, Ezekiel, Gabriel, Ariel, King Arthur, Lucifer, Millie, and of course, Kathleen. His friends, his oath-sworn. No, The Oathsworn. Never had he felt more powerful. He smiled.

"Ready to go meet with the Devil?"

Falstaff laughed and slapped him on the back. "Pity the poor bastard. He doesn't know what's coming."

"Let's go," Rex said. I have never met a real devil before. Should be interesting."

Arthur stepped off with Kathleen on his right and Loki on his left. The others followed.

"Uh, got a question," Loki said.

"Yes?"

"Just where in the woods is he? A little vague, meet me in the woods." Waving his arm. "I mean there is a hell of a lot of trees out here."

Millie pointed to a large number of crows circling a section of the woods. "Maybe there?"

Loki shrugged his shoulders. "Maybe. As good a signpost as any I guess."

They began to walk towards the dark birds.

"Many believe that the crow is a harbinger of death," Thor said. "My father always believed that they were symbols of wisdom."

"Not the owl?" Millie asked.

"No owls on Asgard," Loki said.

"Explains it, I guess," Arthur said as they stepped into the shadow of the trees.

Under the cawing birds was a small clearing. Satan stood in the middle. He was not alone. Three tall, red, athletically built figures were with him.

The crows fled.

"I mean no harm," Satan said. "I have given my word. I am never foresworn."

"Isn't that nice," Loki said.

Arthur stepped forward. "Stay here." He approached, alone, stopping five feet from Satan. He rested his hand on the sword at his side. "Many Shadows and their disciples attacked me and mine today."

"They did not do so at my behest."

"Then by whose? Do Cain and his master not serve you? Can you not control your own?"

One of those with Satan stepped forward and an ebony sword appeared in his hand. Satan put out his hand and stopped him. "No. I have given my word." He looked at Arthur. "Do not push me, boy. I have given my word but will accept no insult."

"If he moves again, he faces me," Lancelot said stepping next to Arthur.

"There will be no violence between us today, Lucifer. I am here solely to talk."

"Then talk," Arthur said coldly.

The hate in the eyes of the evil lord made the hair on the back of his neck raise, but Arthur stood his ground.

"This attack was not of my doing. We have a common enemy, First Dragon. Until this situation is resolved you and your people have nothing to fear from me or those that serve me. The truce between us stands. We will speak again at the conclusion of this unfortunate state of affairs."

"And those that you have taken?" Arthur asked.

"Taken?"

"Cain has taken one of mine."

"We do not take home what we feed upon here."

"Then where is he?"

Satan looked at one of the others with him. He shook his head.

"I will look into it. I do not want chattel in my home. If it is there it will be returned. If it still lives."

He nodded and one of his followers turned raised his hand and a dark door opened. Satan turned his back and stepped into the black doorway. His minions followed and the door closed.

"What the hell was that all about?" Falstaff asked.

"I believe it is important to him that I know he has not broken his word. Strange sense of honor. I also believe he is letting us know that there will be no reprisals for the killing of those that follow Cain. He wants a two-front war. We are sort of an ally."

"One that would destroy us all given the chance," Thor said.

"Something like the Soviets in your Second World War," Sif said. "Allies of necessity."

Arthur looked at her.

"I am a student of history. Even yours. Freya insists."

"Second World War?" Rex said. "There were two world wars between people? Humans?"

"Unfortunately, yes," Arthur said. "Not all evil is perpetrated by Satan."

"He may have had something to do with it," Thor said. "The Shadows have influenced events before."

"That may be true, but I don't think so. It was people that spread the twisted and evil policies that led to the death of millions. There was no mass feeding by Satan's minions."

"And it was people that stopped it," Sif added. "Something to remember."

"There may have been," Loki said. "We do not know what all happened in those camps. A lot of evil took place there."

They all stood silent, the thought of those words disturbing.

"Do you think Randy is still alive?" Kathleen asked. "If he is, will Satan return him?"

"I want to believe he is and hope that he will be brought home," Arthur said. "But ..."

"In what condition?" Lancelot asked. "Will he be sane?"

"We can only hope."

"Do we tell Liz and the kids? If so, what do we tell her?" Kathleen asked.

"For now, nothing. Let's wait a little while. And hope."

"This is unsettling," Ariel said.

"What is?" Arthur asked.

"The window. They are gaining more control."

"I can see that," Loki said.

"But it should not be possible. This is a significant leap in technology. I do not understand."

"Just what we need," Loki said. "Another dammed mystery."

"He said we have a common enemy," Arthur said.

"Who is it?"

"I'm not sure, Loki. But I think it's important we find out. And soon."

"We should go back. The others will be worried," Michael said. "We can discuss this later."

The guards standing outside the house saluted as Arthur approached. He returned the salute and looked at Loki. "I wonder what that is all about."

"Respect?" Loki said.

"There were no smiles," Kathleen said. "Warriors are always happy to see Arthur. They usually smile when they salute."

Stepping into the hallway they were met by Charlotte.

"Something wrong, Mom?"

Wrapping her arms around him and stepping onto her toes she whispered, "Zeus is dead."

CHAPTER TWENTY

The list of the fallen lay on the desk before him. He looked at the names. Twenty-seven dead, nineteen wounded and one missing. Warriors from Olympus and Duat. One a king. A friend.

What about Randy, missing or dead? How was he going to tell Liz? What was he going to tell her? Maybe he should wait. Until he was sure. There was always hope wasn't there? He looked up when the horns sounded. He walked to the open window. Below were assembled thousands of people from all the worlds of the Alliance.

"Arthur, we have to go. They are waiting for you," Kathleen said.

"Waiting for me. Waiting for me to lead the procession for their king. Hell, he's dead because of me."

"Don't be foolish. Zeus is dead because one of Cain's disciples shot him."

"And would they be attacking the house if I wasn't there?"

"Zeus has been fighting these things for centuries. Long before he knew you. He was there because he wanted to be there. He needed to be. To do what he believed needed to be done. He felt it was his duty. Just like it is your duty to lead us."

"She's right," Loki said. "We all know the risks. We take them because all of us know what is at stake. And for what it's worth, Arthur, I think we have a better chance of success, and surviving, with you. Think about that."

Kathleen took his hand. "You need to think of Hera and the others that are waiting for you. For their First Dragon. You do not have time for self-recrimination. The people cannot afford to see doubt within you."

"You're right. I'm sorry. I'm not used to losing friends."

"You never get used to it. Nor should you," Loki said. "We need to go, little brother. The others are waiting for us."

As Arthur started for the door Kathleen took his arm. "You need to wear this." She handed him Excalibur.

He took the sword and belted it over the red tunic with the large gold dragon embroidered upon the front. Loki offered him the helmet he had been given during the assault on Duat. Taking it and placing it under his arm he nodded. Loki opened the door and the heat of the city assaulted him. The people cheered as he stepped into the street.

His oath-sworn fell in as he stepped forward. Kathleen and Loki beside him. An air car hovered at the curb, the honor guard coming to attention as he approached.

"First Dragon," the officer of the guard said saluting. "Her Majesty awaits."

Stepping into the car he nodded. "Thank you."

The crowd parted as the car drifted slowly towards the waiting procession. Kathleen and Loki walked on either side easily keeping pace. More than a thousand Olympian warriors stood in tight formations waiting for his arrival. Their Corinthian helmets glistening in the sun, the red plumes moving gently in the breeze. Each carried a large aspes, the traditional round shield, and the image of a man holding a lightning bolt painted on the surface of each. The eight-foot long leaf bladed spears, traditional weapons of Zeus's honor guard, stood like a forest of perfectly aligned limbless trees.

Another car hovered just ahead. It was adorned with green laurels. A gold coffin rested upon it and a tall raven-haired woman, wearing an exquisitely ornamented bronze cuirass, stood next to it, her red cloak moving slightly in the currents of air generated by the car. Upon her head rested a gold laurel. Arthur stepped down from the car. He bowed.

"Your majesty."

She stepped forward and wrapped her arms around him. Returning the hug he whispered.

"I'm so sorry, Hera."

"I know. We all are. My husband was loved by many. He will be missed."

"I wish ..."

"There was naught you could have done. He was a warrior. He knew the risks. Zeus loved you, Arthur. He believed in you. He felt you were the answer to our prayers to finally end this war."

She kissed him on the cheek. "You are our hope, First Dragon. Honor him by finally putting an end to these things that threaten us all."

Before he could say anything she stepped onto the car that held her husband's body. Hercules and Apollo stood silent on either side.

"It is time, First Dragon. I would be honored if you would join me."

Arthur climbed up onto the other side of the coffin. He put his helmet on. Hera turned to the commander of the guard.

"Now, Hermes. If you would."

Hermes signaled the leader of the musicians standing at attention in front of the royal car. A chorus of trumpets sounded and twenty drummers began striking the stretched leather heads of the instruments. The guard commander called forward and the entire procession began to move reverently down the center of the boulevard. The crowd became still. As the aircar drifted down the street the only sound that could be heard was the beating of the drums and thousands of marching feet. Then Arthur heard the cries. Men and women overcome with grief. Some fell to the ground, others tried to touch the coffin only to be held back by members of the honor guard. Looking down Arthur saw Hercules holding his head high while tears streamed down his cheeks.

As they approached the palace the car slowed and then stopped. Arthur helped Hera step down as eight officers of the household guard walked forward and lifted the coffin onto their shoulders. Arthur and Hera, joined by Hercules and Apollo, followed them as they carried Zeus into the palace. Inside Ra, King Alfred, and Freya waited. They nodded in a solemn salute as the coffin was carried past them.

The drums stopped. A moment later the one thousand warriors of the procession slammed the hilt of their spears upon the ground and yelled Zeus's name three times with such force that the walls seemed to shake. As one they kneeled and lowered their spears to the ground, blades facing the palace, then lay their shields upon the wooden shafts. They stood, removed their helmets, and bowed their heads.

The coffin was reverently lowered onto a golden platform by the King's honor guard. Stepping back they drew their swords, placing the blades point down, they kneeled.

"He will remain here for the next ten days," Hera whispered. "The people will wish to bid him farewell." She turned to Arthur. "At the end of the ten days, he will be interred in a crypt that was built when your people still believed him a god. I thought, hoped, it would never be used.

"I would like your word, First Dragon that those responsible for my husband's death will be dealt with."

"It shall be done if I have to follow them to hell itself. You have my word."

Hera kissed him on the cheek. "I know you will."

She turned back to the coffin. Ra, Alfred, and Freya stepped up beside her to offer their condolences. Freya put her arm around her. Arthur watched for a minute, his chin upon his chest. Then he turned and walked forcefully out of the building and into the heat of the day.

At first, he did not react when the warriors raised their heads and saluted. He started to walk down the steps then stopped and looked at the crowd below him. It was strange. Thousands of people watching him and no noise. Not even a whisper; no dog barked, no child cried. The city was still. All looking at him. Waiting.

"You need to say something, Arthur," Kathleen whispered.

He looked at his oath-sworn and then back at the people standing below.

"Do it, son," Paul said. "They need you to say something."

Arthur took a deep breath then lifted his head and gazed at the multitude.

"Today we mourn the loss a great man. A warrior of incalculable courage and honor. A wise king who loved his people. He died fighting the evil that threatens us all." He hesitated, holding back the tears, he swallowed hard.

"He was my friend. Someone that I relied on for his wisdom and advice." Regaining his composure he withdrew Excalibur. With the blade pointing down he lifted the hilt, his hands on either side of the crosspiece. A ray of sunlight struck the ruby in the hilt bathing Arthur in a crimson glow. His hands began to radiate light that cascaded down the blade as if it had been struck by lightning.

"Let all here accept this, my solemn oath, that I, Arthur, First Dragon of the Alliance of Worlds, swear upon my honor and my life that I shall not rest until Zeus, King of Olympus, has been avenged and this evil finally destroyed."

There was silence. Suddenly thousands of voices began calling out, The Dragon, over and over."

Putting his sword away he looked at the others. Kathleen smiled. His mother stood with tears in her eyes, Paul holding her arm, back straight radiating pride.

Loki shook his head. "Spoken like a true king." Brushing a tear from his eye he added, "I guess we have work to do."

Arthur walked down the steps, the others falling in behind. When he reached the street the waiting warriors turned and opened a path. The crowd parted as he walked amongst them, chanting his name.

Hera stood at the top of the steps. The leaders of the other worlds beside her. She smiled.

"Rest my husband. We are in good hands."

Sitting on the couch in the guest quarters of the palace, Arthur tried his best to unwind from the events of the day. He was alone, insisting the others retire to their rooms and rest. They would return to Earth in the morning. Kathleen was reluctant to go but Loki took her by the arm and escorted her out explaining Arthur needed some time alone.

He reached for the glass on the nearby table unsure what exactly was in it but it was cool, sweet, and refreshing.

"Art?"

Dropping the glass he looked around.

"Art, can you hear me?"

Standing he gasped, "Randy?"

"Yeah, it's me. I got to hurry though. The lady says it's dangerous to do this for too long."

"What lady? How? I mean where are you? Are you okay?"

"I don't know where I am. It's dark and cold. I woke up here. Can't see a thing. Weird voices all around me. I can't understand them. Except for the lady. She showed me how to talk to you."

"Who is the lady? Can she help you?"

"Don't know. Can't see her. Just hear her voice. Only thing keeping me sane. She says you need to come and get us. That things are heating up and we may not be here for long."

"Be where?"

"I don't think she means here. I think she means being alive. You gotta hurry, Art."

"Randy, I don't know where you are. I don't know how to help you."

"Times about up, buddy. Can't talk anymore. The lady says that if we are discovered we're done for. She almost got caught once already. They don't know we are here for now. If I keep talking she says they will find us."

"Who will find you?"

"She calls them the Ghasst. She says you need to ask him for help."

"Ask who?"

"Tell Liz and the kids I'm okay and that I love them."

"Who do I need to ask, Randy? What kind of help?"

I know this sounds weird, old buddy, but she says the only way to help us is to get help from him. He will know what to do."

"Him, who?"

"*Satan.*"

CHAPTER TWENTY-ONE

Arthur sat in the leather chair looking down the long table at his oath-sworn and the leaders of the Alliance. Two members of the Royal Guard of Olympus stepped out and closed the doors.

"We will not be disturbed," Hera said.

"Thank you for allowing us the use of this room. It is most generous of you, Your Majesty."

Waiving her hand Hera smiled. "Arthur. Excuse me, First Dragon, please do not call me that. You referred to my husband by his name. I would be honored if you would do the same with me."

"I've been telling him that since I met him. Good luck getting him to listen," Alfred said.

"As for the room," she continued. "Please consider it the home of the Alliance until the building in Cleveland is once more functional."

"That could be a while," Loki said.

"Probably," Merlin agreed. "But the portal has been cleared and it is under heavy guard. As is the building. The FBI does not intend to allow another attack on one of their facilities."

"Do they know what happened?" Alfred asked.

"Propane truck exploded," Arthur said."

"They bought that?" Falstaff asked.

"Some did, some didn't. It's the official story and so far that is what the papers are selling. We need to keep what is going on as quiet as possible for as long as we can."

"Why? Don't you think it is about time they knew?" Millie asked. "We could use the help."

"And how do you think they would they react," Arthur asked. "The few that believed us? How many more idiots would join Cain if they knew? What about the anti-war folks that would insist we stop what we are doing.

Blocking the portal with their signs and protests. How long could we keep the portals safe?"

"The portal is being guarded by a group of Valkyrie I selected," Freya said. "I do not envy anyone attempting to approach unannounced."

Sif added, "They are a ruthless group of warriors. I trained them myself."

"Imagine the press pushing their way in. Especially if some of the protesters were killed. The government sending troops to secure it or demanding they have access, or worse demand we give it over to them since it is one their land. We would have to secure the portals on all the worlds."

"Maybe that is why Bael and Cain are doing what they are. Creating fear and chaos. To prevent us from using the portal," Hera said.

"Something to think about," Arthur agreed.

Merlin nodded towards Arthur. "You said you had something important to tell us?"

"I do. I'm just not sure where to start."

Ra chuckled. "I have often been told by Isis that it is usually best to start at the beginning. That way it is easier for those not in the know to follow along."

"Like she follows her own advice," Anubis said.

"I have often found that women are big on giving advice they feel it is not necessary for them to follow," Paul added.

Charlotte kissed him on the cheek. "And that is how a marriage works, my dear."

Arthur smiled pleased that his parents had settled into this crazy situation. Especially his mother.

"Does this have something to do with Satan?" Hera asked, the bitterness in her voice unmistakable.

"It does. But not in a way you would expect; or like." He stood. "I heard from Randy."

"What? How?" Kathleen asked.

"He spoke to me."

"As we do?" Michael asked.

"Yes, I think so. He was in my head but it was different than when we talk. It was, somehow distant — hollow. Like he was speaking through a tunnel."

"You are sure it was him?" Merlin asked.

"I am."

"How was he able to reach you? Has he ever done so before?" Apollo asked.

"I don't know how and I don't think he did either. He said a lady showed him how."

"A lady?" Thor asked. "Who is this lady? Can she be trusted?"

"He didn't know. As far as being trusted, I think Randy does and for now, that is good enough for me. Apparently, they are unable to see each other. He said he can't see a thing."

"Then how did he know it was a lady?" Rex asked.

"When I hear a voice in my head it is the same as if the person was speaking to me. I recognized their voice."

"Where is he?" Falstaff asked. "Is it possible to launch a rescue?"

"I don't know. He said it was dark and he was cold. He could hear voices all around him but couldn't understand what they were saying."

"Could he see anyone else? Maybe whoever was talking," Merlin asked.

"No. Wait. Randy said the lady called the things speaking, Ghasst."

Gabriel stood knocking his chair over. "What did she call them?"

"I think it is pronounced Ghasst. It sounded almost like a hiss."

Ariel grabbed Gabriel's arm. "It can't be them."

"Be who?" Lancelot asked.

Ezekiel stood. "If it is, we have a new problem."

"Who are you talking about?" Lucifer demanded.

"If you know something then tell us," Arthur said.

"It happened while you were gone, Lucifer. After that day on the hill when we first came." Ariel explained. "An exploratory vessel returned from a mission mapping many solar systems within our galaxy. They discovered a planet on the rim."

"You use space ships?" Merlin asked. "I thought you traveled through your doorways."

"We do. But others on our world use ships. Not all are aware of the doorways."

"You keep it from your own people?" Sif asked.

"We were concerned about what some might do with the technology. Not all of our world are as we. Believe as we do. Although the technology of Haven far surpasses what you presently possess, it does not equal what we ourselves have."

"Aren't they your people?" Hera asked.

"They are but ... we are ... different in some ways," Michael said. "I do not believe it is the proper time to discuss the differences in our people."

"Then when?" Loki asked. "It's nice to know who we are dealing with. If for instance, you happen to have any other technology you are keeping from us that we could use."

"We have shared with you all that we have in our possession to fight our common foe," Gabriel said coldly.

Remembering what Michael said about their lack of a childhood, Arthur began to understand why Remiel felt it necessary to keep Gwen's arrival secret.

"You are not the same as the others on your world?"

"No. I will explain later," Michael said.

Kathleen looked at Arthur.

"You heard him?" Arthur asked.

"Yes. But how? He wasn't speaking to me."

They heard Michael chuckle. *"Because you are as one in many ways. The strength of your feelings for one another brings you closer."*

He heard the discomfort in Kathleen's voice when she asked. *"Can he hear my thoughts?"*

"Only when you address them to him. When speaking with others you may hear what is being said. Private thoughts are private unless you make them otherwise."

"Except ours."

"To each other, they remain yours. If one of you speaks to another both will hear," Michael explained.

"Good to know," Arthur said.

Lucifer looked at Ariel. "What did they find?"

"Chaos."

"What does that mean?" Loki asked.

"The captain reported the planet was covered in a dark mist that extended from the surface to the upper atmosphere. An attempt was made to land but the crew was bombarded by noise, sounds almost as if thousands of voices were attacking their minds all at once. The atmosphere itself seemed alive. The captain ordered them to pull up and they orbited the planet afraid to reenter the atmosphere."

"Did they hear the voices from space?" Alfred asked.

"Not well."

"Were they able to identify any life forms?" Ra asked.

"There was something there. A force, but like no lifeform they had ever experienced. It was not biological as we know it.," Ariel said. "I had the opportunity to review their findings and was looking forward to delving deeper into the mystery of these beings."

"What is the significance of the word Ghasst," Freya asked.

"It was the name they assigned to the lifeform," she said. "It was the only word they were able to decipher."

Lucifer looked at his sister. "Do you know what this means?"

Trying to downplay the revelation she simply said, "We do not know it is them, Lucifer."

"But this is beyond coincidence. Where else would Randy have heard that name?"

"What is going on?" Millie asked taking his hand.

"The planet they discovered. The mist. The voices," he said. "It can only be one thing."

"Shadows," Arthur said.

"Are you telling me that they found the planet the Shadows come from?" Loki asked.

"It is a possibility," Ariel said. "There was no connection until now."

"It is probable," Lucifer said.

"Why is this a problem?"

"It means, Millie," Merlin said. "That the Shadows come from a planet in their galaxy."

"Which means Ot probably does as well," Arthur said. "But why wouldn't Satan attack Haven? It would seem you are a lot closer."

"A good question," Gabriel said.

"Could it be they do not know we are there?" Ariel asked.

"Maybe they don't have a form of space travel," Paul said. "You don't travel in your galaxy with your door do you?"

Michael was quiet for a moment then he looked at Ariel. "Why haven't we?"

"It never came up. I never even considered it."

"Then why did you come here? How did you know about the Shadows?" Charlotte asked.

"We ... ah ... sensed them," Ariel said. "I have never really considered it before. We had the doorway and knew we had to open it here."

"Do you get the feeling that we are nothing but pawns in a bigger game?" Loki asked.

"I didn't until now," Ezekiel said. "This is most disturbing."

"You think?" Loki said.

"All right," Arthur said. "We can figure all that out later. Right now we need to decide how we can use this knowledge to rescue Randy."

"And the mysterious lady," Kathleen added.

Arthur smiled. "And the mysterious lady. Okay, we think we know where Randy is. How do we get to him?"

"The doorway of course," Loki said.

"It does not work that way," Ariel said. "We cannot open a doorway into a world that is unlike ours. What if there is no air? We would need some kind of coordinates, some idea where to open it so we don't step into a rock or open space."

"And we would be surrounded by thousands or possibly millions of Shadows," Ezekiel added.

"How did you know where to open your door on Earth?" Charlotte asked.

Ariel was silent. She turned to Michael. "I just knew."

"And now?" Arthur asked. "You have come to more than one of our worlds. Your doorway seems to work across dimensions."

"Not until recently," Michael said. He turned to Arthur.

"I believe it locks onto your location."

"That may be it," Ariel agreed. "It may lock onto the location of a Blocker."

"That doesn't work," Freya said. "I remember Odin telling me that someone stepped through the black opening on that first day with the power of a Blocker. It wasn't already there."

"Lancelot," Kathleen said.

"Yes," Arthur agreed. "But Lucifer came with the others that day. There was no Blocker here. He was the first."

"Yep, pawns," Loki said.

"Could Satan do that? Lock in on a Blocker?" Millie asked. "Maybe we shouldn't be here. Maybe we should stay on Earth."

"I don't think it works the same way," Arthur said. "I've been on the other worlds several times and Satan's forces have always needed to use our portals. And as Freya said, Ariel did not need a Blocker to lock onto that first day." He turned to Ariel. "You developed the ... what do we call it ... space doorway?"

"Window. It was my idea but the others helped me with it."

"When?"

"What do you mean?"

"How soon after you had the idea did Lucifer get the power?"

"We did not know about his power. In the early stages of the development of the window we could not travel, only monitor. It is how we discovered what the Shadows were doing here. Lucifer did not reveal his power to us until we had stepped through."

Arthur looked at Loki. "I don't know if we are being used or helped. Either way, our problem remains. What do we do about Randy?"

"We go get him," Thor said.

Arthur looked at Ariel. "Can we do that?"

"I suppose it is possible for you to cross through the doorway. It would very uncomfortable due to our gravity. But you're healthy."

"Okay, so we can get to Haven. How do we get to the Ghasst?" Arthur asked.

"Oh," Ariel said. "I have a space ship."

CHAPTER TWENTY-TWO

Arthur set the empty glass down and pushed his chair back. He sighed. "That was good."

Charlotte smiled. "Thank you. I had a hard time convincing Hera's staff that I wished to cook the meal myself. And the idea of a meatloaf appalled them."

"Well, I for one am happy you did. I have missed your cooking," Paul said.

"Me too," Arthur agreed.

He and his family sat alone in the quarters Hera had provided Charlotte and Paul. Except for Kathleen and Merlin, they were alone. The others had retired to their quarters albeit reluctantly. Loki especially did not wish to leave Arthur alone. But it was to be a family dinner. His parents and his bride to be. Something they had all missed and Arthur insisted, unsure when they would have another opportunity.

"It would have been nice if Gwen and Loki could have joined us," Charlotte said.

Arthur took her hand. "I thought it would be difficult for him without her."

She nodded. "Have you heard anything from Remiel?"

"No. Michael says it is too soon. But he is hopeful. There is no one better to help her he said. I believe him."

"But these tiny robots. How long will they remain inside her?"

"They will be with her always, Mom. Areal says that there is no way to retrieve them once they are injected. But she also said they have a single function and once it is complete they become inert."

"But what if they wake up? Could they hurt her?"

"From what I understand, Charlotte, they will be unable to do so," Merlin said. "The machines have a limited amount of power. Just enough for their basic programming and then they shut down. They cannot be reactivated."

"Seems a bit creepy havening a bunch of little machines rusting inside you," Paul said then smiled. "I bet the airport scanners will go nuts when she passes through."

"Airport scanners?" Arthur asked.

"Oh, sorry, Art. I keep forgetting how long you were gone. While you were ... away, there were several terrorist attacks throughout the world. People pushing their political or religious agendas. Airplanes being their favorite targets. Several were hijacked. There were passengers killed and a few of the planes were blown up. All around the world governments began to increase security in their airports. Some have armed guards. In several, they have installed scanners that detect metal. In the US you have to pass through a metal scanner for all international flights."

Arthur chuckled. "I can see where that could be an issue."

"This is nice," Kathleen said.

"What is, dear?" Charlotte asked.

"Sitting around the table with family." She looked at Merlin. "There was always just us at home. Freya and the others tried to make me feel like I was part of their families but, well, it wasn't like this."

"I'm sorry, Kathleen," Merlin said. "I didn't realize."

Taking his hand she smiled. "Do not misunderstand. I have always been happy, Father. You did what you could, I know. I just didn't understand what I was missing until now."

"Well, you are a part of this family now," Charlotte said. "As are you, Merlin."

"Thank you."

"Not that I wish to break up this wonderful moment, but I have had something bothering me since the meeting with Ariel," Paul said.

"What, Dad?"

"Well, Ariel said she had a ship. A space ship. How big is it? How fast can it travel? We are talking about the outskirts of her galaxy. I mean how long would it take her to fly this ship to the planet Randy is supposedly on? Months? Years? What happens while you are gone? What will the Shadows and Satan be doing? And more important what will Bael and Cain's actions be? Something else. What did Randy mean when he said you will have to seek help from Satan? What kind of help? And why him?"

"I don't know. Ariel didn't get into details. I'll have to ask her. And Satan, I have no idea what that is all about."

"I have been wondering about the ship myself," Merlin said. "But I think I may understand how Randy's rescue and Satan my be connected."

"How?" Kathleen asked.

"It's best we wait for me to better organize my thoughts. I will discuss it with Areal. I could be wrong and there is no sense in causing any more confusion."

"Always with the mystery," Kathleen said.

"Well, I am Merlin."

Rising Charlotte started to pick up the empty plates.

"Let me help you with those," Kathleen said.

"Thank you. Anyone for dessert? I have a peach pie and coffee."

"Peach pie?" Arthur asked. "Where did you find peaches?"

"In the store. This is a civilized world, Art. They have grocery stores and everything. It may look like ancient Greece out there but I can tell you, they surpass us in many areas. You should see what they have in some of their stores."

"Sounds like you have been busy," Arthur said.

"Your mother is a professional shopper, Art. There is no way she would pass up the opportunity to visit a store on another world."

Charlotte stuck her tongue out at him. Kathleen looked at her and laughed.

"I see I have much to learn from you ... Mother."

When they had left Arthur turned to Merlin. "What are you thinking?"

"I wonder if we could use Satan's door to reach Randy."

"Can you feel your toes, Gwendoline?" Remiel asked.

"I feel something. A tingling?"

"That is good. I did not expect this so soon. This is very good. Is there pain?"

"Not really. I still can't move though."

"I have given you something to immobilize your body while the machines work. It is somewhat like placing you in a medical coma. Your body sleeps even while your brain functions."

"Remiel?"

"Yes?"

"Do the robots talk?"

"Talk?"

"Yes, do they talk to each other?"

"Their programming requires them to work in harmony. I suppose they use some kind of rudimentary communication. Why?"

"I hear them."

"Hear them?"

"I hear them talking. I can't understand the words but they are defiantly talking to each other."

"The machines are not alive, Gwendoline. They have no ability for conscious thought. It is like two parts of a single machine working in concert. Each robot is like a cog designed to work with the others as part of the overall machine."

"Don't think so. They are talking. They seem excited."

"I am afraid that is your imagination. They can have no emotions for they are not sentient."

Gwen moved her foot.

"They liked that. They just cheered."

"That cannot be."

"Have you ever used them like this before?"

"Not on one of your species and not with injuries as severe as yours. That is why I told you I was not sure this would work."

"Well, they seem pretty excited for not having emotions."

She lifted first one, and then the other leg. She opened her eyes.

"So am I."

"Gwendolyn! How? This cannot be. The medication I used to immobilize you requires an antidote. Careful."

"I'm okay. Really. I feel no pain." Rising on her elbows she looked around. "As a matter of fact, I feel pretty damned good. Better than I have in a long time."

She sat up.

"Wait!" Remiel cried reaching for her. "You'll fall."

Jumping off the table she stood staring down at herself. The sheet that had covered her had fallen to the floor.

"Don't think so. Ugh, I'm nude."

"I'm sorry, what?"

"I said I'm nude. You know. Buck naked. Makes me a little uncomfortable. Where are my clothes?"

"Oh, yes, sorry. Wait, I'll get you something. But how?"

"Fred says they are done with my back. He says they are beginning work on the rest of me now."

"Who's Fred?"

"I think he is the head robot. He just spoke to me. I think he just figured out how. Funny guy. Told the others he had a major breakthrough. They cheered."

"This cannot be. It is impossible. They are simple machines."

"Well, it is. And they don't seem all that simple to me. The clothes, please."

"Sorry." Remiel recovered what looked like a blue lab coat hanging from a hook on the wall.

"I am sorry. This is all I have at the moment."

She pulled the coat on. Designed to be worn by Remiel, it fell to her ankles.

"Thank you."

"Why Fred?"

"He needed a name. I had a pet hamster when I was a girl. His name was Fred. He made me laugh. It seemed appropriate. And he seems to like it."

"This is remarkable."

"I'm not sure, but I think they were a little surprised themselves. I knew they were working on my back, I could feel it, tickled actually, and then I heard Fred. All work stopped for a moment and then, bam! All of them started talking. The only one I can understand though is Fred."

"But they are simple machines. Programed with a single purpose. I programmed them myself before injecting them. For them to become aware is impossible."

"Guess not. They still have one purpose, however. But it is a bigger one than the original. And one they have decided to pursue. They now wish to keep me healthy. Not just my back. All of me. I can feel them everywhere.

And they are happy. Apparently, they enjoy what they are doing. Wait...Fred says thank you."

"Thank me?"

"For providing them with a purpose. I can tell he means it. Like I said. They are very happy and I have never felt so good."

Gwen looked a little closer at Remiel and then down at herself. "You look the way you did when I first saw you. But I'm still me."

"Yes, I resumed my original form as soon as we arrived."

"Cool."

Gwen walked to a window. The view was spectacular. Grass covered hills leading to a distant forest, the ground bursting in a spectacular blend of colors from what she assumed were wildflowers. She smiled when she saw the two moons. One blue and the other covered in a reddish cloud encasing the orb like a massive dust storm.

Remiel walked over and stood beside her.

"It's beautiful."

He smiled. "My favorite place. I built my lab here away from the city. Away from the chaos. It's peaceful here. It allows me to think."

A bird, the size of a large eagle, gracefully soared by and settled in one of the trees. It was flaming red with bright blue feathers mixed into the wings and tail.

"It is called a Phoenix." He chuckled. "Born from an egg, not a flame."

"It's glorious." She turned. "I thought you were a doctor."

"I am the healer of our family but, along with Ariel, I am a scientist. Michael, Gabriel, and Lucifer are warriors."

"And Ezekiel?"

He chuckled. "I suppose you could say he is a philosopher. He is the conscience of the family. It was he that suggested Michael wait on your world for a Blocker. In case he needed our help."

"I'm glad he did." Gwen was silent for a moment. She turned back to the window to look at the wonders of this new world. Taking a deep breath she sighed. "I think we need to go back. Arthur needs us."

Remiel walked towards the door. "I am sorry about the clothes."

"That's okay. This will be a nice souvenir. You know, of my first visit to another planet. I can pick something up when we get back."

"I will prepare the window."

"To Olympus. I think they are there."

"How?"

"Fred told me."

"Gwendolyn."

"Yes."

"You understand that Fred will soon become dormant. He and the others have a limited power supply."

She smiled. "Oh, they've taken care of that. They are juicing up on me."

"Not yet, Gwendolyn. There are things you need to learn."

"Remiel, wait. Seems there will be a delay in our return."

CHAPTER TWENTY-THREE

Patricia moved from shadow to shadow doing her best to avoid the debris that littered the buckled and melted blacktop of the alleyway. Her query turned and she stepped into the damaged doorway of what at one time had been someone's home. She held her breath as the small man scanned the dark passage. Convincing himself that he was alone he approached the metal door of what appeared to be an old storage building, a small warehouse. Once again he turned and searched his surroundings. Patricia waited until she heard the sound of a rusty door being pulled open. Chancing a look she saw her target disappear into the building.

Moving slowly she crept forward until reaching the door. Trying the handle she smiled. It was not locked. Carefully opening the door she stepped through hoping the creek of the door would go unnoticed. Reaching into a pocket of her loose-fitting slacks she withdrew a short-barreled .38 revolver. Keeping it next to her leg she continued to move deeper into the room. It was large, dimly lit by several overhead florescent lights dangling precariously from the ceiling on rusty chains.

Huge unmarked wooden boxes stacked almost to the ceiling created a narrow corridor down the center of the room. Patricia advanced quickly ducking between boxes when she suspected her quarry was checking his surroundings. When the disciple reached the far wall he stopped and looked at his watch. He waited for a few moments then stepped back, falling to his knees.

A distant hum began to radiate from the concrete of the wall and the lights flickered. Trying to control the knot that suddenly grew in her throat, Patricia watched as an ebony doorway appeared. Cain stepped into the room. The doorway closed behind him.

"Where are they?" he demanded.

"We have been unable to find any of them, Lord. They have vanished. Possibly to one of the other worlds."

"And the building?"

"Several armed people presently secure the area. I believe they may be FBI. No one but the police and fire personnel have been permitted to approach. Half-a-dozen men entered the building an hour ago and have not returned. I assume they are attempting to secure the outsiders' room."

Cain backhanded the man and he fell to the floor. Wiping the blood from the corner of his mouth he slowly regained his knees keeping his head low.

"And Zeus?"

"No word. We know he was badly wounded."

Cain looked down the corridor and sniffed the air.

"You were not followed?"

"No, Lord. I made sure."

Cain sniffed again. Hearing him take a few steps in her direction, Patricia held her breath.

Cain stopped, then turned back to the man. "Find them. I don't care how many people it takes, I want them found."

"And when we do?"

"Kill them. I don't care what it costs, I want them dead. Do not fail me again."

"I understand, Lord."

Cain pulled a small object from his coat pocket and pointed it at the wall. A doorway appeared. He looked down the aisle again, sniffed, shook his head, turned, and stepped through the doorway. It closed and silence returned to the room.

The disciple got to his feet and spat at the wall. The bloody phlegm dripping down the concrete. "Bastard."

He stood staring at the wall, checked his watch then turned. Almost running he worked his way down the open floor towards the door. Patricia leaned back against the boxes as he passed and let out a sigh of relief when he reached the door. She waited to hear it close then gasped as she heard him lock it.

Reaching into her pocket she withdrew a small radio.

"Sheriff, this is Pat."

There was a momentary delay and then, "Go ahead."

"I followed the guy we spotted. He met with Cain."

"Where are you?"

She hesitated and then with a little nervous chuckle replied, "In a warehouse, I think. A storage building in the alley near what is left of the Federal Building. Where you told me you thought the bomb when off."

"You alone?"

"I am now."

"Okay, meet me back at my office. Did you see where Cain went?"

"Sort of."

"What does that mean?"

"Better I tell you when we are alone."

"Oh. Okay, I understand. Hurry back. We will need to brief your boyfriend."

"Uh, about that."

"What?"

"I seem to be locked in."

"Any windows?"

"Nope."

"Okay, I'll send someone."

"Thanks, boss. Have them be careful with the door. I think this guy is planning to return. And I'm pretty sure he is waiting for someone else. Kept checking his watch. If we keep this on the down-low, we might catch them both."

"We watch and report. We aren't equipped to handle Cain. Leave that to your boyfriend and the others. And, Pat ..."

"Yes?"

"Good job."

"Thanks."

She settled down to wait for her rescue when the humming returned. The door opened and Cain stepped through. With him were three figures. Not human. What Arthur had called The Friends?

"I think Joseph was followed. Someone is here. Find them. When you do, kill them."

Patricia worked her way between the boxes until she reached the wall. She heard the large beings as they pushed the heavy boxes around searching. Searching for her.

The room was brightly lit by a pair of halogen work lights mounted on tripods. Dust still permeated the air while men and women continued to move the debris to the outer walls. Dozens of large green trash bags stood like misshapen rocks near a metal ladder, waiting to be hauled to the surface. The hum of a distant generator mingled with the hushed tones of those working to clean up the portal room.

As Arthur stepped off the platform he and Kathleen were handed paper masks which they quickly attached behind their ears.

"Sorry, sir," A uniformed and masked worker said. "We are working to get fresh air piped down here but things are still pretty crazy up top."

"Thank you. And you are?"

"Nimix, sir."

"Thank you, Nimix."

Arthur moved away from the platform as it was engulfed in a swirl of multicolored lights. Thor and Sif stepped down and donned the masks they were handed.

Sif looked around. "I believe we should find somewhere else to wait for the others. This room will not hold many more."

Arthur looked at Nimix. "Did you receive my request?"

"We did, First Dragon. Several of the upper floors have been cleared and the engineers have declared them safe. I was told that a room off the lobby has been set aside for you and your people."

"Can we be seen from the street?"

"No. Your instructions were clear. No one knows of your arrival except for those of us here and the commander above. Steps have been taken to ensure you cannot be seen from the street."

"Who is in command?" Thor asked.

"Hilda Sorenson."

"Good officer," Sif said. "Valkyrie, tuff."

The portal activated again and Rex and Loki appeared.

"A little crowded in here," Loki said as he stepped off the platform.

"The only way out is up the ladder," Nimix said. "The elevator shaft will take some time to clear and get functioning again." He looked at Kathleen. "I am sorry, Your Ladyship, it is a long climb."

"How long?" Loki asked.

"Eight stories."

The portal activated and Lancelot and Millie stepped down.

Kathleen looked at the ladder. "I guess we better get going." She turned to Arthur. "You follow me."

Smiling he nodded. "As you wish."

Sif shook her head. "Men."

"Let's get going before we have to stand on each other's backs," Loki said.

"Be careful, Your Ladyship. The ladders are twelve feet long. We have spiked them into the wall and tied them together. It is a bit tricky where they connect."

"Thank you, Nimix." Kathleen hopped onto the first rung. Without turning around she called back as she started to climb, "Keep your eyes on the ladder, Arthur."

Chuckling he looked up. "I shall try."

Shaking her head Sif turned to Loki. "You will follow Thor"

"It would be best if the rest of you waited until they have reached the next ladder," Nimix said. "I'm not sure how much weight the spikes can take."

"Good idea," Rex said. "It would be most embarrassing if we were all to fall back down."

"And painful," Millie added.

The shaft was lit with a series of emergency lights connected to the surface by wires. Kathleen worked her way around the first of the ladder connections. She looked up and immediately regretted it.

"I think it looks further than it is," Arthur said.

"Do you honestly believe that?" Kathleen asked.

Arthur hesitated. "I'd like to."

She chuckled. Once she reached the top a strong arm was offered to help her over the lip of the shaft. Gaining her feet she began to brush herself off.

"Long climb?"

Kathleen looked up. The woman who had spoken was tall, almost as tall as Thor. Her long blond hair was braided and fell to the beltline of her worn jeans which sported the holster of a large caliber pistol.

"Hilda."

"It is good to see you, Kathleen. It has been a while."

"Too long. How are the kids?"

"Sven is seven now and a real handful. Katie is four and talks your leg off."

"I have not seen them in so long."

"You will have to come by the next time you are in town. By-the-way, congratulations on the engagement. Won't be long until you will be having a few young ones of your own."

Turning a little red Kathleen watched as Hilda helped Arthur up.

"Yes, well. Maybe not for a while."

Hilda laughed.

"What's so funny?" Arthur asked.

"Nothing," Kathleen said doing her best to hide the crimson glow to her cheeks.

Looking around Arthur asked, "Where do we go?"

"Follow the panels until you come to a door. They will prevent you from being seen from the street. The guard at the door will unlock it for you. Go down the hallway and you will see a second guard. He will let you into the conference room. Power has been reestablished and phone lines are available."

"Thank you, Hilda."

"It is an honor to serve, First Dragon." She winked at Kathleen.

Patricia squeezed between two boxes closest to the wall. She held the pistol out in front of her unsure if such a small bullet would do much damage to the massive beasts.

She listened, terrified, as they got closer. They were speaking in a language she did not understand as they searched. She heard Cain call out.

"Hurry. I need this room secure."

A shadow passed in front of the crawlspace she had taken shelter in. She held her breath.

CHAPTER TWENTY-FOUR

Arthur signaled the guard to close the door. The small twelve-by-twelve room was not designed to accommodate the fourteen people that jockeyed for position. Although there was a table and six chairs everyone decided to stand. No one spoke, each lost in their own thoughts as they contemplated the destruction that lay around them.

"How many?" Sif asked.

"We aren't sure," Merlin said. "All in the lobby and the lower offices perished. Many on the street outside were injured. Those nearest the alley were killed outright. Our people were lucky. Most of the damage was confined to the first three floors. The fire did not spread due to the overhead sprinklers."

"Aren't all of those lost our people?" Rex asked.

The room was silent for a moment. Kathleen placed her hand on his shoulder. "Of course they are. My father simply meant those working below were from our home dimensions."

"Rex is right. We must never forget that we are one people," Arthur said.

"And not all of us are human," Michael said.

"What the hell does that mean?" Loki asked.

Ezekiel smiled. "Not all of us have used that phrase to identify ourselves, Loki. We are as one not because of where we come from or our outward appearance. I mean look at the Friends. But we all share what is inside. What makes us who we are."

"What Satan and the others wish to destroy," Kathleen said.

"Not destroy," Merlin said. "Consume."

"Couldn't wait for me?" Anubis asked walking into the room.

"Or me?" Hercules asked stepping in behind him.

Arthur smiled and held out his hand. Anubis gripped his forearm.

"How's Bast?"

"She will recover, but the doctors are keeping her in the hospital for now. She is not pleased."

"I bet she isn't."

Arthur turned towards Hercules. "Should you be here? I would think the doctors would want to keep you as well."

Hercules took Arthur into his arms and squeezing him barked, "I escaped their clutches once more. Besides, doctors know nothing. Do I feel unfit?"

Whispering into his ear so the others would not hear Arthur said, "You have just lost someone dear to you, my friend. No one would think less of you if you needed some time."

Releasing the pressure Hercules whispered back, "I am fine, Arthur. It is better that I am busy. With friends."

"I am pleased to have you both back. I'm afraid we will all be needed in the fight to come."

"Which fight?" Loki asked. "Satan or Cain."

"Cain first."

"And his boss," Thor added.

Lancelot slammed his hand on the table. "Bael."

Hercules looked at Lancelot. "Those bastards will suffer before they die. I swear it."

The room was quiet and Arthur stared at his two friends. "They will pay. I promise you that."

Hercules looked at him. Tears threatening to flow. He nodded.

One of the two phones on the table began to ring. Arthur reached for the receiver. "Yes?"

"Where?"

"Is she all right?"

"Okay. Keep your people away. Watch the alley and let no one enter or leave. Be careful. These people are dangerous. We will get her out."

He hung up, hesitated for a moment then looked up. "Patricia is in trouble."

"Patricia?" Merlin asked.

"She followed one of Cain's people into a small warehouse. She is trapped inside."

"Why would she do that?" Merlin asked.

"She is a police officer, Merlin. It is her job. She knows the danger these people present. She asked the Sheriff to allow her to help. She was only supposed to watch the suspect. When he went into the warehouse she followed." Arthur hesitated.

"There is more?" Merlin asked.

"A portal opened and Cain met with the man. When the suspect left he locked the door before she could leave."

"She's okay?" Merlin asked.

"Yes."

"There is more?" Merlin asked.

"She thinks he may return. I told the Sheriff we would get her out."

"Where is she, Arthur?" Kathleen asked.

He smiled. "Just around the corner."

"Well then let's go," Merlin said anxiously.

"If someone is watching the building we will be seen," Falstaff said.

"I hope so," Arthur said with a grin. "I'm counting on it."

Patricia could hear those that were searching for her. They were getting closer. She knew there was no way they would miss seeing her once they reached the aisle she was in. Holding the small pistol in both hands she waited for what she knew was coming. The only thing she was sure of was that she would fight and would not be taken alive. There were five bullets in the gun. She would save one.

I'm sorry, Merlin.

She shuddered as the sound of shuffling feet suddenly stopped near her hiding place. The light faded as the aisle was blocked by the body of one of the enormous beasts. Turning its head to the side it seemed confused as it stared at her. Taking a step back it looked down the hall for a moment then returned its attention to her. She pulled the hammer back on the pistol. It shook its head and what she thought was a smile appeared on its elongated face. Raising a hand it placed a single finger to its lips, then turned and said something as it walked away. A moment later she heard Cain.

"All right. Whoever it was must have found a way out. I will leave one of you here. I will tolerate no more intruders. Do you understand?"

She heard what she assumed was an acknowledgment.

"The others will be here within the hour. I shall return then," Cain said.

Patricia remained pressed against the wall, unable to move. The room became still.

Cain must have left, she thought. She looked at her radio hoping to get a message to the Sheriff. It was dead.

Lowering the gun she started to edge her way to the main aisle. She had to get away and warn someone about Cain's plan to return and meet up with what she assumed were disciples. The sound of shuffling footsteps brought her up short. Her heart racing she stood and raised her weapon once again. She almost burst out laughing when a large brown hand appeared, the fingers spread in a peace sign.

"Tsgra meltras ... Okay?'

Patricia lowered the gun and stared as the seven-foot being with leathery brown skin and elongated head stepped forward and offered her its hand. She lowered the hammer and put the gun in her pocket then hesitantly took the offered appendage. Walking into the light of the main hall she realized with relief that they were the only two in the building.

In a gentle voice, it spoke to her. The language was strange but she could feel the kindness within the words. It led her to a small table at the end of the aisle and offered her a seat. Then it lifted a large pitcher and poured something into a plastic cup.

"Grriet," it said and mimed drinking.

Patricia took the glass and carefully raised it to her nose. She sniffed and then took a small sip of the cool liquid. It tasted like a fruity wine mixed with gin. Very strong gin. She swallowed, coughed, and offered the glass back. Taking the glass it nodded, took a drink, and smiled.

Arthur stopped and holding up a fist signaled the others to do the same. "It's down this alley."

"Any guards?" Thor asked.

"The Sheriff didn't know if there were any outside. He said that the last thing he heard from Patricia before her radio went dead was that there was someone else inside. That's all he knew."

"So we should be careful," Loki said.

"An excellent idea," Sif said a little sarcastically.

"Maybe we should try not to alert anyone of our presence," Kathleen said.

"And how would we do that, Princess?" Falstaff asked.

Kathleen smiled and looked at Sif and Millie. "Well, maybe a couple of working girls checking out the alley would not be considered suspicious."

"Working girls?" Thor asked.

Sif took his arm and smiled. "Sometimes, my love, you seem very unworldly. It is one of the things I love about you. What Kathleen is suggesting is that she, Millie, and I assume the mantle of floozies."

"Prostitutes!"

"An act only I assure you."

"Not a bad idea," Merlin said. "But we must hurry. Patricia may be in danger."

Thor smiled at his wife. "This could be an entertaining ruse. My mother will enjoy the telling of it."

Sif pulled at his shirt bringing his face close to hers. "I strongly suggest you reconsider that idea."

Thor smiled at her. "I already have."

"Okay. So the ladies stroll down the street to see if the coast is clear. And if it is not?" Rex asked.

Falstaff laughed. "Then the ladies will make it so."

"The world has changed much since my time."

"It has, my friend," Lancelot said. "In many ways for the better. In others not so much. But the acceptance of ladies as equals is one of the better changes."

"Not all would agree with you, Lancelot," Millie said.

"They will all wake up to what is right someday," Merlin said. "It is so on our worlds. Earth just lags behind a little. They are learning."

"I hope it is soon," Millie said. "However, many religious groups may never wake up."

"Their loss," Arthur said then turned and drawing Kathleen to him, kissed her. "We will wait here. When you are sure everything is secure signal me."

"And how will we do that?" Millie asked.

Arthur looked at Sif. "I'm sure you will find a way."

"What if there are too many guards for us to handle?" Millie asked.

Thor laughed. "I do not see that possibility. But if you think you need assistance, just scream. Like a woman in distress."

"Really," Sif said.

Thor shrugged his shoulders. "I say this only to give Millie comfort, my love. I know it will not happen."

Kathleen unfastened the top three buttons of her blouse. Sif watched and did the same.

"I can't do that," Millie said holding her arms out. "Pullover."

Lancelot stepped forward and whispered in her ear.

"I will not!"

He smiled and pointed around the corner. "I will assist. Trust me."

Taking her hand he led her into a doorway.

"Be careful. That's me under there."

They heard Lancelot chuckle. "I am aware. Now don't move."

A moment later the two returned. Millie's pullover now had no sleeves and the bottom of her garment had been removed just below her breasts exposing her midriff.

Sif looked at her for a moment and then nodded. "I believe that will do."

"I like it," Kathleen said as she pulled up her blouse and tied the tails of the shirt.

"Kathleen!" Merlin said.

"Father, I must look the part I play."

"I like it," Arthur said.

"Then perhaps I will need a new wardrobe. One with less material to please my husband to be."

"That would be nice."

Merlin turned to him in surprise. "Really!"

"It is a new world, Merlin," Rex said with a smile. "Is that not what you told me?"

"I think it is time we go," Sif said taking control of the situation.

Michael stepped forward. He offered Sif one of the weapons of his people. "This is small enough to hide," he hesitated. "Almost anywhere."

"Thank you." She pushed the tube into a back pocket of her jeans.

Gabriel and Ezekiel offered theirs to Millie and Kathleen. Millie shook her head but Kathleen accepted hers and intending to follow Sif's example realized she had no back pockets. Sif nodded and smiled.

"Oh." Kathleen pushed the tube between her breasts. "That should work."

Merlin shook his head.

"If you ladies have no objections, I would like to accompany you," Ariel said as she pulled her blouse up and began to tie it."

"Offer accepted," Kathleen said smiling.

Sif nodded her approval, turned, and started down the alley. Before Kathleen could join her Arthur took her hand.

"Be careful."

She nodded solemnly, turned, and followed Sif.

"They will be fine," Apollo said. "They are warriors, First Dragon."

Arthur leaned against the wall. "I know. But that doesn't make it any easier."

The main avenue was deserted except for the clean-up crews clearing the damage from the explosion. City police cars with their lights flashing blocked the road in both directions allowing only maintenance vehicles to enter. Arthur watched as a bulldozer lifted a pile of bricks from in front of what used to be a coffee shop and dropped them into the bed of a large dump truck.

"Can you imagine the amount of damage that could have occurred if the bomber had made it into the lobby?" Hercules said.

"And the loss of life," Loki agreed.

They all watched in silence as the work to reestablish order continued.

"The ladies seem to be taking a long time," Gabriel said. "Should we ensure all is well?"

"I'm sure they are fine," Falstaff said. "Kathleen and Sif know what they are doing and I pity anyone that tries to prevent them from completing their task."

Arthur chuckled. "That's for sure."

And then they heard a scream.

CHAPTER TWENTY-FIVE

With weapons drawn, Arthur and the men of The Oathsworn ran down the alley watching for danger. Arthur suddenly stopped dead in his tracks holding up a fist to signal the others to follow suit. "What the hell?"

The four women leaned casually against the large trash dumpster next to the door to the warehouse. Kathleen and Millie were smiling.

"I've never done that before," Ariel said. "It was invigorating."

"Done what?"

"Scream."

Looking around for some kind of threat he asked, "Why did you do that?"

"Why did I scream?"

"Yes."

"Sif told me to."

Arthur turned to Sif and waited for an explanation.

"Are you injured?" Thor asked.

"I am fine, thank you. There were no guards and the area seems deserted."

"Then why the scream. You scared the hell out of all of us. We thought you were in trouble," Loki said.

"You told me to signal you when it was okay to join us. Did you hear our signal?"

Arthur chuckled. "We certainly did."

"Then it was a good signal," Sif said with the hint of a smile.

"The door is locked, however," Kathleen said. "We may need to break it down. Falstaff ..."

"Yes, Princess."

"Would you mind?"

"Not at all."

"Wait," Loki said. "There is no need for such extreme measures. Besides, in case anyone inside did not hear Sif's signal, we may want to be a little quieter as we enter."

"True," Merlin said. "If Patricia has been captured, we do not want to panic those that hold her. Who knows what they will do."

"If you will step aside I shall take care of our little dilemma," Loki said. He reached into a pocket and pulled out a small leather case. Opening it he withdrew two small metal bars and knelled in front of the door. As he began to work on the lock Thor stepped behind him to watch.

"Where did you learn to do this?"

"Mother taught me."

"Mother?"

"Okay, big brother. Dad taught you a great deal about being a warrior. Where do you think I was during all that time? Mother decided I needed a few kills she felt you would not understand or have the ability to accomplish."

"Like breaking into locked rooms?"

Standing Loki smiled. "And war chests."

"You broke into my war chest?"

"It was just for practice. Mother told me to see if I could get away with it. I never took anything. By the way, your attempts at poetry are abhorrent."

"You read my private letters?"

"Not all of them," Loki said and quickly turned to Arthur. "The door is open. How do you want to handle this?"

"We will go in first." He nodded at the Havenites. "Your weapons will stop any disciples that may be present and Lancelot and I will take care of any Shadows. The rest of you wait outside and ensure we are not disturbed. Once it is clear we will signal you to join us."

Hercules chuckled. "You going to scream?"

Smiling Arthur shrugged his shoulders. "If I do, come quickly."

Sif wrapped her arm around Thor. "I like your poetry."

Arthur pushed the door open pointing his toothpaste tube down the center while Michael and Lancelot watched the side aisles.

"Arthur?"

Patricia stepped into the light. Another figure rose from the shadows. All three men pointed their weapons at what was standing behind her.

"Don't shoot. He's a friend."

The Friend held his arms out palms up showing he was not armed.

"Stand down," Arthur said as the others entered the room.

"***Chet ret Arthur***?" It asked.

"***I am***," he replied in the same language. "***And you are***?"

"***I am called Yeshem. I have heard of you and was hoping to find you.***"

"What is it saying, Arthur?" Michael asked.

"Arthur asked him his name. It is Yeshem," Lancelot said.

"You understand him?" Gabriel asked.

"I can understand but would not try to respond. The words are beyond the ability of my tongue."

"But Arthur?" Ariel asked.

Lancelot smiled. "He is First Dragon. I am not."

"***You are not under the control of Cain or his master?***" Arthur asked.

"Cain believes that I am. I have never seen the other you speak of. I have heard of him of course.

"Those of my cast cannot be used by the intruders. They enter and we destroy them. Those of Ot believe they are still inside us. We allow them to believe so."

"But I know they can possess your kind. The Shadows I mean. I have seen this."

"They were not of the Studiers. Those of the Worker and Warrior class can be infiltrated by the intruders. It is a difficult process and the intruders cannot stay long or they too will perish. The Devalies do not like using us for we are hard to take but when they have trouble controlling a new feeding ground they use us to crush any resistance."

"Devalies?"

"Those of OT."

Arthur turned to Michael. "Please ask the others to join us. Explain there is no threat here. Yeshem is a friend."

"I am sorry, Arthur First Dragon, I understand only a little of your language and find what I do know very difficult to pronounce. Is there something amiss?"

"Everything is fine. I just asked him to tell the others to join us."

Yeshem turned and pointed to the table. ***"Shall we sit? I have refreshment. There are urgent matters we must discuss."*** He turned to Patricia. ***"The little spy is very brave but also very foolish. If it was one of the others that discovered her she would be a shell for an intruder or dead. The others were not of the Studiers and were all occupied."***

Running down the aisle Merlin took Patricia into his arms.

Kathleen joined Arthur and smiled at her father. "It looks like there may be more than one wedding in the Emrys family to plan for."

"It looks that way." Arthur turned to Yeshem. "Kathleen, this is Yeshem. He is a friend."

"I can see he is a Friend."

"No, I mean he is a friendly Friend."

"Okay ..."

Turning to Yeshem Arthur placed his arm around Kathleen's shoulders. ***"Yeshem, this is Kathleen. She is to be my wife and also has the power of a Blocker."***

Nodding his head Yeshem offered what Kathleen assumed was a smile. ***"I understand the concept of your formal mating ritual. It is a pleasure to meet the future mate of Arthur First Dragon. I assume Blocker means one that destroys intruders."***

"Sort of."

Kathleen turned her head and nodded. "Please tell him the pleasure is mine. I understand what he says but find the words difficult to pronounce. You will have to speak for me."

"Kathleen understands your words but is unable to reply. She is pleased to meet you."

"I understand. It is good that you two and the tall Havenite understand me and that you are able to respond."

"You recognize that Lancelot is from Haven? You know about Haven? But how do you know he is from there. He looks like one of us."

"I know. Their world lies within our galaxy. The Devalies fear them and have kept themselves unnoticed for centuries. They learned from us of their existence. Haven lies far from our worlds. Long ago my people explored the far reaches of our known galaxy with remotely controlled craft.

We discovered Haven but we feared to make contact. As to how I know he is of Haven? Those of the Studiers can see the true form of a being. That is how we can tell when one is intruded upon. I can see that you are not as the others, First Dragon Arthur. I have not encountered one of your kind before."

"***What does that mean?***"

"***I do not know what you are. But you are not as the others.***"

Kathleen took his hand and looked hard into his eyes.

"I don't know what that means. Honest."

"We can discuss it with Michael and my father later. For now, I think I recall that Yeshem has something urgent to tell us." Kathleen gripped his arm tightly with both hands. "I think you need to ask him what is so important."

Arthur nodded. "***Yeshem, what is this urgent business?***"

"***Cain and many of my kinsmen will be returning shortly to meet with several of the people of this world.***"

"***How?***"

"***He will open a door from his world where my kinsmen wait. The others will come from beyond this room. The ones that follow him from this world.***"

Arthur turned. "Loki, you, Thor, Rex, and Falstaff make sure no one from outside gets into this room. Do whatever is necessary but they cannot be allowed in. The rest of you take shelter. Cain will be returning shortly using a doorway. He is bringing a small army of Friends with him. Shoot Cain but allow the Blockers to take on the Friends. We will try to destroy the Shadow within them. They can survive possession. We will do what we can to free them.

"Patricia, please contact the Sheriff and tell him to notify the FBI that the terrorists that blew up the Federal Building are coming back and plan to meet in this building. See if they can stop them."

"My radio is dead."

Merlin offered her one of the small communicators. "Use this. I will get you one of your own."

"We must be ready to defend ourselves. I think the weapons you have," Arthur pointed to the Havenites, "would be most effective keeping any disciples that show up in check, in case the FBI doesn't get here on time. You will have to take up positions in the alley. Millie will stay with you in case there are Shadows.

"Kathleen, Lancelot, and I will do what we can to free the Friends of Shadow. I'd rather not kill any potential allies."

"Cain is mine," Hercules said.

"And mine, brother," Apollo said slapping the big man on the shoulder. "He has much to account for."

Arthur nodded. He reached into his pocket and withdrew his Havenite weapon. "You may need this. We will be busy with the others but I will be nearby in case you need my help. He is not like other men."

"Thank you, Arthur," Hercules said.

"Our weapons can stun," Ezekiel reminded him.

"Damn! I forgot. Okay, two of you stay here. Try to stun the Friends that come through the door just in case a direct attack by a Blocker isn't enough to free them of Shadow."

Ariel and I will stay," Michael said. "Gabriel and Ezekiel will go to the Alley."

"Good."

"Okay," Loki said. "So the Havenites are going to kill people..."

"Or stun them."

"Right, or stun them. So, the plan is for you and the other two Blockers to destroy Shadows while Hercules and Apollo take on Cain. That leaves four of us to watch the door. So what do you want us to do if no one tries to come in, oh great leader?"

"There is a good chance Cain will bring more than the Friends with him. If so, stop them."

Falstaff laughed. "Sounds like fun. I was afraid you had forgotten we are warriors."

"Could never do that. You guys are family."

"Just remember that little brother," Loki said.

"Okay, find a place you can cover that wall and not be seen. Yeshem says that is where the door will open."

"And me?" Merlin asked.

"I want you to take Patricia outside and make sure the FBI doesn't shoot us when we come out. Be careful, Merlin. There is something else I'm going to need you to help me figure out later."

"What is that?"

"Something Yeshem said. But later, okay?"

"As you wish."

Patricia walked over and took Merlin's hand. "Every agent in the area is on their way. The Sheriff said they wanted you to know how much they appreciated the opportunity. They lost people in the explosion."

"Thanks. Now, you and Merlin have a job to do so you best be going. Ezekiel and Gabriel will back you up if need be."

Merlin, holding Patricia's hand, walked away without saying a word.

Kathleen stepped onto her toes and kissed Arthur on the cheek.

"What was that for?"

"I know why you sent my father away. He is not equipped to be a part of this. His power rods would be useless against what we are about to face."

"Well, I need him safe. He has a lot of work to do when we are done here. He has to walk you down the aisle."

Smiling she rubbed her fingers down his cheek. "Of course."

Yeshem placed his large hand gently on Arthur's shoulder. ***"Cain said he would be back within the hour. It is getting close to that time."***

"Thank you, Yeshem. What will you do?"

He gave that strange smile again. ***"I will do what I always do. Pretend. If you free my brethren from the intruders I will do what I can to help them quickly adjust. We do not want them to think you are an enemy. That would not be good."***

Arthur chuckled. ***"No, I don't think it would."***

Yeshem poured himself a drink. Arthur turned to Kathleen, Millie, and Lancelot. "If the stun setting works I don't know how long the Friends will stay still. As soon as they fall hit them. The Shadow may or may not emerge. And remember that once the Shadow is destroyed the Friend will be disoriented. Yeshem intends to help them understand we are on their side. But be careful. If you are threatened, shoot to kill. These guys die hard."

"I remember," Lancelot said.

Arthur's communicator beeped. "Yes? Already. That's great. Be careful." He listened for a moment. "I'll tell her." He reached behind his back and withdrew his automatic. "The FBI has arrived. They were close by using a building down the street as a temporary command center." He turned to Kathleen. "Your father says to wish you a safe outcome to this affair."

"He is always so considerate." She shook her head. "I know he is worried. Sometimes I wish he would just say what he means instead of covering it with formality."

"You know he loves you," Arthur said.

"I know."

A gunshot rang out from the alley.

"Arthur!" Loki yelled.

They all looked at the door as the sound of a crash and an explosion was quickly followed by more gunfire.

"He comes, First Dragon."

"Take your positions."

CHAPTER TWENTY-SIX

"Name's Agent Sam Johnson. I take it you are Mr. Emrys, and you miss must be the deputy that sent the message. My boss told me to look for you. That was a gutsy thing you did." He smiled. "Maybe not smart, but gutsy. You armed?"

"I have a .38."

He reached under his coat and withdrew a compact submachine gun called an MP5. Unclipping it from the strap over his shoulder he handed it to Patricia. "Take this. I'll get something else." He turned to Merlin. "What about you, Mr. Emrys?"

He pulled out a Browning 9mm."

Johnson smiled. "Okay, let's get to the end of the alley before the fun begins. We have more agents coming."

"Wait." Merlin pulled his communicator from his pocket. "I need to let those inside the warehouse know you are here.

"Arthur, the FBI has arrived. We will coordinate with them. I wish you a satisfactory and safe outcome to this affair.

"Thank you, we will." He closed the device and returned it to his pocket.

"Fancy little radio you have there."

"You should see some of his other toys," Patricia said.

Several well-armed FBI agents, recognizable by their blue jackets with white lettering, stood around talking near a pile of debris that had been pushed to the curb. A variety of weapons were evident, scoped rifles, shotguns, and a few had the small submachine guns like the one given to Patricia. One man even had an old Thompson submachine gun slung over his shoulder. He was talking on a radio, saw them, and signaled they should join him.

"My boss. John Fredrik."

A shot rang out and Fredrik stumbled back grabbing his chest. He looked at the blood leaking through his fingers then crumbled to the pavement.

"No!"

Patricia grabbed Johnson's arm as he tried to run to his boss. "Get down!"

A garbage truck turned the corner less than a block away. It slammed into the cruiser blocking the road causing it to twist on its front bumper as it flew into a nearby building, crushing the officer standing behind it. The car exploded knocking many of the FBI agents to the ground. Behind the garbage truck, armed men came running down the street shooting in all directions, taking down several of the agents trying to regain their feet. Those that could sought shelter and returned fire.

Agent Johnson stepped into the street and took careful aim at the truck. He fired two shots from his service pistol. The windshield shattered and the truck came to a rolling stop. As he turned to rejoin Merlin and Patricia he was struck twice throwing him onto the wall where he slid slowly to the sidewalk. Patricia rushed to him as Merlin returned fire. She grabbed Johnson by the lapels of his jacket and pulled him into the relative safety of the alley.

"That hurt," he said with a smile looking up at her. "My wife is going to be pissed. She just bought me this jacket."

Patricia removed his tie and wrapped it around the wound to his arm. Tearing open his shirt she undid his bulletproof vest. Blood oozed from a wound to his stomach. She turned him to the side and checked his back.

"The bullet is still inside. Your vest slowed it down. I will do what I can to stop the bleeding but we need to get you to a hospital."

"They're using cop killers," he grimaced. "Military-grade ammunition. Vest won't stop them." Listening to the increased volume of gunfire he shook his head. "I'm not going anywhere anytime soon. Please prop me up against the wall and give me my piece. Then you two get out of here."

Merlin handed him his weapon. "I'm afraid this will have to do for now. There is no way we can reach yours."

"Thank you."

"You are most welcome. I think we should try to get back to the warehouse. All of us."

Patricia tore the sleeve from her blouse, folded it, and placed it on the abdominal wound.

"Keep pressure on it."

He nodded, smiled, and the pistol fell from his fingers. His head dropped to his chest.

Patricia checked his pulse. "He's still alive."

Merlin picked up the fallen weapon. "We need to move. I'll help you drag him."

A shot rang out from the end of the alley and Merlin fell. Pamela picked up her weapon and fired several rounds into the shooter.

"Merlin, are you all right?"

There was no answer.

No sooner had Arthur taken shelter with Kathleen behind a stack of crates then Yeshem rose. He stepped back watching the wall. A dark doorway appeared. Assuming Cain would be the first to enter Hercules stepped into the aisle. First one, and then several more of the Friends stepped through. Seeing Hercules the first to cross quickly brought up a weapon reminiscent of an antique shotgun. There was a loud crack and Hercules flew back against the boxes settling motionless on the warehouse floor.

With six of the Friends in the room, Cain stepped though. He yelled something as several more of the large beings appeared. They lifted their weapons searching for enemies.

"What the hell is going on, Yeshem?" Cain demanded. Pointing at Hercules he shouted, "Someone get that asshole and bring him to me."

As two of the Friends walked towards Hercules Yeshem approached Cain.

"Now!" Arthur yelled.

Two blasts from the Havenites weapons struck the Friends trying to pick Hercules up. They stumbled but did not fall.

"Again!" Michael yelled.

Once again the beams from the small tubes struck the Friends. This time they fell. As they struck the floor Shadows erupted from their open mouths. One was struck by a blast from Kathleen while the other went for Apollo who was trying to help Hercules. Rex threw himself between them and the

Shadow seemed to bounce off the prior king. Lancelot lifted his arms and the Shadow was struck by two blasts of intense light and exploded.

Apollo pushed Rex aside and fired two rounds at Cain while the others were busy incapacitating the Friends and destroying the Shadows attempting to escape their fallen hosts.

"I thought you were watching the door," Apollo said firing again.

"Nothing happening there and I thought you might need some help."

"Thanks, Rex." He again leveled his weapon at Cain and fired. "Die you bastard!"

Cain stepped backward as several holes appeared on the front of his jacket. He looked at them seeming to be surprised that he had been attacked. Apollo fired twice striking Cain in the head and his ear. Cain turned and tried to step into the doorway. Yeshem grabbed his arm and attempted to pull him away. A solid purple rope jetted from the head wound and struck Yeshem causing him to fall backward tripping over one of the chairs. Arthur watched in horror as the snaky mass ebbed back into Cain. He looked at Arthur in contempt then stepped through the doorway. It closed.

Arthur wanted to go check on Yeshem but the fight was not over. Taking aim he fired the tube Michael had given him striking one of the large warriors. A second blast and it fell. As the Shadow attempted to desert the fallen Friend, Arthur opened his mouth and the room glowed. The Shadow burst, ending the threat.

Kathleen looked at him. "Four other Shadows died when you did that. How?"

"Is that all of them," he asked not wishing to explain what he was beginning to suspect about himself.

"They're all down, First Dragon," Rex said. "What happens when the big fellas wake up?"

"A good question. Kathleen, would you please check on Yeshem. We are going to need him."

Kathleen approached the 'man' and kneeled beside him.

"He's alive," Kathleen said.

"Good, see if you can revive him." He turned and listened to the intensity of the gunfire outside. "This is not over yet."

"I need some help!" Patricia called dragging Merlin behind a large steel dumpster. His face was covered in blood. She lay her fingers on his neck and gave a small smile. "You still live."

"I do, but I fear I will have a massive headache for the near future."

"On my way," Gabriel said.

Patricia wiped some of the blood from Merlin's face revealing a long gash above his eyebrow running to his ear. It was bleeding profusely. "Damn face wounds bleed like crazy. I need something to stop it so I can see."

Tearing her other sleeve from her blouse she wrapped it around his head.

"You keep this up and you will soon be out of blouse," Merlin said with a chuckle.

"And wouldn't you like that."

"I believe I would."

Several bullets struck the dumpster. Patricia handed Merlin her .38. She dropped the magazine from the MP5. "About ten rounds left." She reinserted the magazine.

More bullets struck the metal box. She peeked around the corner which resulted in several rounds striking the dumpster and the wall above it. She fired two rounds and stepped back.

"Bastards can't shoot worth a damn."

Merlin chuckled and touched his head. "Some of them seem to be lucky, then."

"A lot of them still in the street. I think they are all trying to get down to the alley. I saw several bodies. Can't tell you which side they were on."

"Can we make it back to the warehouse?" Merlin asked.

"We can try. Can you walk?"

"I think so. What about Johnson?"

"He's safe for now."

Merlin pushed himself up the wall and tried to maintain his balance. "A bit dizzy. I am not sure I can walk." He fell to his knees and vomited.

Gabriel stumbled into the dumpster bumping into Patricia. He looked at Merlin. "Is he okay?"

"Not sure. We need to get him out of here."

"Ezekiel and Millie will cover us. Let me help."

Patricia looked around the dumpster, fired twice more then helped Gabriel pull Merlin to his feet. “Put your arm around me.”

“No. You go. Give me the gun. I will keep them busy while you run. Send help once you reach the others.”

“Bullshit.” She placed his arm over her shoulder while Gabriel did the same with the other. “We go together. I’m not about to lose you now. Just try not to puke on what’s left of my blouse.”

Yeshem slowly rose to his feet. Kathleen tried to help him but it was like a child trying to aid a gorilla.

“Are they dead?”

“No. Just stunned. The Shadows, I mean the intruders, are gone,” Arthur said.

“I shall endeavor to ensure there is no misunderstanding when they awaken.”

“I would appreciate that.”

“Arthur, there is one hell of a lot of gunfire out there,” Loki called.

“I would venture to say there were a few more of the bastards than expected,” Falstaff said and stopped as someone banged on the door.

“Open up. It’s me, Patricia.”

“Open the door,” Arthur said. “Be ready for anything.”

Thor pulled the door open and Patricia stumbled in releasing Merlin who immediately fell to the floor. Gabriel, Ezekiel, and Millie followed.

“Father!” Kathleen ran to the prone figure.

“Close the door!” Arthur yelled.

“What happened?” Kathleen asked cradling her father’s head in her lap.

“There were too many. No one was expecting this kind of attack,” Patricia said. “There is a wounded agent near the end of the alley. I couldn’t bring him.”

“We provided covering fire for them to bring Merlin but were unaware of the fallen agent. We would have tried to reach him. There are a lot of people out there, First Dragon.” Ezekiel said. “They will reach us soon.”

“Okay. Millie, see what you can do for Hercules. Apollo, go with her. Loki, Thor, we will see if we can reach the agent and bring him here.”

“We will go with you,” Michael said.

"Sounds good. Sif, organize the others, and build something we can use to fight behind in case they aren't stopped outside. I'm sure they probably believe that Cain is in here waiting for them. Lock the door when we leave. Don't open it unless one of us calls out."

"I understand, First Dragon."

Arthur looked at Kathleen. "How is he?"

"I think he may have a fracture to his skull. I can't tell for sure but something moved when I touched it. He is breathing okay but we need to get him real medical help soon."

"Move him away from the door. Watch over him you two. I'm afraid things are going to get a little hairy." He looked at Sif. "Now."

Sif pulled the door open and they rushed out. As soon as they hit the alley bullets started to fly all around them. They rushed towards the metal dumpster firing their weapons as they moved.

"Well, this is cozy," Loki said squeezing beside Arthur.

"Anyone see the agent?" Arthur asked.

"There is a man in a suit lying on the ground about ten yards up on the right," Thor said catching his breath. "Wasn't enough time to see if he was breathing. Hell a lot of shooting going on in the street."

"Think we can reach him?" Arthur asked.

"I'll try," Thor said. "The rest of you cover me. If he is still alive I will bring him back."

The shooting stopped.

"What the hell?" Loki asked.

"Don't know, but I can't think of a better time to go." Thor darted around the dumpster and ran to the downed agent. He slid to a stop and while watching the entrance to the alley placed his hand on Johnson's neck. "He lives."

Gently picking the man up and carrying him as if he were a child Thor hurried back to the others.

Arthur nodded. "Take him to the warehouse. We will watch your back. Tell the others to expect company."

Five men, and then five more, and another five stepped into the alley from the street. They stood silent and watched Thor as he worked his way to the warehouse. Shooting resumed with less intensity in the street. Walking slowly backward Arthur remained focused on the crowd that continued to grow at the entrance to the alley and wondered why they did not shoot. When he reached the door he called out. "It's us. Open up."

As they stepped across the threshold he pushed the door shut. "We need to block this door. Several dozen disciples will be here in a moment. I think they realize something is wrong."

"Arthur!" Millie screamed. He's coming back."

Who?"

Arthur spun around and raised his weapon as a dark circle appeared on the surface of the wall. It grew quickly into a pitch-black doorway.

"Shit! Everyone get ready."

Kathleen, Lancelot, and Millie stepped beside him, their arms spread wide. Michael and his kin aimed their tubes at the expanding door.

A tall figure dressed in a long purple robe appeared, turned, and reached back offering its hand to another. The second figure stepped through wearing jeans and a hooded pink sweatshirt with "where's the beef" printed in bold lettering. Arthur had trouble catching his breath as he recognized the second figure."

"Need some help?"

"Gwen!"

CHAPTER TWENTY-SEVEN

"You can walk. You're okay."

"Gee, big brother, I can talk and use the bathroom all by myself too."

He wrapped his arms around her and squeezed. "How?"

Seeing Loki behind him she gently pushed him away. "I'll tell you all about it, but later, please. When we are alone."

Turning and seeing Loki he smiled and stepped aside. "Okay. Later."

Loki took her hands. Gwen jumped up and wrapped her arms around his neck, her feet dangling free.

"You're okay," he said, his voice breaking.

She kissed him then slipped back to the floor. Reaching up and brushing the tears from his eyes she smiled. "I will never leave you."

"Open this door! Now!"

Loki turned. "Don't!"

Falstaff pushed a heavy crate in front of the door. "Nope. Don't think I will."

A bullet burst from the metal door barely missing his face.

"Now that is not polite." He raised his pistol, pushed his hands apart as wide as a man, looked down at his chest, lowered the gun near his waist, and fired two quick shots. They were answered by a yell. He turned to Thor. "He was rude and needed to put in his place."

"It is a good thing that the door opens in and not out," Thor said.

Falstaff looked at the door. "Never thought of that."

Sif lifted a heavy box on top of the crate Falstaff had placed. "That bullet was close to taking that ugly head of yours off your shoulders. I would suggest you not stand in front of the door. Next time they may get lucky."

Falstaff looked at the hole in the door. "Good advice."

Michael walked up to Remiel and embraced him. "You have performed a medical miracle, brother. How did you heal her so fast? I did not believe she would ever walk again."

"To be honest, I wasn't sure she would either. The damage to her spine was catastrophic. I injected her with the medical nanites and introduced the biofiber hoping they could do something. They did and then the damn things woke up."

"Woke up?"

"I can't explain it. They worked on all of her body not just her spine, and one of them spoke to her."

"Spoke to her! That's impossible."

"I thought so too. But you can see for yourself. They did this, not I. The one in charge she calls Fred."

"Fred?"

"She named it after a small rodent she had as a pet when a child."

Remiel dropped the bag he was holding and fell to his knees. He looked up and smiled. His form now as the others, human. "Should have worn something else. Robes a bit baggy."

Ezekiel pointed to the bag. "Bring us lunch?"

Remiel stood and opened it revealing a dozen of the small Havenite weapons.

"You brought flashers?"

"For The Oathsworn. Thought they might find a use for them." He looked at the Friends sitting in a circle as a tall one spoke to them.

Michael chuckled. "These Friends are our friends. I mean as in on our side. The one talking is called Yeshem. He is explaining that we are allies. The true danger lies outside that door."

A series of shots rang out and the lock on the door disintegrated. Remiel looked at the hole where the lock used to be "Obviously."

Arthur walked to the wall and placed his hands on the concrete. They began to glow.

"What is he doing?" Loki asked.

Gwen smiled. "He is closing the door. No one from Satan's realm can use this building as a gateway. Like Mentor." She turned to Loki. "Did they?"

"Oh yes. Cain was using this place to bring his forces together. His disciples. He was the one that brought the Friends through."

"And the Blockers removed the Shadows within them."

He looked at her a little surprised. "How did you ... "

"Don't know. Just do. Beginning to understand a lot of things."

"You doing this Fred?"

"No, my friend, Gwendolyn. We can support your body, not your mind.

"The lady?"

"She was here for a moment before you stepped through the window. She smiled at us but did not speak."

"Thank you, Fred. And please call me Gwen."

"You are as always, welcome. Gwen."

"Arthur, This door is not going to last long," Sif called.

Michael pointed to the bag. "These might help."

Arthur looked in and smiled. He slapped Remiel on the shoulder. "Perfect. Thank you.

"Everyone grab a tube."

"We call them flashers," Remiel said.

"Good name. Everyone get a flasher. Have one of the Havenites show you how they work. I want them on stun. Remember, red end toward the target."

"And my people?" Yeshem asked.

Arthur turned to him. He looked around the building then at the weapons the Friends brought with them.

"How many times will those shoot before they need to be reloaded?"

"Many. Each weapon holds several small projectiles. The propulsion is produced by a device in the stock."

"Okay. We are going to use the weapons Michael's people have provided. Like the ones used on your people. They will not kill. We may not be able to stop all of them. They will be dangerous. If that happens, have your people stop them."

"They will die."

"I know. Can't be helped."

Yeshem spoke to the others and they retreated to the rear of the building where they began to make a barricade of crates and boxes.

"Trust 'em?" Loki asked.

"I do."

Gwen squeezed his hand. "So do I."

"Good enough for me.

A series of shotgun blasts threw the hinges of the metal door into the room. It remained upright for a moment, then, accompanied by a deep groan, slowly slid forward about ten inches coming to rest against the stacked crates.

"Bet they didn't expect that to happen," Kathleen whispered.

Arthur chuckled. "Probably not.

"Listen up, when they come in, stay where you are. If you can stun any from your position, do so. Do not expose yourselves. These guys aren't pros but the guns they carry are deadly even in the hands of an amateur."

"Push the door out of the way you idiots," someone yelled from the other side of the doorway.

"Looks like there may be at least one with a little brainpower," Loki said.

"Kathleen," Arthur called. "Are Merlin, and the agent safe?"

"Patricia and I have them behind several big crates. They are packed with some kind of metal. Automobile parts I think. We should be fine."

Bullets began to ricochet from the walls and ceiling.

"They come, First Dragon," Rex called out.

Three big men pushed the door to the side and began to push the crates. Several others fired wildly into the warehouse.

A loud crack sounded from within the building and one of the men trying to move the barrier no longer sported a head. What remained of it flew into the faces of those standing behind. They disappeared and all activity stopped. Arthur turned towards the Friends.

"I apologize, First Dragon. Tzrot is young and untried as a warrior but I believe he is capable of learning. It will not happen again."

Tzrot looked a little dizzy from the blow he had received from Yeshem.

It became very quiet.

"What now?" Gwen asked working her way over to Arthur.

"I'm sure they will try something else. Maybe they think we are holding their gods. I don't know.

"I can't believe they killed all the law enforcement that was outside. I wonder what is going on."

"I would assume they have pulled back waiting for reinforcements. Maybe a SWAT team," Patricia said.

"Swat?" Rex asked.

"Professional warriors within the police force," she explained. "The Cleveland SWAT team has an armored vehicle."

"Makes sense. So why don't these idiots leave? They have to know they can't win. And where did they all come from?" Sif asked.

"I think the more important question is what they were planning to do with all this firepower. What's Cain up to?" Arthur asked. "It is obvious that they no longer wish to remain in the shadows."

"Shadows. Funny, Art," Gwen said.

"You in there." A voice called out. "Come out unarmed and we will not harm you. We just want the building. I will give you five minutes. If you do not come out then you will all die. I saw women in there. Do you want them to die?"

"You fool," Sif called out angrily. "The women in here are warriors not a bunch of witless fools playing at war. It is you that should be afraid, you insignificant worm."

"He should never have mentioned her gender. My wife is sensitive about not being considered an equal by the people of this world," Thor said. "Big mistake. I almost feel sorry for him."

"You tell him, Sif," Millie said. "Why don't you come in here and face one of us women. Alone. Afraid? You should be, asshole."

Silence again.

"I think you scared him, Sif," Loki said chuckling. "You sure scared me."

"Do you think they will try again?" Kathleen asked. "Maybe they have decided to leave. Even a dedicated disciple has to see when something is hopeless."

"I don't know," Arthur said. "These people don't think rationally. I am beginning to think Cain has done something to them."

"Arthur"

"Yes, Patricia?"

"We need to get these two to a hospital." "Agent Johnson has lost a lot of blood. Merlin has had two spasms and remains unconscious. I'm not sure how much time they have."

"Arthur leaned back against one of the large crates lining the center aisle and took a deep breath. "We can't wait for the police. We need to break out of here." He looked at Arial. "Is there any way you can open one of your doors and let us get them to safety?"

She shook his head. "I am sorry, First Dragon. It is not possible. Whatever you did to the wall has interfered with any doorway opening."

"Shit. Okay here is what ... "

Two metallic objects bounced into the room as Kathleen ran towards Arthur. "Get down!"

An explosion, quickly followed by a second, filled the warehouse as the two hand grenades detonated.

Arthur climbed to his feet. Kathleen lay beside him, blood oozing from her ears. He checked her pulse. She was alive.

"Anyone hurt?" he called out. For a moment there was no answer.

Gwen stepped from behind a crate. "Arthur! You're bleeding!"

He looked down. His shirt was in tatters and his trousers were torn. Blood flowed from numerous wounds on his torso and left leg.

"I'm Fine, check the others."

"Where are you going?"

"To end this." He began to stride down the aisle pushing debris aside when it threatened to infringe upon his progress, a ghostly aura radiating from his body. He tried to ignore the moaning of his friends as he focused on the door. A man appeared and aimed a pistol at him.

"Arthur!" Gwen screamed.

The gun went off. Arthur spun to the side, the bullet striking his shoulder.

A gunshot and the man fell. Arthur looked at the smoking gun in Rex's hand. He nodded his thanks then continued toward the opening.

"Arthur, don't. They'll kill you," Gwen screamed doing her best to catch him.

Arthur reached the barricades and pushed the crates aside as if they were empty cardboard boxes. He backhanded the man that to block his way and he flew as if struck by a car. Arthur stepped into the alley.

CHAPTER TWENTY-EIGHT

Police sirens wailed, rifles barked and people screamed. Arthur heard none of it. All he could hear was the reverberation of the explosion and the cries of his wounded friends not knowing if any had died.

Satan, Cain, Bael; evil, Gwen called them. But it was people that were the true evil. People that killed for pleasure, for profit. The worst being the fanatics that tortured and killed in the name of their twisted religion.

He stepped forward, heedless of the men shooting at him. Someone grabbed his arm. He turned and looked down at the intruder. Gwen.

"Arthur, please. Come inside. You're going to get yourself killed. You can't do this. Think. They need you. I need you. This stupid world needs you."

A bullet ripped through his shirtsleeve and the fleshy part of his bicep. Another came at Gwen's face. She moved her head a fraction of an inch. The bullet passed by. Another and she twisted her body while the projectile whizzed by her breast.

"How?" Arthur asked.

"I don't know. It's like I can see them coming. Please come back inside. We can talk about it later. You're hurt."

"I'm fine. Get behind me, Gwen."

"But, Art."

"I'm not out of control. I know exactly what I'm doing. This has to stop. I can stop it."

From his outstretched arms, a mist began to materialize. More than a dozen men entered the alley and began to shoot. The white fog thickened and the bullets seemed to slow and lose their direction as they entered it. Dozens of lead projectiles fell at his feet, spent. The fog continued to grow, spread, and thicken until he and Gwen were completely obscured. Arthur lowered his arms and the dense cloud suddenly rushed forward as if being pushed by a gigantic fan. The shooting stopped. The alley became still. The fog began to ebb.

Gwen stepped from behind him and looked towards the street. As the mist cleared she could see people on the ground. Thirteen bodies lay upon the asphalt of the alley floor. Unmoving, with no apparent wounds. Many more in the street.

She took Arthur's hand. "Are they dead."

"No."

"Are you all right?"

"Yes, I'm fine. We need to check on the others. Our people."

"Your wounds."

"What?"

"They're gone."

Arthur looked down. "So they are."

"How?"

"To be honest with you, Gwen, I don't know. Something has changed. I have changed."

"You could have been killed."

He shook his head, turned, and headed back towards the warehouse. "I am not sure I could have."

"This is getting weird."

He stopped, looked at her, and smiled. "Tell me about it. I have no idea what is happening to me."

"Did he tell you to do this?"

"No. I have not heard from him in quite a while. I just knew it had to be done and that I could do it. I didn't know I wouldn't be killed. To be honest, I didn't think about it."

She stepped in front of him and took his hands, not allowing him to continue. "Well, you should have! Art, you can't do this anymore. You are not invincible. You act like this fight is yours alone. It's not. We have been brought together for a reason. Do not push us away. We are more than just your oath-sworn. We are The Oathsworn. We are as one. Sworn to each other as a brotherhood." She smiled. "And a sisterhood. Each of us bringing something special to the fight. We believe you are our best hope to defeat this abdominal enemy but not alone. You need us. And we need you."

Arthur took a deep breath. "I know. I'm sorry. But this had to be done before anyone else was hurt and I knew I was the only one that could do it. Because I do know what The Oathsworn is. That all of us are going to be needed. I know that it is the only thing that has a chance to stop the evil that is coming." He smiled. "Not me. Us."

He looked down the alleyway. "I have done all I can here."

Sirens began to fill the air. "It is up to the locals now."

They walked through the damaged doorway, stepping around a couple of bodies and over a lot of debris. Yeshem was waiting for him. His people helping the others.

"They all live, First Dragon."

"Thank you, Yeshem."

Kathleen rushed forward and threw her arms around him.

"Are you okay?" He asked.

"I'm fine. I think one of my eardrums may be ruptured. A few cuts and brushes. Nothing to prevent you from holding me.

"Are you hurt? Your shirt?"

"I'm fine. Not a scratch."

"But ..."

Gwen took her hand. "Art has a few things to explain. But now is not the time. He is not hurt. I promise you."

Kathleen hesitated then nodded.

"How bad?" Arthur asked.

"Sif and Thor were close to the explosions. They received several deep wounds and are burnt over much of their upper body. They are alive but in a great deal of pain. Anubis and Rex are fine outside of a few cuts that may need stitches. None of the Havenites or Friends were hurt. I have no idea how. Patricia, my father, and the FBI agent were protected by the crates."

"Someone needs ..."

"Remiel is checking on them."

"And Apollo?"

She was quiet for a moment. "I don't know?"

"What do you mean?"

"We haven't found him."

Arthur looked around the room. "I don't understand."

"We have looked everywhere. We cannot find him. He's not in the warehouse."

"Excuse me?"

"Everyone okay in here?" A man in a blue FBI vest asked pushing himself past the overturned crates near the door. He froze when he saw the Friends.

Arthur walked towards him while Gwen and Kathleen stepped around the intruder and blocked the doorway. Small white tubes in their hands. Gwen looked outside and shook her head.

"He's alone."

"I saw what you did out there. At least I think I did. I'm not sure what I saw actually. But thank you. You saved a lot of my people."

He looked at the Friends tending the injured. "Or what I'm seeing right now for that matter."

"You are?" Arthur asked.

"Sorry. Bill Spinelli. I'm the Agent-In-Charge of the Cleveland office. Are you the one they call First Dragon?"

"He is," Loki said joining them while holding a bloody cloth to his forehead. "And we are his oath-sworn." He smiled. "And the beautiful blond is his fiancée so hands-off. Her father is a powerful wizard."

Spinelli gazed at Kathleen and smiled. "Lucky man. Oath-sworn?"

"My team."

Spinelli looked at Yeshem who had stepped up beside Arthur. Nodding his head toward Yeshem the agent asked, "Him too?"

"Be this a friend, First Dragon?"

"I believe so."

"He's a friend from out of town," Loki explained with a crooked grin.

Spinelli smiled. "So I see. I am assuming from way out of town."

"I would say that is accurate, agent," Arthur said returning the smile surprised at the man's reaction.

"I was told to look for you," Spinelli said. "My bosses in Washington said you might be around and that I was to ensure you received any help requested. With no questions asked. I can see why. I was told you were the lead on this terrorist thing. I have a feeling he didn't tell me everything."

"Seems that way," Arthur said. "We kind of work on the outskirts of what you might call normal criminal activity."

"But the bad guys are the same?"

"Sort of. I think you and I need to sit down and discuss what is going on. It is impossible anymore to keep this quiet. And we are going to need help. Once my people are taken care of and I find a way for my large friends to get somewhere safe, unobserved, we can talk. I promise to tell you everything. I will let you decide what information should be shared."

"How can I help?" Spinelli asked.

Arthur turned to Remiel who was making his way around the debris carrying Merlin. "Agent Spinelli, this is Remiel. We call him Bob. He is our medic.

"Is there something the agent can help you with, Bob?"

"I can treat most here, First Dragon, but Thor, Sif, and Merlin must be taken to my lab. Hercules has reopened his wound and should go as well. His armor stopped the Friend's weapon from killing him. I will need a quiet room with no windows and little furniture." He looked at Ariel who shook her head. "Somewhere other than here."

"Is it safe to transport them?" Arthur asked.

"I believe so. They are not of this Earth and are stronger so I do not believe a suit will be necessary."

Spinelli shook his head. "Not of this Earth? Thor, Hercules, I don't know, Arthur. I'm not sure you are going to be able to explain any of this. I feel like I have fallen through Alice's looking glass.

I'll keep my people away. There is a small storage facility we sometimes use just down the street. I will make it available for your friend although I think a hospital would be better."

"Not for what he needs it for. Thanks." Arthur turned to Remiel. "Do you need an ambulance?"

"I will need some kind of vehicle. And I could use four stretchers. One of them is for one of your people, agent. I am afraid you will have to take care of him yourself. I cannot take him with me."

"What? Where is he?"

"Over here," Patricia called kneeling next to the man cradling his head.

Seeing who she was tending Spinelli rushed towards them. "Fred!"

"I'm afraid his wounds are bad, sir," Patricia said. "We have done what we can. Slowed the bleeding but he has lost a lot of blood. Bullet is still inside. I don't know if it has moved. If you don't get him help soon I'm afraid it will be too late."

"I'll be fine, Bill," Johnson said weakly.

Spinelli pulled a small radio from his coat pocket. "Control, this is Spinelli. I am at the warehouse. I need an ambulance and four stretchers here ASAP. You will remain in the alley. Someone will come out and get the stretchers. I repeat you will not enter. I will meet you at the door. We have an agent down."

"No questions. You have some well-trained people, Agent Spinelli," Patricia said.

"Thank you for what you did. I assume you are the deputy that led us here. Brave thing you did." He turned to Arthur. "And thank you, all of you."

"It is what we do, Agent Spinelli," Arthur said.

Spinelli stared at him for a moment. "It's Bill. I'm going to wait outside to ensure no one tries to get in. I'll see if I can get a step-van to move your big friends."

He started to leave, stopped, and turned. "And, Arth ... ugh, First Dragon, I am looking forward to our conversation. Any idea where you might be going?"

"I have a house in Hudson. We will go there. Could you arrange for transportation? We could use a van to move our wounded."

"I will see what I can do." He worked his way to the doorway and disappeared.

"Took all this well. Impressive. What now, Arthur?" Loki asked.

"Get the others over here. But not your brother and his wife."

"Why not?"

Arthur looked at him. "You don't know?"

"Know what?"

"I'm sorry, Loki. They were both wounded and badly burned. They were the closest to the grenades. Remiel is taking them to Haven."

"I need to see them."

"I'll get the others," Gwen said.

"Thank you. Loki, tell them I'll see them before we leave. Tell them I am sorry."

"No need to be sorry, little brother. They are warriors and understand the risks. This was not your fault. Besides, it will take more than a few cuts and burns to stop those two." He turned and hurried away.

"What now?" Kathleen asked.

"We find Apollo."

"How?"

"I don't know. He couldn't just disappear."

Lancelot joined them and took Millie's hands. "You are uninjured?"

"I am. But you?"

"Just a few minor cuts. Nothing to worry about." He turned to Arthur. "I discovered something I believe you should see."

"What?"

"It is best that I show you."

Knowing that Lancelot would not mention something unless it was important he followed him without any further discussion.

"It is over here." Lancelot pointed to a pile of crates that had been tipped over from the blast. "When the Friend helped me up I noticed this. It must have been hidden by the crates."

Behind one of the large boxes was a hole. More of a tunnel. Maybe three feet wide and four high.

"Did you check it out?"

"I thought it best to show it to you first. I understand Apollo is missing. It is possible he crawled in here or ..."

"Was taken," Arthur said.

"That is my concern," Lancelot said.

"But who would take him, and why?" Kathleen asked.

"I have no idea." Arthur squatted and looked down the tunnel. "*Michael. I need you and Ariel.*"

"*We will be there momentarily. Something is amiss?*"

"*Yes. Please hurry. Apollo is missing.*"

Lancelot looked at him questioningly. "*Why?*"

"*I do not wish to announce my intentions. Cain has been using this building for a while. It might be bugged and I do not wish to share my suspicions with whoever might be listening. We do not know what is down this tunnel. Or who.*"

"*Disciples?*" Kathleen asked.

"With luck."

"What's going on?" Patricia asked Lancelot.

"Arthur is speaking with Michael."

"Oh. Merlin told me about this. Just a little unsettling watching it."

"I'm sorry, Patricia," Arthur said. "I will explain all. I promise."

Michel and Ariel climbed over some of the overturned boxes. "What can we help you with?" Michael asked.

Arthur pointed to the hole. *"Ariel, you're the scientist. Could you open a doorway in there?"*

She got on her knees and looked down the tunnel. She started to crawl into it. Arthur took her arm.

"It might be dangerous."

She smiled. *"I am aware."*

"Be careful."

"I always am." She withdrew her flasher and disappeared down the dark passage. "I can see light at the end of the tunnel," came the slightly echoing sound of her voice.

"Really," Patricia said with a chuckle.

"I am sorry," Michael said. "Ariel is new to this planet. She has never heard that line before. It was said in innocence and ignorance I assure you."

Arthur chuckled. "I think that makes it even funnier."

"I see something."

Silence for almost a full minute. "There is a room here. Strange, no windows or doors. A chair with restraints on the arms and legs is the only furniture. It is metal and bolted to the floor. There is blood on and around the chair."

"Fresh?" Arthur asked trying to hide the worry he felt.

"I don't think so." She was silent for a moment. *"In answer to your question, First Dragon, it is possible to open a doorway in this room. I have examined the walls and what you did in the warehouse does not affect this room."*

Arthur looked at the others. "Cain has him."

CHAPTER TWENTY-NINE

"What did you do with the Olympian?"

Bael looked down at Cain from a raised platform of dull metal. He stepped back and seated himself.

Although the room was dimly lit, Cain was able to see how close the chair resembled a throne. He tried to hide the smile as the thought came to him. "He is with the others on Shree."

"The Ghass can not reach him?"

"The containment units are similar to those we use to harness the Shadow. Nothing in or out without a key. They will remain safe until we are ready to use them."

"And the Shadows?"

"I have personally selected those to be implanted. They are being programmed as we speak. Once ready they will be introduced and the prisoners will be returned."

"You are certain they possess the required intelligence? Are they strong enough?" Bael asked.

"I have selected them with care. They will do."

"Good. I want them able to integrate themselves into the group the First Dragon calls oath-sworn. They are to be released only when all are together. I want them dead, you understand? All of them."

"I do. But what if she finds out what we are doing?"

"Once it is done I believe she will be pleased and Satan's time will come to an end."

"And if he suspects?" Cain asked.

"Insure he does not. What happened in Cleveland? I see that the body you wear is damaged again. I believe it is time to prepare a new one."

"I like this one. I have worn it for a long time. It has meaning. If it can be repaired I will keep it for a while longer. As for Cleveland, it did not go well. Somehow the First Dragon's people discovered the warehouse. And

I was betrayed by one of those brown bastards I left behind to guard the building. The Dragon and his followers were waiting for me. I don't know how, but the local authorities were also aware and set an ambush. Many of my followers died and a few dozen were captured. I had prepared a safe room in the warehouse and returned there to monitor events. The Olympian was injured and lying near my hiding place so I took him."

"You have more of the human followers? We must secure Cleveland."

"I have many. The covens in Akron, Toledo, and Youngstown have been notified to assemble at the Mentor facility within the week."

"How many?"

"Several hundred. If need be I can draw more followers from Pennsylvania and Indiana. We will not run out of human soldiers or hosts. Those that don't believe in us do believe in the power of money."

"Can they be trusted?"

"Of course not." Cain thought for a moment. "When the apparatus is secured in Cleveland, will it allow us to travel to the other worlds?"

Bael smiled. "That is something we will have to wait to discover."

"Whose there?" Randy asked. "I know they dropped another cage. I heard you yell. Are you hurt?"

"Just my dignity."

"You are from Earth?"

Apollo chuckled. "Sometimes. That is where I was taken, yes. But I am not from there. Is that where you are from?"

"Yeah," Randy said. "Doubt I'll ever see it again though. Or my wife and kids."

"How long have you been here?"

"I have no idea. Time works funny here. I can't tell if it's been days or years. The lady says she thinks she has been here for many years. She is trying to teach me to visit home with my mind. She says she has done it many times. Kind of like astral projection. It's like being a ghost. No one can see or hear you."

"What lady?"

"A friend. Another prisoner. A mysterious lady. She never reveals her name. Sometimes I think there may be more than one."

A female voice chuckled. "As you are a fellow prisoner, I am your friend as well. This place allows us to speak to each other with our thoughts. You may continue to speak out loud but it is not necessary and may draw the attention of the Ghass."

"Ghass? Wait, you can read my mind?"

"A chuckle again. "No. Only if you are speaking to one of us can I hear you."

"Okay, so where are we?"

"We are on a planet called Shree. It is the home of beings that are harvested by the Devalies and transformed into Shadows."

"Shadows?"

"Yes, you know of them?"

"I do.

"He said you can project your mind to your home?"

"Sometimes, yes."

"But no one can see you?"

"Except for one time," the voice said. "I met a young man that could see me and talk to me. At the time I made light of it assuming it was a dream. I no longer think that is so."

"Who are you?" Apollo asked.

"A friend," Randy said. *"The mysterious lady. Never tells me her name."*

"And yours?" Apollo asked.

"Randy."

"You are Randy? The First Dragon's friend. He is worried about you. He is trying to find a way to rescue you."

"You know Art? Who are you?"

"I'm Apollo."

"No! Not you too!"

"Lady, what do you mean?" Apollo asked.

"This is more than I can bear. Not you too, brother."

A warrior from Duat knocked on the wall then stepped into the dining room. "First Dragon, a vehicle has been stopped at the barricade. The driver insists he was invited."

Arthur looked up from the map he was studying. "Does he have a name?

"He showed an ID secured in a leather case. It has his photo and a small metallic badge. Said his name is Spinelli and he is from the FBI. I understand that is some kind of national peacekeeping organization."

Arthur chuckled. "It is and yes I was expecting him. Please allow him in and show him where to park. Then bring him here."

The warrior saluted. "Yes, First Dragon." He turned and rushed out of the room.

"Good kid," Loki said lifting a coffee cup from the table and blowing on it before sipping the dark brew. "Just got here. Never been to Earth before."

"Anyone else for coffee," Gwen asked. "I'm going to get one for myself."

"That would be nice," Kathleen said. "I'll help."

"Is there any tea?" Gabriel asked. "I am still trying to find my way around that bitter brew you refer to as coffee."

"That's what cream and sugar are for," Falstaff said wincing a little as he adjusted his arm in the sling. I use a lot."

"I will try to remember that my large friend," Gabriel said. "How's the arm?"

"Not broken, just dislocated Remiel said. Feel silly wearing this thing."

"Your entire rotor cuff was destroyed, Falstaff," Ariel said. "Remiel has repaired the damage to your shoulder but it will take several days for the swelling to go down. If you mess around with it now you will destroy the wonderful job he did to repair it. That will displease him. I strongly suggest you keep it in the sling. If not, do not be surprised if he doesn't sedate you and tie you to a bed."

Falstaff smiled. "Yes, mother." He looked up at Kathleen. "Is there any ale or mead in the house?

"Afraid not."

"Disgraceful! Barbaric!" he said. "What about beer?"

Kathleen smiled and patted him on the shoulder. "I will check, Uncle."

Arthur turned to Michael. "How are the Friends doing?"

Falstaff looked at Loki. "Loki has introduced them to the game of pool."

"Strange but at least they are busy."

"He has also introduced them to the art of wagering."

Loki shrugged his shoulders. "Thought they could use a little fun."

"As long as they do not kill each other," Michael said. "Or one of us."

"Everything is fine. Yeshem said he would keep an eye on them."

"I noticed he was playing as well," Michael said.

"Oh. Didn't see that coming," Loki said.

"First Dragon."

Arthur turned as the guard escorted Agent Spinelli into the room. The young guard saluted. Arthur stood and returned the salute. "Thank you. No one else is to be admitted to the property. Is that understood?"

"It is, First Dragon. I shall inform the others."

"Do you mind?" Spinelli asked reaching out with an open palm.

The guard looked at him then at Arthur who nodded. He pulled an automatic from his belt and handed it to Spinelli.

"Thank you."

The guard nodded, then left.

"Impressive young man. Cautious. Looking at the damage to the property and the bullet holes in the house I understand the need. What is he, eighteen?"

"The guards may be young but all are experienced warriors." The speaker entered from the kitchen carrying two cups of tea. Handing one to Gabriel he placed the other on the table and offered his hand. "He is thirty-two. He is one of my household guards. My name is Ra."

"Ra?"

"Yes, I am the one you are thinking of. But I am not originally from Egypt. I just spent some time there. And I am not a god. My homeworld is Duat."

"Ra and the others have been assisting the Earth in its war with the Shadows for a very long time," Arthur said.

"There's that word again," Spinelli said, then returned his attention to Ra. "You must be hundreds of years old if you are truly him. Centuries!"

"Not really. I'm actually just reaching the prime years of my life. I am only one hundred and sixty. Time on our worlds works differently. Or did. And our technology, especially in the areas of medicine, allow us to live longer and healthier lives than those of you of Earth."

Arthur pointed to an empty chair. "Have a seat, Bill. I will try to explain. These people, these warriors, are from an alliance of worlds that have fought the Shadows from a time before the Hebrews began to write their version of history. They are from dimensions who until recently, had timelines that flowed at a much different rate than our own. What were centuries to us were measured in mere years on their worlds.

"Long ago they discovered portals that allow them to travel to different dimensions. The rulers of these worlds were present when the first of the invaders presented themselves here on Earth. Their sudden appearance and strange weapons seemed like magic to those that saw them push the Shadows and the Devalies back to their own realm. They assumed they were gods come to save them."

"We were never gods, Arthur."

"I know but they didn't and began to worship if not you then the idea of you."

"And sometimes we were maligned," Loki said. "Even though we came to help our names became associated with evil. My rep got so bad that I spent years unable to return without someone wanting to string me up as soon as they heard my name. Had to change it while I was here."

Bill leaned over to Arthur. "Don't let him see the comic book."

"Oh, I've seen them. Sif loved the way I was depicted. Thought it was hilarious. Especially the horns."

"Sif? Really?" Bill said.

"Yes, my brother's wife. Wonderful lady, a Valkyrie. Why she ever picked Thor over me I don't know."

"Are you sorry?" Gwen asked setting a tray on the table."

Looking up he smiled. "Never."

Bill," Arthur said, "This is my sister Gwen. You know the lady with her. Kathleen is the daughter of Merlin and Gwynivere."

Kathleen chuckled. "If you think that is bad," she walked over to Rex. "This good looking man is Arthur Pendragon. The first King Arthur."

"The first?"

"Some consider my future husband to be the second."

Bill leaned his elbows on the table and gripped his face in his hands. He looked up. "Okay. So I came to work today and now I'm in Wonderland." He sighed. "I think we should focus on the enemy and I'll do my best later to get a handle on the fact that I am working with a bunch of ancient gods." He pointed at Arthur and Rex. "And the King Arthur twins."

Kathleen leaned over the table and whispered, "If it helps, my father is not a wizard. He is just a scientist."

Bill smiled. "Thanks, young lady. But it doesn't. So who is the real enemy here? The folks we locked up, the few that surrendered and the ones you—knocked out—said they were either witches or followers of Satan. Nut jobs."

"Not really," Arthur said. "They believe they are followers of Satan. But the truth is they are being conned. Satan has sworn he is not a part of this and I believe him. The one that orchestrated the attack today was Cain."

"Satan is real! You're not going to tell me this is the Cain. The one from the Bible."

"We believe he might be. I have watched him die more than once and he always comes back. Today Hercules shot him several times. The wounds should have been fatal but once again, he did not die. It was Cain that attacked my home and is responsible for the wounding of Odin and the death of Zeus."

"You mean Zeus, of Olympus, is dead?"

"I am afraid so. He was a good leader to his people and a good friend." Loki said.

"But we do not believe he is working alone." Michael stood and bowed. "Forgive me. My name is Michael. My siblings and I are from Haven and were with Zeus on the first day Satan and the Shadows crossed to this world."

"Heaven?"

"No, Haven."

"And your siblings are."

Each stood and introduced themselves one at a time.

"I think I've lost it. Now we have angles in the room."

"We are not divine, Agent Spinelli, and we have never spoken face-to-face with God," Ezekiel said.

"Arthur has," Loki said with a smirk. "Tell him how you became a Blocker, little brother."

"Little brother?" Spinelli asked.

"Odin and Freya adopted me so the aristocracy would accept me as the First Dragon."

He looked at Arthur. "And the speaking with God? What is a Blocker?"

"I'm not sure that is who he was. A Blocker is one given the power to fight the evil we face. We will talk about all this later. Right now let us continue with who the enemy is. We believe that Cain is working for Bael who is trying to wrest control from Satan. For centuries the Devalies have used beings called Shadows to possess people and use them for their own purposes. Sometimes they were alive."

"Now zombies?"

"Zombies?" Ariel asked.

"The dead brought back to life that survives by consuming human brains," Ra said. "We had them on Duat for a while. They are gone now. Nasty things. Created by a scientist priest that was trying to use the Book of the Dead to bring people back from the grave. The fool would not accept that it was simply a novel and not a powerful religious artifact. Still found a way though. Trust me, the Shadows are not zombies."

"So what do we do about these Shadow things? Stakes through the heart?"

"No, Bill," Kathleen said. "You need a Blocker to stop them. Arthur is the most powerful Blocker to ever live. Lancelot, Millie, and I are also Blockers but we are not in the same league as he. We can identify who is possessed and destroy most of the Shadows that possess them."

"It is for that reason that we need to work together, Bill," Arthur said. "We do not know how many of the terrorists will be possessed when you face them. They can change bodies and they can kill from a distance without a firearm. Some of your own agents may be possessed."

"But why here?" Bill asked. "I mean I haven't heard of this kind of shit happening anywhere else in the States. Or overseas for that matter. Just the Cleveland area."

"Disciples have operated elsewhere in the country. Some may have been possessed. As far as the rest of the world, we think they can only access this area with their doorways through space. They used to be able to use them in Europe and China. But not for hundreds of years. This is the only place they can travel now. We don't know why. We have two portals that allow us to travel to the other dimensions. We believe they wish to control them."

"Why?"

"To cross over and feed."

"On what?"

"Souls," Kathleen said.

"I have an idea why they concentrate on the Cleveland area," Ariel said. "I think it has had something to do with the location of active portals. They tune in to them. But that is changing. I believe it is only a matter of time before they will be able to cross the dimensional barriers."

CHAPTER THIRTY

"It's been two weeks since the warehouse," Arthur said looking out the window of the dining room. He watched as close to a hundred warriors worked building fighting positions in the yard and the surrounding woods. "I mean look at this. We are living in an armed compound in Ohio. In the United States for God's sake. This isn't supposed to happen."

"Satan and the Shadows aren't supposed to happen either, Art," Charlotte said leaning on the table where she had been reviewing reports.

"Nothing! Not a word or sighting. I know they are up to something but I'll be damned if I know what it is." He slammed his hand on the window sill. "I'm sorry. It's just ..."

Kathleen reached up and placed her hand on the side of his face. He looked at her and she smiled.

"They will be all right, Arthur. Thor and Sif will recover. Look what Remiel was able to do with Gwen." She stepped on her toes and whispered into his ear. "As will my father and Hercules."

"I need your father's advice. There is so much I don't understand."

"Was Yeshem able to identify where Randy and Apollo may be being held?" Paul asked entering the room carrying two cups of coffee. He handed one to Loki.

"He thinks they may be on a planet called Shree. The home of the things that become Shadows. He overheard Cain speaking to Bael. He said the Studiers, that's like a bunch of scientists, infiltrate the Devalies by allowing themselves to be possessed. They can kill the Shadow without their masters knowing it is gone. Then they act as if still possessed to gather information. They have been doing this for a long time. He has heard of what he thinks is a human girl they have kept imprisoned there for many years. He believes that is where they would keep Apollo if he is still alive. And hopefully Randy."

"Can we get there? I mean do they have a spaceship or something that we could use."

"They might. The problem we are trying to work out is how do we get to Makaran, their planet, unseen by the Devalies and procure a ship sufficient to carry enough of us to conduct a rescue. Not to mention finding someone foolish enough to pilot it, none of us can fly a space ship. Then pinpoint where on the planet Apollo is being held, rescue him, and hopefully Randy, without being killed or possessed, and then get back."

Loki chuckled. "Piece of cake."

"I see the problem," Paul said.

Freya pulled out a chair, sat, and sighed. "And in the meantime, we need to find Cain." She looked at Arthur. "How is the training going?"

"Pretty good I think. Agent Spinelli seems pleased."

"How did he convince you to include more people from Earth," Gwen asked sitting next to Loki and taking his hand.

"He embarrassed me into it. Why should people from other worlds protect this planet alone? It's our world."

"He has a point," Paul said.

"Caught me off guard, Dad. I mean we have all been trying to keep this quiet. It is still going to remain a secret to most people but they, we, will begin to provide warriors. People who can keep their mouths shut and know how to fight."

"So who are we training?" Gwen asked. "The guys in uniform. They don't talk much."

"From what I understand these guys are used to missions that can never be talked about."

"So who are they?"

Arthur leaned against the wall. "Four Special Forces teams out of Fort Devens in Massachusetts. A Hostage Rescue Team the FBI provided from Quantico, and the local SWAT team from the Sheriff as a start."

"I understand the SF and the HRT, but can we be sure the Sheriff's people will keep quiet?" Paul asked.

"They are from Patricia's department. Some of them have been involved with the Alliance for a long time. Without asking a lot of questions. I trust them. They're good people."

"Good enough for me," Paul said. "I wish I was in the room when they were briefed on who the others really are. And who and what the enemy is."

Arthur smiled. "I must admit, it was pretty funny."

"How did you convince them we aren't nuts," Gwen asked.

"Well, I introduced Yeshem. And I shot one of them with a Havenite weapon on stun. They are quick studies and understand the mission. Although I still think most of them are skeptical of the idea of possessed people and demons that eat souls. Aliens they had no problem accepting."

"You should have introduced Lancelot and told them who he really is," Loki said.

"I think we will keep that to ourselves for now."

The telephone rang, Freya answered and then offered it to Arthur.

"Yes?" He looked at the others. "How many? ... They sure? ... Damn. Okay, have them remain where they are. Don't move any closer. Wait, I think it would be better if they fell back. I don't want them hurt and I don't want to take a chance that Cain knows we are aware of where he is. ... Okay, thanks. How are the troops doing? ... Good. Well, let them know what is going on. I think we may need everyone on this. ... Okay. See you then."

He handed the phone back to Freya. "That was the Sheriff. He's been keeping an eye on the warehouse in Mentor. It has been used twice now that we know of so I figured the disciples might return. I think they look at it as some kind of shrine or holy place."

"We should have blown it up," Ra said. "Leveled it."

Anubis shrugged. "I offered. Poseidon had a ship nearby that could have turned it into a smoking pile of debris."

"Hindsight," Freya said. "Hindsight is always clearer."

"So what is going on?" Charlotte asked.

"The scouts reported a lot of cars arriving," Arthur said.

"What's a lot of cars?" Paul asked.

"Last count, about one hundred and seventy-five."

"Shit," Falstaff said.

"So what are we going to do?" Ra asked.

Arthur shrugged his shoulders. "Try to prevent any of them getting away. See if we can negotiate their surrender, and if not..." he looked around the table. "If they resist, we kill them."

Loki looked up at Arthur. "You have changed, little brother."

Lowering his head Arthur mumbled, "War does that to you. These people kill children. I will not allow that to continue."

"What's that noise?" Randy asked.

"A ship I think," Artimis said.

"What do they want? Could it be a rescue?" Apollo asked.

"Who would rescue us, brother? No one knows we are here and how would your friends get a spaceship? This is another planet, who knows where. There is no portal here."

"Then who?"

"The Devalies."

"What do they want?"

"Us."

Bill walked with Arthur while reviewing the training. "Who are these people assembling in Mentor? What do you think they intend?"

"Regular people. Maybe some are possessed, but most are just people. Misguided, fanatic, dangerous people. They worship Satan and his followers. Some see themselves as witches or warlocks seeking acceptance, approval by the devil. Others are just plain evil, sadistic. Some are greedy, people wanting power over others. The Devalies offer them that and money. Lots of money. The poor fools don't understand they are not selling their souls to the devil. They are providing him with a meal."

"I still don't understand that. They eat our souls. How? Why? And exactly what does that mean?"

"The Devalies and the Shadows gain power from consuming what we are. That thing that makes us individuals. When gone, we die. Sometimes they don't take it all at once. That way they keep the body alive longer so they can use it during possession. People are aware of what is happening and it drives them insane. I don't know if a soul can be registered on any kind of machine but I know it exists. And I know what happens when it has been taken. That is what we need to stop."

"But Gwen said they can't open a doorway at that warehouse in Mentor anymore. How would they get there?"

"I would assume by car. Open a door somewhere else and just drive there."

"So what do you think they plan with this small army?"

"I'm not sure. A campaign of terror maybe. Something to draw attention to themselves. To cause chaos. Maybe to recruit more to their cause. I don't know. This is something new. But if allowed to continue unchecked and the press gets ahold of this, all hell is going to break loose. Not just here but worldwide."

"Can we stop them?"

"I don't know, Bill. But we sure as hell are going to try."

Arthur allowed Bill to continue his inspection and started back to the house. Suddenly he was not alone. Walking beside him was a tall man in a dark trench coat.

"You really should wear something other than that coat. You stand out."

"Old habits." He stopped and raised his hands. "Better?"

Arthur smiled. "Much. A little warm for a sweatshirt and the Pen State logo will not go well around here. We are in Ohio."

Arthur smiled when the shirt turned brown and lost the logo. "I have not heard from you in a while. Things are not going well."

"They are what they are. Your friends will recover. You will need all of them soon."

"What happened to me in the alley?"

"You are growing into your power."

Arthur stopped and turned to the man. "What am I?"

"You are who you are meant to be. You are Arthur Pendragon, the First Dragon. Champion of your people."

"Are they my people? Yeshem said I was different."

"You are no longer the boy you were. You are becoming what you need to be. What all your friends need you to be. Human and not."

"So you aren't going to tell me."

"You are on a journey of discovery. You must this road yourself."

"I have never used my power to kill people."

"And you still have not."

"But ... will I?"

"That is up to you."

"Can I?"

"That is also up to you."

"Why are you here?"

"To tell you two things. First, trust your sister. She is more than she was."

"What does that mean?"

"It means what it means."

Shaking his head Arthur said, "Please don't take this wrong, but you can be very frustrating at times."

He chuckled. "You are not the first to tell me this."

"And the second thing?"

"Beware the wolf in the devil's clothing."

"Okay, what is that supposed to mean?"

There was no answer. The stranger was gone.

"Pendragon?"

He looked up as one of Ra's warriors came running towards him.

"A message, First Dragon." He handed Arthur a folded piece of paper.

He scanned it, looked toward the house, and began to run. "Damn!"

Kathleen was waiting on the steps. She grabbed his arm. "Wait. Let me explain."

"Where is she, Kathleen. What happened?"

"A door opened in the kitchen. Gwen walked into it."

"She walked into it. What the hell does that mean? On her own?"

"No one forced her. I did not feel the presence of a Shadow and saw no one else. Before I could reach her she was gone."

CHAPTER THIRTY-ONE

Arthur rushed into the kitchen. Kathleen did her best to keep up but as she passed the dining room Loki reached out and took her arm forcing her to stop. She had tears in her eyes.

"What's wrong, Kathleen. Where is Arthur going?"

"Gwen is gone."

"Gone. What do you mean gone?" Charlotte demanded.

"A doorway opened in the kitchen and she walked into it."

"Walked into it? On her own?" Loki asked.

"Yes. Now, please release me. I need to go to Arthur."

Loki let go of her arm and she rushed into the kitchen. He, Charlotte, and Paul close behind. Freya looked at the others around the table. "Stay. Leave them. They will tell us what we need to know soon enough. For now, we leave them alone."

"Your Majesty," Falstaff said placing his hand gently on her shoulder. "You are family as well."

"My family has suffered much. I have to ensure that I do all in my power to stop this evil before any more of them are hurt. Now show me the outline of this warehouse."

Arthur stopped when he reached the kitchen. Ariel was examining the wall with a small device, running it back and forth over the drywall. She turned when she realized she was no longer alone.

"What happened?"

"I don't know, Arthur. The three of us were at the sink washing out a few coffee cups. Gwen was helping Kathleen dry. Your sister suddenly looked at the wall and took a step towards it. She said something but I do not believe it was addressed to us."

"What did she say?"

"Okay, I'll come."

"Did she say anything else?"

"She turned to us before stepping through. Said to tell you it was okay and you need not worry. She would be back. Then she stepped into the doorway and was gone. I've examined the wall and the signature of the window does not correspond with either ours or the ones used by the Devalies."

"Then who?" Paul asked.

"I do not know. I am sorry."

Paul took Charlotte in his arms. "She went willingly and said she would be back, dear. We need to trust that our daughter knows what she is doing. Remember she is all grown up now. And one of The Oathsworn."

"I know that. But to me, she was my little girl only a few months ago."

"I know."

Arthur walked over to Loki who was shaking. He placed his hand on his shoulder. "No one took her. She was not afraid."

"So it seems, but these bastards have a lot of tricks."

Arthur turned to Kathleen. "You said you did not sense a Shadow?"

"No. There was nothing. Just that damned hole in the wall."

Taking a deep breath he sighed. "Someone recently told me to trust Gwen. I think we should all do as he says."

"Was it him?" Kathleen asked.

"Yes."

"Did he say anything else?"

"I asked him what happened to me in the alley."

"And his answer?" Loki asked.

"He said that I was growing into my power."

"Anything else?" Loki asked.

Thinking of the response he got about not being like the others he shook his head. "No. That was it."

Loki continued to stare at him. Arthur could see he didn't believe him. He turned away. "Okay then. We need to get back to what we were doing. Gwen will return when she is ready."

Paul took Charlotte's hand. "He's right. We have work to do." Hand-in-hand they walked back to the dining room.

"Don't seal the wall, Arthur. She will be back."

"I know Ariel. I won't."

"So what now?" Loki asked.

"My dad is right. We get back to work."

Loki and Ariel walked out leaving Kathleen and Arthur alone.

"What did he really say, Arthur? You may have fooled your parents but Loki and I know there is something you are not telling us."

"Do you trust me?"

"Of course."

"Then please let it go for now. I'm still working it out."

She reached up and took his face in her hands. "Soon. You do not need to handle this burden alone. I am here. We are here." Then she kissed him. "Please do not wait too long." She took his hand and led him out of the kitchen. As they entered the dining room Freya looked up. "May I assume from the look on your face that everything is okay?"

"I'm not sure I would go as far as to say that, but I don't believe she is in danger."

"That is good news."

"I'm sorry, Freya. With everything going on I forgot to ask how Odin is doing."

"Mad as a winter bear. The doctors will not let him out of the hospital."

"But he's Odin. I know he shouldn't come back but how are the doctors able to keep him in bed. He is not one to take orders," Falstaff asked.

"He will mind. I instructed the doctors to keep him there. He knows they act upon my orders."

Loki chuckled. "And that my friend shows you who is the real ruler of Asgard."

Freya smiled. "Don't tell your brother. It would destroy his understanding of the world."

"No problem, mother. You know I never tell him anything."

"And that is why I have done my best to teach you all I can. You are like me."

"Talented?"

"Ruthless."

"Are you ready, Arthur? Whoops, First Dragon. Almost forgot. I work for you now," Bill said as he stood in the door. "By the way, been meaning to ask. What is a First Dragon?"

Freya placed a hand on the shoulder of her adopted son. "It means he is the Warlord of the Alliance. He commands all military forces of the four worlds. Answering to no one during time of war."

"Wow. But it isn't four worlds, madam. It's now five, and the warriors of this planet await their instructions from their, uh, warlord. Best we call him commander for now with my guys I think. Or general. I'm not sure they would understand the whole First Dragon thing. At least not yet."

Arthur laughed. "Probably a good idea."

"Besides, what are you, thirty? Awful young to command so many."

"Twenty," Charlotte said. "I think. Maybe he is still nineteen or even twenty-one. With all this time travel thing I'm not sure anymore."

"Time travel?" Bill held up his hands. "I don't want to know. But don't tell anyone your real age, First Dragon."

"I understand. Where are they?"

"In the back with the others. They seem to be getting along. But I'm not sure they believe them when they are told where they are from."

"None?" Falstaff asked. "No fighting at all?"

"Not that I'm aware of."

"That is not right. Something must be wrong. Are you sure there are warriors from Asgard out there?"

"There are, you big oaf," Freya said. "And the word has been given that any who pick a fight with one from this world will answer to me."

Falstaff burst out laughing. "Well, that explains everything."

Shaking his head Arthur said. "We need to go. We are running out of time."

As he stepped into what could easily be considered a parade ground behind the house, he looked at the people waiting in ordered groups. The eighty-some personnel from Earth stood directly in front of a raised platform. On either side stood those of Olympus, Duat, Asgard, and Avalon. All armed with modern military-style weapons although some from the Alliance, the original Alliance, carried edged weapons as well.

Freya took his arm. "Wait." She reached into a pouch at her side and removed a broach. It was about four inches in diameter. She pinned it to his jacket. A red dragon, with wings outstretched, glaring at the world in defiance. The emerald eye seeming to be alive.

"Odin insisted I have these made." She turned to those that had followed him from the house. On their coats, a similar two-inch pin was attached. A smaller version of the one on his coat. "For the First Dragon and his oath-sworn."

Doing his best to hide the strong emotion building inside he nodded. "Thank you. But it is The Oathsworn. We are a fellowship. I have sworn to serve them as well."

She smiled. "As a king should."

Ignoring what she said he stepped onto the small platform. He looked at each group for a moment. He was surprised to see Hera standing in front of the Olympian contingent. She nodded. Tilting his head he returned the salutation.

He took a deep breath. "For those of you that do not know me, my name is Arthur. I am called First Dragon. A title afforded me by the leaders of the original four worlds of the Alliance. Odin of Asgard, Ra of Duat, King Alfred of Avalon, and the king of Olympus, Zeus. A brave warrior and a good friend who was recently slain by the enemy. I see his Queen standing with the contingent from Olympus. We are honored, Your Majesty.

"The people standing behind me wearing the red dragon are my oath-sworn. The Oathsworn of the Dragon. We have sworn to serve one another until this war is won or we fall in battle. It has proven costly. Not all are with us today. Horus of Duat has fallen. Thor, Sif, and Hercules are recovering from wounds. Apollo and my sister Gwen are missing."

The contingent from Earth looked at each other having trouble with some of the names.

Freya stepped onto the field and stopped in front of the Asgard contingent. She accepted a rifle from one of her warriors.

Loki stepped forward. "Mother, no."

"Quiet, Loki. It is where I belong. You of all people should know that."

He stepped back to stand with the others of The Oathsworn. Pride showing on his face.

Arthur smiled. He turned to his parents who were standing at the edge of the house. Paul took a step forward. Arthur shook his head no. Charlotte smiled and took her husband's hand.

"It may be that not all of us will survive the upcoming fight. Think hard about following me today. No one would fault you for having second thoughts. Many of you have families. I am First Dragon, but I only lead with the consent of the warriors. No one will think less of you if you decide not to remain."

"Risky, brother."

"I mean what I say, Loki."

Hera took a knee and bowed her head. The warriors of Olympus followed suit. She raised her head. "We of Olympus swear we willingly serve the First Dragon."

Freya kneeled and the warriors of Asgard followed her example. "We of Asgard swear to serve until we send these bastards back to hell."

Her warriors cheered.

"Mother has a way with words," Loki said.

Ra looked at Freya and smiled. He kneeled and the warriors of Duat joined him. "As is right, we of Duat so swear."

Sir Gawain took a knee. "In the name of King Alfred, we of Avalon swear to serve the First Dragon to the end."

"Forever," Kathleen whispered behind him.

Bill Spinelli watched in awe as the warriors of the Alliance kneeled and swore their allegiance to Arthur.

Captain Dunbar, the company XO from Devens who commanded the Special Forces Soldiers, shook his head. "Like some kind of movie." He did an about-face and looked at the men questionably. One after the other they simply said, sir. He turned back to Arthur and whispered. "The colonel is going to kill me."

He presented a parade ground salute. "We are with you, sir."

Bill smiled as the leader of the HRT looked at the three rows of his men, turned, came to attention, and saluted. The Sheriff's people followed their example.

Bill Spinelli, AIC of the Cleveland office of the FBI, stood tall, raised his hand in a salute. "We don't kneel, First Dragon. It is not our way. Even to the generals we normally follow. But we are yours as long as you need us."

"Thank you. I will do all in my power to live up to this honor. This is going to be a hard fight. The enemy is well-armed. I understand from our intelligence people that there may be militia elements within their ranks. Trained soldiers. We cannot underestimate them. We may also face Shadows. There may be knights. And there may also be Devalies. Let The Oathsworn handle them. We are best equipped to do so. No heroics, please. Most of you know you cannot stop a Shadow."

He looked at the Earth contingent. "I need to explain what that means to you before we depart. Please wait when the others are dismissed."

Bill nodded.

"I wish to see the leaders of your respected worlds. The rest of you get something to eat, something to drink." He looked at Falstaff. "In moderation. Then gear up and head for the busses. Your leaders will brief you on the way." He smiled. "Remember, not too much ale. You have a long march ahead of you once we arrive and we do not have time to wait for weak bladders."

Many turned toward Falstaff. He looked offended. "I can hold it longer than any man alive."

His words were met with a good deal of friendly banter.

The formations broke up and the area became full of the sounds of people talking and laughing. Arthur took Kathleen's hand and leaned against the house to wait for the leaders of the various worlds to join him.

"First Dragon," Hera said joining the growing crowd. "Kathleen, I was sorry to hear about your father. Any word?"

"He is stable. And he is in the care of Remiel. I understand from Lancelot that there is no one better to take care of him."

"That is good to hear."

"Your Majesty," Arthur said. "Should you be here?"

"I rule Olympus now, First Dragon. As my husband did before me, I shall lead our warriors into battle. Besides, I need to exact a little payback. To make me feel better."

He looked at Ra and Freya. "And you?"

Freya smiled. "Men often underestimate me, Arthur. Your step-father often did. He has learned. I have been in battle before. I am Valkyrie. In the old world, we were called shield-maidens. Do not be concerned for me. After all, your future wife fights at your side. She is a Knight. Allow your step-mother the same honor."

Arthur looked to where his mother and father stood at the edge of the assembled warriors. She smiled. "Can't fight. I'll stay here and keep an eye on things. Sometimes it is good to have two mothers."

Paul kissed her on the cheek. "I will look after her, Art. Shadows can't hurt me."

He smiled knowing that his father could not follow even if he wanted to. He was still recovering from his wound.

"And you, sir?" he asked Ra.

"How could I face my people if I stayed safe at home? I am where I should be. Where I wish to be."

Gawain gripped Arthur's forearm. "King Alfred sends his regrets. He wished to come but his doctors forbid it. He broke his leg in a joist last week. He asked me to stand in his stead."

"I am glad to have you."

Lancelot stepped forward and gripped Gawain's forearm. "It is good to see you; old friend."

Gawain squeezed his arm. "I understand there is much you need to tell me, brother."

"There is, and I shall. When this day is over. You have my word."

Arthur looked at the men from Earth. "Gentlemen I know that you probably think you have fallen into a black hole and are living in a bad science fiction movie. I understand. But believe me when I tell you this is real. The presence of the Makarans should have shown you that. Today you will face trained soldiers and fanatical disciples of Satan. There will probably be some possessed by Shadows. Kind of like demons. Shadows use people, kill people in service to their lords the Devalies and Satan."

One of the HRT members spoke out. "I'm not a religious man, but are you saying we are about to pick a fight with the devil himself? And a bunch of demons."

Arthur smiled. "Something like that. But don't worry," He turned to the Havenites. "We have four archangels on our side. Meet Michael, Ezekiel, Gabriel, and Ariel."

"You're shitting me," Captain Dunbar said.

Arthur laughed. "The Devalies and the Havenites are people from worlds far from here. From another galaxy. As are the Shadows. They are not devils or demons but are almost as dangerous."

"It's true, John," Spinelli said. "I've seen some of this. It is definitely real."

"So we have been invaded by aliens. Ones that use magic and possess people. That are led by Lucifer himself," Dunbar said.

Arthur smiled trying not to look at Lancelot. "Not him, Captain, Satan. They are not the same being. But the ones you may face today, these aliens, are vicious, dangerous, and as close to true evil as one can get."

"What do they want?" Captain Dunbar asked.

"Souls," Kathleen said.

"Souls? You mean like people or, uh, real souls?"

"They consume the essence of a person. What is often referred to as a soul." Michael said. "They can reach out of the body they possess and destroy another. As the First Dragon said, if you come across one, stay away. Let one of the Blockers handle it."

"What exactly is a Blocker?" Captain Dunbar asked.

"Some of us have been given the power to identify possessed people and destroy the Shadow that controls them."

"You best tell him the rest," Loki said.

Taking a deep breath Arthur nodded. "There is a good chance that we will face Cain, Bael, and possibly Satan tonight. Cain looks human. He is not and is dangerous. There is nothing that distinguishes him from any other human except he will probably be surrounded by Shadows. Possessed people. We will find him. We know what he looks like."

"And we will kill him," Lancelot said in a steely voice. Millie took his hand.

"As for the Devalies. They will be easy to pick out. Seven-foot beings with red skin. Hard to miss. Leave them to me. I am the only one that may be able to defeat them."

They stood still and quiet, doing their best to absorb what they had been told. Finally, a big soldier wearing the stripes of a master sergeant raised his voice. "Okay. People we shoot, anything that ain't people we leave to you. Got it."

A voice called out from one of the teams, "You tell em, Bear."

"We got it, First Dragon," Bill said smiling.

Kathleen looked at Arthur as he suddenly stiffened.

"Be careful, Art. There is more going on than you are aware of."

"Gwen?"

CHAPTER THIRTY-TWO

Ten large school busses and one fifteen-passenger van stopped alongside a large open field two miles from the warehouse. It was a still afternoon, quiet except for the more than three hundred pairs of boots shuffling on the damp grass.

Section leaders stood with outstretched arms to let their warriors know where to assemble. Sentries were set as the leaders joined Arthur near the end of the field.

He kneeled while the others crowded around him.

"We are a little over two miles from the warehouse. It is all forest until you reach the beach. The only road is the one we just came down. About a quarter of a mile east of the target is a large dirt parking lot. The Sheriff has secured it. There were no guards."

"I love to be underestimated by an enemy," Freya said.

Arthur smiled.

"The Sheriff has cordoned off the area three miles down the road on either side of the warehouse. His people will allow no traffic in or out until we're done."

"What about the press," Bill asked. "Things are going to get a little noisy."

Patricia chuckled. "My boss is an expert handling the press. Don't worry. They will be told we are conducting a military training exercise. Classified. No press."

Arthur looked at Patricia. "You sure you should be here. I doubt Merlin would approve."

"He's not here," she said and winked.

Kathleen chuckled. "I do like you, Patricia. My father is fortunate to have found you."

"I found him. And I have no intention of letting him go."

"Okay," Arthur said. "Back to business. Bill, can you provide Olympus, and Duat with sniper teams?"

Bill turned to Captain Dunbar who nodded.

"I have three. One on each team. A shooter and a spotter."

"Good. Please have them see me before we leave," Arthur said.

"All three?"

"Yes."

"Roger that," acknowledged Dunbar.

Bill nodded to the two civilian teams. "I have one and of course so does the Sheriff's team if you need them."

"I will need them with us. Arthur looked at Hera. "I would like your people to come in from the East." He turned to Ra. "And yours from the West. Stay in the woods. I need you to keep your folks back at least two hundred yards until I give the word. Have your sniper teams keep surveillance on the target."

"Will they have radios?" Ra asked.

"Yes," replied Arthur.

"Won't they be heard?" Loki asked.

"Not necessarily," Captain Dunbar said. "My guys all have whisper mikes and the frequencies are secure. And they won't get too close."

"What's that?" Bill asked.

"Something we've been testing. It's a bone conduction microphone that operates off the vibration of, well, your jaw. Something they started working on a few years ago. You don't have to say a word. Just mouth them and it transmits through your radio and sounds like someone speaking out loud on the other end."

"My father would be interested in looking at one of those," Kathleen said.

"I'm sure that could be arranged, Miss."

"It's Kathleen."

"Kathleen."

"Okay, where do you want us, First Dragon," Freya asked.

"I want you and Gawain with me along with the Special Forces and the police folks. We are the main strike force. Lancelot, Kathleen, Millie, and I will need people to keep the disciples off us while we take care of Shadows or Devalies.

As we go forward I will want Avalon, the FBI, and the Sheriff's people to go down the east of the building," Arthur directed. "Lancelot and Millie will be with you in case you run into Shadows. Asgard and the Special Forces will be with me and we will go down on the west side. We remain in the woods behind the building until I give the signal. Then stay close to the building" Looking at Hera and Ra he added, "Your job is to keep as many of them on the beach as you can while we sweep them into the open. Get as close as you need to but do not get in front of the warehouse. We will take care of that. You do not have anyone to handle Shadows and I don't want you to get caught in the crossfire.

"The only door, other than those that lead to the beach, is on the east side of the warehouse."

Arthur turned to Spinelli, "I need you to take as many of your folks as you feel you will need to breach that door. Lancelot will be with you. Millie will remain with the others. When the attack begins, I believe any possessed in the building will try to reach the beach. I intend to be waiting for them."

"Are we to try to take prisoners?" Bill asked. "Will there be any non-hostiles in the building?"

"Fair question. I do not have an answer but take no chances. I doubt anyone in there is innocent."

"Explosives?"

Arthur thought for a minute then turned to Patricia. "Did you see anyone in the building that wasn't one of them?"

"If they are in there they are part of this. They allow no one but their own in that building. They treat it as a shrine."

Dunbar nodded. "Okay. No friendlies in the building. I will leave it to the teams."

Arthur continued. "Poseidon is already on station two miles off the coast with several armed swift boats and a forty-foot yacht that I understand is heavily armed."

Hera nodded. "He does like his toys."

Arthur continued. "Their job is to make sure no one comes in or leaves on the lake."

"Do you want to talk to the sniper teams?" Dunbar asked.

"Yes. I need to brief them. We have about three hours before it starts to get dark. I want them in place ASAP. I need eyes on the target and I want to brief them on what I need them to do. The rest of us leave in twenty minutes.

We are going to be moving fast so make sure they make good use of the trees and relieve themselves now. We can't stop once we get going."

"Not all our warriors are men," Freya said with a smile.

"Sorry, Freya. You know what I mean."

She smiled. "Just teasing."

Dunbar and Bill ran back to their teams while the others went to brief their elements. Arthur sat on the grass and looked towards the heavens. *What did you mean, Gwen? And where are you?*

"Are you okay?" Kathleen asked sitting beside him.

"I'm fine. Just thinking."

"About the battle? You have a good plan, Arthur. And the best of people. You have done all you can. Now it is up to fate."

"I hate that guy," he scoffed.

Kathleen chuckled taking his hand. "She does occasionally do something nice

He looked down and smiled. "Yes, she does and no, I was merely reflecting on what the man in the suit told me. I wish he would tell me who he really is. I can't keep referring to him as 'He'. And I'm worried about Gwen."

"I believe she is safe. It was her idea to go. She wasn't forced." She shifted position so she could look at him. "And the other thing?"

Arthur took a deep breath and looked around to make sure no one could hear him. "Yeshem said I am not like everyone else. That I am something different. Not human, not Havenite. I asked my visitor about that."

"And his answer?" she asked.

"He said I've changed."

"How? What does that mean?"

"I don't know. That's what's so frustrating. He never explains."

She took his hand and brought it to her lips. "You will never be anything but Arthur to me."

He smiled. "Thank you."

"Here they are, First Dragon," Bill said as ten men representing five individual sniper teams squatted near him. Arthur let go of Kathleen's hand and looked around. Half of them had scoped rifles slung across their backs while the others carried long pouches containing the small telescopes they would use to feed information to the shooters.

"I need you to move as quickly as you can to your positions. There will be people inside but what I want is information about those on the beach. I need to know if there are any boats tied up at the pier or beached and if any vehicles are parked nearby. We will need a rough estimate of their numbers. And if you can, identify those in charge. They will be your primary targets when I give the word." He looked at them. "Any questions?"

Some head shaking but no questions.

"Good. Agent Spinelli will designate who you will be working with and where you need to deploy. Coordinate with them."

They nodded and moved away with Dunbar and Spinelli.

"You have turned into a true Strategos, Arthur," Michael said squatting beside him. "I am most proud of you."

"Thank you. But it is you I have to thank. You trained me."

"Nonsense, Arthur. I simply opened a door. You have become who you are by yourself. I did not, and could not bring you to this."

"You and the others know what to do?"

"We do. Ezekiel will go with Hera while Gabriel will accompany Ra. I will remain with you. Ariel will go with Gawain. All of The Oathsworn have flashers."

"And Remiel?" Arthur asked.

"He and the medics from the Special Forces teams will set up a triage station. His patients on Haven remain in stasis, healing which has allowed him to join us."

Arthur looked concerned. "If something happens to him?"

"I am certain it will not," Michael assured Arthur. "And we are all trained to retrieve our friends from stasis if necessary."

"Good. Thank you. I guess that's about it. We need to go."

Sergeant First Class James (Junior) Woolcroft slowly crawled through the grass and brush making little to no sound. He carried a Remington M25 sniper rifle in the crook of his arm. A few feet behind him and to his left crawled Staff Sergeant (Wiz) Worchinski. Woolcroft held up his fist and his junior weapons sergeant froze. He reached up and tapped his left shoulder signaling him to move into position. Wiz crawled up beside him. Junior activated the spring-loaded bipod on the upper stock of his weapon while Wiz pulled out his small telescope and tripod. They pulled up the hoods of their camouflage gillie suits making them practically invisible.

"Good spot," Wiz mouthed.

Junior gave a thumbs up.

As SFC Woolcroft scanned the beach through the scope on his rifle, SSG Worchinski viewed the same area with his more powerful device.

Several people meandered along the beach. All armed. Most with military-style weapons. Several men stood on either side of the dock behind stacks of OD green sandbags. Wiz tapped his partner on the shoulder pointing at the sandbags.

"Are those...?"

"M60s. Two of them." He touched the push-to-talk on his radio. "This is Alpha Three, he mouthed. Two sandbagged bunkers along the dock with MG's. I say again, two medium Mike Golfs."

"Roger," Captain Dunbar said. "Primary target. Out."

"Shit," Wiz whispered. "There are more near the building."

"On a shingle," Junior agreed.

"Roger," Dunbar said. Keep your heads down. I'll let him know. Six Out."

Captain Dunbar turned to the command group. "Snipers report fortified positions, sandbags, and machine guns. Two at the docks and one each on either side of the open beach in front of the building. No vehicles. No boats. About one-hundred and fifty armed men milling around. Team Five, the HRT guys, thought they saw movement on the roof."

"Makes sense. Anything else?" Arthur asked.

"No, sir."

"Damn! Seems they are expecting trouble," Arthur said.

"Looks that way," Dunbar agreed.

"If not us, then who. And if us, how did they know." Arthur took a deep breath. "Okay, tell them to stand by. As soon as I hear from Poseidon we will go. They have their primaries?"

"The machine guns in the bunkers and anybody that looks like they may be in charge," said Dunbar.

"Good. Thanks."

"The teams will coordinate with each other so they don't share the same target," Dunbar said looking back to the waiting soldiers.

"Get in position," Arthur said. "Signal is the snipers engaging their targets.

Dunbar nodded.

"Good man," Falstaff said. "The other soldiers respect him. Was one of their team leaders a few months back. Wish we had time to outfit those boys with body armor."

"So do I. The others?" Arthur asked.

"All the Alliance members wear armor," Loki said.

"Prior four," Spinelli said with a smile.

"Right. Sorry, the old Alliance." Falstaff smiled.

Arthur turned to Michael. "You?"

"Never thought of asking for any. Lancelot may have a set. He has been around longer."

"Then be careful. There is a lot of firepower out there."

"We will. What about the flashers?"

"Try stun, but don't take any chances. Stunning may help ID Shadows but with the chaos that is about to be unleashed, I'm not sure how much help that will be. If there are any knights I doubt stun will work."

"Understood."

"Now what?" Kathleen asked.

"We wait."

"Admiral, radar reports several fast-moving objects heading in our direction."

Poseidon picked up a pair of binoculars from the armrest of his chair on the bridge of the forty-foot yacht he used as his command vessel.

"Thank you, XO. From where?"

"Due west, sir."

"What are they doing?"

"Picking up speed and spreading apart. Looks like they intend to attack."

Poseidon stood. "Full speed ahead, helmsman. XO, contact the others. Battle stations. Possible incoming hostile vessels. Do not engage until we are certain they pose a threat. Don't want to sink some local idiots having fun. You said they are heading towards us and not the beach?"

The XO asked a question through the mike of the headset he wore. "Correction, sir. Five smaller craft coming towards us. Two larger vessels have turned towards the beach and picked up speed."

"Get the First Dragon on the radio," Poseidon ordered.

The XO reached for a series of switches on the control station. "He's on, sir."

"First Dragon, two vessels have turned in your direction. It looks like they intend to land. They are large enough to carry a lot of people. I believe I am about to come under attack. I will dispatch one of my Fast Boats to intercept those heading towards you. Once the situation is stable here I will move in and provide support."

He listened for a moment as Arthur provided instructions. "I understand. See you soon. Poseidon out."

"XO, dispatch the Medusa and have her intercept those vessels heading for shore."

"Rules of engagement?" The XO asked.

"Don't wait for them to engage first. If they appear a threat—sink them."

"Aye, sir."

The XO spoke into his headset and Poseidon watched as a twenty-foot fast boat broke formation. He turned back to the XO. "Status on the others?"

"No doubt their intent is hostile."

"Readiness status?" Poseidon demanded.

"All guns manned and ready. Four remaining fast boats up and standing by."

The helmsman gasped and Poseidon looked towards the shore as he heard the explosion. His heart stopped as he saw the burning remains of the Medusa began to vanish below the surface.

The XO suddenly slammed into him knocking him to the deck, covering him with his body. The windscreen of the bridge shattered in a hail of bullets. Looking around the shoulder of the XO, Poseidon watched the helmsman as he sagged to the deck, his upper body covered in blood, his hands still on the wheel.

Poseidon pushed the XO from atop him. "Jason?" He looked into the glazed and staring eyes of his friend and realized there would be no answer. Crawling to the communications panel he pulled down the microphone. The sounds of gunfire and emergency alarms making it hard to hear. He turned as a large man in the bloodied uniform of the boats Chief pulled at him.

"Sir, we are going down. Some kind of torpedo or rocket almost took the aft section from the boat. We're going down fast. We need to abandon ship."

"I need to radio the First Dragon, Chief. He needs to know."

The Chief looked at the XO and the helmsman. Water was beginning to flood the bridge. From the shattered windscreen he saw the survivors of the command vessel swimming for their lives amid the chaotic battle taking place between the attacking boats and the remains of the Alliance flotilla. He reached for his admiral but a massive wall of water rushed in pushing him away from Poseidon.

"Poseidon's gone," Arthur said putting the mike down. "His remaining boats are engaged. At least two have been sunk to include the command vessel. Two large boats are heading our way with armed men on board."

"This was a trap," Loki said.

Before Arthur could respond he looked up at the rooftop of the warehouse. The sound of several thumps echoed from the flat surface.

Arthur was knocked to the ground as Loki screamed, "Get down!"

CHAPTER THIRTY-THREE

Six M79 grenade launchers propelled their forty millimeter high explosive projectiles into the Alliance forces waiting in the trees. Arthur watched in horror as one of the shells landed in the middle of the Special Forces soldiers preparing for the assault. Captain Dunbar and two others were launched into the air, their bloodied bodies coming to rest on the sandy soil. Several more of the soldiers lay unmoving on the detritus of the forest floor, unmoving.

The machine guns from the bunkers opened up and the sound of gunfire erupted from those on the beach redirecting his attention.

Several single shots, louder, deadlier, silenced the chattering machine guns. A man fell from the roof and the M79s went silent.

"Go! Go! Go!" Arthur screamed and the men and women of the Alliance began to work their way towards the beach, while supported by the constant fire from the snipers.

Falstaff picked up one of the discarded M60 machine guns abandoned by a wounded Special Forces soldier. The HRT and SWAT were quickly organized by Bill Spinelli while one of the team leaders, Captain Ricadelli, took charge of the remaining SF soldiers.

"Let's go."

One husky soldier, his torn and bloody sleeve identifying him as a master sergeant, stepped up beside Falstaff. In his hands was an M60. "Names Master Sergeant Swisher. Friends call me Bear. That's my team you see lying around you. It's just me now. Let's you and me go kill some of these sons-a-bitches. I'm seventeen coats of brushed coated pissed."

Falstaff smiled at him. "Ever heard of Valhalla?"

"Where the Vikings go when they die? Swisher replied.

"Something like that. There's a great pub outside of the castle called Valhalla. Let's get drunk when this is over."

The sergeant looked at him for a moment. "What the hell. Sure."

They stepped forward and opened up with the heavy guns.

"Stay at my side, Kathleen," Arthur said.

"I can fight."

"I know," he yelled over the sound of gunfire. "I will need you if there are Shadows. You need to watch my back."

Pulling the charging handle of her M16 to the rear she smiled. "I thought ... never mind."

Members of the HRT ran up the stairs on the side of the warehouse. The first man up tried the door then stepped back. The agent with him aimed a shotgun at the handle and fired. The door flew open, a shot rang out and the team leader was thrown over the railing. The man with the shotgun jumped after him. The next two on the steps ran up and threw satchels through the door then vaulted over the railing.

One of the two sat up and looked at the other. "How long did you set the charges for?"

"Fifteen seconds."

"Why so long?"

"Figured some idiot would try to see what we threw in. Thought it would be funny when he found out."

"You idiot what if ..."

He never finished his question as a massive explosion knocked them down. A blast of flame jetted from the open doorway. Six agents ran up the steps and entered the building firing as soon as they cleared the opening. Lancelot followed. He raised his hand and the single Shadow remaining in the room was reduced to a shower of hail.

The agent beside him stared. "Damn."

Stepping onto the landing a man held his thumb up. "All clear."

An agent at the base of the steps slowly lowered his wounded commander to the ground and looked up at the remainder of the team. "Okay. That's the easy part. Let's help clear the rest of the beach."

Hera led her people to the edge of the trees. More than two dozen were down with head wounds or broken bones. The armor prevented penetration but not injury from ballistic impact. She knew that several of her people had already been killed or badly wounded but she had no time to check on them.

Wiping a wisp of hair and the blood that seeped from the wound to her scalp she waived her people forward.

"For Zeus," she yelled.

One of the snipers assigned to her looked at his spotter. "Zeus?"

"Yep, now let's keep the lady safe while she and the other gods kill these assholes."

He picked up his rifle and sweeping the area fired whenever he saw a weapon aimed at Hera.

"Let's go, Bill. Keep her in sight. Bill?"

His partner and friend lay on the ground, a hole just above his right eye. "Shit!" He jumped to his feet and followed Hera.

"Leave me," Ra screamed leaning against a tree while holding a bandage to the seeping wound to his abdomen. "Keep them moving!"

"I'll be back, My Lord," Seth promised.

"Just go, Seth. Don't let any escape."

Seth turned and waved his hand at his remaining troops. "For Ra!"

"For Ra!" They screamed and bounding from tree to tree moved slowly but doggedly forward.

Ra looked down at the bloody bandage, then at his people as they fought and died. "I am with you, my friends." He sighed, closed his eyes, and slipped to his side settling on the floor of the forest.

Bullets zipped over his head, on either side of his body and at his feet. None made contact as if Arthur walked within a bubble of energy that moved the lead projectiles. He heard the firing of his people, constant, relentless. The zap of the Havenite flashers. He saw one strike. They were not on stun. The people on the beach were struck from three sides. They had no chance and yet continued to fight.

Arthur tripped over the body of a disciple. Around him, people kneeled and fired into those enemies still fighting on the beach. None tried to surrender. Rex reached down and offered his hand. As Arthur regained his footing Rex spun around and fell. Arthur turned and saw Cain near the door to the warehouse. He held an assault rifle, the barrel smoking, and aimed at him. Before he could react, Cain was struck by more than a dozen bullets as several of The Oathsworn stepped forward. Cain was thrown back, two of his disciples grabbed him by the arms and dragged him towards the water.

Several more stepped in front of them preventing anyone shooting at their leader.

"Shadows!" Arthur screamed.

Kathleen joined him as seven clouds of dark mist rose from fallen disciples that lay on the sand. Those that had protected Cain as he was carried away. Cut down by Falstaff and his new friend.

A glow began to emanate from Arthur as a similar light began to radiate from Kathleen's hands.

"You take the one on the far right. I will handle the others."

Kathleen smiled.

"We will keep the others busy," Arthur heard Michael say.

Flashes of light zipped past Arthur and Kathleen as those from Haven increased their volume of fire.

Bear looked at them. "What the hell?"

"Alien ray guns. Now, watch Arthur, little man," Falstaff said. "See why he is called First Dragon. He breathes fire!"

Arthur brought his hands together and a wave of light leaped from his body as Kathleen expelled her own at the remaining Shadow. Black hail pelted those still standing around the fallen disciples. Arthur saw beams of light from the other Blockers strike Shadows rising from the fallen to his right and left. Several of the disciples, having seen their friends vaporized by the Havenite weapons, and their deities killed by the jets of light dropped their weapons and fell to their knees, begging for mercy.

"No time for prisoners. Stun them, Michael."

Those on their knees fell.

"Arthur!" Kathleen yelled pointing toward the lake where two large boats appeared moving swiftly towards them.

"No more!" Arthur yelled. He stepped forward. Without taking his eyes from the host of his enemy he flicked his coat back and withdrew Excalibur. Those that stood in his way were cut down so rapidly it seemed the blade never moved. Three, then four, and five more times his shoulders snapped back as bullets struck him but he never slowed his pace.

The Oathsworn gave him room to use the sword, falling in behind him, shooting at anyone foolish enough to keep fighting. Arthur felt rather than saw, first Millie, and then Lancelot move in towards him, joining Kathleen, destroying Shadows as they escaped from fallen bodies. Without looking he knew that the remaining special forces soldiers flanked The Oathsworn, shooting, striking the enemy that got too close with rifle butts and fists never seeming to slow down. The Havenites fired their flashers so rapidly it seemed they were blades themselves carving a path.

The remainder of the Alliance warriors stopped and kneeled, placing well-aimed shots at any that turned their weapons towards him.

Arthur stopped. *"Step back!"*

The others stepped away forming a half-circle as a bubble of light began to expand from the place where Arthur stood. Not even those from Earth questioned the unspoken order they all heard in their heads.

"Enough!" He screamed and the orb ignited with the luminance of the corona of a star engulfing the remaining enemy.

They fell.

"Are they dead?" One of the Special Forces soldiers asked.

Kathleen looked at him as Arthur focused on the approaching boats. "No. At least not yet. We shall see what happens next."

She turned her attention to the vessels. Lancelot and Millie stepped up beside them. Lancelot wiped the blood from his brow.

"Do you feel it?" Arthur asked.

"Shadows," Millie said. "Several. Powerful."

"Something else," replied Arthur.

"Bael," Lancelot growled.

"And he is not alone," Arthur added.

The sound of a helicopter drew their attention to the trees behind them. Arthur smiled. "About time."

Arthur heard Icarus's voice through the radio on Captain Ricadelli's belt.

"Sorry, I'm late. An issue with the ordinance. Local FAA rep was concerned when we loaded the bird. We worked it out. He will wake up before we get back."

"Tell Icarus the boats not on the beach are his target."

Ricadelli relayed the message.

"Piece of cake," exclaimed Icarus.

The helicopter banked and dropped until the skids seemed to brush the water. The lead boat opened up with a machine gun kicking up small geysers in the otherwise calm surf. The aircraft bucked and then from one of the round pods on the outside of the helicopter a trail of smoke erupted. As Icarus fought to gain altitude the boat exploded in a ball of flame engulfing the small aircraft.

Arthur sighed with relief when the bird broke through the fireball and banked sharply to move away. It started to shake as it was riddled with bullets from another boat and burst into flames.

"Stay here," Arthur ordered.

"Arthur we cannot," Falstaff said. "Our duty. Our oath."

He turned to them. "I release you all from your oath. What is coming is something you cannot deal with. It is up to me alone to try and stop it. If I fall it will be your duty to save who you can and prepare for what is to come."

They stared at him as if he had slapped them all. Kathleen took his hand. "They will not leave you, Arthur. I will not leave you. We will face this together. We stop them or not. We live or die, together."

With tears in his eyes, he dropped his head. "Then you all will die."

He turned as he heard the sound of a boat hull crunch into the sand. They stood and waited.

"Shadows," Mille whispered.

"Knights," Kathleen said."

"And something else," Lancelot said.

Eleven Makarans carrying long spears jumped from the beached boat and stood poised with their arcane weapons resting in the sand, the gentle waves of the lake lapping at their feet.

"And now it begins," Arthur whispered as Bael and five of his kinsmen leaped from the deck, splashing as they marched forward. They stopped when they reached the large beings from Makaran. Ebony swords slowly sprouted from their dark blue hands.

Excalibur began to glow.

"Or it ends."

CHAPTER THIRTY-FOUR

Arthur knew that this was the end. In his heart, he knew that even he could not defeat six Devalies.

"Michael, you and the others use your flashers on the Makarans. On stun, if you can, but you will need to strike them several times. When they fall I need the Blockers to take out the Shadows as they try to find another host. Use everything you have. These are knights. They are intelligent and strong. Take them one-at-a-time with all of you working together if you have to. They can launch darts of Shadow at you so beware.

"Loki, make sure that no one is attacked by a Shadow seeking a new body. The rest of you watch out for the Makarans. If they get back up and are aggressive, kill them."

"Lancelot, use a shield if they launch darts. Protect the others."

"And the Devalies?" Kathleen asked.

"There is nothing you can do. Stay away from them. I will do what I can to slow them down. If I fall, get the hell out of here. No heroics. Leave me. The Alliance will need you."

"I will not leave you," Kathleen said.

Arthur took her by the shoulders. "You cannot fight them and I cannot be worried about you when I do." He turned to Loki.

"I understand, little brother."

Lancelot stepped up beside Arthur.

"What do you think you're doing?" Arthur asked.

"I will stand with you. I am the First Blocker. It is where I should be."

"Then you will need this."

Arthur turned. "Patricia? You need to get back with the others,"

"Not until I take care of this. I know it sounds nuts, but Gwen gave me this. Before ... you know, before she left. She said I was to give it to Lancelot at the right time. He'll know what to do with it. I think this is what she meant. Been carrying it around in my rifle case."

She withdrew something wrapped in white linen from the cloth rifle bag she had around her shoulder.

Lancelot undid the strings and smiled. "I thought she was lost."

The cloth fell revealing a sword sheathed in a silver bejeweled scabbard. The slowly fading rays of the sun struck the partially drawn blade causing it to glow.

"Galatine. I carried her on that first day. I brought her with me from home. She was lost the day we rescued Pendragon and took him to Avalon."

His reverie was broken by a shout from the shore.

"I see you still live, Lucifer," Bael yelled stepping from the boat. "Today I shall remedy that. You will soon join your sister in the unending darkness of death."

"Thank you, Patricia," Lancelot said not taking his eyes off Bael. "Now you must go. Tell the others to stay back. There is nothing they can do here. It is up to Arthur and me."

MSG Swisher stepped beside Falstaff. "Lucifer? You mean like the Devil. The Prince of Darkness himself?"

Falstaff turned. "What are you doing here?"

"The fights not over is it? I lost some good friends back there. I'm here for some payback." Master Sergeant Swisher looked at Lancelot. "Did I hear him say Lucifer? We are fighting with the Devil? I thought he was who we were trying to stop."

"That's Satan. He's Lucifer."

"Well, that explains everything."

Falstaff looked at Bear and laughed. You are a true warrior, my little friend. We shall have such fun together. But Lucifer is one of the good guys. A strong warrior and a friend."

"Why aren't they coming at us?" Millie asked.

"They are waiting for the sun to set. Their power is strongest in the dark," Loki explained. "Shadows do not need to possess bodies in the dark."

"I suggest we not wait, Arthur. It's getting dark," Lancelot said. "We take the fight to them."

Arthur nodded and took a step forward. As he did Excaliber burst into flames bathing his body in light. Lancelot walked beside him drawing the sword and throwing the scabbard aside. Galatine began to glow.

Arthur looked at the sword and smiled. "Did it do this before?"

Lancelot took a glance at the weapon in his hand and a grim smile grew on his face. "No. This is different." He took another step. "I am different."

The Devalies remained stationary, their long ebony swords poised and ready. The Makarans began to trot forward, long spears lowered, their deadly blades extending eight feet in front of them. Directly at Kathleen.

"Don't these assholes use guns?" Bear asked.

"Sometimes. Not always," Falstaff said.

"Why not? Some kinda alien thing?"

"Don't know. Bother you?"

"Nope. Just asking. Let's go help the lady stop the ugly aliens."

Beams of light passed over their heads striking the large creatures as the Havenites launched their attack.

"Now!" Arthur said and he and Lancelot burst into a sprint. Shields of light materialized as they threw themselves into the air. Their sudden movement caught the Devalies off guard as they were focused on the unexpected attack by the Havenite weapons.

Turning his shield lengthwise, Arthur struck three of the Devalies at once driving two to their knees and knocking the third on his back. Rolling quickly to his feet he raised his shield just in time to prevent a Devalie sword from taking his head while simultaneously deflecting another to his face with Excalibur. He stopped the razor-sharp blade from taking his eyes but not before it cut a deep furrow across his cheek. The burning pain as it sliced through the flesh was excruciating. The pain stopped as light began to shine from within the wound. It closed.

The Devalies stepped back. One of them called out, "How can this be?" What are you?

"I am Arthur. Arthur Pendragon. First Dragon of the Alliance of Worlds." As he spoke his eyes started to glow. The light from Excalibur's blade crawled up his arm like a serpent. When it reached his shoulder a small bolt of lightning flashed, striking the dragon pendant on his chest. The red emblem seemed to move in the light and spit fire at the Devalies, the emerald green eye, focused, menacing. Taking advantage of their shock Arthur thrust his blade into the neck of the closest of his foes. The stricken Devalie reached for its throat as it dropped to the sand dissolving into a black goo that momentarily stained the beach. A dark mist rose into the still sky. Then it was gone.

Arthur backhanded one of the remaining Devalies with Excalibur while striking the other with a burst of power from his left hand. His blade removed the head of the first while the other simply was no more. It was over in seconds. A thick black fog drifted towards the water reviling Arthur standing in a crouch, Excalibur at the ready.

As Lancelot came down he drove his blade into the shoulder of Bael's bodyguard. Galantine cut smoothly through the Devalie. The lifeless body melted into the surface of the beach. Lancelot crouched at the ready facing Bael. Flicking the last of the dark goo from his blade he stared at the thing responsible for his sister's death.

Bael took a step back shocked at the ferocity of the attack.

Lancelot sneered, "Just you and me now." As he spoke he changed to his original form. His clothes fell from his body replaced with a flowing white robe.

"What are you?" Bael hissed.

"I am retribution. I am your death."

The Havenites fired over and again at the Makaran warriors and yet the large creatures continued to move inexorably towards them.

"This isn't working," Falstaff said. "Let me shoot them."

"Not yet," Kathleen said.

"But, Princess."

"Wait, Uncle. They may yet be saved."

The first of the Makarans fell to its knees and then onto its face. Kathleen and Millie sent bursts of energy at the Shadow that rose from the fallen body. It resisted their power and began to take shape. The featureless face turned to Falstaff's friend Bear and shot towards him. Loki jumped onto the man and wrapped his arms around him dragging them both to the sand. The Shadow writhed around them seeking an opening into the new host. Kathleen placed her hands onto the Shadow and focused. She felt the intense cold of the thing as it pulsated beneath her hands. A faint glow flowed from her fingers slowly into and around the Shadow. It arched its back, a terrible scream exploding from an unseen mouth. Kathleen stepped back as it burst into thousands of small crystals.

Bear looked into Loki's face with shock and then humor as the two seemed locked in a lover's embrace.

"Thank you, friend. But whatever the hell that thing was it's gone now, and you're not my type. I would appreciate it if you would get off."

Loki patted his cheek. "You don't know what you are missing."

The Makarans stopped fighting and turned to Bael as if seeking guidance. Locked in mortal combat with Lucifer he provided none. First one, then the others began to step back towards the grounded boat, their weapons remaining pointed at the Alliance warriors. When they reached the water they stopped.

"The sun has set," Kathleen whispered. She turned to the others. Form a circle. Loki, remain in the center and prepare to aid any that are attacked. Michael, I believe it is time you take your weapons off stun."

"And ours?" Falstaff asked.

"They are useless now, Uncle. Your bullets will not stop Shadows."

Bear picked up his fallen weapon. "I think I'll keep mine just the same. Makes me feel better."

The remaining Makarans fell as one to the ground like puppets whose strings had been cut. From each, a thick stream of black liquid flowed from what seemed every opening in their bodies. As the Shadows grew they solidified. The large featureless figures stood tall, massive seven-foot beasts. They looked down with their eyeless faces at the abandoned bodies. The Makarans sat up and crawled to their feet."

"Like Asgard," Falstaff said.

"You've faced these things before?" Bear asked.

"Once. And that was too many."

"Can we stop them?"

Falstaff looked at his new friend. "I don't know. Wish I had my ax."

"I'd settle for a flamethrower."

Kathleen looked at Millie. "Do you think you can help me make a shield? A big one. Like Arthur's."

"I've never tried."

"Neither have I but we can't beat these things. We need to protect the others until Arthur and Lancelot arrive."

"In time?" Millie asked.

"I hope so."

Lucifer parried a thrust by Bael and responded with a swift swing towards his face. Bael stepped back raising his shield and swiftly drove the edge like an ax at Lancelot's neck.

Raising his shield Lucifer laughed. "You think a trick like that will work with me? I am a true Knight of Camelot, beast. I am a master of the tournament. I fought with King Arthur and Merlin against men whose whole life was dedicated to the sword. I know the shield is as much a weapon as a blade."

Pushing with his shield while driving under it with his sword he added, "And I know how to use both."

Bael lowered his shield but not before Lucifer's steel had found purchase along his inner thigh. It was wet when he withdrew it.

Bael stepped back. It was the first time in his long life that he had felt fear. Raising his shield before him, Bael drove it down on Lucifer's glowing shield. Sparks flew. Black ice and red flames engulfed both and then the shields were gone.

Bael smiled. "And now I will finish this."

Arthur took a step forward.

"No, Arthur. He must be mine. For me, for Michael, and for Gwendolyn."

Arthur stopped, understanding his friend's need for closure. In his head, he heard two voices. Familiar. On calm. One near panic.

"Thank you."

"Arthur!"

He turned at Kathleen's call for help. A cold panic took hold as he saw ten Shadows and their prior hosts move relentlessly towards her and the others. He began to run terrified he would not be in time.

Kathleen held her hands in front of her forcing her will forward, trying to create a shield.

"Concentrate, Millie. Push."

Gabriel turned to his kin. "Stand close. Together we fire on one of the brown beasts at a time. If it falls, follow my lead and we will move to another. We must help."

"But will not the shield stop us?" Ariel asked.

"I do not know. We must step outside of it to be sure."

"On stun?" Ezekiel asked.

"No."

The Havenites stepped away from the growing shield of power. Raising their weapons they concentrated on the closest of the Makarans. As they did two Shadows jetted towards them.

"Can I shoot now?" Falstaff asked.

"I'm not sure you can penetrate their armor, Uncle."

"Won't know until we try. I need to do something." He looked around. "Anyone see Rex or Anubis?"

"Here," a strained voice called.

Anubis pushed his way into the circle while helping Rex walk. "Sorry." He pointed to his head. "Grazed, lost consciousness. When I woke you were gone. Started to make my way to the beach when I came upon Rex."

Rex hopped on one leg, Anubis helping him as he moved. "Bullet to my chest and one to my leg. Not sure, but I think the one that hit my chest stopped my heart for a moment. Strange dreams. Some man kept saying do it now, over and over. It was disconcerting. I couldn't walk. The one to my leg broke it just above the knee."

He looked at Kathleen and Millie.

"They are trying to hold a shield," Loki said. "We have a bunch of Shadows coming. Big ones. Knights. I may need your help keeping them off the others. One tried already."

"And them?" Rex asked indicating the Havenites.

"Targeting the Makarans."

Rex looked at Anubis. "Help me stand."

"Where?"

Rex smiled. "There." He said pointed at Kathleen. "I understand what the voice meant."

Seeing the Shadows about to strike the Havenites he screamed and threw his hands forward. Two, fine, thin beams of intense light struck the approaching Shadows. They stopped dead, dark crystals of ice dripping onto the ground from the fine holes that suddenly appeared in their bodies. The wounded Shadows stumbled back toward the waiting boat.

"They are talking," Kathleen said.

"I think they're scared," Millie added.

"Of us?" Loki asked.

"I don't know," Kathleen said. "I don't think so."

Another Makaran fell. The others stopped their attack and became still. Throwing down their weapons they moved back to the water, climbed onto the boat, and stood silently watching.

"What the hell are they waiting for?" MSG Swisher asked.

"Which ones?" Anubis asked. "And you are?"

"Name's Swisher. Friends call me Bear. Both I guess."

"I'm Anubis, Bear, and I would guess that the big guys just woke up and don't want any part of this. The Shadows I believe were caught off guard by the power of our newest Blocker."

"Not, new," Rex said. "Second oldest really. I wish Merlin could see me."

"He will, old buddy," Loki said.

Lucifer moved forward striking relentlessly with Galantine, the blade growing brighter with each blow. Bael stepped back, his arms and chest weeping dark blood from dozens of small wounds. He pushed and blocked as best he could unable to grab the initiative, always on the defense, never finding an opening. Growing weaker by the moment.

Raising his blade over his head, Bael rushed forward in a rage. He did not notice Lucifer suddenly kneel and he impaled himself on Galatine. Bael's sword disappeared. He looked down at the sword. Raising his eyes he stared at Lucifer, a look of surprise and terror etched on his face. Lucifer thrust the last few inches of Galatine into his foe. Bael fell to the ground. Lucifer pulled his sword free and watched as the Devalie melted into the sand.

"Lancelot!"

Hearing Millie's call he turned. "I am coming!"

"Wait," Arthur yelled.

The Shadows suddenly stopped. They turned their heads as if one being and looked across the beach to the trees. Ten ebony darts flew from the wood line ending their existence in a shower of black ice. A lone figure stepped from the shadows.

Arthur turned to Lucifer. "Satan is here."

CHAPTER THIRTY-FIVE

Satan stood at the edge of the trees, waiting.

Lucifer stepped up beside Arthur.

Arthur heard the others approaching. He held out his hand. "Stay, Do not move."

They stopped. Kathleen watching him while the others tried to see what it was he was looking at.

"What do you intend to do?" Lucifer asked.

"Speak with him, I guess."

Lucifer stood silent for a moment. He turned and looked at the others. Kathleen started to move and he shook his head. She stopped fear and understanding on her face.

"Do you wish me to accompany you?"

"No. I think it is better if I go alone. You two have a history. If he wants to talk I'd rather not tempt him. Or you for that matter."

"Beal is gone."

"But he served Satan at the time."

"He is formidable. Is this wise?"

"I doubt it." Arthur looked at Lucifer and smiled. "But what choice do I have? Pretty sure he is waiting for me. Besides, if he wanted us dead those darts would have struck us and not the Shadows."

"What do you wish me to do?"

"Go back to the others. Tell them what is going on. Do not let them approach. If things go bad, get them out of here."

"You can beat him."

"To be honest, I don't know. Six months ago I would have said absolutely not. Now, I just don't know. But don't take any chances. If it turns out he wants to fight, take everyone, and get to the portal. I will hold him off as long as I can."

"I would rather stay."

"I know you would but I need you to make sure the fight will continue in case things don't work out. And, Lucifer ..."

"Yes."

"Take care of Kathleen."

"As if she were my daughter."

Lucifer turned and walked towards the small group of warriors that had sworn to fight for Arthur until the end. As he did he changed, Lancelot once more.

"This is some crazy shit," Bear said.

Arthur griped Excalibur a little tighter.

"I love you, Kathleen."

"I know."

He started to walk towards the trees.

Kathleen waited for Lancelot.

"It is Satan. He must face him alone."

"I know," she said. "I heard."

Of course, she did. They are as one now.

"Then you understand why he must go alone."

"I do not like it, but I understand."

She has grown. So much like her mother.

"If it comes to a fight take the others. I shall remain here."

"No, Kathleen. I have given my word to serve you in case ..."

She placed her fingers along his cheek. "Would you have me abandon him?"

"But I promised."

"I shall wait. If he should fall." She hesitated. "I will return. You have my word. I just need to know."

He stared at her for a moment, understanding, and nodded.

"Lancelot." Millie stood beside him. She handed him his scabbard.

"Thank you."

"You are uninjured?"

"I am."

"I'm glad."

Kiss her you dumb, stuck up, twit!" Loki said. "You know you want to."

Lancelot lifted Millie and drew her to him. He kissed her long and passionately then gently put her down."

"That's better. Now, what is Arthur doing?" Loki asked.

"He is going to meet with Satan."

"What? No! Not alone."

Lancelot took Loki's arm. "You cannot help. He wants us to get the others, those that live and those that are injured, and prepare to retire to the portal. We will not be an asset to him now. He needs all his skill, all his power in case this is more than a mere meeting. If we involve ourselves it could distract him and that would certainly lead to his death."

Loki looked at him and then at Arthur walking along the beach towards the woods.

Bear looked at Lancelot. "All you guys change like that?"

"Nope, just the angels," Falstaff said.

MSG Swisher watched Arthur walk towards the lone figure at the edge of the trees. "Who's that?"

Loki placed his arm around Kathleen's shoulder. "Satan."

Arthur stopped and Satan stepped into the open and walked towards him. Seeing Excalibur in Arthur's hand he hesitated and looked at him quizzically. Arthur pushed the sword into the sand and took two steps forward.

"I am not here to fight, First Dragon."

"Then why are you here? Is this your doing"

Satan looked at the multitude of figures lying upon the beach. "Such a waste. No one benefits from this kind of butchery."

"This is not something you would enjoy?"

He looked at Arthur. "The essence of those that have fallen is gone, wasted. They do not live, we do not feed. Wholesale slaughter serves neither of us, Blocker. To cull the heard is one thing. This is wasteful."

"Why are you here? And why stop the Shadows? They might have killed me."

"I am not so sure that is true anymore. And I told you this was not my doing. We have a truce and we have a common enemy. It is that enemy who is responsible for this incident. An enemy that disrupts the order of things.

They must be put right. When they are we shall meet again." He smiled. "And when it is time for you to die. It will be by my hand."

"Bael is dead. Isn't it over?"

"It is not. Bael was but a puppet. A power-hungry fool. He believed he was the master but the true master has departed."

"Cain?"

"Not Cain but that which lies within him. And she they serve."

"And who is that?"

"Cipactli." She who claimed alliance." He looked once again at the body littered beach. "But wants only to conquer." He looked up. "We shall meet again in two of your moons, First Dragon. On the day your kind calls All Hallows Eve. I will expect your answer then."

"And if our problem has not been resolved?"

"You will know."

"And until then?"

"Until then, young Blocker, none of my kind will enter this domain. Those that followed Bael will be hunted down and disposed of. But understand this. If you decide not to accept my offer ..." He pointed to the bodies that littered the sand. "This will be as nothing to what will come. I will take the essence of every living creature upon this planet. I will leave it a barren ball of dirt and water."

He turned and walked back into the shadows of the trees.

Arthur watched and waited until he was sure Satan was gone, felt for the presence of Shadow, then turned, recovered Excalibur, and walked towards his oath-sworn, his friends, and his future.

Kathleen rushed forward and wrapped her arms around him. Arthur kissed her forehead. "I'm fine." He looked at the bodies that littered the blood-soaked sand as they joined the others.

"Do we know how many?"

Anubis reviewed a paper that had just been given to him. "Of the enemy, an estimate of more than four hundred, including those in the warehouse. It is not a complete list. We are still searching."

"Prisoners?"

"Just those you knocked down. There are fifty-seven and they are still, uh, asleep?"

"Did any escape?"

"None," Loki said.

"Our losses?"

"We are still looking. Many fell in the woods. There are wounded. Broken bones and internal injuries. Our armor stopped most of the bullets but there was ballistic damage. And there is no armor on the head. We have causalities."

Arthur took a deep breath. "Please let me know their names. If they had families."

"I will."

Arthur looked up when Bill Spinelli came forward. The look on his face told him where their greatest losses occurred. "How bad is it, Bill?"

"The HRT was lucky. If you want to call it that. Three dead and nine wounded. The Sheriff's people a little worse, seven dead and eleven wounded. Some of those may not make it. The Army guys were hit hard. Fourteen dead and nine badly wounded. Those are some brave sons-a-bitches. Rushed in and pulled a lot of my guys to safety after they were hit. Cost them. The grenades got five. Another six badly wounded. Dunbar is dead."

MSG Swisher looked at Arthur. "With your permission, sir, I would like to check on the guys."

"Of course. Let me know if you need anything."

Falstaff placed his hand on the big sergeant's shoulder. "I'll go with you." He looked at Arthur for approval.

"Get them ready for transport, Falstaff. Have the Alliance medics do what they can." He looked at Michael. "Tell everyone to get the wounded ready to be moved. Take them to the portal. I want them, all of them, taken to Alliance hospitals." He turned to Ariel. "Ask Remiel if he can help with the worse cases. Take them to Haven if he has to. We are one people now. We share all."

"What about those that are not injured?" Loki asked.

"They go too. I do not want anyone involved in today's action on this planet by morning. Those from Earth are all to be taken to Avalon. See if they have families. Make arrangements for them as well. I want no one that can be hurt by Cain left on this world."

"The dead?" Anubis asked.

"Ours go home or to Avalon for now. The others need to be disposed of. Completely. This place needs to look like nothing happened here. Have Michael and his people use their weapons. And Anubis,"

"Yes, First Dragon?"

"Destroy everything. The building, the dock, everything. I want no trace of this place to remain. I want it clean. Like it was never here."

"I understand. It shall be done."

A bloodied warrior rushed up to Anubis and took his arm.

"What is it?"

Fighting for his breath he blurted out, "The Pharaoh is dying. Ra is dying."

Grabbing him by the shoulders Anubis demanded, 'What do you mean he's dying."

"He has been shot. He lies close to death. He sent me to find you and the First Dragon. We must hurry."

"Take us," Arthur said.

As they neared the tree where Ra lay propped up, the warriors of Duat stepped aside allowing them to approach.

Ra looked up and smiled when he saw them, a bloody bandage around his middle.

"What happened?" Arthur asked.

"Somehow a bullet pierced my armor." He tried to laugh but it started a coughing fit. Ra wiped the blood from his lips. "I think I should fire the armorer."

Arthur leaned down and examined the wound. He looked up at Lancelot. "It's a dart. That's how it got through."

Anubis looked at him. "A dart. There were no Shadows or Devalies this deep into the forest. They were all on the beach."

"None that we knew of, "Arthur said. "They knew we were coming. Lancelot, you, Kathleen, and Millie check for the presence of Shadow. Check the warriors of Duat. Check the dead. Make sure they remain that way. This is the work of a knight."

"I'll go with them," Loki said. "In case I'm needed."

Arthur nodded. He turned back to Ra. "Sir, I am going to check for the presence of Shadow in the wound. You will need to trust me. If there is I need to remove it or you will die."

Ra looked up at him. "Young man, there is no man I trust more. Do what you have to do." He smiled. "But remember, if I die my wife is going to kill me."

Arthur lay his hand on Ra's head and he lost consciousness. Several warriors stepped forward and Anubis yelled, "Stand back!"

"He is simply asleep," Arthur said gently. I will not harm him. Laying his hand on Ra's face he closed his eyes. He felt himself drift and then he was one with the Pharaoh of Duat. He moved as quickly as he could until he found what he was looking for. The Shadow of the shard moved along the inner wall of an artery. Its goal Arthur knew was the heart.

This is what Yeshem meant. It is seeking nourishment. Not the beasts we face. The Shadows. The dart is a Ghass. Raw, unchanged.

Arthur placed his will in front of the thing, doing what he could to make it understand he did not want to hurt it, but that it must stop. But he quickly discovered there was no reasoning with the thing. He felt nothing but raw aggression and hunger. A hunger for Ra. For what Ra was. A powerful soul. Arthur generated a ball of light and the thing was gone.

He opened his eyes. "Take Ra to Ariel. Tell her he is to be taken to Haven."

Anubis nodded.

A man rushed from the woods, a large curved knife raised above his head, missing an eye and a part of the skull. A dark cloud covered the head wound. Four feet from Arthur he fell to his knees, struck by four intense jets of light. Dozens of leaves fell from nearby trees as they were peppered with a maelstrom of black hail.

Arthur looked at Lancelot. "Call ahead. No one goes into the portal until we are there. Or to Haven. We have been infiltrated."

He was about to say something else when he collapsed. The last thing he heard was a voice in his head.

"*Rest now. You have more to do.*"

CHAPTER THIRTY-SIX

"Would you like me to refresh your tea, First Dragon?"

"No thank you, Iona. And please, call me Art."

"Arthur," Kathleen chimed in.

"I shall remember."

"I will never get used to the house talking to me," Paul said.

"Iona is more than just an artificial intelligence," Kathleen said. "She is family."

"Thank you, Kathleen."

"You are welcome, Iona."

Family. A word that brought images of peace, safety, and comfort, Arthur thought as he looked around the table. His family. Whisked from Ohio to Merlin's apartment to keep them safe. He looked down at the dog lying at his feet. Even Sampson is here. He looked at Kathleen. Yes, my family.

"How are you feeling, Art?"

"Better, Mom, thanks. Just thinking. I'm okay, honest. I don't know what happened back there. It was like someone pulled a plug from my heel and all the energy in my body just poured out. I've never felt so weak in my life."

"I was surprised you could stand at all," Kathleen said. "Remember what happened when you faced Satan the first time. You expended a lot more energy this time. You need to be more careful. Let the other Blockers help you. Why else do you think we have been gifted the power. Don't try to do everything yourself."

"You did help. And it was amazing. Your powers have grown. And Rex, I'm happy for him. But you're right. Next time I'll let you take care of Satan."

Kathleen stared at him, crossed her arms, and focused on the others.

Paul cleared his throat. "I understand they found no more Shadows. They did find the body of a disciple in the woods where the warriors from Duat had assembled. Lancelot thinks it was the one that attacked Ra. He must have been killed by one of the warriors from Duat."

"And played dead until I arrived," Arthur said. "I think he wounded Ra instead of killing him knowing I would come. Lancelot is pretty sure I was the target. That's one of the reasons we brought everyone here. Killing or kidnapping someone I care about could draw me into another assassination attempt."

"Satan has never done anything like that before. He's kind of upfront on his killings," Loki said. "Never made it personal."

"It wasn't Satan that set this up."

"Then who? Bael?"

"I don't think so."

"And the Makarans that were possessed?" Charlotte asked. "What happened to them?"

"I spoke to them. They were a little confused. Did not know where they were or how they would get home. I mentioned Yeshem's name and suddenly we were all friends. It seems he is important to them. They are with him now on Olympus."

"How is Ra?" Charlotte asked.

"He is going to be okay according to Anubis. He lost a lot of blood but Remiel was able to help," Kathleen said. "He didn't need to take him to Haven."

"He should set up shop here."

"Not a bad idea, Dad. We wouldn't need to risk our seriously wounded taken to Haven. I'll talk to him about it."

"What about the Shadow that struck him? Did it cause any permanent harm?" Paul asked. "I know that once possessed most hosts go mad."

"It didn't possess him. It was trying to feed on him. There was no real intelligence in the thing. It didn't think, it just acted. But I've never felt such aggression from a being before. Even by the Shadow's that were trying to kill me."

"That is because the Shadow's we face are a mutated form of the original."

Sampson looked up at Merlin standing in the doorway but refused to move from Arthur's feet.

"Father!" Kathleen ran and wrapped her arms around him. "You're okay."

Chuckling he hugged her. "I am. I could spend a lifetime studying the technology on Haven and never see it all. Remiel is a wonder."

"It is good to have you back, Merlin," Arthur said. "You have been sorely missed by even those of us that are not presently draped around you."

Kathleen let him go and looked him up and down. "You are sure you are well enough to be back."

"Don't worry, Kathleen," Patricia said stepping into the room and taking her father's arm. "He is his old self. I promise."

"And the others?" Arthur asked.

"Thor and Sif are almost ready to leave the reconstitution beds Remiel has had them attached to. Amazing things. They remove damaged tissue and replace it with new live tissue grown from the host."

"Painful?" Paul asked. "I understand that severe burns are excruciating."

"No pain at all. I believe there is something in the debridement process that dulls the pain. They are both alert and in good spirits."

"And Hercules?" Arthur asked.

"He will survive."

"I don't understand. Will he get better?"

"Remiel is unsure about the extent of his recovery. Hercules should never have left the hospital."

"So many lost," Paul said.

"Zeus, Icarus, Poseidon ..."

Arthur was cut off when Loki came bounding into the room. "They found him! He's alive."

"Who's alive?" Arthur asked.

"Poseidon. The search boats found him. Several of his crew as well."

"That's great news," Paul said. He turned to Arthur. "I have not heard much about the battle on the lake. How bad was it?"

"I don't have all the details yet. I know that all the enemy boats were destroyed as were Poseidon's flagship and two of his fast boats."

"Enemy survivors?" Charlotte asked. "It would be nice to speak with one. Well, I think Freya would like to. The ones you knocked out have not come to yet."

Arthur smiled. "Sorry. And I'm not sure. I sent word not to allow any onboard our vessels until one of the Blockers insured there are no Shadows."

"How the hell are they doing that?" Loki asked.

"Rubber boats and fishing nets. Once a survivor is located, they are netted and dragged to a rubber dinghy where they are pulled aboard using grappling hooks. The dinghies are then towed behind the fast boats, their catch well contained, without anyone coming close to a potential Shadow. Lancelot and Millie meet them at the dock. Those that are clean will be transported to Asgard."

"That is why I am here. Mother wants me to make sure they are taken to her. I almost feel sorry for them. She is not in a good mood."

"That's the plan. Lancelot is to make sure they are delivered to Asgard."

"Thanks, Arthur." He walked over and scratched Sampson behind the ears. "My father asked me to bring him with me. He wants to speak with you. Mother would not allow it. He would like you to stop by the hospital when you can.

"I will."

Smiling when Sampson licked his hand he ruffled the small dog's neck. "Where has your friend been?"

"With Becky. He will stay with her until we get settled into our new place," Charlotte said.

"New place?" Arthur asked.

'We have decided to stay here. Freya wanted us in Asgard but I think you will be spending more time here. I hope that is okay. You father and discussed it and decided there was nothing for us on Earth anymore."

"I'm glad. What about Aunt Janie?"

"We sent her a letter saying we are touring Europe."

"She bought that?"

"You know how she is. Aware we exist but not overly concerned with being involved in our lives."

Loki picked up the list of prisoners Arthur had been reviewing. "What about them?"

"I'm not sure they know much," Arthur said. "Based on the ones we have dealt with before."

"Whatever it is, we will soon know. Mother is very good at attaining information. What are we going to do with them when she is done?"

"I understand from Anubis there is a lot of open land on Duat. He suggested they go there. They will become farmers. Under strict supervision, of course."

"They will become slaves?" Charlotte asked.

"No one in the Alliance keeps slaves," Loki said. "They will be as free as any citizen of Duat. Each will be given land and the means to work it. But they will never return home and they will be watched. If they start to preach their hatred, additional steps will be taken."

"And their families?" Charlotte asked.

"Will assume they have been abandoned. I would guess that most of them will be better off."

"I see.

"I have been speaking with Yeshem," Arthur said thinking it best to change the subject. He thinks he knows where Apollo and Randy are being kept, and although he believes any rescue attempt is doomed to failure, he is willing to help in any way he can."

"Can we trust him?" Loki asked.

"It's funny, but when you can see one's thoughts it is hard for them to lie. Yes, I trust him. Besides, he intends to speak with the leaders of his world about joining the Alliance."

"Well, having a few of the big guys on our side isn't going to hurt, I suppose," Loki said. "Think he can do it?"

"It seems that Yeshem is a somewhat influential individual on his world. That is why the others of his kind were so easily swayed to our side."

"How influential?" Charlotte asked.

"He is a prince."

"Anything he and his folks can do to help us?" Paul asked.

"Actually, quite a lot. He is a treasure trove of information about the Shadows and the Devalies. And like the Havenites, he has spaceships. Ones that can travel where they have never been. And he knows where Ot is."

"It's a shame no one can talk to him but you," Loki said.

"I'm working on that. Freya has a lot of questions but at the moment I am the only translator. Kathleen can hear him but not respond so she can't ask any of the questions Freya has. At least not yet. I am going to check with Lancelot. I think he might be able to."

"You mean since the upgrade," Loki said.

"Since that, yes. A lot of us changed on the beach."

Kathleen took his hand knowing how worried he was about what Yeshem had said about him not being as the others.

"You sure as hell ramped up," Loki said looking at Arthur. "Do you have any idea how much power you now control? Or what you can do with it?"

"I don't. I know something has changed within me but I don't know what it is. Or how to control it. What happened in the alley and on the beach just — happened. I knew I could do it at the time. It frightens me. I was unable to hurt people before. Now, well, I held back on the beach."

"Held back?" Loki asked a bit astonished.

'I knew I could have killed them all."

"But you didn't," Kathleen said. "Because that is not who you are."

"Is it?"

"It seems there is much I have missed," Merlin said. "Patricia has told me of the battle on the beach." He looked at her. "Where she should not have been. But her details were a bit sketchy when it came to what you did. You will need to tell me about this new power of yours, Arthur." He looked at Kathleen. "And yours."

"Later. I promise. For now, I want to tell you what else Yeshem told me. As I said, he thinks he knows where Randy and Apollo are. And he thinks he knows a way to get to them. It will be dangerous but he is willing to help.

"By the way, Merlin, have you spoken with Rex?"

"No."

"You need to. He has something to tell you."

"As do you, Arthur. I have been told about Galantine and Excalibur. I am not responsible for their power."

"I know."

"So, what happened?"

"Not sure. Magic maybe?"

Arthur and Kathleen walked across the plaza on their way to the Emery's conference room. Lancelot, Loki, and Falstaff walked on either side and behind them. All armed with swords. He could see the others mingling with the people going about their daily routines. Watching them.

"I don't think all this security is necessary. We know the Shadows can't get here without going through a portal. And both are secured. Besides, we can feel the presence of a Shadow before it can strike."

"But not a disciple, little brother. And it is they that have tried on more than one occasion to kill you. We will remain close. Get used to it."

"And when we are married?" Kathleen asked.

Loki laughed. "You will not even know we are there."

"That's because you won't be," Arthur said.

Loki laughed.

Lancelot was waiting when they reached the steps to the building. "Everyone is present, First Dragon."

"And my special guest?"

"Is waiting in Merlin's office. Patricia and Millie are with him. Millie can now understand him."

"Can she speak to him?"

"Not yet."

"And you?"

"A little."

"Good. Have Gabriel go to them and wait for my signal."

Falstaff nodded and slipped away from the group as they mounted the steps. Once inside the main hall the remainder of the oath-sworn stepped forward and led them to the conference room. Apollo opened the door and announced, "The First Dragon."

It was a large room. And it was crowded. Those sitting around the single long table rose as he entered. Hera, Freya, and even King Alfred who rose unsteadily while balancing on one leg. The chair at the head of the table was empty and he stepped behind it, placing his hands on the backrest. "Please be seated."

Bill Spinelli stood near the far end of the table next to a soldier wearing the eagles of a full colonel. The Sheriff himself stood beside Bill, obviously uncomfortable.

"I know you are all busy and I thank you for coming. I would not have asked you here if it was not of grave importance to us all."

He looked at the Sheriff and the colonel. "I know some of you from Earth are here for the first time. Thank you for coming and welcome to Avalon.

"The battle at the beach was hard-fought and hard-won. I am proud of all that were there and am deeply saddened by those we have lost." He stopped. "Somehow the enemy knew we were coming. They were waiting. If it were not for the skill and courage of our warriors this could have proven to be a disaster."

He started to stroll around the table. "So how did they know? I don't think they had agents on your homeworlds. Most likely they had people watching us on Earth. Cain has recruited many."

Stopping behind Bill's chair he continued. "Warriors from Earth have joined us in our fight and taken their rightful place within the Alliance. Their warriors have fought and died beside us. They did so with commitment and courage. It is only a select few that represent their world at the moment but their numbers will grow. Their wounded are in our hospitals and the others are recuperating in our cities. The existence of our worlds is no longer a secret."

Our worlds, Merlin thought. *He has indeed grown.*

"For centuries the people of the Alliance have kept the existence of the Shadows and this war quiet. The people of Earth were not ready to understand the nature of the enemy. I believe that has changed."

Arthur nodded to Lancelot who opened the door and signaled Falstaff.

"Our enemy becomes more complicated the more we learn about him. We believed the enemy was the Shadows. Then disciples infiltrated our ranks. The Devalies themselves increased their attacks in an attempt to seize a portal. We never understood why they needed one when they were able to open doors to Earth. Why it was so important for them to reach the other worlds? Or what prevented them from doing so.

"After consulting with the chief scientist of Haven, I now believe it is because their doors can only operate through space and not from one dimension to another. As for why they are trying to come here, we believe they need additional feeding grounds. With their ability to travel through space, access to the other dimensions would open up new galaxies with countless planets where they could feed. It is why we can never allow them to cross.

"The truce with Satan continues. I met with him. He claims we have a common enemy. That Cain is an agent of this enemy. And he is not a Shadow or Devalie. I believe him.

"Until what we call All Hallows Eve on Earth, Satan has sworn he will honor the truce while he tracks down this enemy. I intend to take advantage of the truce."

He nodded and Millie led Yeshem into the room.

"Oh shit," the Colonel whispered a little too loudly.

"This is Yeshem. He is a Prince from a planet called Makaran that orbits a star in another Galaxy."

The Havenites entered the room. They had resumed their true forms.

The colonel looked at Spinelli who smiled and shrugged his shoulders. "It gets better, wait."

"Our friends from Haven have discovered that Makaran is within their galaxy. Yeshem has confirmed that the Shadows and the Devalies are from there as well. He knows where both planets are and believes he knows where our people are being held. I intend to raid that planet and free them."

CHAPTER THIRTY-SEVEN

"First Dragon — Arthur." King Alfred leaned back in his chair shifting his injured leg. "No one in the Alliance is capable of travel to another galaxy. We have just begun to explore the space within our own solar systems. How do you propose we get there? Can their ships reach us?"

"No, they cannot. So we will do it the same way the Devalies and the Havenites do. We use a window. One that folds space allowing almost instant travel between galaxies."

"From where would we open this door? And where would it take us?" Alfred asked.

"We would open it on Earth and take a team to Haven. From there we open another and take it to Makaran. Yeshem's people have spacecraft that we can use to reach Shree, the home of the Shadows. They have been there before. That is where Yeshem believes we will find our friends. It is where the Devalies keep their test subjects."

"Test subjects?" The colonel with Spinelli asked.

"According to Yeshem the Devalies take beings from different worlds and experiment on them. Their goal is to find a way to possess an unwilling host while keeping them alive and sane."

"Not very successful are they?" Loki said.

"That's barbaric!"

"I agree, Colonel ..., I'm sorry, we have not been introduced."

He stood. "Colonel William Shrift. I command the Group that provided the teams attached to, hell, I don't know, you? My orders were to provide people to the FBI for a classified mission, something called Operation First Dragon. Earlier today I got another call from the SECDEF himself telling me to accompany agent Spinelli to a highly classified meeting." He smiled. "I defiantly did not expect this."

Arthur laughed. "I'm sure you didn't. And I am sorry for your loss."

"Thank you. They were good men." He hesitated. "I wasn't given much of a brief on what is going on." He looked around the room. "Like nothing at all, but my orders were clear. A POTUS directive attaching my command to provide whatever assistance is needed for this project. That means until I am told otherwise, I work for you."

Bill shrugged his shoulders. "After I briefed the Director he called the President and filled him in. Took some convincing but he finally agreed to help."

"I'll bet that was an interesting conversation," Loki said.

'The picture of Yeshem helped."

Shrift looked around the room. "So let me get this straight. We are at war. The people in this room have been fighting monsters and devils to keep my planet safe for centuries without anyone knowing."

"Not many, true," Arthur said.

"And now we are finally going to be allowed to know what is going on and help."

"Something like that."

And the man in charge of this Alliance of Worlds is you, a young man barely out of his teens with a magic power that kills demons. One given to him by who...God? Not to mention I'm sitting here with Lancelot, Ra, and Hera."

"That about sums it up," Loki said. "Oh, King Arthur is one of the oath-sworn of the First Dragon. He couldn't be here today. He broke his leg in the last encounter with the Devalies."

The Colonel looked at Loki. "And you are?"

"I am Loki, brother of Thor and son of Odin."

"Of course you are." He laughed. "Why not, it makes about as much sense as anything else today."

"You are in Camelot, Colonel," Arthur said. "On the planet Avalon. Which, like Asgard, Olympus, and Duat, lie in parallel universes with Earth."

"That portal thing crosses dimensions?"

"And sometimes time," Loki added with a smile.

"Don't confuse the man, Loki," Freya said.

"Yes, mother."

Colonel Shrift looked at Freya. "Too late, ma'am."

Arthur smiled when Shrift shook his head, pleased and amused that he seemed to accept everything he was being told.

"Do the Russians know?"

"Not at the moment. The enemy activity has been restricted to the Ohio area. We don't know why yet. There are some theories, but nothing concrete. We have seen no crossings in Europe or Asia for centuries. Until that changes, we thought it best to keep things quiet."

"Probably a good idea. This is some crazy shit" He looked at Freya. "Sorry, Ma'am. "I mean demons invading America. I can imagine the diplomatic issues that could cause.

"So it's just us. What the hell. 10th always gets the crazy missions while the other Groups get the simple blow things up ops. God, wait until I tell my deputy that I attended a meeting today in another dimension with Merlin and Loki."

"Should be fun," Bill said slapping him on the shoulder. "You might want to mention the aliens also. He's not going to believe you anyway."

"True enough." He looked at the Havenites and Yeshem. "A picture might help. Would be fun to see his face when I show him." He looked up at Arthur. "A truly interesting day, young man. Gods, legends, aliens, shapeshifts and of course the Devil himself and his demons. Just another day in the Forces."

"Are you all right, Colonel?" Arthur asked.

"Are you kidding, I'm having a ball. But two things are bothering me."

"What's that, sir?"

"Have they ever invaded one of these other worlds?"

"At this time they are unable to cross to our dimensions without using one of the portals. They have tried. We have stopped them. And your other question," Freya asked."

"Why don't these Devalies use guns? From the briefing I received from my soldiers, they used magic swords that grew out of their arms while only the humans with them used guns. If they are so advanced that they can use wormholes to travel across galaxy's I would expect them to have ray guns or something."

Merlin rose. "They are powerful beings, Colonel. With abilities similar to the Blockers, but they have never used firearms. Even Shadows seem to need to possess one to use a gun. The true reason for this is unknown."

"I believe something or someone is providing them the technology they use to get to Earth," Arthur said. "It is not theirs. Yeshem's people have never seen a Devalie use spacecraft. They always arrive through a doorway." He looked at Yeshem. "When they come to harvest his people.

"Harvest them?"

"They are possessed by Shadows and used as warriors."

Shrift looked at Yeshem. "I am sorry for what is happening to your people."

Arthur translated and Yeshem tilted his head in thanks.

"Satan told me we had a common enemy. When I asked if it was Cain he said no. It was what lies within him."

"Did he say what it was?" Ra asked.

"No. Just a name, Cipactli. He said that he served someone else. He didn't say who."

Hera stood. "This news is disconcerting, First Dragon. It might be prudent to wait for the rescue attempt until we know better what we face."

"I agree, Arthur," King Alfred said attempting to stand.

"Please remain seated, Sire. You need to stay off that leg," Gawain said.

"Why not use one of the doorways?" The Sheriff asked. "Wouldn't that be quicker and safer?"

"A window through space requires that you know where you are going or you could end up stepping into the bottom of an ocean or the middle of a star," Ariel said.

"Then how did the Havenites find Earth the first time?" Freya asked.

"I was told where we were to go," Lancelot said. "I opened it."

"By whom?"

"I do not know."

Arthur looked at him.

"Is it possible there are Devalies and Shadows on other planets within our dimensions?" Alfred asked.

"Possibly," Ariel said. "But I do not think so. If that was the case I believe you would have had contact by now."

"But you can travel here?" Hera said. "To our worlds, our dimensions."

"We were not able to do so until we were first brought here by a portal."

"And they have been here. So there is a chance in the future that they could open a doorway here," Hera said.

"That is possible," Ariel agreed. "But I think it unlikely. If what I have heard is true, no Shadow or Devalie has ever returned to Earth after coming here."

"I believe we should try for the rescue," Michael said. "Among other things, it will allow us to mark the location of the planet for future reference. It would allow us to travel there using our space window. But I do not agree you should accompany us on the raid Arthur. Yeshem and a few Havenites will be more prudent. If we are discovered the Devalies may not associate us with the Alliance."

"But ..."

"He is right, Arthur," Freya said. "We should not let them know the Alliance is aware of their home. Or that we could reach it. A surprise to be saved for a later time. And you are needed here."

"Your forms would give you away. That you do not belong in our galaxy," Ariel said.

Kathleen took Arthur's hand. "I understand you wish to save your friends but Freya is right. You are not just a warrior, you are First Dragon and your responsibility is to us all."

Although it hurt, Arthur knew they were right. "Okay. When can you go?"

"This afternoon," Ariel said. "Yeshem and I have already worked out the details."

"How long will it take?"

"Yeshem says it will take a day to get there from Makaran."

Lancelot turned to Arthur. "I will need to accompany them. To translate."

"And you can speak to him."

"I understand him and he understands me. We communicate. And more importantly, I will be able to defend the others from Shadows. I am the logical choice."

Millie took his hand. He looked down at her. "You will wait with the others. I will be back. This I promise."

With a tear working its way down her cheek she smiled. "I know."

"Who will you take with you?" Arthur asked Michael.

"Lucifer and Ariel as well as Yeshem. Fewer to risk and we will need room on the ship for the return. If any of Yeshem's people are there we will do what we can to free them as well."

"Be careful."

"As always, my friend."

Kathleen took Arthur's hand and pulled him aside as the meeting broke up.

"We need to talk."

Walking to a corner he took hold of her shoulders. "Is something wrong?"

"Yes, well, not really. It's just that for the first time since I met you we are not fighting someone. Two full months before you have to give Satan your answer."

"Unless we have more trouble from Cain's people."

"Let the locals take care of that. Bill and Colonel Shrift. Now that they know what to look for they can handle the disciples. If Shadows appear they can send for one of us. Or use one of the other three Blockers"

"What's this all about?"

She looked down.

"Kathleen, what's wrong?"

She looked at him tears marking her face. "You have almost died more times than I can count. As have I."

"I'm sorry. I can't help what has happened."

"But you can do something about what will happen."

"Like what?"

"I want to get married."

He kissed her on the forehead. "So do I. That's why I proposed."

"I want to get married now. I don't know what tomorrow holds for us. Whatever it is I want to face it with my husband."

He smiled. "Two weeks okay? My mother will need time to plan."

She stepped onto her toes and kissed him. "I love you."

CHAPTER THIRTY-EIGHT

The four members of the rescue team stepped through the doorway into a dimly lit room. Ariel waved her hand, the lights came on and the doorway folded into itself and disappeared.

"This is my home and my lab," she explained. "Excuse the dust. It has been empty since I joined the others on Olympus. Remiel's lab is quite a distance from here. On the other side of the city."

"I have been gone for a long time." Lucifer looked out a large window overlooking the city. "Much has changed."

"It has been but years for you Lucifer, but it has been centuries for the rest of us."

"I do not remember a city near your home."

Stepping next to him she placed her arm around his shoulder. "It was not here when you left. About five hundred years ago litiniam was discovered in the mountains across the river. It is an important element in the development of our spacecraft. The city grew around the need to support the miners."

He turned to Michael. "Do you remember this?"

"Yes. I was here most of the time you were gone. It was long after the first battle that we discovered the intelligence within Excalibur. Although crude, we knew it did not belong in that time, on that world. It had to have been created by someone from one of the other dimensions. That someone felt it was necessary to introduce advanced tech to fight Shadows. We had wished for a long time to help but were always concerned our appearance might create some ... confusion."

"You would probably have been burned at the stake," Lucifer chuckled.

"Our concern as well. So we saw this as an opportunity. We decided that Ariel should merge my thoughts to the artificial brain in the sword. I tried to link with the Pendragon but he never heard me. Nor did Merlin. When Pendragon was struck down I returned home. I remained here until the day

Arthur touched the sword. I felt him somehow. It was like a voice told me to return.

"Ariel placed me in the chamber and I was linked immediately. I was surprised to find myself in another dimension. We had never crossed before. I assumed it was the sword. We had no idea you had accompanied Merlin to Avalon. It must have opened a pathway. We thought you dead."

"You never went home?"

"When Gwendolyn died I had no desire to go back so I stayed here. When I was not in status I worked with Ariel."

"And Gwendolyn's family. My family? Our family?" Lucifer asked.

"I did not want to try to explain how she died. I couldn't stay, didn't want to really. Too many memories. She and you."

"And they would not have understood our longevity," Ariel said.

Michael leaned against the wall next to Lucifer. "Gwendolyn was the only one that knew of our difference. When we were wed I told her everything. I even explained that you were not her real brother, that you found her abandoned and raised her. She didn't care. You were like a father to her. Decided not to tell you she knew. She loved you. If I hadn't had her in the lab the day we went to the hill she would not have died. I did not realize she would follow us. It was my fault."

"It was the beast that killed her," Ariel said. "Not you, brother."

"Over time we changed our names claiming to be relatives that inherited the places where we lived and worked," Ariel continued. "We moved a lot making sure we did not run into people we might know.

"Remiel grew tired of the subterfuge and moved far from the city. He had married several times over the years and could not suffer the loss of his loved ones as they aged anymore."

Lucifer looked at Ariel. "And you?"

"The rest of us enjoyed friends but never allowed ourselves the pain of a long time relationship. I suppose we learned from Remiel. Eventually, I retired to my lab."

"You must have been very lonely."

The three turned and stared at Yeshem. He smiled.

"I am as surprised as you that I understand your words."

"How?" Lucifer asked.

Ariel chuckled. "I believe that the one that gave you the power of the Blocker, and that sword, and steered us to Earth, is not yet done with us. As we all understand each other on the other worlds, we can here."

"But why could I not make myself understood there except to those with the power?"

Ariel's eyebrows deepened. "Maybe it is because you were a newcomer to their galaxy. Or maybe it is because we are all in the same dimension in this galaxy. I don't know. But it will make our job easier."

Lucifer turned his head as he heard a woman's voice.

"As it is meant to do."

Noticing the expression on his face Ariel asked, "Are you all right?"

Michael stared at him. "You look like Arthur when he hears the voice."

Hesitating for a moment he nodded. "I am well. I do not think it is the same."

"Thank you, my lady."

"You are welcome, my knight. And I am not him. We shall speak again."

"How do we go about getting to your world," Lucifer asked Yeshem not wishing to share what happened with the others."

I never asked Arthur about the voice. Why he always referred to it as male. Interesting.

Ariel waved her hand over the window and it changed into a dark wall covered by a star chart. "Can you show me where your world is, Yeshem?"

He stared at the chart and walked to the far right of the room. "I recognize these stars but they are on the outskirts of the space we have mapped."

Ariel waved her hand again and the area he had indicated swelled and became clearer. "We have sent probes to this area allowing us to map most of it. We did not identify any habitable worlds, however. Strange. I would think we would have picked up life signs on your world."

"Is there any way they could be masked?" Michael asked.

"I suppose it is possible. But who would want to do so and why?"

"Questions for a later time," Lucifer said.

"Maybe," Michael whispered.

"Here," Yeshem pointed to a spot on the chart. "And this is Shree, the home of the Ghass."

"I cannot open a door there but with your help, I should be able to do so on your world." Ariel studied the numbers flowing across the chart. "Let us see about locating a safe place on your world. Can you use your star coordinates on this map? I have equipment that can convert your identifiers to ours. You will have to give me an idea where best we should open the door. I'd rather not drown."

Yeshem gave what the others assumed was a chuckle. It sounded somewhere between the purr and the angry growl of a large cat."Little chance of that. The only water on Markaran is underground."

Lucifer looked at the pinpoints of light. "You are sure you can do this?"

"It will take a little time, but I think so."

"What can I do to help?" Michael asked. "Arthur is depending on us." He turned to Lancelot. "And Millie is expecting you home safe."

Ariel walked to a panel of computers. "You need to record all Yeshem can remember of the area he wishes us to use."

Several hours later Ariel stood and stretched her back. "I am ready to test the door." She walked to a cabinet and removed a small box. "I will send my little friend through and see what lies on the other side."

She opened a dark door on the window and held the box in front of her. Dropping her hand the box hovered momentarily then jolted through the opening. After just a few minutes it returned and gently settled on her palm. The door closed.

"Let us see what my friend recorded." She pressed a series of buttons on the surface of the box. A desolate area of brown rock and sand appeared on the window. She rotated her hand and the view changed reveling a large number of buildings and an airfield containing several tube-like craft a short distance away.

"That is Nesheti. A major spaceport and home of many thinkers. It is where I live. Or where I lived before I volunteered to be harvested."

"You volunteered to allow the Devalies to take you? To be possessed?" Michael asked.

"Of course. It is my duty. I can resist occupation. We of the thinking class often allow ourselves to be taken so we may gather information about the actions of the Devalies. They always return our people so they may use them again. We have been collecting information this way for many generations.

It is our hope to someday use this knowledge to destroy the Devalies. This is why I know where the friends of First Dragon will be held."

"This is where we need to go?" Ariel asked.

"It is. We can get a ship in the city. We will not need a crew. I can fly."

"They are just going to let you have a ship? And what about us?" Lucifer asked.

"I am a prince. There will be no issue with me using a craft. They all belong to my circle. As for you ... we get many visitors. It will not be an issue."

"From other planets?"

"Yes."

"We need to compare notes when this is all over," Ariel said. "How could there be inhabited planets within this galaxy and I do not know about them?"

"I did not say they all came from this galaxy," Yeshem said.

"Interesting." Ariel reached into a drawer and withdrew four flashers. She offered one to Yeshem who shook his head.

"If it becomes necessary for me to have a weapon I will find what I need on the ship."

Lucifer walked over to a wall where several swords hung. He turned to Ariel. "For display?"

She smiled. "I travel a lot. No, they are not ornaments."

He handed one to each of the other Havenites. He ran his hand down the scabbard that lay at his side. "In case the flashers don't work."

"It is good you two have been reunited."

It was hot. Hot like in the belly of Death Valley.

"It is good that it is a cool day," Yeshem said.

Lucifer looked at him, sweat dripping down into his eyes, but said not a word.

"This way." Yeshem started to walk towards the airfield. Reaching one of the long cylindrical craft he placed his hand on the side and a door slid open and a ram appeared. He climbed aboard and walked towards what the others assumed was the cockpit. As soon as all were aboard, the ramp withdrew and the door slid shut.

"Please take a seat. I am contacting the control tower and telling them who I am and that I wish an immediate departure."

"The ship is ready?" Ariel asked.

"All ships are ready. They are fueled and provisioned before being parked on the field. It would make little sense to park a craft that was not prepared for use."

Ariel smiled. "That does make a lot of sense."

"The internal dampeners will compensate for the effects of gravity as we accelerate to reach escape velocity. I would ask that you utilize the safety harness attached to your seats in case something has not been properly maintained. It does not happen often but it is best to be prepared."

The three Havenites quickly buckled their harnesses.

After a few minutes, Yeshem climbed out of his seat. "I have set the coordinates. We should arrive in approximately fourteen hours. There is food and drink in the galley."

He pointed to a small cylindrical bulge in the hull that rose from floor to ceiling. "That is a relief room."

Michael's eyebrows rose.

"We have departed your atmosphere?" Ariel asked smiling at Michael's discomfort.

"Yes. As I said we are moving towards our destination."

She looked at the control station he had just left. "I will enjoy studying your vessel."

"If you wish I can provide schematics. We are allies after all."

"That would be wonderful."

Yeshem turned in his seat. "We will be docking in a few minutes. There are no other vessels at the prison but the Devalies don't use ships so I cannot confirm that they are not present."

"Who else would dock here?" Michael asked.

"The Devalies used another race to construct the facility. It was they who used the docking facilities."

"Do we need to worry about them?" Lucifer asked.

"No. They are gone."

"Gone?" Michael asked.

"The Devalies used them up."

"Used them up?" Ariel asked.

"When they were of no further use they consumed their essence."

"All of them?" Michael asked.

"They no longer exist as a people. That is what they do. They take, they use, and they destroy.

"We are here. I am checking the airlock and insuring there is an atmosphere on the other side."

"Can you tell if anyone is aboard?" Michael asked.

"It seems to be clear. And there is air. We can enter."

As the airlock opened Lucifer fell to his knees. Ariel grabbed him.

"What is wrong?"

Lucifer gasped out, "Shadows, thousands of them. Screaming. Insane. I can hear them. I can hear them all."

"You better stay here. We will be right back," Michael said.

"No." Lucifer slowly regained his feet. Sweat flowing down his face he shook his head. "I need to block them. I am so attuned to look for Shadows I was caught off guard. Give me a moment."

Taking a deep breath he nodded to Michael. "I have it under control now. I am blocking them but by doing so I am afraid I will not be able to detect one possessed."

"We will be careful. Are you ready?"

Nodding Lucifer worked his way towards the airlock.

Yeshem stood at the end of the connecting ramp gripping the wheel of the hatch. He spun the wheel and it and hissed as he pulled it open. One-by-one they stepped into the gray, twelve-by-twelve room. Outside of a small control panel attached to one wall, the room was empty.

"The Devalies keep their subjects in small containers outside this room. The specimens are surrounded by Shree. They cannot reach them but they constantly try. The Devalies think this helps condition the subjects."

"How do they stay alive? And sane?" Ariel asked.

"The Devalies usually come once a day to provide nourishment and check on the condition of the subject. When they feel they are ready they are taken back to Ot where they are introduced to processed Shadows."

A dark door materialized on the wall.

"No!" Ariel screamed drawing her weapon.

A Devalie and a Makaranian stepped through the doorway. The Makaranian was carrying a metal tray of what they assumed was food.

Lucifer threw a bolt of light striking the chest of the Devalie driving him into the wall as he drew Galatian. An ebony blade appeared in the hand of the Devalie. The door closed and the Makaranian threw the tray at Michael. Yeshem struck him along the side of his head and the large being fell to the floor.

The Devalie launched himself from the wall and drove his blade at Lucifer. The blow was deflected as it struck the white shield that had materialized on Lucifer's left arm. He struck back and the thing quickly parried his blow.

"A Blocker!" It screamed. "Here? How?"

"I am Lucifer, know that I am here to end you, beast."

Ariel and Michael fired their flashers at the Devalie who brushed off the beams.

"Take it off stun," Michael screamed.

"Leave it. It's mine." Lucifer rushed forward and slashed at the Devalie striking its arm. It screamed in pain and fury. A tentacle of black tar worked its way down its wounded arm wrapping itself around the ebony sword at the end of his wrist.

The Devalie flicked its hand throwing the blade forward striking Lucifer in the face. The sword returned to its hand.

"Lucifer!" Michael rushed to his aid and pushed his blade into the side of the Devalie. It turned swinging its sword opening Michael's torso from navel to shoulder. He dropped his blade and fell to the floor.

Lucifer crawled to his knees. "No!"

The Devalie turned and raised its blade again. Lucifer knocked it aside and launched himself into the beast wrapping his arms around it. He began to glow. The Devalie screamed as the dark blade withdrew into its arm and pushed with both hands to free himself. The light intensified encasing the Devalie. Lucifer squeezed and the light of his body entered it. The beast fell limp.

Lucifer worked his way to Michael, brushing the blood from his eyes he lifted his head. "Stay with me, brother."

Michael looked up at him. "Promise me you will take care of Arthur."

"We will do so together."

Michael closed his eyes and fell limp.

Yeshem removed his shirt and wrapped it around Michael's wound. He gently lifted him.

"I will return him to the ship." He nodded to the panel." The red button will identify occupied cages. It will give you the number. The panel next to it will recover the cage. It will appear there," he nodded his head to the wall where the door had appeared. Get your friends. We should hurry. They will soon wonder why those two did not return."

"And him?" Ariel asked indicating the fallen Makaranian.

"I struck him too hard. He will not be coming with us."

Yeshem walked from the room. Ariel pushed the red button on the control panel. Nothing happened. She tried again. Still nothing.

"What does that mean?" Lucifer asked.

"They are empty."

CHAPTER THIRTY-NINE

Yeshem lowered Michael's still form to the floor of the ship and rushed to the control station.

"I will get us back as soon as I can."

"Any chance of pursuit?" Lucifer asked.

"No. The Devalies have no spacecraft. Nor allies that do. They have never had one of our occupied warriors fly them anywhere either. I do not know why. There will be no pursuit."

"The Makaranian in there had no Shadow."

"A traitor. A collaborator." Yeshem said in contempt.

Ariel checked the wound on Michael's chest. Through tears, she called out, "I need to get him back."

"Back where?" Lucifer placed his hand on her shoulder. "He is gone, Ariel. There is nothing we can do for him."

"There is. There has to be. I need to get him back to my place, my lab. We need to call Remiel and have him meet us there."

Helping Ariel to her feet Lucifer held her at arm's length. "You know we cannot call him until we return to Haven. And it is too far for us to fly there even if this vessel could make the trip. I love him too, Ariel. But we must accept the fact that he is gone."

"He is not! I will open a door and get him home. I can help him there."

"You cannot open a door from a moving object. Nor can you do so from an unknown point."

"Yeshem, stop the ship."

"You can't be serious," Lucifer said.

"I said stop the ship. We have to keep him warm, Lucifer." She turned to Yeshem. "You must stop the ship from any movement. And I need the exact coordinates of our location."

"I can give you that. And I will endeavor to hold the ship steady, but it will be difficult."

"I understand, but for this to work, it must be completely still."

"You can't do this," Lucifer said. "If you make the slightest miscalculation you could end up inside the walls of your own home. Or somewhere between worlds."

She looked up at him. "I must try."

Lucifer stared at her for a moment, then nodded. "I will help Yeshem. Let me know when you are ready. I will carry him."

"I will do it. If I am wrong you could die."

"I am aware of that. But I will carry him. You open the door. I will go first. If you do not hear from me within two minutes it will mean I was not successful. Return with Yeshem and then go on to Haven. Let the others know that Randy and Apollo were not there. Explain what happened to us."

"I'll go."

"No."

They stared at each other for a moment and then she nodded.

Yeshem turned in his seat. "I have the coordinates. The ship is stable for now but I do not know how long I can keep it that way."

Ariel stepped to the front of the ship and looked over his shoulder. She typed a series of numbers into the control unit then turned to Lucifer. "Ready?"

"A moment." He kneeled and lifted the still form of Michael. "Now."

Ariel aimed the device at the bulkhead and the window appeared.

"You must hurry. The solar waves are strong and the ship is trying to drift," Yeshem called without turning around. "I do not know how long I can keep it steady."

Lucifer stepped through the opening. There was silence. Then Ariel's communicator chirped. She lifted it to her ear and wiping away tears smiled. She turned to Yeshem. "Thank you. I will come for you."

Concentrating on the controls he said, "Not right away. Give me some time. I need to speak with my elder. We need to take a more active role in this war. I will return to the place we arrived on Makaran in seven days."

"I will be there. And thank you."

He turned but she was gone.

Lucifer caught Ariel as she stumbled. "The door opened three feet above the floor. Not perfect but considering I did not think this was possible I am impressed we are alive."

Ariel broke free and looked at Michael lying upon the floor. There was no fresh blood.

His heart has stopped. Rushing to the cabinet facing away from the windows she pushed a series of buttons and a long covered shelf slid from the wall. "Quickly, place him in the chamber."

Lucifer gently lifted Michael and lay him on the cushion.

"Help me with his clothes. There must be nothing between him and the device."

Carefully removing Michael's blood-stained robes Lucifer spoke softly."The heart has been damaged, Ariel. He is dead."

"I know about his heart. Help me with these." She handed Lucifer a series of padded wires. While placing two directly on his heart she nodded towards his head. "Those go on his temples. Quickly."

Ariel stepped back closing the dome. It was translucent allowing them to see the still body within. A mist formed obscuring the body.

"This is where he initially lay while his consciousness was transferred to the sword."

"A stasis chamber? But he is gone, Ariel."

"I must try, Lucifer. I can't lose him."

Arthur paced around the room occasionally stopping to check the communication device lying open on the table.

"She will call when she gets back. Stop worrying. Freya, two FBI agents, Patricia, who carries a gun remember, your father, and three of the Special Forces soldiers are with her." Loki leaned back in his chair, picked a bottle off the table, and took a drink. "I think I prefer the beers of Earth. So many different varieties and tastes. The Alewives here do their best but, well, it's not the same."

"Why couldn't I go with her? I should be there in case of trouble," Arthur demanded.

Loki wiped the foam from his mouth and leaned his elbows on the table.

"Because, little brother, your mother is taking her to pick out a wedding dress and according to tradition, on your planet, not mine, you are not permitted to see the bride in the gown until the day of the wedding. Stupid I know, but your mother insisted and I am not about to argue with the lady."

"Why couldn't she get one here? There are plenty of stores. Or on Asgard. Or Olympus for that matter."

"Or Duat."

"Not Duat. Cleo showed me what they wear at weddings there. My mother would have had a heart attack."

"Well, Charlotte said it was important that she have the proper dress. A real wedding dress, whatever that means. Personally, I think it is a waste to wear a garment only once, but as I said, your mother insisted. Worse yet, my mother loved the idea and couldn't wait to see what Charlotte had in mind. I defiantly was not going to argue with her."

Gabriel and Ezekiel stepped into the room. "Any word from Michael or the others?"

Loki stood, walked toward a large refrigerator, reached in, and pulled out three bottles of Iron City Beer. Opening his he handed the opener to Gabriel. "I've been saving these. Picked them up on a trip to Pittsburg. I haven't tried them yet. Seems like a good time. And no, we have not heard. It's only been two days. I doubt we will hear from them before tomorrow.

"Hear from Remiel?" Loki asked.

"Yes. Thor and Sif are well enough to return. Hercules is much improved and demanding to come home as well." Gabriel laughed. "Remiel considered using restraints to keep him in bed. He demands to be allowed to attend the wedding."

"Did that work?" Arthur asked. "The restraints I mean."

"Didn't try. Didn't want to annoy the big fellow too much."

"So what did he do?" Loki asked.

"Drugged him," Ezekiel said. "Never knew what hit him. Remiel just opened his IV line and boom. Sleepy time."

"Wouldn't want to be there when he wakes up," Loki said.

"Remiel says he may ask you to be there when it's time."

"This beer isn't bad," Gabriel said.

"I should have brought more."

"How much did you bring?"

"I smuggled a case. Merlin has convinced everyone we shouldn't bring things from Earth."

"I won't tell him," Gabriel said.

"Tell who, what?" Merlin asked as he walked through the door. He pointed to the bottle in Loki's hand. "Got another one of those?"

"I thought you didn't approve."

"In theory, I don't. But a decent beer is worth a little indiscretion." He turned to Arthur. "Hear from the ladies?"

"Not yet."

"Well, they will be fine. Kathleen has an army protecting her. Thought it was kind of nice that Colonel Shrift insisted on providing additional security. Said his guys were good at clandestinely watching for bad guys."

Ezekiel placed his empty bottle on the table and walked towards the refrigerator. "He seems to have adjusted to the situation rather quickly."

Loki jumped from his seat. "Whoa, one to a customer. That's all I have."

Merlin pushed him back into his seat. "Don't worry. I'll send you a couple of cases of Heineken. Good stuff."

"You ..."

"Of course. Do as I say not necessarily as I do. Besides, I'm the Emrys. Now, what were we talking about?"

"Nothing really. Just that I should be with Kathleen," Arthur said.

Merlin chuckled. "I suspect that would be a little dangerous. The ladies can be quite formable when angered. Best we wait here, drink beer, and worry."

The phone rang and Arthur rushed to answer. He listened for a moment then hung it up.

"That was Odin. Thor and Sif just arrived. They are on their way. Should be here any minute."

"Sif is going to be pissed she didn't get to go on the shopping spree with Kathleen."

"She can help with the bridesmaid dresses," Arthur said.

Loki placed his bottle on the table. "That is a term I do not understand. I mean maid. Isn't Sif going to be one of these maids?"

"Maid of honor," Arthur said.

"I'm pretty sure she is no maid. I can ask my brother but I don't think that is necessary. They have been married for quite a while."

"Ask me what?" Thor asked as he held the door for Sif. "Got another one of those?"

Sighing Loki pointed to the refrigerator. "In there, and nothing."

The others laughed.

"Where is Kathleen?" Sif asked.

"Shopping. She, Freya, and my mother, along with a small army of security folks, are looking for a wedding dress in Cleveland."

"Remiel said the wedding was to be soon. I am sorry I missed going with them."

"I'm sure they would have loved to have you along," Merlin said.

"On Earth?" Thor asked.

"I didn't want them to go but was overruled. Only place to find what they are looking for," Arthur said. He walked over and gave Sif a gentle hug. "How are you feeling?"

"Good. No scars, no nerve damage. That Remiel is a wonder. His machines are incredible. We suffered third-degree burns and now there is no trace of the injuries."

"He is well on his way to healing Hercules and I did not think that was going to be possible," Thor said emptying the bottle. He reached into the fridge and pulled out another. Loki started to protest then gave up.

Thor tossed the empty bottle into the trash. "Remiel told us about the rescue mission. Any word

"Nothing yet. Probably won't hear until tomorrow," Arthur said.

Odin walked in carrying a package. He placed it on the table and reached for the door of the refrigerator."

Loki grimaced. "Getting a little crowded in here. Help yourself."

"Last one," Odin said reaching for the opener.

Seeing Loki's expression Merlin patted him on the shoulder. "I will have a case sent right away.

Odin took a drink and raised his eyebrows. "Not bad. So what is going on? I feel a little out of the loop having been tied up in that damn hospital for so long."

"You been briefed on the rescue attempt?" Loki asked.

"I have. Gutsy move. I hope they are successful."

"Kathleen and Arthur are getting married next week," Gabriel said.

"I have been told that as well. Which is why I have brought this." He unwrapped the package exposing Excalibur. "The groom needs to be properly dressed. It is cleaned, shined, and sharpened."

Arthur looked at the sword and smiled. "Thank you. Didn't think I'd be carrying a sword on my wedding day."

"It's tradition," Odin said.

"Not on Earth."

Odin looked at Gabriel. "How come you look like that here but not on Earth?"

Gabriel smiled. Raking his fingers through his purple hair he shrugged his shoulders. "Don't know. Kind of fun though. Keeps folks guessing?"

"How is Rex?" Thor asked. "I heard he was injured."

"Some broken bones, bad one in his leg, and a few cuts here and there. He's fine. Seems Becky has taken a liking to him and is tending to his needs," Merlin said.

"Becky?"

"Yes, Arthur. She came with Randy's wife to see if there was any word on Randy as we were sorting out our wounded. I told her Rex was one of your oath-sworn and introduced them. She offered to take care of him until he is back on his feet."

"Did you tell her who he was? How old he is?"

"I did. But the Pendragon is in reality but a few years senior to Rebecca. It did not seem to bother her."

The phone rang again and Arthur picked it up. He listened solemnly then turned to the others. There were tears in his eyes. "Lucifer has returned. He is waiting in the conference room."

"Did they get Randy and Apollo?" Loki asked.

"They weren't there."

Merlin walked over and placed his hand on Arthur's shoulder. "There is more?"

He struggled to control his voice. "Michael is dead."

CHAPTER FOURTY

Arthur watched the rain as it bounced off the floor of the stone balcony. His dark mood matching the clouds that filled the sky. Hearing a whistle he turned and walked to the small kitchenette and picked up the kettle.

Tea, he thought. Merlin's ban on the import of goods from Earth should not include coffee. He'd need to talk to him about that.

"You have a visitor, First Dragon."

"Thank you, Eva," he said to the artificial intelligence that managed his apartment.

"It is your father. Shall I allow him access?"

"Yes, please."

Paul worked his way through the door, a large box in his arms.

"Need help, Dad?"

"I've got it," he said as he lay it carefully on top of the table. "Isn't heavy. Freya asked me to bring it over. Said you'll need it for tomorrow. I understand she and your mother worked on the design together. They seemed excited about the results.

"Oh, and Loki said he would be up later. Had a few things to pick up for tonight."

"Loki planning my bachelor party worries me a little."

"You asked him to be your best man." Paul looked at him. "Something wrong, son? Worried about tomorrow?"

"A little maybe." He smiled sheepishly. "No, that's not it. Just thinking too hard about things I can't do anything about."

"Such as?"

"Randy and Apollo missing. The deaths of Michael, and Zeus. They should be here, with me tomorrow. And Gwen. I wish I knew where she was. That she is okay."

"We are all worried about Gwen. But we must remain optimistic. She went willingly and Gwen is no fool. She wouldn't have gone if, well, if she thought she was walking into danger.

"As for the others, it is our responsibility to ensure they are never forgotten. And as long as we remember them, they are never truly gone.

They stood quietly for a moment.

"Thanks, Dad. You're right. But it's hard. I guess I've had too much time to think lately. Not used to it. And not seeing Kathleen, well, that doesn't help."

"Traditions can sometimes really suck."

Arthur chuckled. "Yes, they can."

Paul smiled. "About the bachelor party tonight."

"Something I'm not looking forward to. I don't trust Loki."

Paul laughed. "I'll do my best to make sure you are well enough to make the ceremony tomorrow. And I've asked Remiel to stand by in case he's needed."

"You're coming?"

"Wouldn't miss it."

Paul noticed the case leaning against the wall. "You haven't opened it?"

"No. They want me to wear it tomorrow. I don't know if I can."

"Why not?"

"Outside of feeling foolish wearing a sword to my wedding?" He hesitated. "It's Michael. We were one for so long because of Excalibur. And now he's gone. "

"He would want you to wear it."

"I guess he would" Arthur walked to the table. "Okay," he said taking a deep breath. "Let's see what my Moms have decided I'm to wear tomorrow." He opened the box. "You have got to be kidding me."

"This is Camelot. They like flashy things. Will go well with the cufflinks Loki gave you. And the ring. At least the pants and boots are plain black."

Arthur chuckled." I hope no one laughs when they see this. I will look like one of those princes on coronation day in Europe.

"You are a prince," the metallic voice chimed.

"I will never get used to those things," Paul said.

The procession worked its way through the multitude of well-wishers. Leading the bridal party was a magnificent white stallion, shaking its head and prancing in pride while the rider fought to remain in the saddle.

"I am no horseman," Arthur gasped. "This is nuts! I'm going to fall off and die. On my wedding day."

Loki laughed. "We are here to make sure that does not happen. Relax. Enjoy the moment."

He and Lancelot rode on either side ensuring the horse did not bolt, and Arthur did not fall off.

"Everything will be fine," Lancelot said. "Ease up on the reins a little. That's good. The horse knows where he is going."

"How's your head, little brother?" Loki asked chuckling.

"I should kill you for last night. Until Remiel gave me his hangover cure this morning I wasn't sure I was going to live."

Loki looked at Remiel walking beside him while Gabriel and Ezekiel flanked Lancelot helping to keep the crowd from the riders. They were intimidating in their true forms with long flowing red robes, swords at their sides, and the dragon of The Oathsworn prominently displayed on the left breast. The remainder of The Oathsworn rode behind. All there except for Hercules and Rex. And of course Apollo and Gwen. The horses that Thor and Falstaff rode were massive beasts that Loki said should be pulling a beer wagon.

"We are almost there," Lancelot said nodding his head at the main hall of Camelot. Along the steps stood two teams of soldiers in their green Class A uniforms and Green Berets. Colonel Shrift, in his Dress Blues, at their front. Behind them were the FBI people in dark blue suits and above them on the steps the Sheriff' and his deputies in their brown dress uniforms and Montana Peak Hats. Being a bridesmaid, Patricia was not with them as Ariel was not with her brothers. As they stopped Colonel Shrift called attention and saluted.

Several grooms came forward and took control of the horses. Arthur was happy to be on solid ground. His oath-sworn fell in behind him two-by-two as he started to mount the steps. Paul and Odin waited at the top along with Ra and Hera.

"Nice outfit, Paul said."

Arthur smiled straightening the coat his mothers had designed. Gold piping lined the hem and sleeves. Twelve gold buttons climbed the coat in two rows ending in a raised collar, also piped in gold. A red dragon outlined in gold was embroidered on the left breast. Its wings unfurled and emerald eyes glowing. Around his waist was a gold belt, five thin red lines running parallel representing the five worlds of the alliance. At his side was Excalibur.

Rex stood just inside the entrance resting on a pair of crutches, Becky beside him holding his elbow to help keep him steady.

"Interesting."

"You have no idea," Loki whispered. "They have become very close friends."

"That's good."

Odin and Paul preceded down the aisle taking seats in the first row next to their wives. Paul leaned over to Charlotte. "Everything good?"

"Everything is fine. Freya is acting as the bride's mother and has taken charge of the bridesmaids." She smiled. "Very organized."

Paul smiled at Freya as she took a seat next to her husband.

The male members of his oath-sworn, in their red coats sporting smaller versions of the Oathsworn's Dragon, entered and lined the aisle. Arthur and Loki walked between them stopping when they reached the raised platform at the front of the room.

As the hall filled with their friends, Arthur had a chance to look around. The room was filled with flowers of all shapes and colors. Beautiful tapestries lined the walls. It was something from a fairytale.

King Alfred hobbled onto the platform. He nodded. The doors opened and Merlin and Kathleen stepped into the hall.

Arthur was surprised when the wedding march began to play.

Standing beside him Loki whispered, "Your mother insisted. Catchy tune."

He could not see Kathleen's face for it was covered in a white veil, never-the-less he took a deep breath. She was stunning. Her gown a gossamer white that flowed behind her, the material seemingly made of spun glass. She looked like an angel stepping down from heaven.

Behind her walked Sif and Patricia carrying the long train trailing more than a dozen feet behind her.

Arthur smiled when he noticed the slim dagger hanging at Sif's side.

"Wouldn't feel dressed without it," Loki whispered. "Formal attire for a Valkyrie."

The remainder of the bridesmaids followed carrying bouquets of brightly colored flowers all wearing long red gowns with small dragon pins attached at the neck. Ariel stood above them all with her flowing purple hair hanging down her back. Even Bast was there having recovered from her wounds

When they reached the dais Merlin lifted Kathleen's veil and kissed her on the cheek. He took her hand and handed it to Arthur. With tears in his eyes, he nodded. "She is yours now, my son. Protect her and love her."

Unable to take his eyes from Kathleen and finding it hard to catch his breath he whispered, "With my body and soul, sir. I swear."

Merlin took his seat beside Freya. She patted his hand.

"She is beautiful, Merlin."

Unable to respond he nodded.

Kathleen smiled at him and whispered. "Do you like it? Your mother said it's what they wear on your world for weddings."

"You look magnificent."

She blushed. "Thank you."

"Are you ready?" King Alfred asked smiling. "I can wait if you want."

Kathleen answered without looking at him as she stared into the eyes of her soon to be husband. "We are."

Resisting a chuckle Alfred nodded towards Sif and Loki. They stepped in and wrapped first gold and then red silk cords around their wrists.

"We are from many worlds and have many customs for the joining of a man and a woman," King Alfred said. "Having spoken to the families of the two young people standing before me we decided to incorporate as many traditions as we could. So with your indulgence here we go.

"Who gives this woman to be with this man?"

Merlin stood and smiled. "I do."

"And who gives this man to be with this woman?"

Paul and Charlotte answered, "We do."

"Do you take Kathleen to be your wife, Arthur? To protect, love, and cherish the remainder of your days?"

"I do."

"And do you Kathleen take Arthur to be your husband. To love and cherish for the remainder of your days?

"And protect. I do."

"These rings symbolize the bond between you for all to see."

Loki and Sif handed them the rings. Arthur placed the simple gold band on Kathleen's finger and she did the same to him.

"Around your wrists are the cords of love and loyalty which symbolize the binding two into one."

Looking out into the crowd he asked. "Is there any here that sees reason these two should not be wed on this day?"

While waiting he noticed that several of The Oathsworn lay their hands on their swords.

"Then as King of the realm and representative of the Alliance of Worlds, I proclaim Arthur and Kathleen husband and wife. You may kiss the bride." He whispered to them. "Your mother told me this was important. I have no idea why I have to tell you that you have my permission."

Arthur kissed Kathleen.

Holding hands they turned.

King Alfred shouted. "To all present, I would like to present Mr. and Mrs. Arthur Pendragon. Prince and Princess of the Alliance of Worlds."

"Arthur looked at Kathleen. Did you know about this?"

"No."

King Alfred placed his hands on their shoulders. "A gift from us all. For none deserve the titles more than the two of you. Now smile and walk down the aisle. Your people are waiting."

"Pendragon?" Ra asked.

"That's what the voice called him. We discussed it as a family and decided it was easier to say then Earsterdrak. And it means the same thing. Since we don't have to explain it to anyone at home, what the heck," Paul said.

"We talked to Rex and he didn't mind. Was flattered actually," Charlotte added." And it is easier to spell. The grandkids will appreciate that."

"Is she ...?" Merlin asked.

Charlotte chuckled. "Not that we are aware of."

"Prince and princess?" Paul asked looking at Ra and Odin.

"We discussed it. All were in agreement. We share them both. They are the first to be granted the title in all our histories."

Everyone came to their feet and roared their approval as Kathleen and Arthur stepped from the dais and started to stroll down the aisle trailed by the bridesmaids. Their parents and The Oathsworn followed to the sound of trumpets.

When they reached the door Arthur was surprised to see Hercules hobbling up the steps.

"You don't think I would allow you to wed without me, do you? And I brought a gift."

Randy, Apollo, and the woman he had met in the woods on Olympus, Apollo's sister Artemis, stood at the bottom of the steps.

"How? Where?"

"They stepped through a door into Remiel's place just as I was about to use his little doohickey to create a door for myself. He left it in case of an emergency. Showed me how to use it. Programed it for me. They said Yeshem opened it for them. Thought you might like me to bring them along."

"I didn't know Yeshem could open a window. This is fantastic!"

Ariel looked at him in concern. "He can't."

Randy ran up the steps towards Arthur while Apollo approached Kathleen. Lancelot looked at Ariel then toward Artimis who was rapidly approaching.

Arthur went to open his arms to hug Randy when his hand brushed Excalibur."

"Beware, Arthur! Things are not as they seem."

"Michael?"

Randy wrapped his arms around him and whispered, "I'm sorry, Art. I can't stop it."

From within his sleeve, he withdrew a purple dagger and plunged it into Arthur's back.

Kathleen screamed and reached for him as Apollo drove a similar blade into her chest. As the two fell Lancelot tried to draw his sword but was stopped when Artimis slashed her dark blade across his throat.

Loki pulled his sword but before he could level it Randy raked the razor-sharp blade across his abdomen eviscerating him. Loki's sword fell from his fingers as he grabbed his stomach trying to keep his internal organs from spilling out.

Thor grabbed Apollo by his neck and Artimis stabbed him in the chest.

Millie threw out her hands and a bolt of powerful light struck Artimis to no effect.

"They are not Shadow!" a voice called. Gwen stepped from a dark doorway. "Do not kill them!"

Sif dove and tackled Artimis who dropped her knife as she struck the ground. She lay as if waking from a dream, confused, frightened.

"Everyone step back!" Gwen screamed. She raised her hands and a fountain of red light exploded from them striking the two remaining attackers who crumbled to the ground. Ezekiel reached for one of the purple blades.

"Don't touch it," Gwen yelled. She approached the one near her brother, and kneeling in a widening pool of blood, placed her hand around the knife, and closed her fingers. The blade began to pulsate, then wiggled like a captured eel trying to escape. Gwen pushed her fingers deeper into the writhing mass and it turned black and stopped moving. She dropped it and moved to the other two. As the last blade crumbled she turned and looked at her brother.

Arthur rolled to his side and reached for Kathleen's still and bloody hand. As his fingers touched hers he whispered, "I will always love you." His eyes slowly closed and he went limp.

Gwen kneeled beside her brother, tears streaming down her cheeks. "I'm so sorry, Art. I was too late."

THE OATHSWORN

Arthur Pendragon, Kathleen Pendragon

Gwen, Millie, Rex

Loki, Thor, Sif, Falstaff,

Hercules, Apollo

Horus, Anubis, Bast

Lancelot, Michael, Ariel, Remiel, Gabriel, Ezekiel

Their story will continue.

www.ingramcontent.com/pod-product-compliance
Lightning Source LLC
LaVergne TN
LVHW091028080826
845145LV00002B/402

9780999517970